Finding MISERY

RUSSELL C. CONNOR

For all those who saw me through while I was finding my own misery.

"Passion makes the best observations...

...and the sorriest conclusions."

-Jean Paul

Chapter ONE

The cop that arrested me looks just like Timothy Olyphant.

That's all I can think about. Even with the pop-eyed Hispanic on one side of me, moaning about how that bag of crystal meth wasn't really his, and the overweight redneck on the other demanding to know how he can get arrested for a DUI when he wasn't even in a vehicle. Which actually *is* a good question, I suppose.

No, at the moment, the only thing I can ponder is how the man with the badge on the other side of the glass looks strikingly like some actor.

Because if I let my mind wander too far in any other direction, I might just puke.

As I watch, he comes out of the jailer's office and heads toward the door of the station garage where we parked a few minutes ago. "Good luck," he whispers as he passes.

It's weird. All the cops that invaded my apartment earlier tonight fired off various forms of the same sentiment.

Sorry to have to do this.

Wish there was another way.

This is for the best.

They said these things as they frisked me in the dingy little storage room I call an office, where I write books that nobody reads. As they cuffed my hands and led me out of my home. The trip wouldn't have been complete without the obligatory march past staring neighbors, my best friend in the world (who clutches Minchi, the Pomeranian my wife and I purchased a few weeks ago) and my sister, who arrived just after the cops and bawled her eyes out through the whole ordeal.

The Olyphant look-alike fed me similar platitudes while he took a single sheet of paper off my battered printer, glanced over it, folded it, and put it in the breast pocket of my shirt for safekeeping.

I realize his 'good luck' means he's leaving. I watch him go—this local Withers County cop who may not even realize he's got a famous doppelganger—and I have the urge to call out. Beg him to stay. After all, we bonded, right? While I sat in the back of his patrol car, in the most uncomfortable and claustrophobic position of my life, and begged for updates about Brynn.

"We're not gonna talk about that," he says over his shoulder. His real name is Reed; I remember seeing it pinned above his badge.

"Was she mad? What did she say? Do you know where she's going?"

"No, and I wouldn't tell you if I did. This is better for now, trust me."

"*Oh, fuck that!*" I waver between despair and anger, with no transition between. Sitting on my handcuffed hands is killing me, and my legs are too long for the narrow space between the front of my seat and the back of his. "I call the cops and *I'm* the one getting hauled off to jail? This is her fault, you know!"

He glances in the rearview. "Your decisions are your own, sir."

I take a deep, cleansing breath. "I know, I know. Just please…tell me if she's all right."

He softens. I see it in his eyes, as he drives us through the sleeping streets of what passes for suburban Withers. "Hey, let me ask you something. Why do you want to be with a person that can hurt you like that anyway?"

I admit, I don't have the answer to that one.

"I'm not a marriage counselor or anything, but I've been in holy matrimony for eight years and…if a person is willing to do something like that to you…trust me, it ain't meant to be." He takes one hand off the wheel to tap his temple. "Think about that."

I do. I have. But I keep my feelings to myself. He doesn't understand. He can't. I'm sure he and his wife of eight years live in a perfect little whitewashed house, with a picket fence and flower bed, and they can say they're so in love only because they've never been tested.

He doesn't understand what it means to sacrifice. To give and give and give, all the while believing each piece of yourself you send out the door is just another fire-hardened glaze across your bond with this other human being.

It's like the Offspring said: the more you suffer, the more it shows you care.

So I don't plead as he strolls from the station. For all I know, such a sign of weakness might be like blood in the water around here. I both read *and* saw *Shawshank Redemption*, after all. As the door closes, the two jailers—one black and pissed off, the other female, chunky, and pissed off, neither of them resembling any actor or starlet—turn back to their three arrestees of the night and tell us to shut up.

I'm the only one that does.

After a few minutes, I'm taken to a side room with the black one. He tells me to stand inside a little square marked on the concrete floor and remove my clothes. I do so.

"*Not* your underwear," he snaps in exasperation.

I repress the urge to tell him he should've been more specific. This is my first trip through the penal system.

He pulls on a pair of rubber gloves, and, I swear, my bowels threaten to fucking evacuate. I almost start screaming I don't have anything up there, I'm not carrying drugs and I'm not hiding my father's watch from the Vietcong. Before things progress as far as my imagination, he pulls an orange, short-sleeved jumpsuit from a stack against the far wall and tosses them at me.

"Put those on, then go back and have a seat on the bench."

I do as told, wondering why the hell he needs rubber gloves.

Crystal Meth is gone when I get back to the bench, but the redneck is still here, alternately demanding his phone call and trying to sweet talk the chunky female jailer. I sit in my cotton jumpsuit and try not to imagine who wore it before me. When black jailer comes back to the office, I'm called up to the window to sign paperwork on a clipboard.

"This one is to verify the objects on your person when you were processed." He holds up a plastic bag full of my shit. "Wallet with eighteen dollars, keys, watch, ring, and one piece of paper."

I stare at the contents. There's my wedding ring, a plain silver band. And, of course, the folded printout that Officer Reed slipped in my pocket earlier. The one that caused this whole mess. I sign the form.

He pulls the clipboard back through. "Who is it you allegedly assaulted?"

Even with that all-important 'allegedly,' the question stings. It's so cold and clinical and absolute. I want to stop him, explain it wasn't like that, I would never hurt her in a million years, but he doesn't care, and it's so obvious.

So I just mutter, "My wife."

"Gimme a number where I can reach her."

I rattle off Brynn's cell, the only number in the world I can pull from memory like that, the one I screamed to a crowd of people last year while I lay in a puddle of my own blood in the middle of a busy intersection. I watch him call and speak into the phone.

I should be mad. After all, *I'm* the victim here.

Pay no attention to the fact that I'm being put in jail as I say that.

Chunky female jailer takes me to another room and poses me for fingerprinting and a mug shot. "Have they explained what's gonna happen?"

"No ma'am." I finish every sentence with a 'sir' or 'ma'am' during my time in the clink, hoping it will somehow convey I'm not like the rest of the sleaze. I'm a good guy, an upstanding citizen, a law-abider even.

Doesn't help. They still treat me like shit for the most part.

"You're probably gonna spend a few hours in here while we get you processed, then you'll be released on your own recognizance tonight. You'll be given a court date and a ticket. It'll be somewhere around 500 dollars."

I nod. No prison tattoos for me, apparently. I'll barely even have time to be anyone's bitch.

"Listen," she says, "I don't know what happened, but… don't see her tonight. Give yourself some time. Otherwise, you're gonna end up right back in here. And it won't be for a few hours next time."

"Okay." Something sharp twists around in my guts like a fork through spaghetti. "Do I get my phone call?"

I'm taken to a phone hanging from the wall in a dingy corridor. I dial the same number I just gave the jailer.

No answer. After four rings, I get voicemail. At just the sound of the recorded message, my eyes tear up.

"It's me," I say. "I'm so sorry. We can work through this. Please."

Hanging up is a little like cutting off an arm.

And the next thing I know, I'm in a cell. Behind bars.

Me. Rudy Compton. 28-years-old. Editor of the high school newspaper. College drop-out. Occasional pot smoker. Pop culture junkie. Wannabe writer.

That's what I try to focus on, as the door trundles closed on its automatic track behind me. How all this will be a great experience for my writing someday. Hemingway said to never write about a place until you're away from it, because it gives you perspective. But one look at that exposed metal toilet in the front corner of the cell reminds me I'm no Hemingway. I have a shy bladder and undiagnosed Irritable Bowel Syndrome.

The place is painted white, but it's chipped and rubbed away in large patches to expose gray cinderblock. The lights are turned low, just a few weak, screened-in fluorescents. Much bigger than I imagined, though. It's communal, with metal bunks hanging from the walls for fourteen people, stacked in double rows; six along each side and two at the back. Only two of them are occupied, by guys asleep in orange jumpsuits on my right. I wait for them to start the hazing, but they don't even open their eyes. One of them is snoring, for God's sake. If you can't trust the movies, who can you trust?

I noticed two other holding pens like this on the way in, both of them packed with occupants. Crystal Meth and Carless Drunk must've been put in one of these.

I trudge across the room with the blanket they gave me and take the lower bunk on the back wall. The front of our cell grants a sliver view of the jailer's office outside in the hallway. A little black and white TV mounted in the corridor is playing *Diff'rent Strokes*, but the sound is down and I can't get the gist of what Arnold and the gang are up to.

I try lying down on the thin mattress. Sitting up. I can't get comfortable. I have no idea what time it is, or how long I've been under arrest.

Luiz, one of the guys who works at the MegaMart with me, did hard time out at Huntsville. Four years for home burglary. It was all unarmed stuff, which is the only reason Josh gave him the job at the Meg. I can't even imagine being stuck in a room like this for four years. He told me the only way to get through a stretch like that is to keep all your muscles busy, and that includes your brain.

But really, I just want to survive the experience. I think about Thoreau, one of my heroes, and his night in jail. I think of all the proud Americans who have served their time. You know, like Lindsay Lohan, Mel Gibson, and Paris Hilton. I think of Nelson Mandela.

Jesus, what I wouldn't give for a joint. Or a cigarette. Or even just something to read.

At some point, one of my cellmates gets up to use the toilet. Somehow he checks the time. I'm not sure how; maybe he *does* have a watch up his ass. When he comes back, the snorer asks him when they get breakfast.

"Seven a.m.," he answers.

"What time is it now?"

"12:45."

"It's only 12:45?" I burst out, forgetting my goal of not drawing attention to myself. I was taken into custody sometime around…9:30 maybe? This is the longest I've ever gone without looking at a clock.

"Yeah," my time-privy cellmate confirms, and then adds with a wry smile before rolling over to face the wall, "but don't forget, at 1 the clocks roll back."

That's right, the time change was tonight. I was excited about it. It was an extra hour I got to spend with her.

God help me, that's actually how I thought about my marriage. Not to sound like an Aerosmith song, but there were some nights where I couldn't go to sleep, because the prospect of time away from her was just too goddamn scary.

Get through this first, I tell myself, *and we'll sort everything else out later.*

Unfortunately, my night in county is just beginning.

Chapter TWO

Withers is one of many micro-cities jammed into the sprawling tangle of the DFW Metroplex. That's Texas. It's on the northern outskirts of this big conglomeration, clustered around a road called 287 that would take you all the way Choteau, Montana, if you followed it far enough.

It's not rural. None of us own horses. It's certainly not New York City or even Dallas, but we're here, we exist. 70,000 people in the last census. Modest-to-low income. Young couples. Elderly. Families. Tract housing. Apartments. Only one trailer park. Plenty of fast food and even a few chain restaurants. Sparse in the job arena. Most folks commute.

Not the kind of place you dream about moving to, just another forgotten road child on the highways of America, but you could do worse. You don't hear about gangs running our streets or prostitutes sleeping with the mayor. Hell, I don't even know the mayor's name.

I guess the reason I'm telling you this is so you'll know that, no matter how much I want to believe otherwise as I sit shivering in my jail bunk, this is a pretty typical demographic for a Saturday night in a Withers County holding cell.

No rapists or muggers or serial killers.

Just drunks, disorderlies, and druggies.

And me, of course. Me and my decisions.

But there is absolutely no excuse for someone like Lennie Kincaid ending up in this stir.

I get my first look at him sometime after I give up finding a comfortable position on the metal slab of a bed. The cell door slides opens and I think maybe they're coming to take me out, but it's the guy who gave me the time that walks instead. He posted bail. As he's let out, another prisoner is pushed inside, and I catch a glimpse of my old friend Officer Reed back at the jailer's window, turning in his report. I assume he's responsible for the new arrival. The man's had a busy night.

The newcomer is a scrawny white kid. He's swimming in the jumpsuit they gave him, and I get the feeling it's the smallest size they make. His hair sticks straight up from his head in stiff, half-foot spikes. His eyes dart back and forth, back and forth, ping-ponging across the cell. I might be inclined to think he's another tweeker, but he looks pretty lucid.

Scared, probably. More scared even than me. Another first-timer. I feel pity.

He takes the bottom bunk closest to the door, farthest away from us, and sits on the edge. The starchy jumpsuit collar is pushed up high enough on his narrow face it would give Elvis a run for his money. Those enormous hair spikes almost brush the bottom of the bed above him. We're the only two awake; the snorer is back to sawing logs. I watch him, and his eyes graze me every few times they rocket around the room.

"Hey," I say.

"H-hey." He doesn't look at me when he talks.

"Don't sweat it, man."

"Huh?"

"I said, don't sweat it."

"S-sweat what?"

"This place. I was the same way, but turns out, it ain't *Oz* in here. The anal rape doesn't come till after breakfast, I guess."

"I know."

"Wait, I was joking. That's not really some little known prison fact, is it? Anal rape after breakfast?"

"I know how th-things w-w-work around here," he clarifies, saving me from hyperventilating. "I b-been in before. Lotsa times."

"Oh." I try to place the accent built around that chronic stutter. It's nasally and abrasive. Jersey, maybe? If so, he's a long way from home. "You mean in here?"

"Naw, I d-done *real* time, not this pansy-ass, Barney Fife shit." He clasps his hands in his lap, but the thumbs stay moving, rolling over and over one another. "I been in f-f-for grand theft auto, robbery, possession with intent, you n-name it."

Funny, I would've thought each of his listed crimes would've called for multiple years in jail; figure five each, minimum. But this shrimp doesn't look a day over 20.

"So...what'd they get you for this time?"

He finally peels his eyes away from the chipped paint and graffiti and looks over at me. "Busted tail light."

I snicker a little, until I see he doesn't. "They arrest you for that?"

"They w-will if you got warrants."

And then, the next thing I know, the guy explodes into motion.

He's at the door of the cell before I even register he's up. Except it almost looks like he's *dragged* to the bars against his will, by a giant, invisible hand. He starts pounding on the metal and wailing, *"C'mon, Jeeeesus, hurry the f-fuck up, I can't be stuck here, I can't!"*

I cringe from the noise. To my left, the snorer grumbles and pulls a pillow over his head.

The black jailer looks up from his desk behind a wall of glass, leans over, and says into a microphone that sends his voice through speakers overhead, "Pipe down, or I'm comin in there, Mr..." A pause while he checks paperwork. "... Kincaid. And when I do, I'm crackin skulls!"

The kid puts his palms against his temples and presses. *"Just lemme out, you pig, you f-fuckin desk pig! I'll pay the fine or whatever, but I GOTTA GET OUTTA HERE!"*

"Hey. Hey man," I say, trying to get him to stop the racket. The jailer said *skulls*, after all. Plural. "Calm down. Take it easy."

I hop off my bunk and start across the cell. He senses the motion and spins, backing away from me into the corner, his eyes wide as a cartoon character.

"S-stay away from m-me!" he screeches, holding up his hands, palms out, like he's ready to do some kind of Shaolin Tiger Claw maneuver. He's quivering, from his knees all the way up to those sharp quills jutting from his head.

"Okay, okay, it's cool!" I'm back across the room in a flash. I can't believe I got myself involved. It's been too long of a goddamned night to put up with this. "Kincaid, is that your name, man?"

He calms after he sees me back off. "Yeah. Lennie. Lennie K-Kincaid."

"Okay Lennie, I'm Rudy Compton. It's all right, nobody's gonna hurt you. Just chill out. I'm sure they'll have you outta here soon."

"Not s-soon enough." His face scrunches up. He grabs both ears and pulls on them—I mean, really *rips* at the fuckers—and then stamps his tiny foot. He murmurs, "I'm comin, all right? I said I was, I said I'd come!"

"Come? I thought you said you had to go."

"Not you, dumbshit, I ain't talkin to *you!* I just...I gotta be somewhere!"

I ignore that bit of weirdness and press on, trying to keep him distracted. "Oh really, well, where you going?"

"None of y-your goddamned business!"

I retreat farther, back to my bunk, ready to give up and let him spaz out. I probably outweigh the guy by fifty pounds, but I'm no fighter, and those small ones can sometimes surprise you. I mean, look at Jackie Chan. "Look, I'm just making conversation here. You want, I'll shut up."

His eyes narrow. He studies me. "...R-Reno, all right? I'm goin to Reno."

"Reno? Wow, that's cool, I've never been. Gotta pay off some gambling debts, huh?"

He shakes his head and looks at the floor. "There's something I gotta get. I *need* it."

I realize we're talking right back around to the problem I wanted to get his mind off in the first place. So I say the only other thing on mine.

"Hey Lennie, tell me…what the hell do you put in your hair to get it to stand up like that?"

He raises his head and grins.

Turns out, it's Elmer's glue.

In the hour or so I know him for, I actually get to like Lennie Kincaid. We sit on adjacent bunks and shoot the shit in the wee hours of Sunday morning. He *is* from Jersey, but he's been living in Fort Lauderdale, Florida for the past two years, which is where he came from before starting on this cross-country road trip. After talking to him for a while, I'm almost sure he's connected to the mob. This is quite exciting for me once the initial shock wears off. I try to imagine him hanging with Tony Soprano.

Just the fact that *he's* calm, makes *me* calm. And the best part is, it gets my mind off the Brynn situation.

The snorer is even awake and chatting now. His name is Duwan, a black guy about my age, and he's actually pretty cool for someone who punched a convenience store clerk this afternoon over the marked up cost of Ramen noodles. We both read comics and watch the same television. We make a date to hit the roadhouse up the street together some night next week and discuss the finer points of Bryan Hitch artwork.

Who would've thought my social network could be expanded so much by a few hours in the slammer? Maybe I just discovered the real reason for the high rate of recidivism in this country.

I find out later that Dutt and my sister have been fighting like mad to get updates on me. My baby sis is giving some receptionist hell about hurrying up and getting me discharged. And the women in my family are experienced at giving hell.

By my calculations, I was just a scant fifteen minutes from release when our cell opens up one more time, and we get another brother-in-orange.

One that changes *everything*.

This one is the opposite of Lennie in every way. Huge. Not just tall, but built like a dump truck. The jumpsuit strains at the seams on him, the short sleeves looking like they might be cutting off circulation to his arms, which are muscled and hairy. Face mean and wide and glowering, with a uni-brow that could be used as a dish brillo. He steps through the jail door and stands patiently as it glides to a close.

And I immediately think this guy has less business here than my Jersey friend.

"Good evenin, my man, and welcome to tha Ritz," Duwan says cheerfully, with legs dangling from his top bunk across from Lennie and me. "Let us show you to yer suite, brutha."

Duwan keeps talking—the guy is a regular comedian once you get him going—but I'm watching Lennie beside me. His eyes have gone all round and panicked again, and they're glued on the behemoth.

The bruiser's gaze shoots right to Lennie in return, like a bloodhound after a fox, ignoring the rest of us. Suddenly the temperature in the room is very OK Corral-ish.

Lennie licks his lips, tugs on his ears, and starts up a stutter I don't think will ever end. "F-F-F-F-F-F-Fiver, man, how'd you find me? What's up, g-good to see you." Something in his tone suggests this is a lie.

"Lennie, you know this muhfuckah?" Duwan asks.

The question goes unanswered. Fiver spins and walks back to the cell door. Whoever escorted him in is long gone, back to the jailer's office. Fiver stands hunched at the point where the bar of the door touches the first bar that makes up the rest of the front wall; where the mobile part of our cell meets the immobile part, in other words. His girth blocks whatever he's doing from view, but over his shoulder, the TV outside is still playing *Strokes*. Must be a marathon.

There's a short buzzing sound. It reminds me of the hum of a microwave. His arms work with purpose, elbows out to the side, like someone milking a cow.

Then he turns back to us and starts into the room, and I catch a glimpse of his handiwork.

A thick, black, rubberized cord that looks like a giant trash bag tie is now wrapped tight around the door connection.

I don't understand what's going on. I'm a smart guy, but not very good at thinking on my feet. Lennie, on the other hand, has no trouble. He scoots back on his bunk, into the shadows.

The bruiser dives in after him without a word. The intensity is spooky. Lennie squeals and tries to scramble from his bunk to mine, I guess with the intent to use me as a 180-pound human shield. The big guy gets a hold on his leg and drags him out so fast Lennie slams to the floor on his stomach. I hear his jaw strike the concrete with a cringe-inducing *thwak*.

All this happens so fast, Duwan and I haven't even moved. We watch in awe as Lennie is grabbed by the back of his jumpsuit and thrown against the cinderblock wall between our bunks, then spun around to face his attacker. Finally, Duwan starts shouting, "Guard, GUARD!"

I still can't move. Even if I could, I know I couldn't help. I'm mesmerized by the sight of Lennie pinned against the wall a foot away from me with one forearm the size of a bread loaf, so high his feet dangle off the floor. Lennie whimpers and weeps and clings to the man's bicep. Outside, the black jailer screams into his microphone, *"BREAK IT UP! BREAK IT UP RIGHT NOW, GODDAMN IT!"*

Inside the cell, next to me, Lennie blubbers in a great rush, *"I d-didn't mean it, I was on my way, I swear, I was g-gonna hand it over!"*

Fiver speaks at last, with a voice like grinding glass. I hear him say what sounds like, "Give me the word."

"Please, p-please, it's not my fault, I got pulled over, I was on my way, just let me finish the j-job, I can—" The rest of this is cut off as Fiver's arm presses into his chest hard enough to crush the breath from him.

At this point, I add a halfhearted contribution to the proceedings: "C'mon, stop, let him go."

Fiver ignores me. "You had a week to finish the job, Lennie. You think Carbini didn't know what you were up to? Give me the word. *Now.*"

From elsewhere, Duwan is screaming his lungs out and leaping off his bunk. The gears that move the cell door are grinding, but that black cord is holding it shut. Like an alligator's jaw, these things are designed to stay closed, not open. There's commotion outside the cell as the two jailers scramble from their office.

But all these things might as well be in another universe as Lennie Kincaid catches his breath, opens his mouth, and says two syllables that I just barely catch.

"*Sedoc.*"

I feel galvanized. Like 50,000 volts just ran through me. Something screeches in the bowels of my brain as that word settles in there, something primitive and sleek and angry. I feel like I could tear a phonebook in half. A single thought gets through the fog—*Elmer's glue my ass,* this *is why his hair stands on end*—and then I snap out of whatever the hell has me, panting like I've just run a 10K. Or, who am I kidding, a *1K.*

Duwan leaps from his bunk and lands on the bruiser's broad back. Fiver lets go of Lennie, who drops to the floor. The behemoth backs casually out to the wide space in the middle of the cell with Duwan riding him. He leans forward and then bucks backward, a tremendous heave. Duwan goes flying. His back hits the edge of the bunk beneath his and he comes down hard to the floor, then scrambles up for another go.

By now, the jailers are at the door. They're pulling on the bars and tearing at the thick black cord holding it closed and screaming for us all to freeze. Over their noise, I hear the hoots and jeers from the other cells.

Fiver turns to meet Duwan head on. As he performs this 180, Duwan is on his right, Lennie on his left, and the door at his back, so that, for just a split second, he is facing only me.

I hear the microwave hum again. Before it starts, his big hands are empty. After it ends...Fiver is holding a wicked little knife with a half-foot blade.

"Jesus, look out!" I yell.

Duwan is coming full throttle; he never has a chance. Fiver swings low and barrels into him with the weapon between them. Their bodies collide with NFL brutality, and Duwan sort of wraps himself over Fiver, his dark head almost on the other man's shoulder, like kids dancing at the prom. He looks at me, completely perplexed.

Then Fiver pushes him away, and I see the knife slide out of Duwan's stomach. The orange jumpsuit is tinged a horrible shade of red. Duwan gasps and falls across the nearest bunk.

I just witnessed a man getting shanked. I've never seen anything so violent in real life. All my prison nightmares are coming true.

Fiver sweeps his eyes over Lennie and me. The smile on his face makes me realize.

We're locked in here with a psychopath.

The jailers have given up yelling. Another cop has joined them and is sawing at the cord with a pocketknife. It's getting through, but not nearly fast enough. I see the black jailer come to the same conclusion. We share a look. The fear is communicative.

"The taser, *get the taser!*" he orders his colleague. She runs as fast as her thundering thighs will carry her.

Fiver starts toward Lennie.

"*S-s-stop man, stop!*" he squeals, as Fiver drives him back against the wall again. "*L-leave me alone, I g-gave you the word!*"

"Don't work like that," Fiver growls. "You're out. *All* of you."

He rams the knife up through Lennie's neck and into the soft meat behind his jaw. The tiny guy with the big hair gurgles and shudders as a torrent of blood gushes down his chest, over the knife hilt, and around Fiver's clenched fist. It looks like a faucet, all that blood. A few of the splatters hit my cheek. Lennie's eyes roll back as he dies.

Which just leaves me.

Fiver yanks the blade from Lennie's corpse—it gets stuck on the jawbone—and swings at me in a wide arc. I fall back at the last second. The dripping red point whickers past my nose. Please don't mistake this for reflexes or instinct, but rather the arm supporting me turning to jelly.

I can't fight this juggernaut. The only option is retreat. But that's a little hard in a rectangular concrete room. I try though, rolling onto the bunk before Fiver can swipe at me again and crawling across to the next one.

I stick as close to the wall as possible, clambering from bed to bed. Fiver follows along, hidden from the neck up by the overhanging bunks. He rolls the knife in his hand.

Then I hit the back wall, and there's nowhere else to go.

I push myself into the corner. Sink into the floor. Brynn is all I can think about, how I'm not going to see her again. Fiver stands over me, his shadow like an eclipse.

And then he starts jittering. His jaw clamps shut. The knife drops from his hand to clatter on the floor. His eyelids flutter and the jitter becomes a full-out convulsion.

The man who has just committed two murders in a locked jail cell falls facedown at my feet with the stiffness and grandeur of a redwood. The prongs of a taser gun stick out of his back. They're connected to wires leading to the horde of cops now outside the door.

I sit there shaking and looking at all the blood and bodies and wonder what the fuck just happened.

~ ~ ~

It takes them less than a minute to get the door open. Three of them cover Fiver with guns drawn, while the black jailer kneels and puts two fingers against the underside of his broad neck.

"Holy shit," he says. "This guy's dead."

Chapter THREE

As you can imagine, this changes my status considerably.

I'm no longer an inmate, but the star witness in the investigation of how three people died tonight while in the custody of the Withers police. This is the kind of thing that brings hefty lawsuits. I'm thinking the working days of Duwan's next-of-kin are just about over.

They make me stay where I am so I don't disturb anything. Within minutes the cell is filled with detectives and forensics, getting in each other's way and trying not to tromp through the drying blood puddles. Withers doesn't have those kind of resources, so they're probably rushed in from Fort Worth or someplace closer to the center of the Metroplex. Once the crime scene photos are taken, they let me get up and rush me to an interrogation room to get my statement.

This seems more formality than anything, but I'm numb. A dense fog sweeps through all those little wrinkles and ridges you see in pictures of the human brain, making all my thoughts slow and drugged. The interrogation room has a two-way mirror taking up the entire wall on my left. The reflection staring back at me is shell-shocked. Some of Lennie's blood is still on my cheek. I scrub at it with the shoulder of the jumpsuit until it's gone.

It's obvious the paunchy detective drew the short straw on questioning me, and would much rather be out where the action is. But he's thorough. I tell him everything I know, which isn't much. He looks like he believes me. He's convinced this was a gangland thing, a Jersey mafia slaying that, for some reason, took place right squat in the middle of nowhere, Texas. His entire interrogation is designed to hammer that square peg of logic into the round hole of this FUBAR situation.

"So, you're sayin he knew the guy?"

"Lennie? Yeah, I guess so."

He takes out a pack of cigarettes and offers me one. I accept with a shaking hand. We light up and he continues the questions after his first drag. "What makes you say that?"

"Well, he called him by name."

"Martin Dunbrough?"

"Huh?"

"He called him Martin Dunbrough?"

"Why would he call him that?"

The detective sighs smoke and connects the dots for me. "You said Kincaid called the big guy by name. The big guy's name, accordin to his fingerprints, is Martin Dunbrough."

"Oh." I try to imagine the psycho out there being called Martin by loving parents and can't quite get there. "No, he called him Fiver."

"Nickname, maybe?"

I shrug. "Is he...really dead?"

"Oh yeah, he's dead."

"Does that...usually happen when you taser somebody?"

"Not really. They're still trying to figure out what happened."

"What'd he do to get arrested, anyway?"

"Went speedin right by a cop. Then, when they pull 'im over for a ticket, he gets belligerent, pushy, keeps goading them, then hauls off and belts one of the officers in the face. My theory, the guy *wanted* to get put in here. Had the whole thing planned out." The detective glances back over his notes. "Okay, so he throws Kincaid against the wall, holds him there, and says he wants to have a word with him."

"No, no," I clarify, for what must be the twentieth time. "He said he wanted *the* word."

"What kinda word?"

"You got me."

"Like a password?"

"Could be."

"And Kincaid gave him this word."

"Yes."

"And what was it?"

"It was..." My tongue flops around the cig filter. I can't remember. I can't even remember what letter it started with. Everything happened so fast, I never had time to focus and commit it to memory. It's been washed away by a flood of adrenaline and fear.

But I can still recall how it made me feel when I heard it. That rush of energy. I have no idea how to explain that to the detective, so I don't try.

"I can't rembember," I say.

"You were right next to him. You musta heard it."

"No, I did, but...I can't remember what it was."

He watches me. This is the only part of my story he seems

to doubt. That line of reasoning is going to be prevalent in my life in the very near future.

"Okay, let's talk about the knife again."

I groan. This is the part he's most interested in.

"You didn't see where it came from."

"Yes, I did. I told you, it came from nowhere."

"Had to come from somewhere. Did he pull it out of his pocket or his sleeve? His ass, maybe?"

I lift an eyebrow. "His ass?"

"You'd be surprised. I've had prisoners hide entire pistols in their ass."

"Bullshit."

"'S true. One even had it go off inside 'im. Guy farted and the bullet tore out the front of his stomach."

"Bullshit."

"Hand to God." I can tell how much he relishes this story.

"Look man, I don't know, all right? The guy had a knife and he killed two human beings with it. Who cares about the fucking specifics?"

The detective holds up three fingers with the cigarette clinched between them. "The newspapers. The court. And there's a jailer out there who's most likely gonna be fired for not friskin this guy thoroughly enough. So anything you can tell me that might prove he did his job is greatly appreciated."

I think about Duwan, stabbed in the chest. I think about Lennie, his blood gushing out of a hole in his throat. And I think that maybe the jailer should be thankful for what he's got.

I look the detective in the eye. "It just sort of...appeared."

They put me in another cell while they get me processed out. Turns out it's with my ol' buddy Crystal Meth. The guy is so hyper—walking the floor, shouting out to inmates in other cells, demanding to know what's going on and for the TV in the hallway to be turned up—that the other cellmates all hate him. Ten or fifteen minutes later, the new jailer on duty comes to get me.

"Hey brother, you gettin out?" Crystal Meth asks me.

"I guess so."

"That's great!"

"Good luck," I tell him, passing on Officer Reed's sentiment.

"Thanks, brother. I don't know if you're religious or not, but pray for me, okay?"

I say I will, but I lie. I only pray for myself. And no one is answering.

On my final trip to the jailer's office, I take a peek in my old cell. The coroner's taken over, and the bodies are zipped up in black vinyl bags now. The cops have mostly filtered out, but I see my detective in there, standing with another man in a somber, blue, three-piece suit, and black cowboy boots with badly worn heels. They're deep in conversation, the detective gesturing at the blood on the floor and then at the mammoth body bag that could only contain Fiver. As I walk past, the man in the blue suit looks up.

I suppress a shiver. He's tall and far too pale, with thinning gray hair and beady little eyes that look like they've been poked back into his skull beneath a protruding brow ridge. He holds his knobby hands in an upside down steeple at the waist. His supreme creepiness brings to mind old-school Sam Raimi movies.

That hollow-eyed gaze firebombs me. I flick my eyes

away, but I can still feel it crawling over my spine as I walk away, like a giant spider scuttling across my flesh.

I'm taken back to the changing room and given my clothes: jeans, work boots, and blue Old Navy button-up sweater. At the jailer's window, I get my belongings back. I put everything in its place, and slip on my wedding band. I'm almost me again.

The last thing out of the bag is that piece of paper. I hold it between thumb and forefinger like it's a dead rodent and slip it back in my breast pocket.

"What about my ticket?"I ask.

"We're, uh, talking to the judge," the new jailer answers uncomfortably. "That's probably going to be excused."

What do you know? A comped room.

They lead me down a long hallway, hold a thick wooden door open, and, just like that, at close to three in the morning on Sunday, my stay in penitentiary is over.

I meet Dutt Lansing the summer before sixth grade.

I've just moved to Withers with my folks. I'm a nervous kid, shy and awkward, and terrified of starting school. As the last days of August wane, I prowl the streets of the new neighborhood on my Huffy, trying to get the feel of the place.

Back then, Withers is still developing. Behind my housing edition is a grid of empty streets that will eventually lead to houses, and acres of woodland waiting to be expanded into. As I coast along a downhill slope far out from the driveways and manicured lawns and basketball goals, I see a figure ahead, squatting down in the dirt beside the curb.

I pull to a stop next to a kid a little bigger than me, formless mop of black hair, hunched over something. He pretends I'm not there for a minute, then finally looks up.

"What the fuck're you staring at, new kid?"

"Uh...nothing."

"Then come over here and get down before someone sees you."

I dump my bike and join him in the gutter. He puts a hand over whatever he's got and asks, "You live in the house on Salado, right?"

I nod.

"That's one street over from me. I'm Dutt."

I think the name is supremely stupid. Still do. But with a handle like Dutton Geneva Lansing, you don't have many options.

"Rudy."

"You seen Miz Hampton naked yet?"

"What the fuck?"

"Miz Hampton. Your neighbor. She goes out and sunbathes naked in the backyard on Saturdays. You can see *everything*. Bush and tits and all of it."

"How do you know?"

"There's a tree in the vacant lot behind your street. I keep binoculars up there. But *you* can probably see her right through the fence, dude! Front row seat, you know?"

I give a horrified frown while making a mental note to try this at the earliest opportunity.

"I know everything about this neighborhood," he continues. "Me and my dad've lived here since they first started building houses."

"What're you doing?" I gesture at his hand.

He moves where I can see. He's got a lighter, and on the ground is a pile of dirty paper tubes, each about two inches long.

"Black Cats," he explains. "The high school kids come way out here to shoot off fireworks on the Fourth. I found a bunch that didn't go off."

What he means is that he's been rooting around in the dirt for moist, two-month-old explosives with fuses too short to've lit the first time. This is classic Dutt Lansing.

The problem is that the lighter is a discard from the high schoolers also. It's out of butane. I watch him flick the wheel a few times and produce only sparks before I get an idea.

I carry around a knapsack with all sorts of crazy shit in it. In the bottom is an old magnifying glass I keep for ant-frying and G.I. Joe-melting. "Try this."

He lays a bent firecracker out on the concrete. Huddles down beside it. Focuses sunlight on the sliver of a fuse, and the thing goes off in his face. The pop is loud to my ears, and I'm a yard away.

He grins, displaying a sizeable gap between his front teeth. "Sweeeeeet."

We take turns until the pile is gone, then search the ground for more, all the time watching the neighborhood in the distance to make sure no one is coming this way. When we reconvene, he's got a fresh supply and a glass beer bottle.

"Let's drop one in this!"

The operation takes a few minutes to work out. The fuses are too short to hold and then try to throw inside, so we come up with a brilliant plan: we'll set the bottle upright on the ground, then I'll hold the Black Cat just inside the lip while he uses the magnifying glass.

"Just make sure you drop it and get away fast," he advises.

He gets in position. A concentrated yellow beam shoots onto the tip of the firecracker held between my fingers.

The little twist of paper that serves as a fuse catches, and Dutt is gone before I can react. I realize too late that my crouched position won't allow me to run, so I let myself kind of fall backward and roll to the side, away from the bottle.

The explosion is muted. I spin around fast to look at our handiwork. The bottle has burst into pieces. Lazy smoke curls out of the remains.

I give a whoop of excitement. "Did you see—?"

Dutt's face is frozen in horror. I follow his eyes and find a three-inch gash on the back of my bare leg, just below the knee. Blood cascades down in a sheet, wetting my sock. Something in the hole looks rough and bumpy and I slap my hand over the wound to block out the sight.

"Oh my God!" I wail. "Tetanus! I'm gonna get tetanus!"

Dutt continues to stare.

"Please, go get my parents!"

Dutt slowly shakes his head, mouth hanging open. "I gotta go," he says slowly.

"What? No, I can't ride home like this, you gotta go get my parents!"

He runs for his own bike, throwing over his shoulder, "Sorry dude, my dad'll fucking kill me if he finds out! See ya at school next week!" He starts to ride away.

"Wait! Wait, you asshole, *you can't just leave me heeeeeere!*"

And that pretty much sums up mine and Dutt's entire relationship.

The two of us cause explosions, and I get left screaming.

Shit changes over time, but we remain constant. We're inseparable through school. We graduate, go to college. He gets into some trouble, and his father hands down a mandate: join the military or get out of his house. I offer to give him a place to stay until he gets on his feet, but Dutt's always been pretty hung up on his father's respect. He ships out for the Army three weeks after my nineteenth birthday.

I drift away from school, start working at the Meg. My folks retire early to a modest house on the lake, leaving my sister and me in Withers. Dutt's father dies. I only see him now when he has his month of leave and crashes on my couch, but we keep in touch the rest of the year. I never let him forget that the scar on the meat of my right calf is because of him.

Three years ago I meet a girl named Brynn that rocks my world. I marry her this past June. Dutt is my best man.

Thank fucking Christ this shit happened while he was home on leave.

In the waiting room of the precinct, my sister jumps up to hug me. Dutt stands to the side and sketches a two-finger salute. He's a long way from that kid that ran home scared after blowing my leg off seventeen years before. His head is shaved to hide his premature baldness, and he wears a pair of those thick, black, military-issue glasses. A few years back they put him in what he called 'the fat boy program' in the Army. He lost the weight, but he's still more imposing than me.

It's only the two of them. She isn't here. I was so sure she would be.

Dutt nods as though answering a question. "God, you look like shit."

"I've been in too long," I say, in my most deadpan tone. "I don't know if I can readjust to life on the outside."

"What the hell happened?" my sister demands. "They wouldn't tell us anything, then all these cop cars came squealing up outside with an ambulance and…is that a *morgue truck* out there?”

“Later.” I don’t want to rehash my prison adventures. Now that I’m back in the real world, my problems are all that matter. Lennie Kincaid and Martin ‘Fiver’ Dunbrough are getting further from my thoughts every second.

I pull out my phone. The battery was end-of-day low already, but now it’s dead. “Can I borrow a cell?”

“Why?”

“…I need to call Brynn.”

“*No*,” they both bark in unison.

Outside, it’s chilly. This is the first week of November. The precinct parking lot is full of cop cars just like my sis said, and a few that are probably unmarked. I wonder if Officer Reed is here somewhere. The morgue truck looks empty, and I don’t want to be here when it fills up. Not so much because I don’t want to see their bodies again, but because I don’t want to catch another glimpse of the freak in the cowboy boots. We hurry past just as the first news van comes squealing into the lot.

While we walk up the street to where my sister parked, I pump them for information.

“Where is she?”

“We don’t know. She left the apartment. The cops wanted to take her to a women’s shelter.”

“A shelter? A fucking *shelter?* That’s stupid, this isn’t *Sleeping with the Enemy*, for chrissake, I’m not gonna kill her!”

“We’re just telling you what they said.” Dutt holds up his hands. “She made some calls, grabbed some stuff, and then she took off right after the cops left with you.”

“Is she with *him?*”

"I don't know, man."

His answer isn't fast enough. I whirl on him and jab a finger in his chest. "Goddamn it, is she with him, Dutt? If she is, you have to tell me!"

He takes my finger and removes it from his chest. "First of all, I don't *have* to do anything. Second, how am I supposed to know where she is? You think she'd tell *me* where she's going? Or that I'd believe her even if she did? The little slut lies as much as she breathes."

"Watch your mouth," I warn. "That's my wife."

"Yeah, and whose fault is that?"

"Don't push me, or I swear to Christ…"

"What's wrong with you, Rudy?" My sister pulls me away. "We're the ones that have been here waiting for your ass all night, so don't take this out on us!"

I rub at my exhausted eyes. "You're right, you're right. I'm sorry. God, Dutt, I'm sorry."

He concedes with a shrug. "My fault, man."

"Just tell me, did she say *anything?* Anything at all?"

"She cried," my sister answers. "Begged them not to arrest you, but they said they had to."

"No, I mean, did she say anything to you two?"

"She said nothing was going on and made a lot of excuses. Said you were crazy and jealous and suspicious all the time."

She's blaming me. Turning me into the villain. My sorrow turns to teeth-grinding, red-filmed fury. My hands clench into aching fists at my side. "What did you say to that?"

"I said you kinda have reason to be."

"There's one other thing you should know," Dutt adds.

We're at my sister's car, a big Chevy minivan-looking thing. She pops the rear loading door, and inside is the little portable fire safe where I keep my life-savings in cash: sixteen thousand dollars, including the seven thou I got for the settlement on my motorcycle accident last year. Pretty much all the liquid assets I have in the world. I only keep a bank account open in case I need it. I find it much easier to save if I can actually see the cash.

"She cleaned you out, man. We tried to stop her, but the cops wouldn't let us. Communal property and whatnot."

So my wife has left me *and* robbed me.

I do the only sensible thing I can think of.

Smash one of those fists into the sidewall of my sister's car, breaking the pinky knuckle on my right hand.

Like I really need this on top of everything else.

We arrive back at my place sometime around 3:30.

I unlock the door and push it open, but refuse to cross the threshold. It's dark and empty. Once I go in and turn on the lights and she's not there, it'll make all this just too god-damned real. Out here, I can still pretend.

The place isn't much, really. A microscopic two-bedroom on the second floor with a mouse problem and far-too-thin walls. The neighbors on the left have loud sex at all hours of the night. Across from us is a Pakistani couple that own a gas station out on the highway; they're almost never home. The furniture is old and worn, the tile is dingy, and the air-conditioner conks out at least twice every summer, but when Brynn and I moved in together almost three years ago, it seemed like a palace.

On our rickety dining table is a little macramé Thanks-giving turkey she bought at some flea market. It looks so forlorn staring at me with its googly eyes.

God, I miss her so much. It's eating me up not knowing where she is. I can't believe that less than eight hours ago, we were having dinner at that table with Dutt, and I still had no doubts that I wanted to spend the rest of my life with her.

Chinua Achebe was right: things fall apart.

Minchi is in his kennel. He's a sable Pom that I named after the dog from some old japanimation Dutt turned me on to. He's proven to be uncannily smart in the few weeks I've had him. I let him out and he crawls between my legs to stare up at me with brown, wet eyes. Just another child of divorce.

A survey of the apartment reveals she's taken a suitcase of clothes. All her bathroom paraphernalia. And every framed picture of us she could grab. The place looks like it's been burglarized by a very sentimental thief.

The thoroughness is frightening. *This is actually happening*, I tell myself. We've had our problems before, but nothing ever felt this...final.

I sit down in my beat-up leather armchair and let Dutt go to work splinting my purple and rapidly swelling hand. My pinky is now at a forty-five degree angle to my other fingers. My sis wants to take me to the hospital, but I don't have the money, especially now. There goes my bowling game.

She makes me go over the whole night again, the fight, the arrest, etc. I go light on the details, but still feel ashamed when I get to that one crucial moment. The one where my brain exploded and I did the thing I can never take back. My sister calls Brynn enough four-letter words to fill a dictionary in a shrewish tone she inherited from our mother. I whine, I bawl, I rant, I lament. I go from cursing her name to pleading for her to come home, and right back again. I beg to call her, but my sister makes me promise I'll at least wait until tomorrow.

Dutt is conspicuously silent through all this.

Finally, she has to go. She's been up all night, and she has to be at work at the salon in the morning. As I walk her to the door, I ask, "Do mom and dad know?"

"*I* didn't tell them. Figured that one's up to you."

"Yeah. I kinda wanna delay that conversation as long as possible."

"They might get suspicious when she doesn't show up for Thanksgiving dinner."

"Aw, Jesus." I hadn't even considered the prospect of getting through the holidays.

I give her a hug and watch her in the parking lot until she's in her car. Sure Withers is a great place, but no woman should be out alone at this time of night.

When I get back in, Dutt is rummaging in the fridge. The dog watches him greedily.

"You want a beer?"

"Naw."

"You wanna smoke?"

"God, yes."

He swipes the bong from the sock drawer in my bedroom and starts packing it with some of this sweet herb he bought nicknamed Cherry Blossom, while I throw on some music. I opt for Soundgarden. Every track on *Superunknown* fits my dour mood perfectly.

My smashed hand is throbbing. It's all bandaged and splinted with a plasticware knife. I can only bend my thumb and first two fingers. In the bathroom cabinet, I find some expired pain pills from my accident and dry swallow two.

Dutt lets me start, and I take two long rips before surrendering the pipe. It cuts my anxiety a bit and helps the pain pills get a toehold, but then my mind opens up and my imagination starts conjuring all sorts of images about what Brynn might be doing with *him* right now. Then it's all I can do to hold my shit together. I reach for the Xbox controller on the coffee table with a shaky hand, but Dutt stops me from the couch.

"We need to talk."

"Well, shit. That sounds serious."

"Deadly."

"Then why the fuck did we get high? You can't talk serious when you're high."

"You don't have to talk. You just have to listen."

I settle back in my chair and gesture for him to continue. Minchi jumps in my lap.

He sets the bong on the coffee table and waits a few moments in silence before saying, "You know you can't take her back...right? Even if she shows up on the doorstep tomorrow in nothing but crotchless panties, with an apology card and a bundle of heart-shaped balloons and begs—I mean, fuckin begs you to take her back, promises anything up-to-and-including unlimited blowjobs for a year—you just...you can't."

I don't say anything, mostly because it's eerie that he rattled off the exact scenario I've been fantasizing about since I ended up in the back of Officer Reed's patrol car.

"She's done this to you three times now. That you know of."

"Yeah, but she doesn't mean it."

"Every time I come back to town this happens."

"So stop coming back to town."

"You two are just...crazy for each other."

I raise an eyebrow. "Isn't that a good thing?"

"No, I mean you're retarded for each other."

"What's the difference?"

Dutt kicks the underside of the coffee table in exasperation. "I'm serious, Rudy. Look, from what I saw here tonight…you two should never be together again. I mean, like, in the same room, together. I've never seen anybody get to you the way she does. Not even me, and I really try. Do you realize I had to call the police on you tonight?"

"I told you to!"

"You were like a mental patient on a rampage. I had to watch while they carted you off. I won't ever be put in that position again. If you take her back this time…I won't come around anymore. You and I are done."

Just for the record, this is my best friend since the sixth grade—the person who, if our thoughts are on a frequency, has a wavelength closer to mine than anyone I've ever met— telling me I have to choose between him and the woman I need more than oxygen.

I feel tears welling again. My buzz is dead and buried. I scratch Minchi's soft little ears with my mummified hand and stare at the thin silver band on the other. That ring meant so much when I finally slipped it on. "You don't understand. She went through a lot when she was young. It changed her, changed the way she thinks. I don't know how to explain it, but it's not really cheating…"

"Yes, it is, Rudy. Another man sticks his dick in her. Hey, listen to me! Doesn't matter if she lets it happen because she's got daddy issues or because she really likes orgasms, it's all the same. I've watched you swallow all the shit she's given you over the past three years with a big smile on your face. It's time to pull your head out of your ass and stop making excuses."

He's right. I know he's right. Hearing the stark truth clicks something in my brain, derails my thoughts out of this funk, and where they land is on Lennie Kincaid.

"I saw…oh Jesus, Dutt, I saw three people die tonight."

He leans forward at the abrupt topic change. "*What?*"

"While I was in jail. This nutjob came in and stabbed the other two guys in my cell. He tried to kill me, but the cops ended up tasing the dude to death, if you can believe it."

"Wait a minute. You're telling me two people were shanked in the temp lockup? In *Withers?*"

I nod.

"That's what all the cops were about?"

"Yeah. I had to give a statement."

"Who was it? Why'd he do it?"

"I don't know. It was a fight between these two mooks all the way from Jersey. Some mobster thing, I guess. This big fucker starts hassling another smaller guy for some password or something. Things got out of hand, and the bruiser pulls out a knife and goes all Michael Myers."

"Whoa. Carpenter or Zombie?"

"Hardest R possible." I'm starting to shake again as I recall what it was like to be trapped in that room with Fiver.

Dutt reaches for the bong and lighter, shotguns, then talks as he exhales. "Wow. That's…goddamn. That's hardcore. But you're lucky this guy died, right?"

"Yeah, my internal organs are very thankful."

"No, I mean, it's a good thing he didn't live *after* the tasing. Otherwise, you'd be witness to a mob execution. They'd have to put you in the protection program and shit."

Minchi scoots up and licks my chin while I consider that. What did I witness?

What the hell was that word?

"C'mon, let's get some sleep," Dutt says, stretching out in his usual place on the couch. "This'll all look better in the morning, man, I promise."

I wish I could believe that.

But it's been three years since I've slept alone, and that queen size bed looks the length of an airport runway without Brynn in it.

We're lying sweaty and tangled in sheets, me on top, crushing her into the bed with my weight, but unable to let go. We don't move, just stare into each other's eyes like they're the only thing in the universe.

She's naked, small and delicate under me, her bronzed skin so healthy it glows even in the dark bedroom. She can go out in the sun for fifteen minutes and come back with a tan. I want to tell her she's beautiful, but there are no words that would do anything except cheapen this moment. Her eyes are wide and piercing, reaching into parts of me I never knew existed.

This is a dream. Well, a dream of a memory. I know it, because I know everything that's about to happen.

This is sometime during the summer after she leaves the abusive foster parents she stays with while she goes to community college, and we move in together. We make love more times than I can count, in every room of the apartment, the pool in the dead of night, my car, anywhere we can get a few seconds alone. Life has a deliciously lazy pace I've never experienced before.

I keep staring at her in the darkness, and suddenly find those words I was looking for.

Marry me, I whisper, without the slightest reservation.

Instead of saying yes, she opens her mouth and emits a loud POP!

Following the intuition that only comes in dreams, I push myself up on hands and knees and look down. There's a shattered bottle on the bed beside us with the remains of a Black Cat firecracker inside. A shard of glass has somehow flown between our mashed bodies and sliced her taut stomach open from one side to the other.

I scream. There's no blood, just a gaping black hole, but something moves in there. Someone is looking out through the wound in Brynn's stomach and it's Fiver and he has a knife and as he starts climbing out I realize I'm back in that cell only this time there are no cops at the door...

I wake thinking someone is pulling on the front of the t-shirt I wore to bed.

I'm still groggy from the pain pill and weed combo, so I grab for Brynn in a panic. She's not there. Everything comes flooding back and I choke on a sob. But there's no time to dwell because there's this invisible hand grabbing me, and the fingers aren't in my shirt but in my *chest*.

My feet find the floor. The apartment is dark and silent except for Dutt's snoring from the living room. That hand stays with me, guiding me, pulling me forward. Its tug is gentle but insistent, like being carried by ocean waves. I follow it, and where it leads me is to the window of my bedroom.

It's still dark out, the sky tinged with the burnt orange of early morning. My window looks out on another building in our complex to the left, the parking lot to the right, and beyond that a section of the street and the dry cleaners on the other side. I can see my Toyota down there. A group of punk teenagers in hoodies strolls through the lot. Nothing the least bit out of the ordinary.

The hand is still pulling. The destination isn't the window, but someplace beyond. There's an undercurrent of... of *yearning* to this sensation, as if this hand is trying to take me someplace important. Something tells me if I went downstairs and started walking, it would lead me somewhere over the dark horizon.

I have a sudden thought. *What direction am I facing?* It takes me a second to orient myself mentally with the freeway a few blocks away, but then I figure it out.

West. This invisible lasso is pulling me in a vaguely western direction. Toward New Mexico. Or California. Or the Pacific.

Or Reno.

And then it fades. Just like that. I wipe sleep from my eyes and try to figure out if it was just left over from the dream. Minchi sits at my feet, his head cocked to one side.

I go back to bed and check the time. It's six a.m. I don't think I'll be getting any more sleep today, and there's no way I can work. Josh will understand if I bail.

My phone is charging beside the clock. I pick it up. I want to call her. The only thing holding me back is anger and pride. The fact that *she* hasn't called is killing me. Don't I mean anything to her? Doesn't our marriage mean anything?

But I have an answer to that already...don't I?

I get up and find my shirt, being careful not to wake Dutt in the other room. That folded piece of paper that came with me to jail is still in the pocket. I sit on the edge of the bed and read the typed words by flashlight. This is the first time I've been able to do more than skim it.

It begins, *I miss you so much.*

Imagine someone has reprogrammed your brain. You're compelled to press various parts of your body against a very sharp, scalding hot knife. You can't help yourself, and yet you know each time you do it, it's going to hurt like a motherfucker, until the *anticipation* of touching the knife is just as bad as the actual pain from doing so.

That's what reading each sentence of this is like for me.

A printout of an email I caught my wife writing to another man.

The tears are flowing again, bitter things that scald my cheeks on the way down because my skin has gone so clammy. This letter is addressed to no one, but I know who it's to.

His name is Chris. He's the new manager of the comic book store I go to every Wednesday like clockwork for the past ten years, and where I've drug Brynn for the last three. A smarmy asshole that wouldn't know Mark Millar from Frank Miller. He looks like the kind of guy who would've pantsed you in high school, or wiped a booger in your lunch. Don't ask me how this thing got started between him and Brynn, because I'm still trying to figure that one out myself.

Various phrases from the letter carve themselves into my memory.

Last week was great.

I need to see you again.

It gets harder and harder to leave you.

This is what I found her doing last night while Dutt and I were in the other room watching TV and *I* went nuts and *she* went nuts and, oh God, I hit her, and yeah, that's so awful my soul feels like a shriveled, rotten piece of fruit, but even worse is the unfaceable truth that if Dutt *hadn't* been there, I might've done a lot worse.

I tell myself, this guy can't possibly mean anything to her. Brynn is all screwed up. She has a pathological need for acceptance. Whenever I find out about her little 'dalliances'—one before we got married, one after, always revealed because one of her bitchy friends ratted her out—I get mad, we have our miniature crisis, but she says they don't mean anything to her, and she doesn't know why she did it.

She cheats on me, but she always comes home.

Except this time.

My wedding ring is so heavy, it feels like it's weighing my whole hand down. I think about taking it off...but that would be too much like admitting I've lost.

I refold the paper, put it on the nightstand and try to get some sleep.

Chapter FIVE

The MegaMart was the first grocery store in Withers, and the last non-chain left. The new Walmart is being built four blocks away, so that may not last long. It looks like a big Spanish mission from the outside, constructed of gray and white stone and a stucco roof, full of high arches and decorative woodwork, with a quaint little cupola bell tower and a railed balcony on the side that leads off the upstairs business office. I don't know if the building was anything before it was the Meg, or if Mr. Peters just wanted to remember the Alamo.

Inside is the kind of shopping experience most people haven't had since the fifties. The aisles are sparkling clean. The shelves are well-stocked and not laid out to facilitate impulse buying. They're low enough so you can see over the top and give a friendly hello to other shoppers or wave to your neighbors. Everyone that works there—from the clerks to the stockboys to the Photolab Twins to Sven the Butcher, who's been here since the Meg opened in 1956—are trained to be cross-knowledgeable and friendly, and we are all required to greet any customer who comes within five feet of us. I know for a fact that this is how Mr. Peters wanted it. He ran the store himself until about four years ago, then he retired and turned operations over to Josh.

I'm a filler, taking care of whatever Josh needs. Sometimes stocking, sometimes clerking, sometimes counting cash at shift end. It's not what I envisioned myself doing back in the halcyon days of youth, but it's peaceful, morale is high, and I can write on a little yellow legal pad if it's not too busy.

I love working here.

But I swear to God, if one more person says hi to me right now, I'm going to knock their teeth in.

"Oh man, and do you remember that pass in the second quarter for that touchdown? They were on fire, just freakin amazing!"

Josh is mid-thirties, clean-cut and goofy, and believes everyone loves the Dallas Cowboys as much as he does. In most cases, he's right. I've told him time and time again I don't watch football, but even the concept is alien to him.

"Best game they played all season! Do you realize they have a shot at division?"

"Josh."

"And the interceptions were UN. REAL. You musta just stood up and cheered when they took that ball at the 20, huh?"

"Josh, man."

"Yeah?"

"I didn't watch the game."

"Holy crow, you *didn't?* I got the whole thing DVR'd if you wanna come over!"

I called him when I woke up to let him know what happened, and that I wouldn't make my shift. I had planned on just staying in bed all day, but Dutt got me up at eleven, starving. There was no food in the fridge, because today's the day Brynn and I would usually do the shopping.

Hence, here we are at the Meg. In a strictly customer capacity.

I should mention, I still have on the rank t-shirt and sweatpants I wore to bed.

"No, Josh, that's cool. I was wondering if I could…maybe…if it's okay…have an advance on next paycheck?"

He grins ear-to-ear. "Oh, sure, sure, kid, no problem! How much you need?"

"Fifty or so, just to get by."

He rummages in the bottom desk drawer and pulls out a cashbox. We're in the upstairs office, which is populated by filing cabinets and decorated with bad movie posters the employees slap up. We have a contest going for who can find the worst. Currently, I'm winning with a bootleg Japanese one-sheet of the Roger Corman directed Fantastic Four movie, in which—due to some poor photoshopping—it looks like The Thing is squatting to take a dump on Human Torch's head. Behind Josh is the bolted screen door that leads out to that strange little balcony.

While he digs in his pocket for the key, he asks, "You that bad off?"

"She took everything. My entire savings."

"What, from that stupid fire safe?"

"Yeah."

"I told you not to keep that lyin around in cash! Didn't I tell you that? You think any of the Cowboys have millions of dollars stashed under their mattress?"

"No. That's where any self-respecting football player keeps his cocaine and dead hookers."

"Hey! Don't talk about them that way," he warns. "That's all in the past."

I roll my eyes. "Anyway, without Brynn's income, I'll probably be evicted from my place in a month."

Josh pulls out three twenties and hands them to me. "So that's it then, huh? It's really over for you two?"

I shrug. "Your guess is as good as mine."

"That's too bad. You guys made a real cute couple."

Thanks, Josh. Twist the knife deeper.

I go downstairs to find Dutt. It's after noon now, and the Meg is packed with the well-dressed, after-church shoppers. I look over the crowd as I walk. Along the way, the cashiers and a few of the regular customers call out greetings. I wave. Tammy and Rebecca, two college girls that work the day shift, make a point of looking the other way as I pass by.

Word has apparently spread fast about what I spent last night in jail for.

Sven the Butcher gives me a grunt. He's not really Sven, but nobody can pronounce the guy's real name, which is all consonants. I swipe one of the free sausage samples from his counter and keep walking.

"'Ey, yo, Rudy, man," Luiz calls from the middle of the aisle where he's stocking cans. As I go down to meet him, he holds out his hand, I hold out my unbandaged one, and he performs a complicated handshake I can never follow. I usually just hold still and let him do his thing. "So check it out, bro, I got a question I need answered." He grins, and I know what's coming. "Just how many packs of cigarettes does it take to buy a hot shower in the clink these days?"

"Oh ha ha, Luiz. Least I didn't get cornholed every night for four years by my roommate Big Steve. Who was, I might add, of perfectly average *height*."

Luiz is still laughing, holding his shaved head like he expects the laughter to burst apart his skull. "C'mon, man, I'm just playin. Gotta tease you a li'l. You the *last* muhfuckah I'd expect to see behind bars."

"Who told everybody? Josh?"

"Yo bro, he told me, but that's only cause I was nice enough to get in here and work your shift. That old dude Kazmer, the one that comes in to get his adult diapers? He told everyone else. Heard it on his police scanner last night. Old fart got nuttin better to do with his time."

I groan. "Great. Now I'm Ike Turner."

As if on cue, I hear behind me, "Whoa, dude, Rudy, dude!"

Two high school seniors with bleach-tipped hair rush down the aisle to me. Sean and Kevin. The Photolab Twins. They're tall and lean, baseball players for their school. Collectively, they have the IQ of a really dumb bag of rocks, but somehow, they're the only two people in the entire place that know how to run the photo-processing equipment Mr. Peters bought before he retired, for the three people on the entire planet that haven't gone digital.

"Dude, is it true you were in jail last night when those mobsters shot up the place, dude?" Sean—or maybe Kevin—asks me. These two begin and end every sentence with 'dude.'

"You were there for that?" Luiz looks at me with new appreciation. "Shit was all over the news this morning."

"I can't really talk about it," I say. Neither the cops nor the detective told me any such thing, but it seems the easiest way to get out of having to rehash the topic.

Kevin waves a hand in excitement. "Dude, well I heard that, like, they were transporting some snitch, and the mafia ran a car right through the building to kill him, dude!"

"Dude, say hello to my little friend, dude!" Sean agrees. They high-five.

"Naw, nothin like that," I say, bursting their bubble.

They calm enough for Kevin to solemnly ask, "But dude, so you and Brynn are like kaputs now, huh dude?"

"I don't know."

"Dude, that's too bad. That chick had a *bangin* little body on her, dude."

"Yeah, dude, we always said she was too hot for you, dude."

Believe it or not, this is their idea of a compliment.

"Get back to work, assholes," Luiz tells them.

They go, leaving me to mourn the fact that Brynn did—*does*—have a banging little body.

I think of the first time I saw her, at the bar around the corner from where I was living at the time. Green sneakers. Short little denim skirt. Children's size t-shirt revealing a lean section of midriff. Eighteen, fresh out of high school, and scamming the bartender with a fake ID. Hottest girl in the place, and somehow she ends up talking to a loser like me.

Two months later and she would've been on her way to school at UT Austin, free of the string of foster parents she's been with since the age of 2, and I probably would've taken the editing job I'd been offered in Oklahoma. Had to be fate, right?

I think about how I could never, in a billion years, get a girl as hot as Brynn again.

"'Ey," Luiz says quietly. "Don't go through this alone, bro. I been down the divorce road, I know how hard it is. You come stay with Graciela and the kids and me, if you need to."

I nod and walk away down the aisle.

Dutt is by the cold case near the back, dropping pre-sliced lunch meat and a case of Miller into his shopping cart. I start over to him, and my phone buzzes in my pocket. I pull it out, banging my injured finger in the process.

It's Brynn. The little window on the phone shows a picture I took of her performing drunk karaoke.

My heart starts thumping. I look up at Dutt. He raises an eyebrow and waves a hand as if to say, *Go ahead, gotta happen sooner or later.*

I push TALK. "Hello?"

"Hi." She sounds tired. And snuffly from crying.

Silence stretches. The moment has so much potential. Too much to express, too many different directions, so I say the only thing that's true for all of them.

"I need to see you."

She answers with a heavy sigh.

"I was in jail last night."

"I know. I told them not to take you."

"How could you do this to me? To us? *Again?*"

"Rudy..."

"You promised last time. You promised it would never happen again."

"Rudy, I don't wanna talk about it." So cold. Her voice like ice in my brain.

"No, we *need* to talk about it."

"Why?"

I consider that for a second. Think about Dutt's ultimatum. And I decide.

"So we can get through this."

"Rudy…I don't know if I *want* to get through this. I've been unhappy a long time, I guess. Last night…what you did…this is probably for the best."

The sentences might as well be poison-tipped darts. I can't move. Can't think. The world swirls away, drains of color, and there is only an ache in my heart that feels like a black hole. I have to lean against the closest shelf just to keep from sliding into the floor. Families in their Sunday best pass by. Over the PA system in the store, Stevie Wonder is singing "Superstitious."

"Let's just get this over with as easily as possible," she says, and starts into a speech that sounds entirely rehearsed. "You can have the apartment and the dog. I want half the dishes and sheets and a few other pieces of furniture. That's all. I'd like for you to go with me to get the cell phones separated, but if you won't, I'll understand. We can let the court settle everything else."

My jaw works. *C'mon Rudy, get it together. If the bitch is actually doing this, don't let her play you for a fool.*

"What about the money?" Voice surprisingly calm.

"What money?"

"*You know goddamn well what money,*" I snarl. Dutt starts to walk over and I hold a hand up. "The money you stole from me while I was rotting in jail. *That* money."

"I…I need it. To get on my feet."

"No, *I* need it. How do you think I'm gonna pay for that shitty apartment on my salary alone? That money is *mine*. I saved it, I almost died for it."

"Can we…can we talk about it later?"

She sounds weird. More than just cold. And then it hits me.

"He's there right now, isn't he? You're there with him."

"I told you, he's just a friend."

"Put him on." The plastic casing of the phone creaks in my hand.

"No."

"Let me talk to him."

"*No, Rudy.*"

"This conversation goes no further until I hear his voice."

I imagine the grimace on her face. There's a rustle. Then a cheerful male voice says, "Heya, sport!"

Blood. Busted teeth. A baseball bat to a human skull.

"Hi," I return, just as cordial. "How'd you sleep last night?"

"Pretty good," he says, in an even more jovial tone.

A hammer to kneecaps. Drill bit to eyeballs. I want to hear what his screams sound like.

"Yeah, you sleep pretty well next to my wife?"

"Are you gonna just run your mouth, or do you actually have something to say?"

"*I WILL FUCKING KILL YOU!*"

The whole store goes dead silent, except for Stevie. All eyes are on me. Dutt is coming, but before he can reach me, I slip through the EMPLOYEES ONLY door next to me and into the back stockroom. I hurry through the dimly lit chamber and out the exit that leads to the side alley and dumpsters. The sudden shock of cold air doesn't even register.

"Whoa, easy there, Compton," Chris says over the phone. "That the sort of thing Captain America would say?"

"You're dead. A fucking dead man."

"Bring it on, sport. I guarantee I can hit a lot harder than a hundred-pound girl."

Ooo. That one stings.

There's some muffled words, and then Brynn is back on the line.

"There, Rudy, you talked to him, are you satisfied?"

"*Him?* You're leaving me for *him?*"

"Yes. No. Look, I don't know. I just need some time to get my head straight, and I can't do it around you. I have to go. Goodbye."

"I love you," I say quickly.

"I love you too," she answers, "I just don't know if I'm *in* love with you."

The phone goes dead, I lean over in case my roiling stomach decides to throw the gears in reverse, and that's when I see the little Honda parked at the edge of the lot, right in front of the alley opening.

In the front seat are two hooded figures watching me.

I go through the first of what could only be called 'withdrawal pains' that night.

Dutt is gone. His only living family is his grandmother, who lives south of us in Richland Hills. She's in the hospital, and he needs to see her before his leave is over. He'll stay at her house, and be back in the morning. Before he goes, he makes me promise not to call Brynn.

I fix a sandwich and eat half of it. I try to write but can't keep my mind focused. Finally, I settle for television.

One second I'm fine, right in the middle of a midnight *South Park* rerun, and the next I'm clammy and shaking, shaking so bad my hands are just blurs, and then I'm clutching my aching stomach and rocking back and forth. I wouldn't be surprised if pink bugs started crawling out of the walls.

I have to call her. I have to know where she is and what's

she's doing and beg her to come back. If I don't have some kind of contact with her immediately, by brain is going to fry like an egg. This raw need consumes all rational thought.

Is it good to be addicted to the person you're in love with?

I'm not talking about any of that psychologist babble like codependency and enabling. What I'm asking you is, wouldn't the world be a better place if we all had someone we loved that...fucking...*much?* If love is truly, as Aristotle said, a single soul inhabiting two bodies, then mine is ripped in half.

And to top it all off, that invisible hand is back, stronger than before, feeling like it wants to pull me straight through the back wall of the apartment and on to parts unknown.

"What do you want?" I mutter aloud, feeling my chest for the fishhooks that must be imbedded there. This is just anxiety on top of anxiety.

Come to me, a small voice whispers in my head. I might be imagining it, just another symptom of my withdrawal. As awful as I feel, I can't be sure of anything.

I can't be alone right now. I need someone to talk to. Dutt said to call him if I needed to, but I can't do that to him. I don't want to bother my sister in the middle of the night and my parents still don't know what's going on. I consider Luiz for a second, but that just doesn't feel right either.

Then I get an idea.

I pick up the phone, and dial the non-emergency number for the police.

Whataburger is really the only thing decent that's open this late. In high school, Dutt and I used to come here at three in the morning, high as apple pie, and eat till we couldn't move. I'm still not hungry, but I order a burger and fries just so I'm not sitting there without any food.

Across from me is Officer Reed, in full uniform, chowing down on a bacon cheeseburger. He doesn't look so much like Olyphant to me anymore. He keeps his head down while he eats, but every few seconds he looks across the table at me and squints, as though trying to figure out if I'm going to jump him. The other weirdos that populate all-night fast food restaurants give our booth a wide berth.

"Thanks for meeting me like this," I say.

He shrugs, giving me another of those looks. "I don't make a habit of taking my lunch break with the people I arrest, but my chief said it would be a good idea. They're all afraid you're gonna sue them over what happened yesterday."

"Oh." And here I was thinking he might as interested in me as I was in him.

"So are you?"

"Am I what?"

"Going to sue the city?"

"I don't really see the point. Nothing happened to *me*." I put a fry in my mouth. I'm sure it's mealy and salty but my senses are so dulled I can't even taste it, so I end up chomping it like gum. "Did they ever find out what all that was about?"

"Not really. Some specialist from the FBI is handling the whole thing."

"What about the big guy? Fiver or Dunbrough or whatever?"

"He's dead. What about him?"

"Yeah, I know, but did they find out why he, um, croaked?"

"They think he had a heart defect. When they juiced him with the taser, it just stopped him cold."

I nod solemnly, but can't imagine anyone shedding tears over this fact. The world can only get better without that maniac in it.

"Is that why you brought me here, to talk about that?"

"I...I don't really know. My head is just so muddled. I needed someone to talk to, and you were the first person I thought of."

"Why's that?"

I force myself to swallow the fry I've been turning into paste in my mouth. "Last night, you said some things. They kinda stuck with me. Plus, I knew you worked the night shift."

He chews through a big bite of burger and asks, "What about you and your wife, you work things out?"

"I haven't seen her."

"That's good."

"Doesn't seem that way. I've never felt this lousy in my life."

"Did you ever find out if she really cheated on you?"
"She won't admit it, but I'm pretty sure. She's staying with the guy now. Plus, she's done it before."

"*What?* You mean this is the *second* time?"

"Well...third."

He sets down his burger and leans toward me over his tray. "Okay, I had to be diplomatic before, what with you being under arrest and all, but right now I say to you, one man to another: Fuck. *That.* Why would you put up with that?"

"It's complicated." My standard excuse.

"No, it isn't. My wife is the love of my life, all right? The queen of my world. I would rather chop off an arm right here and now than be without her. But if she ever cheated on me...even *once*...either she's gone, or I am. Guaranteed."

"You could really walk away like that?"

"You bet your ass I could. Once the trust is gone, it's gone. It changes the entire relationship, turns it into a whole new animal. You can't rebuild it, you can only live with whatever it becomes, which is usually this sickly, pale imitation of what was once something really good." He shakes his head in disgust. The emotion in the gesture is so genuine, I think, *who broke* your *heart, Officer Reed?* "Let me ask you something, after she did this the first time, did you ever really get over it? Or was it always lurking in the back of the closet? Be honest, now."

"I...not really."

"See? And I bet you'd be willing to open your arms if she came back right now, wouldn't you?"

"Probably," I agree. This guy—this virtual stranger—is reading me like bad Danielle Steele, and I hate it.

"My friend, that goes beyond naïve and into the realm of pathetic. I mean, damn, what hold does this woman have on you to make you stick around after she did it twice?"

"I didn't really see it that way." I want to explain this to someone, the thing I could never make Dutt or my sister or anyone else understand. "She had a rough past. Her childhood...it sucked. Abusive parents, abusive foster parents. She's restless, can't be happy with life. And she has this need for attention, so she goes out and looks for it with strangers. Sex is just sex, but she *loves* me. I *know* she does."

"Well then you have a problem." Officer Reed wraps up the remains of his food in the paper from the bottom of the tray. "If that's what you truly believe, then by acknowledging the situation, you're signing a release that frees her from any wrongdoing. You can love her through it, pray to God she changes, but if it doesn't happen, you have no one to blame but yourself. You can't go losing your temper when the alley cat comes dragging back home after a night on the town."

"I know," I say defensively. "But you have to believe me, nothing like last night has ever happened to me before. I just saw that email and…something snapped."

He points at the bandaged nub of my right hand. "Correct me if I'm wrong, but you didn't have that yesterday, did you? What was it, brick wall?"

I look at the table. "Car door."

Officer Reed nods like Sherlock Holmes after finishing a case and leans back in his seat. "I see it all the time. Perfectly rational, friendly, loving guys—guys without an ounce of violence in them—completely lose their shit over a woman. Love is such a weird, scary, intense thing."

"I don't even know if I believe in love anymore." The statement sounds small and petty coming out of my mouth.

"Why do you say that?"

"I used to believe in fate. In soul mates. All that crap Hollywood feeds us about there being someone for everyone. And I thought she was it. I was so sure. There was never a doubt in my mind that I'd spend the rest of my life with her. If love is real, then how could a person feel something like that and be so far off base?"

He waves a hand. "Oh, love is real, trust me. People look for it every day. They steal for it, they kill for it. The problem is, they think it's something they can go out and grab for themselves. Take control of it. But love is balance. A seesaw. You gotta work in unison, or one person's gonna end up on the ground. Kelly and I are like that." His wistful smile as he says this makes me feel very hopeful that someone can find happiness in this universe.

"This thing though…it's killing me," I say, with tears in both eyes. "I want to keep calling her, keep begging."

"Well, on the opposite end of the spectrum, divorce is like a death. You're grieving right now. But pretty soon, your pride is gonna outweigh your grief. One day—maybe not tomorrow, maybe not this week, but one day—you'll wake up and say 'enough is enough.' It'll be like a light switch—BOOM—and you'll be done with the bullshitting phase of the break-up. You'll be ready to reclaim your dignity. After you reach that point…it's all smooth sailing."

He slides out of the booth and stands up, brushing away crumbs from his uniform shirt. "All right, I gotta go."

"Thanks again," I say. "This really helped a lot."

"No problem." He digs a business card out of the breast pocket and slides it across to me. "You need to talk again, just gimme a call."

I accept the card with the intention of taking him up on the offer.

I just never get the chance.

Chapter SIX

I am a robot, grinding through the days.

I may look authentic—working, eating, sleeping (not so much these last two)—but what you see is not a thinking, reasoning human being, but a shell going through motions. Like that part of your brain that regulates your breathing and heartbeat without you concentrating on it.

In the five days following my incarceration, the pain fades from my hand even though it's far from healed. I drop ten pounds, grow roots in front of the TV, and blaze up until I'm floating on a neverending sea of smoke that even Min-chi gets high on. Any time I close my eyes and manage to breach the sleep barrier, my nightmares are steeped in sex and blood. When I'm not home, I escape into music, wear my iPod everywhere, but skip over any song that reminds me of her. Since this constitutes three-quarters of my collection, the playlist is limited.

Dutt is with me all the time except when I go to work, but he's leaving in a couple of days to fly back to his base in Korea. I'm terrified. He's the only person I can stand to be around, and the only thing keeping me from collapsing into a puddle of Jell-o. My mom calls several times about Thanksgiving plans, but I never pick up.

Trying not to call Brynn—or worse, go to her job at this freight warehouse out by the airport—is a constant struggle. For the first few days after my sit down with Officer Reed, I'm losing badly. Deep in my heart, I know it's over—it *has* to be, just like Dutt said—but I can't let go. I call until she hangs up on me, then call some more. Sometimes I cry, sometimes I yell. Sometimes I beg and then call names. I text message so far over my limit, AT&T checks to make sure my phone hasn't been stolen. The most I get from these conversations is that if I don't stop, she'll file a restraining order against me.

The wedding ring stays on my hand every second now, even when I'm showering.

Some nights…when sleep has completely abandoned me…I go and sit in the closet and smell her clothes.

This is my life, and I don't know how I got here.

Work is the absolute worst. Things I used to love about my job seem trivial; the things I tolerated are nearly unbearable. I know the Meg is dead-end, I always knew it, but until now, it never mattered that I gave up my ambitions to teach or get into the publishing industry while I waited for one of my novels to be discovered. As Huey Lewis once said, I was doing it all for my baby. But you know what, fuck him and his lyrics for the common man. In my opinion, "Stuck With You" is the least romantic song ever written.

I try to ignore Luiz and all my coworkers, but everyone wants to cheer me up. And when you're going through a serious break-up, the advice always comes in one of two flavors.

First, there's the Give-It-Timers. They tell you to be patient, that things will get better, time heals all wounds, the same sort of jazz Officer Reed told me, just not quite as eloquent. Telling that to someone in my position is the equivalent of strolling up to a GI that's just had his legs blown off and telling him not to worry, someday he'll learn to get around on the stumps.

But then there's the other little piece of wisdom the world tries to feed you: someday you'll meet someone who makes your heartbreaker pale in comparison, someone you'll love even more, the person that was *really* meant for you.

All I can think at the moment is that if there's a bigger love than the one I had for Brynn out there, then my heart would never be able to contain it.

It would burst my chest like an over-inflated balloon.

"Rudy, you in here?"

I am, but I don't want anyone to know that.

Where I am, precisely, is wedged under the dog food shelf in the back storeroom of the Meg. Josh has been understanding enough to let me stay away from customers and take care of inventory and stock the last few days. Moving things takes a lot longer with my busted hand, but I don't care. I'm transferring dog food from the shelves to the pallet cart when I notice a few bags of Kibbles 'N Bits have fallen off the back and lay wedged in the two foot gap between the bottom of the wooden shelves and the cold concrete floor. I lie down full out and slither under on my belly, wiping away cobwebs, then pause after I reach the offenders.

It's cool and dark and closed in down here. Like a cave. I rest my head on my cheek and feel protected from all my problems for the barest of moments.

And then I'm yanked forward by my chest so hard I start sliding against the tile.

My hands catch the metal crossbars that hold up the shelves before I can fly out and slam against the wall. My broken finger screams in outrage. I brace my feet against the opposite end of the shelf and struggle against the invisible force that has me. Sweat pops out across my brow. Imagine hanging from parallel bars with a metal cummerbund around your waist and a big supermagnet below and you'll get some idea what this feels like.

West, a voice whispers in my ear. It's so faint, and fading in and out like bad radio reception. *Come to me.*

"*Stop*," I plead through clenched teeth. The tension is so great, if I let go, it'll be like an arrow fired from a taut bow. These attacks or whatever have been getting stronger, but this is by far the worst.

And then it's over. I'm released and lie gasping on the floor under the shelf.

That's when the door to the stockroom opens and someone comes in looking for me.

At first I don't answer because I'm still trying to catch my breath. I see a pair of size 11 Nikes come around the corner into the main stock aisle, and when the voice calls out again, I realize it's Luiz. I'm just about to speak when his sneakers are joined by a pair of black cowboy boots with worn heels.

"Sorry, sir, I thought he was back here," Luiz says, using his forced cheerful, customer-interaction tone.

"Not a problem," a gravelly, officious voice answers.

Beneath the shelf, a long, slow shiver starts at the base of my spine and travels up. I hold my breath and shrink back into the shadows. The invisible hand is forgotten.

"You can wait out front, if you want. I know he's working today. Maybe he just went to lunch."

"Won't be necessary," the man in the boots says. "If you would, just let Mr. Compton know I stopped by."

"Is he…in some kinda trouble or somethin?"

"I just have some questions for him about the incident last week. Here's my card. Please have him call me."

I can tell, even from under here, that Luiz is hesitating. Can't say I blame him. I wouldn't want to accept anything from that basement dweller I saw at the jail either. But then he must take the card, because the cowboy boots turn crisply and clack out of the storeroom.

I'm out of my hiding spot in a flash. Luiz is still watching the door where the owner of the boots just disappeared. He jumps a good foot in the air when I come up behind him.

"Jesus, Rudy, man, where the hell were you, there was this guy—"

I grab the card from his hand and run out of the stockroom.

In the shopping area, I catch sight of a narrow head covered in slicked back gray hair. I follow it toward the front of the store, being careful to keep my head below aisle level. Customers are sparse on a Thursday afternoon. No one sees me sneaking along like an escaped con. On the way, I glance at the card I took from Luiz.

Douglas Hillman, FBI. Then a phone number.

The automatic door chimes as he exits. I slink past the registers to the front windows and watch him through the glass. Hillman doesn't look like any FBI agent I ever saw. He's gangly, like a scarecrow come to life, and today he's wearing black dress pants and a white, long-sleeve shirt buttoned all the way up to his bulging Adam's apple. His forehead is Neanderthalic, his nose a shark's fin. He heads out to a brown Ford sedan parked in the first row, opens the driver's door, and pauses.

Then his head turns, and his dead eyes go right to where I'm crouched in the display case.

I dive sideways, down behind the newspaper dispensers. Through the crack between the Star Telegram and Dallas Morning News machines, I watch as he scans the storefront for another second and then folds his long frame behind the wheel of the car. He drives away.

I raise up a little at a time behind the dispensers, terrified he'll come squealing back into the parking lot and not knowing why this idea scares me so much, and as I pass the square window where today's newspaper is displayed, Officer Reed stares at me from the front page just a few inches away.

The headline reads, 'SEARCH FOR COPKILLER GOES ON.'

Apparently, this is all anyone's been talking about. A dead cop in Withers, a city whose murder rate is in single digits for the decade. I've been so wrapped up in my own world of shit, I never heard a thing.

I carry the paper back to my stockroom sanctuary and skim the article. On Tuesday night, two days after our midnight meal, Officer Nathan Reed's body was found in his patrol car on Stardust Drive, in a sleepy residential area. This is, I realize, the same patrol car I was cuffed and forced into on Saturday. Nearby residents heard no commotion, but the authorities suspect possible gang activity due to a report from down the street about four individuals wearing 'matching hoodies or hooded garments.'

I read that phrase several times.

However, it's the manner of Officer Reed's death that has them most puzzled.

His body was riddled with arrows fired from all directions through the vehicle's windows.

The picture that accompanies this article is a young, academy snapshot of the cop I knew, looking a lot less seasoned and a lot more innocent. I stare at that photo and think of his smile when he talked about his wife.

Kelly. She's mentioned also. Pregnant with their first child.

The world blurs through a film of tears. There's a big stewpot in my brain, and in it is swirling all my problems: Reed, Hillman, the invisible hand that's going to be yanking me through walls soon. And Brynn, of course. Always Brynn. I don't know what to do about any of them. Then again, I'm so wrung out it's a wonder I can tie my shoes.

I fold up the paper and start back to work just as a random thought bubbles up:

I'm not the only one who rode in the back of Officer Reed's car that night.

Lennie Kincaid did too.

Dutt's been using my Toyota to get around while I'm at work. I go out to wait for him after my shift ends, still thinking about Agent Hillman's sharp, angular face. I'll have to talk to the man eventually. I didn't do anything wrong, so I really don't have any reason to be worried.

My phone rings. Brynn.

For a heartbeat, I consider not answering. I'm not her slave anymore. I don't have to jump when she calls. Officer

Reed said one day I would just be done with all the bullshit, that I would be ready to reclaim my dignity.

Today is not that day.

"Hello?"

"Ruu-uu-uudy." My name, stretched into multiple syllables by sobs.

"Baby? Brynn, what's wrong?"

"N-nothing," she says, audibly pulling herself together. "I was just thinking about last year. Your accident."

A quick series of jagged memories slice through me. Seeing the car pull out from my right. Braking too hard, feeling the back wheel of the bike lock up. Flying through the air. Then lying facedown in a puddle of my own blood.

"Rudy? You there?"

"Yeah, I'm here. Why were you thinking about that?"

"I was. I was just...so scared you were going to die."

You're the only thing killing me, I almost say. Instead I ask, "What do you want, Brynn?"

"To come by the apartment."

In a heartbeat, all the stones piled on top of me are lifted away, and I can breath again, I can think again, I can *feel* again, it's like that wonderful sensation when your ears pop after you get over a cold and you can hear, only this is all over my body, my mind, my soul, every molecule and atom in me awakening at the same time.

"Okay," I say, trying not to sound too eager. "You want to come...tonight?"

"Um, tomorrow would be better, if that's cool."

"Why not tonight?"

"I just...I can't, Rudy."

"What are you doing?"

"Stuff. I have plans."

"With Chris?"

"…maybe this is a bad idea."

"*Nonononono*," I blurt, "tomorrow's fine, I'm off work, I'll be there all day."

"Okay. See you around one."

Dutt and I are supposed to go miniature golfing today. Just to get me out of the apartment. But I lie and tell him I need some alone time and feel like shit for doing it.

"You can't wallow," he says.

"I'm not wallowing. That's a stupid word."

"I agree. But you're still doing it."

"Pigs wallow. Are you calling me a pig?"

He grins, but it's off his face almost immediately. He peers at me through his thick glasses. "You know, I'm outta here in a few days. What are you gonna do when I'm gone?"

I'm not as scared of that anymore, because I'm sure that by tonight Brynn will be back, and things will be on their way to normal. And if my best friend doesn't like it, that's his problem.

I shrug. "I'll survive."

"I'm coming back here to get you at five, and we're gonna grab dinner."

"Sounds like a plan."

He borrows my car and heads out on one of his 'culture runs,' which is really just him stockpiling DVDs and video games he can take back overseas with him.

I hear the knock at the door and answer it.

She stands on the stoop. It's been a week since I've seen her, and she looks amazing, cute and sexy and adorable and sultry and practically edible. This is my wife: raven black hair in a Tinkerbell mop, dark chocolate eyes, button nose, imbedded dimples in either cheek when she smiles, perfect skin the color of sand on a warm beach, down near the waterline, with a dusting of freckles. An angelic face you would never believe capable of deceit or betrayal. I know I never could. She stands a good foot shorter than me. Her breasts swell against the tight, green, half-sleeve sweater she's wearing, which is just short enough to give a hint of midriff and show the top of her hips before they're hidden by a pair of curve-hugging jeans.

God, I *love* that. She knows it drives me crazy.

We open our arms and hug. She's small against me. I put my arms around that tiny waist and something south of the equator begins to stir.

"I missed you," I say.

"I missed you too," she whispers in my ear. Her breath against me is electrifying. My lips find hers.

I pull her into the apartment, but don't get farther than the living room. I'm kissing her with such urgency, consumed by the smell of her, the taste of her. Her hands are moving, running down my chest and caressing me through the front of my pants. I grab the backs of her legs and lift her off the ground. Her legs lock around my hips and I can feel that tight heat at the center of her pressed right up against me.

We cross the living room and make it as far as the couch. I'm rushing this, I know I am, but I want her in a way I never have before, want to consume her, hide away deep inside her where the misery can't find me. She seems just as urgent as she unbuckles and unzips us both.

She guides me in. I'm trembling. We both are. We rock together, grasping, touching, licking. I bury my face in her smooth neck as I get ready to finish. And when I'm right there, right on the verge of total ecstasy, she makes it even better by panting, "I want to come home."

Yeah. That's the way it'll happen.

I clean the apartment first. Top to bottom. It takes three hours, and the vacuum has a meltdown halfway through. I have to stack the filthy dishes Dutt and I have been accumulating on the short stretch of bar countertop to dry after I wash them. I clean myself up, something I haven't done properly in a week, and change out the funky bandage on my hand. I even give Minchi a bath.

I put on something sexy. Something I know she can't resist. Black Skechers work boots. A pair of faded dungarees, boot cut, just about to wear through in several spots. A plain white tee that clings to my non-existent abs. And, to top it off, a black velvet sport coat she got me for Christmas last year.

In the mirror, I examine myself. My sandy blond hair could use a cut, but otherwise, I look like me again.

It's only about 12:15. I throw on Chris Isaak's *Heart Shaped World*, the album guaranteed to take any woman from zero to wet in six seconds. I decide against making lunch for her in case that's presumptuous, and spend the rest of the time pacing the apartment. For masochistic reasons I can't begin to fathom, I grab the printout of her email and read through it one more time, then slip it into my back pocket.

At 12:30, there's a knock. She's early, and thank God. The suspense is killing me.

I throw open the door wide without checking the peephole, ready to live out my fantasy.

And that's how I get the broken nose to match my hand.

Before I can see who's on the landing, a fist smashes into me hard enough to cause a flare of light across my eyeballs.

I stumble back, clutching my nose, my eyes already tearing up. My feet get caught on one another and I go down on the slick tile of the entry. Blood seeps between my fingers as I look up.

There are two figures on the threshold of my front door, standing in golden fall sunlight.

The one on the left is squat and froggy, but my attention glosses right over him and centers on the huge guy beside him, the one that hit me.

Because this guy is Fiver.

Chapter SEVEN

I haven't told you what I write, have I?

It's sci-fi, mostly. Some dark fantasy. Horror, when the mood strikes. All the stuff that falls under the 'speculative fiction' category nowadays.

When my sis and I were kids, our father kept us on a pretty regular diet of the strange and macabre. If my mom was traveling for work on a weekend, the three of us had a movie marathon. I remember watching *Them!* in elementary, *Alien* in junior high, and *The Exorcist* in high school. I liked high concept stuff. My imagination was spurred by authors like William Sleator and Charles Sheffield. And somewhere along the way, I decided it wasn't enough to be fascinated and horrified; I wanted to have the same effect on others.

I started writing short stories my senior year, on any number of screwed-up subjects. Got up the courage to submit them during my doomed college experience. To date, I've even sold six or seven, for enough money collectively to buy one of the more expensive meals on the menu at Mickey D's.

Just before Brynn and I got married last year, I start

working on my first novel. It's this cheesy zombie story, very Romero-influenced. In it, the main character's husband claws his way out of the grave and chases her around the house with a hacksaw, intent on taking the hand with her wedding ring. There's a great scene where he's battering down the front door and she's trying to hold him off with a pizza cutter.

So with all my experience in the odd and unthinkable, and in light of the novel I've been scribbling at for eleven months now, you'd think I'd be prepared for the sight of a dead man on my doorstep.

Not even close.

They both step inside, the shorter one first, then Martin 'Fiver' Dunbrough, who shuts the door and locks it. I can't tear my gaze away from the sight of his massive form filling the entryway, now dressed in gray jogging pants and a black sweater with the sleeves rolled up, instead of prison orange. The last time I saw him, he tried to gut me with an eight-inch hunting knife.

Not true. The last time you saw him, he was in a body bag.

I flip over and scramble to my feet, boots slipping on the tile. I run across the living room, but have no idea where I'm going. A hand clamps on the back of my sport coat before I can get more than a few steps anyway. I hear the fabric rip as I'm lifted off my feet and pitched forward by collar and seat of my pants.

The kitchen bar stops my fall, but does nothing to soften it. Clean dishes fly off the other side, exploding against the stove and dishwasher. The wind is walloped out of my lungs.

I slide into the floor on my stomach, choking silently, the world muted by shock and pain.

Fiver stands over me once more. The other guy comes in, takes a casual glance over at us, then walks further into the living room.

I finally remember how to breathe. Gasping and sputtering, everything coming back into crystal clear focus.

My nose throbs. Minchi barks from somewhere. Chris Isaak warbles the end of "Wicked Game." I try to roll over, and Fiver puts one of his huge feet on my back to hold me down.

"Nah uh, get comfortable," he rumbles.

I can cock my neck at an odd angle and roll my eyes to look around. The other guy is checking out the apartment. He's half a foot shorter than even me, so Fiver dwarfs him. Got a wide build too, but it looks more fat than muscle. Hair is buzzcut brown, and his face could've been hit with a shovel; lips wide and thin, nose flat, eyes squinty and too far apart. He's wearing khaki Dockers, and a black leather jacket unzipped to reveal the front of a New Jersey Trenton Devils sweatshirt stretched over his gut.

He goes to the stereo, listens for a second, then pushes the stop button. I hear him mutter, "Fucking faggoty music."

Minchi is still issuing shrill little yips at the guy and bouncing around like he's looking for the opportunity to sink his teeth into an ankle. The guy spins and kicks out at him, landing a sneaker in the dog's small haunches with a brutal thud. Minchi squeals and leaps away, then limps for the bedroom with one leg dragging behind him.

"*You fucking asshole!*" I scream. With a mouthful of carpet, it comes out '*Ooo uh-eee aaa-ho!*'

The guy grabs one of the rickety wooden chairs from the scarred plastic table Brynn and I use for dining, the one with the macramé turkey. He plops it down in front of me and sits with the toes of his shoes about a foot away from the small puddle of blood my nose is creating on the beige carpet. It groans from his weight.

Now that my brain isn't coated in adrenaline, I can think. Obviously Fiver wasn't as deceased as the cops thought, although why he isn't behind bars, I can't say. In any case, there's only one reason for these guys to be here.

And suddenly I see just how deeply in trouble I am.

"Let's get off on da right foot, how 'bout dat?" Nasally voice. Jersey accent, of course, but a lot more gutter. From this angle, I can't look up enough to see past his knees. "I'm Weldon. Dis is my associate Five-Spot. And *you* are Rudy Compton, recently an inmate of da temporary correctional holding facility on Young Avenue, here in Withers." In his accent, it comes out *Widders*. "Nod your head if you're wit me so far, friend."

I nod, trying not to jostle my nose.

"Okay, good. Now, ya might not believe it Rudy, but Fiver and I are here today because we got business wit ya. When dis business is over, we'll be outta your life forever. It's a beautiful day, ya look like a guy wit places ta be, so let's just get through dis quick and civil. Dat sound fair?"

I refrain from pointing out that 'civil' usually doesn't include breaking the host's nose and just give another nod.

"See dat Fiver? He wants ta be civil. Let 'im up, help 'im over ta da couch here."

The pressure on my back disappears. Fiver picks me up like you would a toddler, sets me on my wobbly feet, and gives me a little shove toward the couch. I make it over and fall back on the cushions as Weldon turns his chair to face me. His legs almost touch mine.

"There, now we can look each other in da eye, like men." He gives me a smile, his lips pulling out into a big slash across his face. It's kind of ghastly, but what happens next is even worse. "Isn't dat—" he begins, then twitches his head twice to the left and yells out the side of his mouth, "*EF! EF! GEE-DEE!*" before finishing the sentence. "—better?"

"Yeah. Better," I agree, snuffling blood. I glance at Fiver, standing next to the arm of the couch. He doesn't give any indication he noticed the outburst.

"Okay, Rudy, here's da deal. Ya met one of our *other* associates recently. A gennleman named Lennie Kincaid. Ya know who I mean?"

"Sure. I remember him."

"Good!" Weldon claps his hands together. I flinch. "According ta our sources, ya overheard a certain word dat Lennie used in front of ya. Correct?"

I look up at Fiver again after Weldon says 'sources.' I can't very well lie about it with him here. But I have no doubt that as soon as I confirm it, I'm a dead man.

"Uhhhh…yeah."

Weldon's head jerks to the side in time with each letter he yells, like it's on a string. "*EF! ES! ES OF A BEE!*" He closes his eyes, swallows deliberately, then opens them and beams at me. "Dat is just fantastic, friend! Have ya said dis word ta anyone else? Da police, maybe? Or dat other guy staying here?"

"No. No one."

"Another correct answer! So tell me…what *is* dat word?"

Something about this isn't making sense. I'd assumed—after getting over the initial surprise of seeing Fiver—that they were here to rub out a witness, just as Dutt suggested. But if that's true, why drag it out, and go through all the trouble of getting me to confirm what they already know?

"Why?" I ask cautiously.

He looks up at Fiver with his grin still in place and hooks a thumb at me. "Look at dis guy, thinks he's Barbara Walters over here! Dis ain't no Christing interview kid, ya just tell me what I need ta hear."

"But...don't you already know?" I point at Fiver. "He was there, he heard it."

Weldon shakes his head. "He wadn't there."

"Uh, yeah he was. He...tried to kill me."

"Nope, not him."

"...I'm pretty sure."

He waves a hand. "Let's not get caught up on details. If it's easier for ya, just pretend dat he wadn't there, and he don't know shit. Now..." He leans forward eagerly. "You say dat word ta me, right here and now, and I *swear* ta ya's... me and Fiver are just gonna get up and walk right outta here."

I don't really believe that, but it doesn't matter. I give them the only answer I have.

"I don't know it."

Fiver reaches out, curls his thick index finger behind his thumb, and flicks my broken nose. It might as well be a sledgehammer. I yelp and twist away as pain lights up my skull.

Weldon bows his head in disappointment. "Rudy...dat was just too quick of an answer. Ya barely even had time ta think! Don't ya want us outta here?"

"Yes. God, yes."

"Then do ya wanna try again?"

"Look…I don't know. Really, I don't know," I babble. "I promise, I would tell you if I could, I have no reason not to, but I just…I don't remember."

Weldon makes a suction noise with his lips, the kind of noise you make when faced with an unfortunate truth. He shrugs. "Well Rudy, ya seem like a good kid. Ya got dat honest kinda face. So I believe ya." His eyes glitter, and I see the malicious glee that's been hiding behind the buddy persona the whole time. "The problem is…Fiver *don't*."

Fiver bends over and grabs my left wrist just below the bandage. He holds it up in front of my face. His grip is so iron that, even with the rest of me is squirming, my arm is dead still. He yanks at the bandage, unraveling it to reveal the swirl of blue, red, and purple bruises across the back of my hand and up my swollen pinkie, which still hangs askew.

"Brick wall?" Fiver asks.

"Car door."

"Yep. That'll do it."

Still holding my hand in front of my face, he brings forward the thumb and first two fingers of his free hand like a pincer and clamps down on my injured knuckle.

He squeezes.

Agony, instant and bright. Something grinds beneath the skin, cracked bones rubbing against one another. I sit bolt upright and shriek.

"Shut. *Up*," Fiver commands, bearing down harder. The pressure is enough to do damage in its own right. I force my mouth shut, but can't stop a steady trickle of whimpers. Everything goes dark as I slip toward unconsciousness.

And then he stops. Holds my crumpled hand where I can see. It's bloated, like a cartoon appendage after someone drops an anvil on it, and pulsing fire with each beat of my heart. He lifts it out of the way so I can see Weldon.

"Whaddaya think now, friend? Dat word coming back ta ya?"

I feel a sudden jolt of red rage. Pain sometimes has that effect on me.

"You stupid guido fuck," I spit through clenched teeth. "It was just some weird word mumbled by a guy I barely knew while I was watching him get his brains beat out by the Hulk over here. I didn't *memorize* it, because I didn't know there was gonna be a fucking pop quiz that involved turning my hand into a juiced orange if I answered wrong."

Except that's a lie. It wasn't just some weird word. I understood that as soon as it wormed into my brain. I just wish I could remember it.

Any trace of joviality fades from Weldon's chubby face. "Ya better—*ES! AY-AITCH! EM-EF'er!*—watch your tongue, Rudy."

Fiver reaches for my hand again. I panic.

"Wait, wait, think about it! *I don't fucking know!* What reason would I have to lie to you?"

Weldon shrugs. "Maybe ya figure it's da only thing keeping ya alive right now. Maybe...somebody's already talked ta ya, and ya know more than ya say."

He sneers. "Either way...we're gonna find out."

The rest of my time in their company is a haze. Despite Fiver's size and brute strength, he has some surprisingly delicate methods of torture. I take it as long as I can, and when my screams get too loud, they stuff a pair of my own socks in my mouth. I could've told them not to bother. No one's around this time of day to hear.

"How 'bout now?" Weldon asks. "Ya remember yet?"

I'm back on my stomach on the floor. Fiver is straddling my torso backwards, putting just enough weight on me so that the slightest dribble of air can get into my lungs. On top of that, he's doing something with my legs that brings to mind pretzels. I'm pretty sure I've got bruises on my side and chest and it feels like a couple of teeth are loose, but other than that, most of the proceedings have focused on pain rather than permanent injuries.

Fiver raises up enough so I can breathe and pulls out the blood-covered sock. "*Please...*" I rasp.

Weldon's chair is in front of me. He leans forward, right to the edge, so he can put his flat nose in my face. "What's dat? Can't hear ya."

"*Don't know...don't know...can't...remember...*"

"Well, think a little more." He leans back. "Den maybe we can—"

The chair collapses under him. It's actually kind of funny. He falls straight back on his ass in the splinters of woods and sits there for a moment with a bewildered expression on his face. I feel Fiver twist around to look.

Once the shock wears off, Weldon's face clouds over. He bounces to his feet. "*EF! EF! EM-EF'er! CEE-ES'er! GEE-DEE!*" He's twitching like crazy all over, those abbreviated curses spilling out of his mouth like machine gun fire. Still spewing, he stomps into the bedroom and slams the door. I can hear him in there screaming.

Fiver climbs off me. He sits on the couch. I focus on catching my breath and not moving. The way my head is turned, he's all I can see.

"Coprolalia." He gestures toward the closed bedroom door as he lights up a cigarette. "Symptom of Tourette's."

"Why the...letters?" I pant.

Fiver leans his head back and forth, stretching his neck muscles. His eyes are on the wall as he talks. "Everyone with Tourette's has a tic disorder, right? Could be anything. Flapping your arms, banging your head, clucking like a chicken. Anything. Only a small percentage of them are coprolalia—the blurting of obscenities and the like—but Hollywood loves that shit, so that's the one everyone knows." The black, dead circles of his eyes drill the far wall as he sucks down the cigarette like it's a straw. "The thing about coprolalia is, it ain't necessarily the blurting of obscenities so much as the blurting of *what your mind considers to be taboo*. And it forms during childhood, based on what you know at the time. Well, when Weldon was a kid, his parents were devout Catholics. Sheltered him and his brothers from the world too much. But his old man loved to cuss. So he was careful never to say the full words in front of his family. Weldon didn't hear a real curse until he was sixteen-years-old. By then, the coprolalia had him, and he's left shouting out letters like a fucking *Sesame Street* puppet for the rest of his life."

I push over on my back and cough. "I think they did an episode where Big Bird had the same problem."

He finally looks down at me on the floor with a little half-grin. "Gets worse when he's angry. My advice to you: don't acknowledge it. *Ever*. Just act like it doesn't happen. Or the pain I just put you through is gonna pale, Compton."

The bedroom door opens. Weldon storms out. His face is red, but he's calm now. He walks over to me and kneels. His face appears upside down over me.

"Here's my dilemma, Rudy my friend," he says. "Ya claim ya don't remember da word, so I have two choices. I can either believe you're lying, or I can believe you're telling da truth, which means da key ta da greatest treasure in da universe is lost in some dumb schmuck's head. And—don't get me wrong—life has a sick sense of humor, so it ain't dat far-fetched. But either way, it's da same problem: I need da word, and *you* got it."

The pain is ebbing, but I'm far from all right. Even so, my mind latches on to the word *treasure*. "What can I do to convince you?"

"You can come wit us."

I swallow. "Where?"

"To an extractor. Someone who can get inside dat head of yours and get what we need. Once we got dat, you're a free man, Rudy. But coming wit us—on your own, wit-out causing a fuss—is gonna go a long way toward making us believe dat you're just an innocent bystander in all dis, and not a liability."

I think about that. Think about how much worse things could get once I'm in their custody. Think about disappearing and nobody ever seeing me again. Think about the term 'extractor.'

But mostly I think how I have no other options.

I nod. "Okay."

They both stand. Pull me up. My legs are rubbery. They help me walk as we head toward the door of the apartment.

"Cheer up, Rudy," Weldon says. "Least ya still got all your fingers and toes. Dat's more'n a lot of guys in your position could say."

"Gee, I really hope that one's carved on my tombstone," I mutter.

Weldon chuckles. "Ya know Fiver, I kinda like dis kid."

Fiver grunts in agreement. And just as he reaches for the knob, there's a knock from the other side.

Chapter EIGHT

Weldon and Fiver look at each other. They look at me. I look at them and then back at the door.

A voice calls out, "Rudy?"

Oh, shit. Somewhere between Tourette's and torture, I completely forgot Brynn was coming home.

Fear blurs the edges of thought. I can't let these two get their hands on her.

"Who is dat?" Weldon hisses in my ear.

"My wife."

"You're married?"

"Separated. Sorta."

"So what's she doing here?"

"She was supposed to come by so we could work things out."

Heavier, more insistent knocking. "Rudy, I hear you! Open the door!"

Weldon and Fiver exchange another glance I don't care for. "Ya tell her anything?"

"About what?"

"All dis. Da word."

"No, I haven't even seen her since I got out of jail! Just leave her alone, she doesn't have anything to do with this!"

"Then get rid of her," Weldon commands. "Nothing funny. Ya don't want her involved in dis, don't get her involved."

I hate complications. Like I said, I'm more of a Thoreau man: simplify, simplify. I think that's probably the reason I dropped out of school, although most people would call it laziness. In any case, when things get complicated, I get flustered, can't think straight, and I make mistakes.

But there can't be any mistakes this time. Not where she's concerned.

Fiver moves out of the opening and stands next to Weldon, so they're both right over my shoulder, hidden by the crevice between door and wall. I turn the lock, crack the door, and peek out.

My apartment opens on to an outdoor concrete landing that I share with the Indian couple, whose door faces mine. The stairs go down immediately to the left as soon as you walk out, along the side of the building.

Standing right beyond the threshold is Brynn Compton.

She's cut her hair.

That's the first thing I see.

It's a lot shorter, almost buzzed at the back and neck, the remaining hair tufted into cute little half-curls on the side and top. Cherubic. Plus there's red in it now, standing out against the stark black. She's not wearing what she was in my fantasy, just sneakers, white capri cargos, and a *Fight Club* t-shirt with a yellow knitted coat over it. It makes me sad to see her different, to know I wasn't the one she came home to show her haircut to, but at the same time, she's so heart-stoppingly beautiful that I forget about the very dangerous men standing right behind me.

She also has the last fading blotch of a bruise across her right cheekbone. *I put that there*, I marvel.

Her jaw falls open at the sight of me. "*Rudy?* Jesus, what happened?"

I can only imagine how much blood is crusted under my crooked nose and slathered down my chin. "Uh. I had an accident."

"Are you okay?"

The concern in her voice could melt me.

"I'm fine."

We stare at each other.

"Can I...come in?"

"I don't think that's such a good idea right now." It nearly kills me to say. "Can we, maybe, reschedule?"

"Why would we need to reschedule?"

"You know, cause we were supposed to get together today—"

"Get together?"

"Yeah, you know. Talk about things. Work this out."

She squirms. Something in the pit of my stomach jabs at me, and I don't think it's from Fiver using my torso as a yoga mat. "Rudy...I just meant...I wanted to come by and get a few things."

I only stand there, crestfallen. Behind me, one of my captors snickers.

"Can I just come in?" she asks. "It'll just take a second. I need clothes and some kitchen stuff."

Fiver steps on my foot, applying pressure not to the toes, but to the bony slope just above them. I feel it even through the leather of my boot.

"Now…is really not a good time."

She puts her hands on her hips. Frustrated. I used to kiss the tip of her nose when she did that. "Rudy."

"Brynn, baby, listen to me. You *can't* come in right now. We can do this tomorrow."

"No, she's doing it now."

That's when the next complication that's been standing just out of sight on the stairs steps out to face me.

Chris is not a big guy. Or all that muscular. And I don't make a habit of checking out men, but I don't even think he's that attractive. He's got the start of a beer gut and he's prematurely balding and…and…and his ears stick out a little too far. But Brynn always had odd taste in men.

He stands next to my wife on the doorstep and inspects me. "She's coming in, and you're gonna let her get her shit."

"Chris, you said you'd stay out of this," Brynn tells him.

"He ain't gonna jerk you around like this. We came all the way over here, and he's gonna let you in." He continues to glare at me while he talks to her. "Okay, wifebeater? You gonna make this easy?"

I talk a big game, especially when that temper of mine kicks in, but under normal circumstances, I'm a pretty docile guy. I would think twice about taking on someone this aggressive, even when he's fucking the woman I'm married to.

But after spending the last half-hour in the presence of my two psychotic houseguests, he just can't measure up.

"The only thing I'm gonna make easy," I say, "is my sentences, so you can understand them, jackass. Get outta here, or I'm gonna make sure your face can do a pretty good impression of mine."

"Oh, I'm real scared, fanboy." He puts his hand on the door and pushes. I'm shoved back, and he forces his way in.

I spin around to Weldon and Fiver, ready to beg.

They're gone.

I'm so dumbfounded, I just stand there as Chris steps around me and strolls into my apartment. Brynn slinks in and raises guilty eyes to me. "I'm sorry about this, Rudy. I didn't want it to happen this way."

"Don't apologize to him. Just get in here and get what you need."

She walks into the home we shared up until last week, and I follow. I half expect to see Weldon crouched down on the far end of the couch. Fiver's shoes sticking out from under the window blinds. But the living room is empty, and the bedroom door is closed again.

I think about trying to signal Brynn, either to get help or run, but decide against it. Just too risky. If they think I tipped her off, who knows what they'll do? The best plan is to cooperate, play nice, and get her out of here. Eliminate the complication. Quick and easy.

But when Chris scowls at me, I can't help scowling back. I'm in too much pain to put up with this.

Brynn is studying me too. "Sure you're okay? Your clothes are ripped."

"I know. Accident."

"What'd you do to your hand?"

"Hurt it at work. No big deal."

She lifts one of her perfect eyebrows. "Where's Minchi?"

I don't miss a beat. "Dutt took him to the park."

"Oh. I was hoping to see him."

"Then maybe you should come home." Oops. That one slipped out.

She runs a hand back and forth across the bar countertop where she used to prepare dinner.

"Don't you want to come home?" I press.

"I do."

"But?"

"But I can't. I…need to think."

Now is not the time for this conversation, but seeing her has overridden all other instincts. "Think about *what?* This is your home, here with me! Brynn, I miss you so much, I'm going out of my mind without you!"

"I'm not…"

"Not what?"

"I'm just not…"

"Brynn, if we could sit down and just talk—"

"Hey," Chris warns. "Leave her alone. She doesn't need you browbeating her."

"And I don't need you refereeing conversations with my wife."

"Someone's gotta make sure things don't get rough."

I groan. "Oh Jesus, would you just get the fuck outta here? This is my home, and I don't want you in it. You can wait outside."

"I'm not going anywhere, fruitcake. She still legally lives here, so you can't kick me out." The way he says it, all it's missing is a *nanny-nanny-boo-boo*.

I whine, "Brynn, would you make this guy leave?"

She puts her fingertips at her temples and squeezes. I notice, for the first time, that she's not wearing her wedding ring. "Okay, just stop. Both of you."

"He started it," Chris and I say in unison.

"I can't take this right now, I really can't. Just let me grab some stuff and we'll go." She heads into the kitchen, sees the dishes shattered all over the floor, and gives me a black look. "You're such a dick, Rudy."

"What do you—?"

"You can't do this. You can't just break our things to get back at me."

"I didn't do that!"

"You knew I wanted these. I thought we could get through this without having to go to court, but I can see we can't."

I try to walk after her, and Chris maneuvers himself into my path. He sneers. "Maybe it would be better if *you* wait outside."

I look around him. "What are you taking?"

"Some plates. My blender. The crock pot."

"Not the crock pot, I use that!"

"Since when?"

I don't answer. I've never used the crock pot. While she goes through the cabinets I ask, "What about the money, Brynn?"

She looks over her shoulder at me and says the most unfair thing imaginable. "Is that all you care about?"

"I'm not the one that chose to end this in the first place! I would burn that money if it meant you were coming home, but if you're going through with this, I have to start looking out for myself!"

I try to move forward again and Chris bumps me back with his chest. "That money is half hers, so back off, okay?"

I snarl, "You touch me again…"

"And what?" He pulls a cell phone from his back pocket and flips it open. "I'll call the cops on you and get your ass hauled back to jail."

Apparently he said the magic words without knowing it, because the bedroom door opens.

~ ~ ~

I understand immediately that my time is up. They gave me a grace period to diffuse the situation, and I didn't. Anything that happens from here on is my own fault.

Chris turns to find Weldon emerging from the bedroom with Fiver right behind. I see the hesitation come into his eyes when he gets a load of them. "Hey. Hey man, what is this?"

"We're afraid we have ta ask ya ta leave," Weldon says.

"Rudy, who are these guys?" Brynn asks, giving them the stinkeye.

"They're right, you gotta go. Just leave now, both of you."

Brynn hears something in my voice. She slips out of the kitchen and comes to stand between us and the front door.

"We…we have every right to be here." Chris' voice holds a little more respect this time.

"Dat may be, but for now, it's time ta go."

Chris knows he's out of his league. It's plain on his face. Fiver's big enough to use me as a toothpick, and him as an anal douche. But he can't back down; not in front of his—*my*—woman. That's the problem with guys like him.

He comes forward and jabs a finger into Weldon's chest. "Look fatty, we're not leavin till we get what we came here for."

Weldon looks down at the finger. His face goes red and cloudy. "Take—*EF!*—your hand—*ES! ES! GEE-DEE!*—off me."

Chris cocks his head to the side. He lowers his hand and takes a step back with a big smirk on his lips. "What the hell, faggot? You twitch like that every time you get too close to a dude?"

"Oh fuck," I moan.

Weldon calmly and deliberately extends his arm straight out through the air, turning his empty palm to the side, fingers and thumb curled in a loose circle, with index bowed out but not pointing. There's something familiar about that shape. His knuckles are right in front of Chris' face, who's still grinning with an eyebrow raised, trying to figure out what this loon is doing.

There's a humming noise I know too well.

A large-bore, Smith & Wesson .40-caliber Sigma semi-automatic pistol pops into existence in Weldon's hand, perfectly fitted to those contours. I realize the shape was familiar because it's the same one children all over the world form when they mime holding a gun.

The trigger of this no-longer-imaginary weapon is now resting under the pad of his pudgy index finger.

Chris has a split second to be very afraid before his brains paint the far wall of my apartment.

You see what complications lead to?

Chris' body flails its arms, and then falls over backward, spilling a chunky red soup from the remains of its skull.

Brynn yells, "Holy shit!" From the corner of my eye, I see her bolt for the door.

Weldon tracks her with the pistol.

"No!" I jump forward, bringing my foot up to connect with his shin. He grunts, and the shot he squeezes off punches through the ceiling. Fiver reaches for me around his partner, and I turn to run.

Brynn is at the door turning deadbolts in her panic that are already unlocked. I give her a hand and we race out onto the landing. Across the way, my Indian neighbor—who I'm almost sure is named Gupta—has her door open too, looking out with wide eyes. I haven't seen this woman in five months, and she picks today to be home. Good for us, bad for her.

I give Brynn a shove toward her. "Go, get inside!"

We bolt through, bumping the dark-skinned woman aside. I turn and slam the door shut just as Fiver comes thundering out of our place. When he hits this side a moment later, the entire wall shakes.

"What the hell is this, Rudy? Who *are* these guys?"

"Not now!"

Mrs. Gupta is screaming high-pitched gibberish and slapping at me. Everywhere her hands land on my aching body sets off a burst of pain.

"Stop, stop!" I try to fend her off with my one good hand. "We need the police! *Policia!*"

"She's Indian, Rudy, not Spanish!" Brynn helps drag her off me while Fiver keeps bulldozing his way through the door. Each smash bows the frame a little more. Mrs. Gupta starts after Brynn until she manhandles the woman down into a chair. "Call the police, Mrs. Gupta!"

"Po-lice!" The woman seems to get the idea at last and runs down the hall to her bedroom.

Gotta get my bearings. Try to think. Fiver will be inside long before the cops can get here. No going out the front door, and these cheap ass apartments don't have back doors or even balconies. That just leaves the window.

I go over, tear off drapes and venetians, raise the glass. Outside is a long drop to the muddy patch that passes for a lawn on the east side of the apartment complex. "Come on, I'll lower you down!"

Brynn comes over and sticks her head out. "Uh uh, no way! You won't be able to hold me!"

"What? Yes I will!"

"With one hand? You got hurt trying to open that peanut butter jar last month!"

Mrs. Gupta's front door cracks down the middle.

"Not like we have much choice!"

She climbs out the window backward without further argument, laying her stomach against the sill and dangling her legs into space. I brace my feet against the wall and grab her wrist with my good hand, preparing to take her weight.

Brynn pushes off. I slam forward against the jamb, almost going out with her. I lean out as far as I can and use my opposite arm for leverage until she lets go and drops to the ground.

"Go!" I shout. "Get outta here! Try to get help!"

She looks up at me, nods, and runs.

The front door smashes open. Fiver charges me like an angry rhinoceros.

I squirt out the window headfirst, slam my shoulder against a protruding dryer vent, and get turned around enough so I land on my leg and hip instead of my face. I ignore the accompanying bout of pain and look up. Fiver stares out the window, weighs his options and opts for the stairs.

I climb to my feet and turn around, trying to decide where to go.

The apartment complex sits on a corner lot, the last in a long line of similar building and mid-income duplexes that string out to the east. That's the way Brynn went. She's already disappeared around the corner of the brick wall that divides properties.

I want to go after her, but it would be better to lead them away. At least then if they catch me, she still might be safe. The freeway is just a few blocks up to the north. I decide that's my best chance.

I start around the buildings and stick to the few mid-afternoon shadows, slinking along the brick exteriors. I'm maybe halfway across the complex when I come around a corner and almost run into Weldon.

He points the gun at me, the one he conjured out of thin air like David fucking Blaine. I freeze. He doesn't do anything.

And then I realize, they need me alive.

I break to the left, hurtling down the narrow aisle between buildings.

Weldon gives chase, but he can't keep up. It's obvious he hasn't seen the rotating side of a treadmill in some time. Of course, I haven't either, but I'm just saying.

I can hear him gasping and wheezing behind me as I leave the apartments and cross the last sliver of weed-strewn lot before the street. He starts bawling out Fiver's name.

'Traffic jam' is not a term you'd hear often in Withers, especially not on a mid-weekday, but the roads are steadily traveled with people passing through on their way to other points in the Metroplex. The intersection on the corner has a green light against me and cars are rushing by in both directions at speeds upward of forty miles an hour. I step out into the crosswalk, cause a little Honda to swerve, and pull back.

Behind me, Weldon stops to catch his breath. Fiver blows past him, legs pumping, arms reminding me of the coupling rods on a locomotive as they churn. His face is stone set in determination.

I cross against the light. Just close my eyes and go. I hear horns honking, brakes squealing, a collision of glass and metal. Something passes so close, I feel it brush against the back of my torn sport jacket. I dare to open my eyes.

The curb is just ahead. I hurtle on to it and look back. Fiver is halfway across, not in any danger since the cars have all stopped, but having to pick his way through the chaos. I keep going.

My legs burn. My chest aches as it sucks in the brisk November air. I have a stitch in my side. There's two blocks of wide storefronts between me and the freeway, and I don't think I can make it. Even if I can, it's no guarantee of safety with Fiver right on my ass. I take the next turn into a dank alleyway filled with dumpsters.

Gotta hide. I'm terrified and exhausted. I would've been willing to go with them, especially to save Brynn, but what's done is done, and now I just want safety and a place to rest.

There's other offshoots in the alley. I take corners at random, but I'm wishing I stayed on the street where there's people. Surely they couldn't do anything to me in public. How far are these two willing to go to have me?

I replay the events of the last hour. And the scene at the jail. Pretty fucking far.

What the hell have I got rattling around in my head that's worth all this?

I make one last turn. Another street is ahead. But between me and it is a chain link fence. I crash against it and hang by my fingers, panting.

Running footsteps halt behind me. I turn. Fiver stands there, flexing his big hands. He's not even sweating. So much for his heart condition.

"Weldon's not gonna like this," he says.

He starts toward me. Then his eyes flick over my shoulder.

A cop car squeals into the mouth of the alley, lights flashing.

"Help!" I scream. "Help, he's right over—!"

I stop mid-tattle.

Once again, Fiver has disappeared.

It's not the same interrogation room, not even the same precinct, but it might as well be. Square room, metal table and chairs, big panel mirror on one wall. I guess there's really not too many ways to design these things. However, there are a few differences from my last experience with Withers law enforcement.

For starters, I'm almost sure there's somebody watching from the other side of that two-way mirror. Probably several somebodies. I've been here a few hours now, and even when I'm alone and doing nothing more than staring at the table, I can feel their eyes. I'm not offered a cigarette or anything else, but I am told that Brynn is safe and here at the station also.

My interrogator is a grizzled, sharp-eyed senior detective named Kitner that does *not* look like he belongs on the Withers police force. His questions aren't distracted; they're sharp and focused and spat with a mean-spirited edge that I don't quite understand. He starts out asking me a short series at a time, with breaks in between, then comes back and takes the line in a new direction. A box anchored to the center of the table records every word digitally.

During the last break, they let me call Dutt, and then a doc came in to do a professional bandage job on my hand and set my nose, a procedure which hurt worse than when Fiver broke it. It's still swollen and tender, but at least I don't sound like Baby Huey anymore. The rest of my body still aches from being worked over, but there are little-to-no marks on me.

I start out just as jumpy as during my last interview in one of these places, but after being stuck here for so long with no one telling me what the fuck is up, the shock of what I've been through and of seeing yet another person die in front of me is replaced by annoyance.

Kitner returns with the same manila folder he's been carrying with him, which gets thicker with new paper each time. He sits across from me and gives a weary smile.

"Tell me again what happened to Mr. Bartell."

He means Chris. I lay my head on my shoulder and let my tongue loll out.

"One more time," he insists patiently.

"He got into an argument with this guy Weldon, and Weldon shot him."

"With the gun that just appeared out of nowhere."

"Yes."

"Like the knife that just appeared out of nowhere in Mr. Dunbrough's hand in the cell?"

"Uh-huh."

"The same Mr. Dunbrough that was killed while in police custody but showed up at your apartment today."

I throw my hands up. "I know it sounds crazy. I don't understand it any more than you do."

He gives a measured nod. "But before Mr. Bartell argued with this Weldon character, he argued with you. Is that right?"

"He is—he *was*—fucking my wife. We weren't exactly on each other's Christmas card list."

The detective sighs through his nose. "Before we go on, I want to make sure I understand. Dunbrough and this Weldon character show up at your place of residence. They torture you for a piece of information you don't have, related to whatever happened in the holding cell on Saturday night. Then your estranged wife and her new boyfriend show up at the wrong time, and Mr. Bartell is killed. You and your wife escape." Both eyebrows climb his forehead. "Is there anything about that story you want to change? Keep in mind, this is an official record."

"Noooo," I answer slowly. I'm stuck on the phrase 'before we go on.' We're at some point of no return, and I'm about to find out why they've been treating me like suspect rather than victim. "That's all correct."

"Okay." He studies me without blinking. His calm demeanor only infuriates me further. "You work at the MegaMart, correct?"

"Yes. Didn't we cover this already?"

We did, during the 'state your name-age-occupation' portion. He doesn't respond to my tone. "And can you confirm you were there on Sunday afternoon, the day after your incarceration?"

"Yes, I was shopping with a friend."

"And you received a phone call from your wife?"

I frown. "Yeah, how did you—?"

"What was the subject of this call?"

"She…she told me she was leaving me."

"And was there some mention of money? An amount you feel she owes you?"

"Yeah, she took my life savings when she ran out on me."

"Uh huh, okay. And what else did you talk about?"

"I don't remember exactly. It was a short call. She was with Chris."

"Did you speak to him also?"

I'm being led. By the nose. I just don't know where. "Yeah, near the end."

He opens up the manila folder and glances at something inside. "And while you were speaking to him, do you recall shouting, 'I will fucking kill you?'"

"*Oh, come on!*" I burst out. "You think *I* did this? You think *I* shot him?"

He closes the folder. "You have the corpse of the man who was having sexual congress with your wife—a man who several of your coworkers have already stated you threatened with mortal injury—on the floor of your residence, and only an insane story about undead mobsters and magical weapons to account for it. What would *you* think, Mr. Compton?"

I wave my hands like I'm trying to hail a taxi. "No, no, no, no, no, that's bullshit! Why do I look like this then? Tell me, did I beat the shit out of myself too?"

"Maybe. Or maybe there was a struggle before Mr. Bartell was shot."

"Jesus Christ, ask Brynn, she'll tell you!"

"She *has* told us. The exact story you have."

"So?"

"So here's the problem with that. Six days ago you were arrested for domestic violence."

I grab a fistful of my hair. "Don't. Don't even."

But he does. "I've seen wives so scared of their husbands, they'll say just about anything to keep them from getting in trouble. 'Oh, these bruises on my neck shaped like hands? No officer, they're not from my husband, I just fell on a bunch of popsicle sticks.' They tell these lies, because they're *that* afraid of what their husbands will do when they eventually get out."

"It's not like that." I shake my head. "What about Mrs. Gupta? She saw them!"

"The only thing Mrs. Gupta saw was you chasing your wife into her apartment, and your wife begging her to call the police."

I slam my hands down on the table. They're shaking.

Kitner doesn't let up. He's on a roll now, trying to keep me off balance while he performs his *coup de grace*. "Can you account for your whereabouts on Tuesday night?"

I squeeze my eyes shut, trying to concentrate. "What?"

"Tuesday night. Where were you?"

High, probably. "At home. With my friend."

"This is Dutton Lansing? Will he confirm that?"

"Yeah. Why?"

He breathes deep. "You contacted Officer Reed the day after he arrested you."

"Oh my god."

"He met with you that same night."

"Oh my god."

"And two days later, he turns up dead."

"Oh my god."

"It seems like that's becoming a habit with the people who wrong you, Mr. Compton."

~ ~ ~

When he puts it like that, even *I* have trouble believing my innocence.

My heart starts thudding. Sweat jumps out of every pore. For a split second, I envision the months of legal battle ahead of me—some *L.A. Law*, *Perry Mason* type courtroom drama—followed by a stint in *real* prison, the kind that's going to make Saturday night look like Hawaii. All for a crime I didn't commit. I can be the A Team of the nerd set.

But there's just one problem with the web of logic he's weaving, one hole I can punch straight through.

One fact that's surely going to save me.

"Fiver," I say, striving to regain composure. "Martin Dunbrough. What did you do with his body? Did you bury him already or ship it off somewhere? Because he can't very well be there and still show up on my doorstep to torture me."

Kitner smiles and nods as though he's been waiting for this. "Let's take a field trip."

He leads me through the precinct, which has to be the main Withers PD because the municipal courthouse and town hall are attached. We take an elevator down to the sub-basement, where a sign points the way to the morgue.

I start getting a bad feeling about this.

They must have been waiting on us because we stroll right in, head down a wall of metal drawers, and stop at one that's already partially ajar. Kitner grabs the handle and pulls it open the rest of the way, straining at the weight.

Inside is a huge body in a black bag, unzipped enough to reveal the individual's head.

Fiver's eyes are closed. His skin appears waxy and cold, his lips blue.

Otherwise, he looks exactly as he did when he squeezed my metacarpals into mush earlier today.

"So you tell me what's more likely," the detective says. "That this big, dead bear climbed out of this drawer, showed up at your residence, and did you a favor by killing the man that your wife is leaving you for…or that you did it yourself, blamed it on him using the information you got from your encounter earlier in the week, and then coerced your cowed spouse into telling the same story?"

Wow.

Even I honestly don't fucking know anymore.

Then it's back to the interrogation room, where I'm apparently going to live the rest of my life.

Kitner goes on grilling me like a well-done steak, and I have no doubts Brynn is getting the same treatment. They're pecking away at our stories, looking for chinks that they can widen until we break open, piñata fashion. He's only just started probing my relationship with Officer Reed when the door opens and another cop waves him over.

They whisper. Kitner is obviously perturbed by what he's being told. I catch something about 'jurisdiction.' Finally, the other guy leaves and the detective says, "Well, you had your chance. The FBI is here now."

He steps out, and a few seconds later, Douglas Hillman steps in.

Today, he almost looks like a preacher. Black, smocky, coat-looking thing with a starched white dress collar visible beneath, buttoned up the front, over a pair of crisp black slacks. Still the cowboy boots though, which add another few inches to his already gawky frame. He carries a briefcase in one hand. He stalks into the room and pulls out the chair opposite me to brush the detective's ass print away.

"Mr. Compton, I'm Douglas Hillman," he intones, setting the briefcase on the table between us. His head bobs on his stalk of a neck, almost birdlike. "I'm investigating the incident that occurred this past Saturday. I made several attempts to get in touch with you, but…" He looks down his hatchet nose. "We must have missed each other. Now I'm looking into the possible connection between that situation and this one."

I start to answer, and he holds up a knobby finger. He leans over, down past the side of the table, and works at something underneath. He comes up holding the plug to the recording device.

"What—?"

"Ut, ut." He looks at the mirror wall. "Give them another minute to clear out."

I sit patiently. After a few seconds, he gives a satisfied nod and turns back to me. "I think we have some privacy now."

"Mr. Hillman—"

"Agent."

"Agent?"

"*Agent* Hillman."

"Oh. *Agent* Hillman. You have to listen to me, I didn't do any of the things they're saying I did. You must have a CSI team or something that can prove that, right?"

"I know you didn't." His hands crawl across the briefcase latches and pop the lid.

"You do?"

"Of course." He removes an 8x10 glossy black and white photograph and places it on the table between us, facing me.

It's a candid shot of a young man through a telephoto lens, halfway turned from the camera as he gets into a beaten Mustang. I wouldn't recognize him if not for the spikes on his head. "Lennie Kincaid. Low-level flunkie and cross country delivery boy for a triangular syndicate that stretches between Florida, Nevada, and the New York-Jersey complex." Hillman's voice is clipped and gravelly, almost robotic. He dips back into the briefcase and places a second photograph beside the first, squaring off the corners. In this one, a large, bullet-headed man is accepting a briefcase from another party hidden in the shadows of an overpass. "Martin Dunbrough. AKA Five-Spot, Fiver for short. Killer-for-hire. Wanted in connection with over thirty-eight deaths, three of them undercover operatives, and suspected in another fifteen. Incidentally, do you know the origin of his nickname?"

I shake my head, thinking, *I'll take 'Questions I Don't Want to Know the Answers to' for $500, Alex.*

"Because he accepted five dollars as payment for the first man he ever killed. When he was twelve-years-old." Yet another photograph joins the others, of a hefty guy in a jogging suit with his foot planted deep in another guy's ass as he crawls away. The look of unrestrained fury on his face is frightening.

"That's him, that's Weldon!" I exclaim. And it is, I'm sure of it, except for the fact that the man in the picture looks a good decade or so older than the one who interrogated me this morning.

"Weldon di Latorio. Enforcer from a long familial line of New Jersey Mafioso. Known for his temper and sensitivity to his psychosomatic condition, he mostly worked his way up the chain of command by executing those above him. These three men have all served multiple prison sentences for a variety of crimes, and all of them work for this man."

The last photo comes out and is placed above the others. A rakish, late 40's, good-looking guy in an expensive suit, stepping to the door of a short limo. He looks approachable, like a politician, but there's a hardness to his features, as though steel runs just beneath the surface of his skin.

"Sullis 'Eels' Carbini. Former head of the Carbini crime family. I take it you haven't had the pleasure?"

"No."

Hillman gives a scarecrow's smile. "Didn't think he would show up here, but stranger things have certainly happened."

I glance over the photos again. "Look, Agent Hillman, I don't know these men, and I'm not affiliated with them. I just want them to leave me alone."

He sighs. "It may not be that easy, son."

Hillman swallows, causing his Adam's apple to dribble like a basketball, and taps the picture of Carbini. "For fifteen years, this man ran a very successful drug cartel, managing operations on two coasts. He made a lot of money doing it. Then, ten years ago, he got his fingers into something he liked a lot more, and gave all that up. Tightened his operations and scaled back his crew considerably. Moved to Reno. The resulting power vacuum started a drug war he completely washed his hands of."

I'm curious, in spite of the fact that I really don't care. "So...what did he do instead?"

"With the smuggling and delivery operations he already had in place and a new set of contacts, Carbini began to traffic in certain...high technologies. Stolen, bartered, some sold to the highest bidder, some kept for his own personal use."

I lean forward over the table. Now he has my attention. "*High technologies?* How high?"

Hillman hesitates a millisecond. "Very. On par with the light bulb in terms of revolutionizing the world, if they were ever made public."

"High enough to make a gun appear out of thin air?"

He nods. "Absolutely."

"High enough to bring someone back from the dead?"

"High enough to make it seem that way, maybe."

I almost scramble out of my seat. "If that's true, you have to tell that detective, you have to tell him I'm innocent!"

"Settle down now, son. There are national security issues to consider."

"Fuck national security, they wanna string me up for murdering a cop! I mean, why are you telling me all this if you're not gonna help me?"

"Because I believe *you* can help *us*."

"How?"

"Intel suggests that Sullis Carbini has taken possession of something new. An object far outside his normal range of expertise. Something he intends to hand off to another party in short order."

"What does that have to do with me?"

"Because you, Mr. Compton, have apparently intercepted the password he needs to make it work."

I don't speak. I just try to digest what it means.

Hillman's eyes glitter. "You've felt it pulling, haven't you? That Word, deep down inside you, urging you to come." I'm pretty sure this is the moment I begin to think of it with a capital 'W'. "It's growing inside you, and it's only going to get worse."

"That's impossible." I search his face for any sign of a lie. "How can a word do that?"

"Because the spoken sounds are only the way it's passed on. The Word itself is pure, raw power. On a long enough timeline, its effects on the carrier become greater and more consistent, but in this initial phase, it's like a Geiger counter. Or a compass. Pointing the way. The Word attempting to join with this object and tugging along the carrier as a consequence."

I feel a knot of panic growing in my stomach. It's like I've just been told I have a deadly virus. I would think he's completely full of shit if I hadn't experienced exactly what he's describing. "Weldon said this all had to do with treasure. The greatest treasure in the universe."

"I'm sure he might see it that way. Carbini also."

"What is this object? What does he have?"

"You wouldn't believe me if I told you."

"Try me."

Hillman scoops up the photographs and places them back inside his briefcase. "You know, the term 'weapon of mass destruction' gets thrown around a lot these days. What if I told you Carbini had acquired what is potentially the greatest weapon of mass destruction ever to exist? That he has, in effect, made himself an arms dealer?"

"Oh shit. Is it nuclear? It's nuclear, isn't it?"

He gives another tired grin. "No, not nuclear. And I've already told you far too much. But it will be worth it if gains your cooperation."

I lean on my elbows and cradle my forehead. "This thing. He's gonna give it to terrorists?"

"In a way, yes. Not al Qaeda, or Hezbollah, or Taliban or any other collection of Middle Eastern vowels, but people who would do this country—and this world—harm."

"Jesus," I whisper.

"Mr. Compton." Hillman's eyes blaze. "We can get you out of this situation. But first...I need you to tell me the Word."

"I don't know it. I really don't. I don't remember."

Hillman watches me. Bites his lower lip thoughtfully. And stands. "All right then." He heads toward the door with his briefcase.

"Hey, where you going?"

"If you truly don't remember the Word, then we don't have much else to say to one another." He pulls something from his slacks pocket and puts it on the edge of the table. The same business card he left with Luiz. "If you think of anything else, feel free to contact me."

He stands outside, pauses, and looks back at me.

"One caution: you're actually quite lucky it was Dunbrough and di Latorio that found you first. If word were to get out—pardon the pun—there might be far more unpleasant individuals that come looking for you."

Chapter TEN

Kitner comes stomping back into the interrogation room after fifteen minutes.

"C'mon, get up," he barks.

"But—?"

"*Now.*"

He escorts me down a long corridor toward the precinct lobby. A couple of new arrestees sit handcuffed to chairs while they wait to be processed. At first I think this is where we're headed, and that my jail experience is about to start all over, but he steers me toward the big metal door to the waiting room.

"What are you, in the witness protection program?" he asks. "An informant or something?"

"I don't understand what you—"

"Your freaky friend back there's got some pull with someone in authority. I just got orders from my chief. We're supposed to put your ass back on the street immediately. No more questioning."

We reach the door, which swings only one way. He holds it open for me to walk through, but I don't.

"Wait, hold on," I argue. "You can't just kick me out! What if those guys come back?"

"Not my problem. Unless maybe you wanna tell me what the hell is really going on. Then I'll see what I can do."

I shrug helplessly, not even knowing where to start.

"All right then. Get outta my face." He shoves me through into the waiting area and slams the door on me.

Dutt is slouched on a bench, reading an issue of *Maxim*. His eyes roll up from the glossy pages. "Picking you up at police stations is becoming one of my least favorite habits."

"Minchi. Is he—?"

"He's alive, but the poor fucker's back leg is broken. The cops wouldn't even let me in the apartment. But they handed him out and I dropped him off at the emergency vet clinic like you said."

"Thank God."

"You wanna tell me what happened?"

Before I can answer, the exit to the waiting room flies open again, and this time Brynn stumbles out. Her mascara's run, but the tears that caused it are long gone. She takes one look at us and storms past, toward the door of the precinct.

"Honey, wait!"

"Don't 'honey' me!" She hobbles down the front steps of the building. It's around five, dusk settling on the horizon. The temperature has plummeted from this morning. "I don't know what you're involved in, but I don't want you near me!"

I grab her wrist. "*Involved?* What do you mean *involved?*"

"Don't touch me!" She yanks free and stands a few steps below. "You and your goons! What is this about, are you a drug dealer now or something?"

"What? No! They're not *my* goons, they're just goons!"

"Oh really? Cause that's a little hard to believe considering they were hanging out in your apartment!"

"*Our* apartment!"

"Goddamn it Rudy!" She pumps her small fists. Her new pixie hair hangs disarrayed and shaggy. "I just watched them shoot my...my...*someone*...and then I get held at the police station and questioned about it all day, like *I'm* the one that did something wrong! The cops don't even believe those guys were real, but if they were, they think you hired them to kill Chris!"

"Brynn, baby...look at me." I hold my arms out to her. "It's me. You know me. You've known me three years. I never met those two before today. They showed up and beat the shit outta me. I was doing everything I could to get you out of there so they wouldn't hurt you. Please, you have to believe me." It's a slightly skewed version of the truth, but it's for her protection.

She looks up at me. Her bottom lip trembles but she reigns it in fast. "Why should I?"

"Because I'm not the chronic liar. I'm not the one that betrayed you over and over."

I don't know why I said it. Other than the fact that I'm suddenly furious at being doubted.

And I don't love her.

I hate her. I fucking *hate* this bitch, for everything she's put me through and everything she's taken from me, starting with my dignity, my confidence, and my peace of mind.

Her face draws up, first in shock and then in anger. "Fuck you, Rudy Compton." She starts down the steps.

I call after her, "Wait, I'm sorry, I didn't mean that! C'mon, where are you going?"

"I don't know! Considering the guy I was staying with is kind of dead, I guess I'll go to a motel!"

She disappears around the corner of the building. The anger leaks out and leaves me feeling horrible. God, I've got to control it. That's how I ended up in jail in the first place.

I turn and find Dutt waiting behind me.

"So that's why you wanted me outta the apartment today? So you could see her?"

"Not now, Dutt. I can't take this from you too."

"What did I tell you would happen if you took her back? Didn't I promise we were finished?"

I stare at his feet and say nothing. I'm so ashamed. His ultimatum, along with the advice I've been getting from everyone since the first time Brynn cheated on me—hell, since we first start dating—comes back to me. About how she's no good, she's all wrong for me. Officer Reed's simple and almost poetic input on the subject.

I'm a tool. Just another horny male dog sniffing after a hot piece of ass no matter how much shit comes out of it. Henry David Thoreau would be disgusted by me.

Dutt crosses his arms and shakes his head. "Lucky for you, I'm as bad at keeping promises as your whore-of-a-wife. Let's get outta here."

I let him drive my car while I explain my day. Dutt gets the full, unadulterated version, including every insane thing Hillman told me.

"Shit Rudy, this is really serious." During my story, he starts checking the rearview every few minutes. "These guys could come back after you."

"I know."

"And this FBI dude didn't say anything about protection?"

"No, this was a total *quid pro quo*. If I couldn't give him this password, he wasn't doing jack for me."

"Bastard," he mumbles. He digs around in his shirt pocket for a cigarette, then can't get one out of the pack. I light one for him, hand it over, then take one myself. We crack both windows.

He says, "Maybe I should try and get in touch with my CO."

"What could he do?"

"Probably nothing, except send it up the chain of command. But if this is about some kinda terrorist plot, then maybe the military should be informed."

"No, let's not get anyone else involved, especially more people who the cops could turn against me. Besides, I get the feeling if Hillman doesn't want any information climbing your chain, he could squash it." I pick at the peeling veneer on my dash and blow smoke at the window. "This Word. This fucking Word. As if I didn't have enough problems without this bullshit."

Dutt checks all the mirrors again, craning his neck to look at the occupants of the few cars around us. He's making me paranoid. "So...have you?"

"Have I what?"

"Felt it...pulling at you, or whatever he said."

I nod. "Yeah. I have. It wants me to go west. Sometimes it's so hard I think it's just gonna take control of me like a puppet. Every day I almost get in the car and start driving. I'm practically sleepwalking toward this thing."

"That is...far out, man. Far. Fucking. *Out*. How is that possible?"

"I don't know. I don't *wanna* know."

"But what kind of weapon needs a password like that?"

"Hillman said it was a weapon," I remind him. "Weldon said it was treasure."

"Yeah, and the truth is probably more fucked up than either of them." Dutt changes lanes. We're on 287, heading northwest from the center of the city where the precinct is. "So what do you wanna do then?"

"Go home, I guess."

"We can't go home. Even if the cops don't have it on lockdown, that's the first place these mafia assholes are gonna look for us."

My eyebrows arch. "What's this 'we-us' business?"

"I'm not letting you out of my sight until this over, shithead. What about your sister? Can we stay with her?"

"Fuck no. I just said, I don't want anyone else involved. If anything happened to her, my parents would do far worse to me than any crime syndicate." I close my eyes and lean my head back. "We need someplace public. Just...take me to the Meg and we'll stay there till we can figure something out."

It's after eight by the time we reach the store. The Meg closes at nine. The parking lot is mostly empty except for employee cars. Dutt parks in a space on the second row and we hurry inside.

I feel the change in barometric pressure almost as soon as I walk in. There's only one checker on duty, a middle-aged MILF-type named Cheryl, and she's ringing up the only customer in the store. As I pass by, she goggles so hard, she scans the same can of peaches four times and has to call for a manager to have it removed. Sean and Kevin are in the process of closing down the photolab machines for the night, but when Sean catches sight of me, he whaps his brother in the shoulder and whispers in his ear while his eyes track me. Kevin spins around fast enough to put Olympic figure skaters to shame. Josh comes down from the office in response to Cheryl's call, sees me, and falters on his way over. At the butcher counter, Sven grunts. Trust me, for Sven, that's like giving the finger.

So much for that ultra-friendly MegaMart shopping experience.

Dutt follows behind me toward the break room at the back. I need some place to sit and think. We make it through the first row of aisles before Luiz heads us off.

"'Ey, Rudy, you okay bro?" He's holding a broom in both hands near the base, slightly crossed over his chest, and shifting his weight uneasily. The stance strikes me as awkward.

"I'm fine, Luiz. What the hell's going on?"

"The cops came in here earlier this afternoon, askin 'bout you. First they just talked to Josh, but then they start callin the rest of us in."

"I know. Did they talk to you?"

"Caught me as I was comin on my shift."

I roll my eyes and nod. "And you told them about the scene I caused in the store on Sunday."

"Bro, by the time they got to me they *already* knew, and they weren't fuckin around! I had to tell 'em the truth! I'm still on probation, I can't be bullshittin the police!" He stops, lets his eyes slide side-to-side, and whispers, "Yo, did you kill somebody, Rudy? Did you kill that cop they been talkin 'bout on TV?"

And then I get it. Why he's holding that plastic broom in front of him like a lightsaber and glancing around for the nearest escape route.

He's scared. This 200-pound Hispanic former gang member with tattoos across most of his body is scared of me.

My friend.

I didn't kill anybody, I start to say, my new mantra, but someone says my name behind me first.

Josh is coming from the opposite end of the aisle, and if Luiz is scared, my boss looks terrified. He approaches with slow, cautious steps, like a zookeeper to a rogue lion. Across the store, the entire skeleton crew—Cheryl, Sven, and the Photolab Twins—stops their closing activities to watch us.

"You need to." Josh halts, licks his lips, and tries again. "You need to leave the store, Rudy."

"What? Why?"

"Management insists."

"*You're* management, Josh."

He flinches at my tone and clutches the base of his throat. He seems transfixed by my broken nose and the red swelling under my eyes. "Until the matter with the, ah, police is cleared up, they…that is, *we*…um, *I* feel it would be better if you, ah, extricated yourself from the premises to avoid any negative associations with the store."

I've never heard him try to sound so official about anything that doesn't involve air wrapped in pigskin. "Am I fired?"

"Let's. Let's not make a scene."

"I'm not making a scene, I'm trying to find out why you're treating me like Charles Manson. You've known me six years, Josh!"

Dutt puts a hand on my arm. "Let's just go, man."

I pull away and raise a finger at my boss. "I'm not going anywhere until he explains this!"

Josh's eyes are pained. He is, above all else, a nice guy. The kind of boss you want. It's clear he hates doing this, and I hate making him. He opens his mouth, and, I don't know, maybe he intends to do just as I ask and give me some answers.

But before he can, an arrow thunks through the side of his skull.

It looks like one of those fake props that lame comedians think is funny. The tip drills through one temple and out the other with enough momentum to drive Josh's head a foot to the right and bite into a tall display shelf of Doritos. He slumps at an angle, his head pinned to the faux wood grain like Tonto listening for approaching hoofbeats, a slightly bewildered expression on his face. Blood leaks from both sides of his eyes and runs down to meet under his chin. The fletching on the back of the arrow quivers for another few seconds, evidence of the shot's force.

I'm still pointing at him, now in amazement. At first, I think I did this with my finger somehow—with all I've seen today, it's really not outside the realm of possibility—but then I realize Dutt and Luiz are staring past me to the left, in the direction this arrow came from. I lower my arm and look out over the store.

Two aisles away from us is a figure revealed from the chest up by the shelves, dressed in a maroon hood and cloak with silver piping, covering what appears to be a green, long-sleeve tunic, all ornate in design. The look is very modern medieval, like something from a Renaissance faire, when you just know those LARPing losers are going for style over authenticity. The only part of him uncovered is the lower half of his stubbled face, visible beneath the hem of that bright, overhanging cowl.

He raises the longbow he just used to kill my boss in one black-gloved fist and shouts, "Death to all Carriers of the Word!"

And then everything goes completely batshit insane.

At the front of the store, Cheryl screams.

There's more of these Legolas-wannabe's pouring in through the automatic entrance doors. Six by my count, all dressed in the same outlandish hooded cloaks and carrying bows and various other medieval-themed weaponry. One stops to smash the electronic eye above the glass with a mallet that looks like something Thor would carry, locking us all in, while the others charge the register kiosks with snarling war cries. The sight is as surreal as watching *Braveheart* in your living room.

And by that I mean *in* your living room.

As they leap over the divider for Cheryl's lane, one of them slices her in half at the waist with a huge broadsword, silencing her scream. Her upper torso lands in the entrance of our aisle in a bloody tangle, arms still flailing.

"*What the FUCK!*" Luiz shouts, dropping his broom.

"*Look out!*" Dutt leaps on me as another arrow hisses through the space my neck was just occupying. We sprawl across the checkered tile with Luiz right beside us. More arrows clatter against the hard floor while others sink into the shelf surfaces, standing out like porcupine quills.

"*Go, go, get outta here!*" I yell. On hands and knees, we crawl toward the back of the store, away from these nutjobs and Josh's upright corpse. At the next cross aisle, I give Luiz a bump to get him to go left. We skip over several rows from where we were, into canned goods, and slide to a stop as quietly as possible.

The store is silent except for a saxophone version of "Annie's Song" playing over the speakers, just loud enough to mask our heaving breaths. From down at the end of the aisle, I catch sight of Sean and Kevin peeking over the top of the photolab counter. I wave at them to stay put.

"Shit, oh shit, they killed Josh!" Luiz whisper-moans.

"Shhh!" I hold a finger across my lips.

"Yo, what the fuck is goin on? Who are those guys?"

Luiz and Dutt both look at me expectantly.

"How the hell should I know? They're a bunch of lunatics with a Monty Python fetish!"

Dutt shakes his head. "You heard what he said! This is about that Word!"

"What word?" Luiz asks.

I ignore him and nod reluctantly at Dutt. "There's something else. I think…they might actually be the guys that killed Officer Reed."

"That is fucked, bro! We gotta get the cops here!"

"My cell's in the car." Dutt looks at me.

"Sorry, I didn't have time to grab mine when I fled for my life this morning. We need to—"

The lights in the store go out.

~ ~ ~

I've been in the Meg plenty of times in the dark—once while having sex with Brynn in the middle of the toiletries aisle—but never has the atmosphere seemed so sinister. The muzak dies, leaving us in even deeper quiet. Dutt, Luiz, and I give one another wide-eyed glares.

And then one of our attackers comes flying over the top of the shelf and our heads like an Olympic gymnast on the dismount, landing on two booted feet in our midst. He draws a sheathed sword attached to his belt as we scramble up on either side of him.

Dutt's back is exposed. The swordsman pulls back to take a swing at him. I react on pure adrenaline and instinct, awkwardly throwing my weight against the guy, shoving him against the shelves and knocking over a whole row of canned peas.

Two more come in from either end of the aisle, surrounding us. Dutt and Luiz each spring at one. Luiz grabs the gloved wrists of his dance partner before he can bring his sword down and starts grappling. Dutt's guy slices the air with some kind of hatchet. Dutt jumps out of the way as it chops a shelf in half and then belts the dude in the face.

By this point, the one I shoved has recovered enough to return the favor, throwing an elbow into my solar plexus hard enough to force the air from my lungs. His sword is on the ground, and I try to stop him from retrieving it by stepping on the blade.

He forgets the sword and just goes for my throat. I can see his face under the hood in the darkness, a kid younger than me with acne scars, gnashing his teeth.

He snarls, "We will purge your infection before the disease inside you spreads!"

His fingers dig into my windpipe. I pry at them to no avail, then gasp as the world turns black and white.

Eyes closing.

So tired.

And then that invisible hand comes roaring back to life inside me.

You remember He-Man? How the overly-muscled, vaguely homo-erotic blond dude would hold his sword aloft and become the overly-muscled, outright homo-erotic Conan-the-Barbarian-type?

Well, at the moment I'm about to surrender consciousness, as the last fading image in my head is of my estranged wife's face, a familiar burst of unnatural strength and energy rips through me like a bolt of lightning. It's the same adrenaline overkill I got back in the cell, the first time the Word got into my head.

This surge of power doesn't cause my clothes to shred or my biceps to bulge, but I do suddenly feel like I can take on a fucking army of teenagers dressed up to play "Dungeons and Dragons."

Which is good, cause I just might have to.

My fist pistons out, only I'm not really in control of it. It strikes the guy strangling me dead center in the chest. Something snaps beneath my knuckles like dry kindling. He goes sailing through the air, his fingernails taking narrow strips of flesh out of my neck. He hits the top of the next shelving unit and tumbles over the backside.

The other two fights come to a standstill as everyone looks at my handiwork.

The guy manhandling Luiz mutters in awe, "My God. You're the Omega. The Wellspring."

I charge forward, still feeling like I'm pumped full of more sugar than a case of Red Bulls. He doesn't even have time to react before I backhand him across the jaw, spilling him to the floor along with a handful of teeth.

The guy trying to eviscerate Dutt is another story. He shoves past my best friend and comes in swinging his hatchet in a high arc meant to scalp me.

Without thinking, I just do what my body wants me to: step forward and bring my forearm up against his incoming wrist. There's another of those unpleasant cracking sounds. His weapon flies past my head. He screams and cradles his broken arm until I give him a right cross that just about caves in his face.

Dutt and Luiz stare at me.

Behind us, there's the sound of booted feet. *Lots* of them. More of our new friends pour in through the entrance to the stock room, first five, then ten, then twenty. All of them have bows with nocked arrows ready, and they take up firing positions in a row like Roman siege combatants.

"Run, go!" I give Dutt a shove toward the front of the store, and then Luiz. We pelt down the aisle. Even more of these wackos stand straight and still amid the store shelves, watching us from under their hoods as we pass in the dark. The flat *whoosh-zing!* of launched arrows sounds many times. The bolts come so hard and fast they might as well be machine gun fire, chewing up loaves of bread and Little Debbie snack cakes and clattering off the floor all around us.

The photolab counter is just ahead. Sean—or maybe Kevin—has started through the batwing door in the side, but then he sees us coming and backpedals in a hurry. Luiz slams through right behind him, Dutt vaults up and slides over the countertop on his hip, and I glide over with less grace on my stomach. An arrow imbeds in the lacquered plastic two inches from my nose just before I fall into the floor in a heap.

We huddle behind the counter as the assault continues, arrows punching through our barrier to form a wall of wicked metal spikes or lodging behind us. I look up, and it's like a river of arrows flowing over our heads. The noise is a constant barrage of pops and cracks.

"*Duuuudes, what's goin on?*" Sean sits with his head between his knees and arms over his neck, screaming at the ground.

Kevin puts a comforting hand on his brother's back. "Is this a robbery, dude?"

Dutt smacks him in the back of the head. "*Does this look like any robbery you ever saw, numbnuts?*"

"*You!*" Luiz jabs a finger at me. "*This is because of* you! *They're gonna kill us and it's your fault!*" He launches at me, knocking me flat against the tile and landing on top of me. His fist pulls back. I make no move to stop him.

Dutt wraps an arm around his chest and hauls him off before he can punch me.

"Luiz, man, I didn't...I didn't...!"

"*Yo, then who did? You heard that muhfuckah! Saw how he looked at you! I got a wife, I got kids, I can't be dyin over some shit that got nuttin to do with me!*"

"He's got a point," Dutt says. "What was that with the Superman routine back there, Rudy?"

"I don't know. I. I." My stammering trails. That energy, that power, is fading again already.

Luiz is right. Regardless of whether or not this is my fault, it's certainly not his or Sean's or Kevin's or Dutt's. And why should they have to die for it?

"*Stop!*" I yell over the ceaseless noise of arrows. The area around us looks like the inside of a pincushion.

I get ready to stand up, and Dutt clutches at me. "Rudy, what the fuck're you doing?"

"*Just stop shooting and I'll come out!*"

They do stop.

But only to give themselves time to light their arrows on fire before resuming the attack.

The back wall—nothing but dry plaster, the photo print machine, and the cabinets for the developing chemicals and blank photostock paper—goes up in a sheet of flame in seconds. The heat is enough to bead sweat on my face. Oily, black smoke curls to the ceiling and quickly works its way down, choking us all. But at least the volley of arrows stops. Why waste ammunition when they can burn us to a crisp?

"*Dude, what do we do?*" Kevin shouts.

That's a good question. The front door is malfunctioning, thanks to the medieval warriors; we'd have to smash our way out through the glass, and then we'd be in the open parking lot. The stockroom and back door are definitely out. That only leaves...

"Upstairs," I gasp. "We have to get upstairs to the office. We can go out on the roof."

Luiz pulls his shirt collar up over his mouth and nose. "Josh has that gun up there!"

"*No, no, I don't wanna die, dude!*" Sean shouts suddenly. Before any of us can stop him, he jumps up and claws his way over the counter.

All of us stand. Kevin tries to go after his brother, but we hold him back. The Meg fills with more smoke as the fire engulfs the area around us, and Sean skitters blind into the darkness.

Further out in the murk, several ghostly figures turn in the fleeing teenager's direction.

"*Sean, no!*"

"*Get down, bro!*"

"*DUUUUUUDE!*"

Arrows fly. We hear the wet thuds of them hitting home. Sean crumples.

I clench my fists hard enough to draw blood under my nails.

"We gotta go," Dutt says. "While they're distracted."

We make our way along the far east wall of the store, keeping low. Kevin is in tears, and we just about have to drag him. The fire spreads fast, eating through the cheap, outdated insulation in the walls, the shelves and paper goods, lapping at the ceiling. The air gets blacker and fills with charred, orange embers. My eyes water with the sting of it.

We're about halfway down, passing the glass cold case full of meat, when a horde of our enemies stomps out to block our way. There's way more than I could probably beat, if my superhuman powers even came back. They advance on us, drawing swords and brandishing maces.

The swinging door to the butcher room bursts open, and two-hundred and fifty pounds of Swedish-made muscle comes barreling into the crew in front of us like a bowling ball into pins. Sven's got a miniature propane canister in one hand and a butcher's knife in the other. He wades into their midst with berserker fury, catching them completely off guard, and takes turns burying his blade into flesh to create streaming geysers of blood and bashing the canister against skulls to make a nice, ringing gong sound.

When they're all on the floor, he holds out a hand to us and curls the fingers three times, beckoning. We run.

The fire—and the attack—are in full swing. Air is scarce and what little there is fills up with arrows and angry bodies. Sven leads the way, shielding us with his broad body as he tosses aside those that come at us for melee warfare.

But there's only so much he can do.

"*Dude, heeeeelp!*"

At the last cross aisle before the staircase door, two of them jump out and latch on to Kevin's arm. Sven is occupied with at least three others, so Luiz and I grab hold and try to yank the kid back. There's more coming to help our opponents in the tug-of-war.

An arrow soars in out of nowhere, arcing high, dropping low, and piercing Luiz's thigh all the way through. He lets go and falls backward with a wail.

Kevin is dragged away, out of my grasp. My last view of him is five hooded douchbags tossing him to the clean tile floor and hacking away with axes and swords.

Luiz sits up, gripping his leg where the shaft of an arrow has lodged in the bone. A circle of blood grows around the point of entry and exit. We're all coughing and gasping, close to asphyxiation, but I still catch the look of anguish on his face. Dutt and I each grab an arm and support him with our shoulders.

Sven has the door to the staircase open, waving us inside. He's riddled with arrows, the feathered tips jutting from his muscled back and shoulders and arms. We start up the stairs with Luiz, but after several steps I turn back.

"*C'mon!*" I tell Sven, this guy I've worked with just as long as Josh, who I've never said two words to, whose real name I never bothered to learn, but who still, not to sound too much like Elton, saved my life tonight.

He shakes his large, buzzcut head and gives me a thumbs up just as another arrow pounds through the side of his neck. Sven stumbles against the door, then slams it closed on us.

The three of us continue up to the office, but it's slow going. Luiz weighs a fucking ton. Right now I'm just glad to be able to breathe again, but the floor under our feet is getting steadily warmer.

The MegaMart, which has stood in this location since 1956, is minutes away from burning to the ground.

We reach the office, all of us panting, and drop Luiz into a chair. He whimpers in pain and clutches his leg, shivering. Dutt kneels to examine the wound while I dig out the little .380 ACP from Josh's desk that he thinks none of us know about.

Thought none of us know about.

"We gotta keep moving." I go to the balcony door, throw the bolt on the screen, and step outside to scan the slanted section of roof around the tiny landing. "Coast is clear!"

Dutt bends to get a grip on Luiz. "All right, we better get started. It's gonna take a while to lift him—"

Luiz shakes his head. "Leggo me."

"What?" I pull back inside the window. "Luiz, we don't have time for this!"

He nods at the window. "Ain't no way I'm gonna make it out there like this, bro. Just gonna slow both of you down." He licks sweat off his lips and grimaces. "Yo, but if you gimme that gun, I'll stay here and buy you some time. Get a little revenge on these muhfuckahs, know what I'm sayin?"

I shake my head. "That's ridiculous, we're not leaving you!"

"Got no choice, bro. It's either me or all of us."

Dutt says quietly, "It's his choice to make, Rudy."

"You know what, fine! Whatever! The whole universe has gone fucking insane!"

I stand and watch while Dutt pulls Luiz' chair over in front of the staircase. He holds a hand out for the gun. I bring it over.

Luiz takes it and then grabs my wrist. His face is twitching with pain. "Hey. Rudy. I'm sorry about what I said, bro. I know none of this is your fault."

"I don't," I whisper, feeling a tear slide over my cheek.

"You were gonna take the bullet for us. Ain't a lotta people in my life been willin to do that."

I stand mute.

"You just tell Graciela. You tell her...a man gotta do what a man gotta do."

At the base of the stairs, the door flies open, letting in a dense bank of smoke and the crackle of flames.

Luiz shoves me away and opens fire to hold them at bay. Dutt and I run for the balcony door.

Surrounding the recessed balcony is a slanting ledge that leads up to the stuccoed roof of the building. Dutt climbs up onto it, but I lean cautiously forward and peer over the railing.

The balcony overlooks the business block nestled against the north side of the Meg and part of the front parking lot to the right. The area is clear of the hooded freaks, but below us, flames eat through the walls and billow out to caress the little café next door, now closed for the night. In the far distance, the first sirens are rising over the sound of Luiz' measured shots.

"Jesus, all of downtown is gonna burn," I whisper.

"Then let's fucking not burn with it," Dutt hisses. "Get your ass up here, Compton!"

I clamber to the rooftop with him. We make our way across the cobbled surface toward the fire ladder bolted to the back of the store. From this vantage point, we have a good view of the entire area. A rusted yellow school bus is parked diagonally in front of the building. There's the sound of breaking glass from the front of the store, and then five or six of the warriors charge from the fire and up the stairs into the vehicle.

The engine rumbles to life. They're getting ready to haul ass. Behind us, Luiz screams.

We run to the back of the Meg. Down in the fenced alley where I talked to Brynn on the phone a few days before, one of these guys is sprinting past, his scabbard jangling against his belt. He's in a hurry, and doesn't even look up.

Without a moment's hesitation, I leap from the edge of the roof as he passes beneath.

I manage to get in a solid heel to his back before I come down on top of him. We both hit the pavement hard, but I'm up first and straddling him before he can get his bearings. I push the hood back and sock him in the face. The impact rattles my teeth; I'm definitely not super strong anymore. For the first time, I notice the symbol on the breast of their maroon cloaks, a little white candle with a blazing yellow flame.

"Who are you bastards?" I growl in his face.

The guy looks to be about 25, with a scar across his right cheek. He wrinkles his nose in disgust at me and says, "We are Acolytes of the Candlemaker. He Who Lights The Way."

I hit him again. "You've been watching me. Following me."

"We were tracing the path of infection."

Once more, just for good measure. This one splits his upper lip. "What does that even mean? What do you want with me?"

He dribbles blood from the corner of his mouth and says, "We are sworn to eradicate the Word wherever it's found, just as we've done for hundreds of years. All Carriers must be purged before the Servant of *Sideris* is awakened."

I hear the clang of Dutt coming down the ladder behind me, but I keep my attention on this lunatic. "I don't know what the hell any of that means, but there's no need for you to do this! I don't even remember this goddamn Word!"

"Doesn't matter, it's still inside you. And your death is the only way to ensure it never gets out."

"You stupid fuck." I grab the edges of his cloak and shake him, trying not to spill tears. "I'm right here, you could've come to my home and slit my throat! But those people in there…they were my friends…and you animals butchered them!"

He grins savagely, and in his eyes I see the same fire that ignited every religious war and crusade since the beginning of time. Rock-hard self assurance, coupled with an inability to compromise. "That's right, Carrier. And we'll kill every single person you've even *spoken* to since you were infected—and everyone *they've* spoken to, if necessary—just to be sure the Word doesn't spread. That it dies here and now."

I grab his forehead and smash the back of his skull against the concrete like a dribbled basketball, knocking him out. Dutt is standing beside me now, and I look up at him in absolute panic.

"Brynn."

Chapter TWELVE

"Everyone?"

"Yeah."

"They're gonna kill *everyone*."

"Yes."

"*Everyone* you've spoken to since the night you went to jail."

"Jesus Dutt, yes, that's what he said!"

We're back in my car again, only I wouldn't let him drive. By the time we got back to the front parking lot of the Meg, the beat-up school bus was gone. The sirens were getting louder and the fire had become a hellish, infernal blaze spreading to everything around it. We didn't stop to watch, just sprinted to my car and tore out of the business block.

"Wow. I mean, *shit*. Do you know how many people you speak to on a daily basis? Do you think they're counting by telephone, or just in person?"

"I don't know, I didn't ask them to explain the semantics of their insane beliefs."

"Whoa." He sits bolt upright in his seat. "Does that mean me, too?"

"Unless they think you're a deaf mute, I'm pretty sure that paints a big fucking target on your head."

Dutt nods and grabs for the dashboard as I squeal around another corner. "Then can you at least slow down before you do the job for them?"

"Can't." In the darkness of the car, my unbandaged hand is almost bloodless on the steering wheel. "We gotta get to her before they do."

Brynn. She's all I can think about. Her being in danger blocks out the trauma we just went through, the sight of all my coworkers being massacred by a hooded cult. If these guys have really been keeping tabs on me—working backward to exterminate everyone I've been in contact with since my night in the slammer—she's bound to be pretty high on the list.

I hit the gas and fly past the next major street at Timmons, running the red light. A fire engine hurtles into the intersection from our right, lights and siren blazing, coming within inches of clipping my rear bumper. Dutt shouts some wordless gibberish. The driver lays on the horn before turning left, heading in the direction we just came from, where the night sky glows orange.

Dutt twists around and watches them through the back window. "Are you sure we shouldn't have just waited? Or called the police?"

"No time. I can't risk trying to explain all this to the cops if they go after her next. We get her, then get help."

"Rudy, I know you'd love nothing more than to go riding in on a unicorn and rescue that bitch, but...do you even know where you're going?"

I chew the inside of my lip as I cut around a VW, run another red light, and hang a left on Merced, heading toward the west side of Withers. Most of the cheap motels are around there. "Not specifically, no."

"Then stop and let's figure this out."

I reduce speed by about ten miles an hour. "Give me your cell, let me call her."

Dutt leans into the backseat and rummages through his knapsack. "You got any idea about these guys? Are they with those mobsters?"

"I don't think so. Weldon and Fiver wanted me to..." I almost say *infect them*, "...to give them the Word. But these hooded guys want to *stop* me from telling anyone. That's why they killed Officer Reed, because I had dinner with him and they thought there was a chance I told it to him." I wipe sweaty soot off my forehead, mostly to hide my wince of guilt. The cops are right. In a way, I did kill Reed. "And if any of that makes a damn bit of sense, then I'm never getting high again."

"Okay, yeah, we got that part figured out, but *think*. What else did he say?"

I go over the interrogation in my head. "They work for someone named 'the Candlemaker.' He said they want to stop me before I can wake somebody up. The Servant of..." I sound out the word for him. "*Sigh-dare-is*."

Dutt sits back in his seat and hands me his cell. "And that other one, the one in the grocery store. What did he say after you went berserk?"

"He called me the Omega."

"What happened anyway? You were getting your ass handed to you one second, and the next you were invincible."

"I don't know, I just got this...rush. More like I was being guided than actually doing those things myself. Hillman said the Word was growing in me. Getting stronger. And that it would have other effects. Maybe this was like…a defense mechanism. The Word's way of trying to protect itself."

"Jesus," Dutt mutters, shaking his head. "What the hell are we in the middle of, Rudy?"

Hillman's parting shot comes back to me.

"I don't know and I don't care, as long as we can get out of it."

She only answers because she doesn't recognize Dutt's number.

"It's me," I blurt. "Don't hang up!"

"I told you I don't wanna talk to you!"

"This isn't about you and me! You're in danger! Where are you?"

"I'm not telling you that! Goodbye!"

"Everyone at the MegaMart is dead, Brynn. They…they burned the place to the ground, along with half of downtown."

When she speaks again, her tone is concerned but cautious, as if this might be a trick. "What are you talking about? Who burned it? Those two guys?"

"No, this was somebody else. They're a cult or something. Very medieval-themed. They're gonna kill everyone I've been in contact with. You have to tell me where you are so we can come get you."

"Um, correct me if I'm wrong Mr. Wizard, but if they're killing everyone you come into contact with, that's just more reason for me to hang up this phone right now!"

"It's too late for that!" I raise a hand to hit the steering wheel and stop myself. Temper, temper. "Look, if you don't want me to come, then call the police. Get in their custody. I just...I need you to be safe."

There's silence. All I want to hear is her agreeing, so at least I have one less thing to worry about.

Instead I hear a crash, a short scream, and then a new voice in my ear.

"Well, well, well, Rudy! Ain't dis a—*EF!*—pleasant coincidence!"

"Oh, you son of a bitch!"

"We lost ya after da cops let ya go, but we managed ta find your pretty wife here."

"Don't you fucking touch her!"

"Relax, friend. If I hurt *her*, den *you* ain't got no reason ta come ta me. See?"

"Okay. All right." I force myself to take a breath. "Just tell me what you want me to do."

"All-Night Motel on Worthington. Room 406. Get here just as soon as ya can. Be prepared ta either give us da Word, or come wit us. And judging by how your place is deco'd, I think ya seen enough movies ta know what'll happen if I even get a whiff of da cops."

The phone goes dead in my ear.

The All-Night Motel sits just off the access road for 287. A sign out front proclaims rooms only cost 35 dollars per night. The cadre of hookers on the corner indicates they probably rent by the hour also. Not much bigger or cleaner than our place, but I still can't believe Brynn stayed here. The place is just a big, four-story rectangle, eight rooms on each floor, in two back-to back rows. I pull into the lot of the apartment building across the street and kill the engine.

"So what's the plan then?" Dutt asks. "You go in first, or me?"

"You're not coming."

"The hell I'm not."

"I'm going in there alone. I don't wanna make them antsy by showing up with someone else."

"I. Rudy. *Jesus!* These guys could kill you!"

"They won't. Not until they have the Word. Listen, out of everyone that's been after me for this thing, these two have actually dealt the straightest with me. As long as they're willing to let Brynn go, I'm gonna do whatever they want."

He smirks and starts to take off his glasses. "Nah uh. Not gonna happen. I'm gonna beat some ass."

"Look, you're my backup. If they try to leave with both of us, you can do whatever you want. And once you have Brynn and you're sure she's safe, by all means, call the cops. Until then, just sit tight and let me handle this." He doesn't say anything, just stares at me. "Dutt, please, I need you to do this." I don't add that I need him not to be hurt in all this just as much as I need Brynn not to.

He scowls and then waves a hand as he looks away. "Fine. I'll be here. But I wanna remind you, you're risking an awful lot for someone who's made it very clear she thinks about the feelings of pond scum about as much as she thinks of yours."

"She loves me. I know she does."

"Spare me, Rudy. Go get yourself killed already."

I leave the keys in the ignition and get out of the car.

The fat guy in the glass corner office eyes me as I walk up to the motel. I give him and the hookers a wide berth and take the first metal staircase I come to, climbing up to the fourth floor and heading down the narrow, Astroturf-covered walkway that rings the building at each story. Room 406 is next to last on the row. I shiver from cold and fear as I knock. A muffled voice tells me to come in.

One lamp glows in the corner, casting crisp shadows. Weldon is stretched out on the bed with a cigarette in one hand, a paperback book in his lap. I sense someone behind me and turn to see Fiver against the wall. The fact that I saw his corpse an hour ago at the morgue is just another drop of weirdness in an ocean of strange. He closes the door after I step inside and then places a large hand on my neck to guide me forward.

"Rudy, I hafta say, after ya ran away earlier, I had my doubts about ya. But ya proved ya got some brains and balls by coming in. We'll just chalk da other up ta first time jitters."

"Where's Brynn?"

"Bat'room." He nods at the closed door beside him.

"Brynn, honey? You okay?"

A burst of high-pitched, incomprehensible syllables from in there.

"She's a trooper, dat one." Weldon swings his legs to the side of the bed and stubs out his cigarette against the scarred bedside table. "Tell me, how da hell'd ya corral a prize filly like her? Cause, looking at da two of ya, I just don't see it."

"If I corralled her, she wouldn't be staying at a motel, would she?"

He shrugs with his eyebrows. "Too true. I'm just saying, when ya got a pair of legs like dat wrapped around your waist—legs ya didn't *pay* for—ya must be a nervous wreck constantly, waiting for da other shoe ta drop. Knowing there's always gonna be a guy out dere with something better ta offer her."

I jut my jaw and glare at him. "Can we just do this?"

"Sure thing, friend. Dis ends as soon as ya give us what we want."

"You let Brynn go first."

His nostrils flare. "It don't—*GEE-DEE!*—happen like dat."

Fiver gives my neck a gentle squeeze that brings to mind car crushers. "Do you remember the Word or not?"

"Ah. Ah, *ah*. No."

Weldon shrugs, trying to regain his composure. "Den ya gotta come wit us."

"Okay. Okay, I'll do that. Let's just go, and we'll leave Brynn here."

"Sorry, new orders. She's gotta come too. My boss is afraid ya mighta told her da Word. And even if ya didn't..." His froggy lips stretch wide. "Well, ya never know when a little leverage might come in handy."

I shrug off Fiver's hand and take a step toward Weldon. He looks at me with open surprise.

"That wasn't the deal."

"I don't recall making any deal, Rudy."

"Well...it was implied."

Weldon chuckles. "Next time, get it in writing. Till then, ya both stay wit us until we get dat Word outta yer head. Fiver, go get da girl. Rudy ain't gonna cause no trouble."

Fiver stares down at me and then walks into the bathroom. Weldon stands up and tucks his book into his back pocket under his coat. I consider tackling him for a moment. Even without my unreliable super strength, I might be able to take Weldon down. I can't see any weapons. Which doesn't mean anything with these two, of course.

But Fiver...man, I probably couldn't take that guy even

with my new abilities. And that would just put Brynn in potential danger. Too many complications.

On the bedside table, I notice the collection of framed photographs of us she took from the apartment. The one taken after our wedding at the JP is right in front, with her wedding band on the wooden surface next to it. My heart swells at the sight of them, displayed so they'll be the last thing she sees before falling asleep.

Fiver comes back out of the bathroom pushing my wife in front of him, hands tied behind her and a gag in her mouth made from an old scarf. She must've been getting ready for bed, cause all she's wearing is a midriff t-shirt promoting a band called Metric, an old pair of my boxer shorts, and her frog slippers. Her gaze latches onto me.

"You okay?" I ask.

She nods.

"All right, let's get a move on," Weldon says.

He goes first, and then Fiver herds us through the door, leaving it open. We all start down the covered walkway, heading to the staircase I came up just a few minutes before. I scan the area for Dutt, but see something else of interest.

A rusted out school bus that comes squealing into the parking lot and broadsides a parked vehicle.

"Hell." Fiver states the word less like an exclamation and more like the dignified admittance of an unpleasant truth.

"Goddamn religious wackjobs," Weldon growls. "I been killed enough times by dose motherfuckers."

Below us, the bus doors open and out files a group of the Candlemaker's Acolytes. They must've stopped to get reinforcements after torching the Meg, because the long vehicle is full again. That's probably the only reason we managed to beat them here. They form themselves into a line four stories down and stare up at us, their breath pluming in the cold air. The prostitutes on the corner disappear like a cloud of smoke in a high wind. The fat night attendant comes out of the corner office, screaming that he's calling the cops. One of the hooded guys turns and launches an arrow that hits him just below the jaw.

"You have all been in the presence of a Carrier," this one shouts. "Surrender yourselves for purging, and we will be merciful!"

Weldon jams a middle finger at them. "Go back and suck dat old man's cock, ya—*DEE! DEE-AITCH!*—lunatics!"

They raise their bows and fire.

Weldon grabs Brynn and me and pulls us below the level of the latticed metal guardrail. The weave is almost a mesh, the holes too tight for the arrows to penetrate. A pistol appears in Weldon's hand. Literally. At this close range, I see it fade into existence a little at a time, like pixels on an old cathode ray tube. Fiver dives around us, summoning an uzi from thin air. When he lands on his knees, he shoves the thin barrel through the guardrail, tilts it down, and begins firing. Weldon does the same.

I turn to Brynn while they're preoccupied. She's on her side, squirming and wincing at the gunfire. I untie the cord around her wrists and help her sit up, then slide the gag down onto her neck.

"You okay?" I ask again.

She answers by throwing her arms around my neck. I could die happy.

"C'mon," I whisper in her ear.

Arrows spang all around us, keeping Weldon and Fiver

busy. I crawl away from them, tugging Brynn the opposite direction, toward where the walkway turns right around the corner of the motel. We pass the open door of her room and she says, "Hold on!" She slides out of my grip and crawls inside, then comes back after a few seconds with her tiny purse slung over one shoulder.

"*Priorities?*" I ask over the gunfire.

"*I need it!*"

We start off again, make it to the door of the last room, and Weldon squeals behind us, "Hey! *Heeeey! Get your— EF! DEE-BEE! AY-EF!—asses back heeeeeeere!*"

Once we turn the corner, we stand up and run. Doors slam closed ahead of us as other motel guests jerk back inside like turtles into their shells. There's another staircase on the far side of the building, but by the time we get there, three Acolytes are coming to meet us. Their hooded faces look up, the lead one's eyes glittering.

My heartbeat jumps. My muscles light up with that raw power. I push Brynn aside and hurdle down the stairs with both feet out in front of me in an improvised flying karate kick.

I hit the first one in the chest. He falls back into the others like a Three Stooges routine, all of them rolling backward. The move is bold and forceful and pays off, but it leaves me crashing down against the metal steps, the breath knocked out of my lungs.

So much for being invincible.

As I get up, trying to suck air into my deflated chest, Brynn rushes down and helps me stand, then clings to my back. One of the Acolytes regains his feet and draws a sword, advancing on us. I rear back to hit him, but lack of oxygen withers me. He jabs forward, trying to ram the blade through my intestines.

Someone slams against us from behind. Weldon leans around us with his pistol pointed down the stairs. He squeezes off two rounds that blow the Acolyte off his feet just as my lungs remember how to work.

More are coming, surrounding both sides of the third floor landing. Rather than retreat, Weldon charges down, firing at the ones coming from the front. I go down behind him with Brynn following, and wade into the others trying to sneak up on him.

For a few seconds, it's utter insanity. Weldon and I are almost back-to-back with Brynn sandwiched between us, his gun reports hard and fast. The Acolytes flood the walkway, but they're too packed in to put their weapons to good use. I let the Word override every instinct and watch in amazement as I break jaws and crush sternums.

One of them careens by after I snap his shin. I hear Brynn shriek, and turn around in time to see her tumbling backward over the rail after being slammed by the Acolyte's flying body.

My movements are a blur. I lean out into space and clamp onto her wrist. She dangles. The drop is a lot higher than the one from Ms. Gupta's window. Her purse slides over her shoulder and she catches it before it falls. I stand there completely vulnerable and try to haul her up just as one of the Acolytes draws his bow further down the walkway.

"Goddamn it, *no!*" Weldon jumps around me and raises his arm just as the bowstring twangs.

An arrow that would otherwise have gone through my eyeball pierces the meat of Weldon's hand and stops halfway through. His drops his gun, clutches the wound, and yowls like a drowning cat, interspersing each shriek of pain with shouted abbreviations.

I yank Brynn back over the ledge. I don't know if it's super strength or plain old adrenaline at this point. Once she's on her feet, I scoop up Weldon's piece. His hand—the one not being used as a shish-ka-bob—latches onto my calf and there's one of those microwave hums followed by a moment of searing pain before I kick him away.

"Everybody, get the fuck back!" I yell, waving the pistol around. I don't stop to see if anyone is listening before leading Brynn down the rest of the stairs, all the way to the bottom.

There's another group of five waiting for us in the side parking lot of the motel. I raise the pistol, but before I can fire, headlights blaze from the dark alley of the buildings that back up to the place. Dutt roars out and smashes my car into them, tossing bodies through the air and cracking my windshield.

"*Get in!*"

I push Brynn through the back door, climbing in on top of her. An arrow punctures the cloth seatback next to my ear.

"*GO!*" I scream at Dutt.

He's already in motion, peeling out of the parking lot and jumping the curb onto the freeway access road, but he still yells, "*Go where?*"

I say the first thing that comes to mind.

"West."

THIRTEEN

"...*considered extremely armed and dangerous. It's un-known at this time if a second male—identified as Dutton Geneva Lansing—is an accomplice, but we're fairly certain the suspect's wife, Brynn Marie Compton, is being held against her will.*"

"Shit," Dutt murmurs. "They used my full name."

We're at a rest stop off 287, about thirty miles west of Withers. Out here, on the edge of the Metroplex, there's no lights, no houses, just the drone of traffic on the freeway. I made Dutt drive until I was sure we weren't being followed. I used the time to get my head straight and explain some of this to Brynn. She sat on the far side of the seat, listening without speaking, until we pulled over to figure out what to do. The best option, until Dutt turned on the radio, was to call the police, tell them where we are, and have them pick us up, rather than try to make it back into the city.

"*Again, we're seeking anyone with information as to the whereabouts of Rudolph Corey Compton.*" I'm fairly certain the voice coming from the car speakers belongs to my old friend, Detective Kitner. The statement must've been hastily prepared, but he sounds as cool as a Russian winter. *"He is believed to be responsible for the fire that consumed the local MegaMart and a large section of the surrounding businesses in downtown Withers, as well as a shoot-out that occurred minutes later at the All-Night Motel, where his wife was staying. We are attributing the majority of the deaths from tonight to him and his accomplice or accomplices, although there may be some unknown parties involved. These deaths include the proprietor of the All-Night, and several bodies found in the debris of the MegaMart that we are tentatively identifying as Compton's coworkers."* There is an audible pause for breath on the other end of whatever microphone he's speaking in to. *"He is also wanted for further questioning in connection with the shooting death of Christopher Bartell earlier today, and is also suspected…in the murder of Officer Nathan Reed."*

The end of the sentence is said hesitantly, and I bet I know why. Once the media puts together today's timeline, they're going to want to know, FBI mandate or not, why a man already in police custody in connection with two homicides walked free a few hours later to kill again. And again.

And again.

"We gotta call them." Dutt switches off the radio and turns around in the front seat to look at me. "We gotta call the police and tell them the truth."

"Won't help."

"Bullshit. We're the victims here. Those guys tried to kill us."

"What guys? Who saw them, Dutt? A couple of hookers and whoever was staying at that crackhouse? Nobody's gonna talk to the cops. Nobody credible, anyway."

"We have proof! The bodies of the ones we killed at the Meg—!"

"Were burned to a crisp along with Luiz and Josh and everybody else. They'll just look like customers. And they obviously cleaned up their mess at the motel before the cops showed. These Acolyte fuckers don't strike me as stupid. Trust me, the police didn't believe me before about Weldon and Fiver, and they won't believe us about this. Hell, I *lived* through it, and I still don't believe it."

"But there's no motive for you to do any of that!"

I bark laughter. "No *motive?* Shit, I couldn't have any more motive if I tried! Reed arrested me! Chris was fucking my wife! Josh was about to fire me and everybody at the Meg ratted me out!" I hike a thumb over my shoulder at Brynn, still sitting across the car. "We kidnapped my soon-to-be ex-wife in the middle of the night!"

"She can tell them the truth though!"

"They think she's a cowed wife who'll say anything to keep me out of trouble. We'll be lucky if they don't skip the trial and execute me on sight."

"Is that true?" Brynn asks suddenly, without looking from the front windshield.

"No, they can't really do that."

She turns to me. Her face is rigid. "I mean about the kidnapping. Am I being '*held against my will*'? If I open the car door right now and run, are you and your little sidekick gonna wrestle me to the ground?"

"I'm more of a wingman than a sidekick," Dutt says.

"What? No, Jesus Brynn, we-we-we rescued you! I came there to *save* you from those guys!"

She nods slowly. "I know. Thank you. I just...I don't understand what the hell this is all about."

Dutt slumps behind the steering wheel and rubs his eyes beneath his glasses. "Join the club. Fuck, Rudy, you got the cops after you, but I'm gonna have the *Army* after me. In seventy-two hours, I'm AWOL."

"So what are we gonna do?" Brynn asks. "We can't just sit here all night!"

"We're listening to suggestions."

"Then here's one: take me back! This doesn't have anything to do with me!"

"Looks to me like they sure think it does."

"Well, it doesn't!" She leans forward to glare at him and bunches her small hands into fists. "Rudy never told me this password or whatever! I demand you take me back right now!"

Dutt grins wickedly at her in the rearview. "So fulfill your needs and damn the consequences to anybody else? Right, sure, sounds exactly like your relationship with Rudy thus far."

"Oh, shut the fuck up, *Dutton!* You don't know a goddamn thing about us! You're in the country like what, once a year?"

"That just means I can call out whores in multiple languages."

"Okay, Christ, just stop," I tell them. "Things are bad enough without having to put up with this."

Brynn sits back, fuming.

Dutt keeps the smirk and asks, "So what do you wanna do then?"

The answer comes easier than I would've thought. "Hillman. He was the only one that knew the truth. He got me out of this before and maybe he can do it again."

"You wanna call him?"

"I lost his card."

"Doesn't matter. Just call an FBI branch office and they'll track him down."

I pick up Dutt's cell.

"Not on that. The cops might be waiting to trace it as soon as we turn it on. Let's find a payphone."

I sit back as he starts up the car and look at Brynn. She has her arms crossed, clutching her purse to her chest while she looks out the window.

And even though I know she's pissed as hell, and that this is far from the ideal situation, I can't help but be secretly thrilled that she's here.

Payphones suck.

The only people who use them anymore are criminals. But another fifteen miles up the road we find a diner that has a bank of three outside: one that looks crushed, one that looks burned, and one that looks like it has semen smeared across the mouthpiece. I go for this one, and dial the operator.

"What city?"

"Um, Fort Worth, I guess. Can you connect me to the nearest FBI office? Or just, any FBI office?"

"One moment."

There's a repeating *burrrrrr*. And then an electronic menu welcoming me to the Fort Worth/Dallas Division Office of the FBI. I huddle out of the wind and hit zero over and over again to skip to a live person.

A bored female voice asks, "How may I direct your call?"

"I'm trying to reach an agent named Douglas Hillman about a case he's working on. He gave me his card but I lost it. Is there any way you can get me in touch with him?"

"Is this an emergency?"

"Depends on your definition, I guess."

"If it's not life and limb, I can put in a contact request."

"Okay, sure, that's fine."

"Your name and a phone number?"

"Do I have to give that?"

"Going to be hard to have him call you without it."

"Okay, it's uh, Rudy. Just tell him…I talked to him about that thing in Withers. He'll know." I give her Dutt's cell number.

"One moment."

A click of keys. "I don't have a listing."

"He may not be from your, you know, your section or branch or however that's all set up."

"Sir, I'm checking the entire FBI contact database. There's a Dilbert Hilton in New York, and a Douglas Hammond in L.A., but I'm not finding any Douglas Hillman with the Federal Bureau of Investigation. Unless he's above my security clearance, but those agents don't make a habit of handing out their cards."

I stand at the payphone kiosk and stare at the white stain across the mouthpiece.

"Now," she says, "are you sure he wasn't with the DEA?"

The diner is one of those truck stop joints you always see in the movies, except more depressing. It's decorated for Thanksgiving, but somehow that just makes the ambience worse. It's pushing ten-thirty, and the only people eating are tired, lonely men in baseball caps, all of them staring at Brynn's legs beneath her baggy shorts. A lone waitress is doing her nails behind the counter, next to a TV playing syndicated *Office* reruns. Not exactly the most low-profile place for fugitives, but it could be worse.

I enter with my head down and go straight back to where Dutt and Brynn sit across from one another in a back booth, him with a half-eaten cheeseburger, her with an untouched fruit plate. After a moment's deliberation, I sit next to Dutt. They ordered me a burger too, and I sit down and take two huge bites before realizing I'm not hungry.

"You talk to him?" Dutt asks.

"Nope. Because Douglas Hillman doesn't work for the FBI."

"Okay. What does that mean?"

"I don't know. Could be a spook. Could've been playing me. But he wasn't who he said he was, and that's enough reason for me not to trust him."

"Which leaves us right back at square one. Wanted and on our own."

"No, it leaves *you guys* at square one." Brynn pushes her plate away and digs a pack of cigarettes out of her purse. She doesn't offer to share and we don't ask. She lights up and blows smoke at the dim bulb over our table. "Way I see it, you two have no option but to go back. I will tell them the truth and do everything I can for you, I swear."

Dutt leans sideways in the booth to rest his head against the wall. "Rudy, you know I would rather cut out my tongue than agree with her over anything besides her STD count—" Across the table, Brynn hikes her middle finger. "—so I hope you know how serious I am when I say...she's right. We need to call the police and turn ourselves in."

I nod and put both my palms on the tabletop. After getting off the phone with the FBI, I stood outside and thought about all this already. And I give them the conclusion I came to. "Yeah. That's exactly what the two of you need to do. Get to the cops and tell them what really happened. Clear my name, if you can. Just…give me a little time to take the car and get a ways up the road before you call."

The reaction is what I expected.

"Whoa, no way, man!"

Brynn reaches out and puts her ringless hand on my bandaged one. "Rudy, sweetheart, shit's been bad between us, I admit, but the last thing I want is for you to get hurt. You *know* that. I really think you should turn yourself in. Running is just gonna make this worse."

Dutt joins in. "Yeah man, they might not believe you initially, but the truth will come out. No way would these charges stick."

"But what if they did? What if I went to prison for murder?"

"You won't. Besides, if you're in police custody, at least you're safe. Out here, you're hunted by too many people. What's your plan anyway, run to Mexico?"

"No." I shake my head. "I was thinking of going west. Reno, probably."

"Oh." Dutt wrinkles his brow. "*Oh.*"

"Oh what?" Brynn looks from me to him. "What does that mean, what's in Reno?"

"The thing. The treasure. Or bomb. Whatever this Word is trying to lead him to."

"*Treasure?*" she repeats.

This time he ignores her and asks me, "Even if you get there and find it, what are you gonna do?"

"What treasure?"

"Depends on the situation."

"Rudy, you didn't say anything about a treasure!"

"Yeah, but what good will knowing where it is do you?"

"Are we talking gold or diamonds here?"

"Because once I know where it is, then maybe I can call the cops and not only prove I'm innocent, but take down everyone after me—after us—at the same time."

"Maybe those Spanish balloon things that pirates carried around?"

"I...I have to say, man...that's not a bad idea."

"Hey goddamn it, one of you answer me, *what treasure?*"

She's finally shrill enough that the patrons—those not already staring at her bare legs—look up from their plates.

"I don't know what it is," I hiss at her. "Weldon, that chunky mobster with the letter-shouting problem? *He* called it a treasure. This fake FBI agent Hillman says it's a weapon. The Acolytes called it the Servant of *Sideris*. All of which adds up to one big question mark. Did those two say anything while they had you?"

"They just busted in, tied me up, and threw me in the bathroom."

"Tell me something." Dutt grabs my shoulder. "Do you really think you can find it? That this Word will lead you right to it?"

I close my eyes and concentrate, for just a second. Look deep inside my own head. And, even though I can't for the life of me remember what that Word was, I can feel its power in there, a constant thrum like distant machinery.

And that voice. No more than a whisper. Begging me to *come, come, come right now.*

"Like Lassie to little Timmy in the well."

Dutt slaps the table. "All right. I'm in."

"No. No way. I don't want you involved in this."

"I'm already involved! I'm a bonafide accomplice! The Acolytes wanna kill me just as much as you!"

I want to argue with him. The thought of him getting hurt is like acid down my spine. But I'm too tired, he's right, and I don't want to do this alone.

"Thanks," I say. "So Brynn, if you'll just let us get—"

She stubs the cig and holds up her other hand. "Uh uh, no fucking way. I'm coming too."

"No you're not!"

"Yes, I am."

"What the hell, five minutes ago you wanted to go back and turn yourself in!"

Her mouth twitches downward. Her eyes get moist. "Sweetie, I'll be too worried about you, not knowing where you are. I wanna come. I wanna help you."

My heart gets carried out of my chest by doves until Dutt says, "Oh bullshit, you wanna go look for treasure."

"Yeah, so what? You think I'm gonna let you guys go off to get rich without me? I don't think so!"

I sigh. "Brynn...there is no treasure."

"You just said you don't know that."

"Even if there was, it's not ours. We'll never get our hands on it."

"We'll see about that."

I shake my head firmly. This is one complication I intend to do without. "You can't come. You have to go back and tell the police the truth."

She stands up and leans across the table until her lips are close enough to kiss. "You listen up, Rudy. If we get divorced, then half of whatever you find out there in Nevada is *mine*. You either let me come, or I'll tell the cops you dragged me out of that motel with your dick in one hand and a dead baby in the other. I'll have the two of you painted as the next Mansons before I'm through."

"Fucking hell," Dutt mutters, and stares out the window at the dull night beyond.

"All right," I say. "You can come."

In case you missed it, she said 'if.'

If we get divorced.

"What are our assets then?" Dutt asks after we all pick at our food a little more.

"We have a gun now."

"Which, if things go right, we won't ever need."

"And the car."

"Which there is now a statewide APB on, I assure you."

"Can't we swap plates or something?" Brynn asks. "They do that in the movies."

"Not much point. If a cop gets close enough to actually check them, that's not gonna do anything for us."

"At least it'll get us there."

"Yeah, if we have gas to put in it. Using credit cards is out. I don't know about you children, but I have about twenty bucks on me, which is barely enough to cover this meal."

"I think I have ten," I add. "Brynn got her purse, at least."

She bites her cheek. "I don't...I don't really have any money."

"Where's my savings?"

"What Chris and I didn't use is back at the motel."

"Great. Fucking great. You don't even have any goddamn shoes on!"

"Well, excuse me, I didn't expect to be tied up by mobsters, shot at with arrows, and leave for a cross-country trip when I got ready for bed tonight."

"We'll figure it out." Dutt points across the room. "But for now, I think it's time to pay and go."

On the TV next to the waitress, the show has been interrupted with pictures of all three of us. Mine is my mug shot from last week.

I nod my agreement. "I gotta make one more phone call first."

"Rudy, my God, where ARE you?"

My sister sounds both frantic and pissed off.

"Are you okay?" I ask.

"I'm fine, *I'm* not the one wanted for murder!"

"Are the cops there?"

"They got here ten minutes ago!"

"Thank God. Stay with them. Stay in their custody. If they won't keep you, then get outta town. Head down to Mom and Dad's place if you have to."

"What about you?"

"I'm going to Canada." That ought to keep them off my trail, since they'll have this payphone number and location within minutes.

"Rudy..." She's crying now.

"I'm innocent, okay? I didn't do any of those things they're saying. Tell Mom and Dad that, okay?"

"Okay."

"And one more thing. Please...pick up Minchi from the emergency vet on Harwood and take him with you."

I see the car turning in front of me, but there's really not much I can do.

I've only been riding the bike for a month, after all.

I try to brake. Try to swerve. Feel the back wheel lock up, the bike's skidding, and I'm airborne.

This is the Tuesday after last Labor Day. We need another vehicle after our small courthouse wedding, and I decide to fulfill a life long dream and buy a motorcycle. I save up a year for the down payment, take riding lessons in the blazing heat of August, and give my car to Brynn so she has a way back and forth to work. We find a beautiful little Honda Shadow I start riding that fall.

Only now this idea doesn't seem so hot. Not while I'm flying through the air toward the driver's side of the idiot who made a right on red without seeing me.

I won't remember the impact. There's a jump in the movie reel of my life, all the way from me doing my amateur Superman impression to me lying face down on the concrete with a mouthful of blood.

People scream at me not to move, swarm over me, their shadows the only evidence of their presence. I think of that Bradbury short story "The Crowd," and curse my overactive imagination. I discover I can't move even if I wanted to. The lower half of my body feels stiff and awkward, and any attempt at motion creates waves of pain.

This is it, I know it, the life is seeping out of me like the blood that's pooling under my chin, and I don't want to go out like this, I don't want to die with strangers.

Her face. Her smile. Her voice. That one cute little crooked tooth of hers. The smell of her hair.

I want these things to be my last memories of the world.

Hands grab me. Rough hands. They flip me over. And now I can see that the hovering crowd is full of familiar faces.

Luiz, charred like a blackened steak. Josh with an arrow through his temples. Sean with the same through his chest, and holding his brother's severed head. Officer Reed and Sven, each with a torso full of feathered spines. Chris with only half his skull intact and the few brains he possesses sloshing inside. Duwan and Lennie Kincaid are there too, bleeding from their still-fresh stab wounds. And Abraham Lincoln for some reason, but I'm pretty sure he's unrelated.

Please, I beg, the same way I did when this really happened, please get Brynn.

You don't need her, *Josh says.*

We'll k-k-keep you company, *Lennie agrees.* Aaaaall the way t-to the end.

I have to see her! Just one more time!

She's a fuckin slut, *Chris' mouth says, just below the bloody edge where Weldon's bullet exploded his cranium.* And she's *great* in bed. Trust me, fanboy, I had her in ways you never dreamed.

For sure, dude, Sean and Kevin second.

Tears run down my bloody face. I...I don't wanna die.

Luiz kneels next to me on the blacktop. Pieces of his fried flesh flake away from the movement. He puts a leathery hand on my forehead. Yo, Rudy...neither did we, bro. But here we are. Here we are.

I'm so, so sorry, man. I didn't mean for any of this to happen.

Then change it, bro. Until then...don't think you're any better off than us, just 'cause you're still breathin.

I jolt awake in the front seat of the car.

Dutt is snoring beside me. God, I forgot how loud he snores. When we were kids, and we spent the night at each other's house, I had to sleep with a pillow over my head.

We put some miles between us the diner last night, then pulled off on a rutted dirt track to sleep. All around us is open Texas flatland, but we're far enough from the road not to be seen. The sky beyond the windshield is streaked with the first auburn rays of sunrise.

I stay very still, letting the last of the dream bleed out. I fractured two vertebrae in that accident, and got road rash on knees and elbows. Considering there was a paint swatch on my helmet the same color as the car that turned in front of me, it could've been a lot worse.

Instead of dwelling, I go to a happier time. A few hours later, when Brynn showed up in the hospital. She didn't speak at first, just came in and laid her head on my chest to cry.

You can't ride it anymore, she said.

Don't think that's gonna be a problem.

I mean it, Rudy. When they called…I thought you were dead.

The love in those words gave me gooseflesh. *So did I.*

I don't know what I would do without you. Promise you won't leave me.

She cried harder against me, and I raised my hands to hold her, ignoring the fire raging through my body.

So please tell me, how the hell did we get from that…to this?

I turn in my seat to look at Brynn in the back. She's not there. My body lurches with panic.

Then I see her outside the car, sitting in the dirt a few yards away with her back to me, smoking a cigarette. I reach down and pop the handle, open the car door, and get out.

The chill of November is increased by the dry air of the open plains, but at least there's no wind. I'm still shivering though, and I can only imagine how cold she is in her bed shorts and tee. I ease the door shut and walk over, then lower myself to sit cross-legged beside her on the hardpan.

She passes me the cigarette without a word, not looking away from the horizon, where the sun's orange fingers creep across the sky. I accept it and take a few drags while I try to think of something to say. Only a bit of her cheek is visible; in the early light, I can pretend the last of that bruise is a shadow. When I hold the cig back out, she turns to me and I see tears leaking from the corners of her eyes.

"I'm sorry," I blurt.

"About what?"

"Chris. I didn't want…that. For him to. You know. I know he was your…" There's no word I can think to say at the end of that sentence that a) wouldn't rip a hole in my chest, and b) that I would be sure was correct in the first place.

She shakes her head. "I don't care. I didn't love him or anything."

"Oh." Part of me is relieved, even though that email she wrote told a different story. Another part is just put off by the coldness of the statement. It's too easy to imagine her saying the same thing about me. "I thought…since you were crying…"

"I was just thinking how pretty it is out here. I've never even been camping."

"We could've gone."

"Yeah, well…we didn't. That would've required you to drag yourself away from the TV. Or the Xbox. Or your writing."

Even though this seems monstrously unfair, I only offer, "We could still go."

"Sure, let's light a big campfire and roast hot dogs while the army of killers is hunting us."

I run a finger through the dirt beside my shoe. "I meant… after."

"Oh don't worry, we could still die a gruesome death. Let's not get ahead of ourselves."

"You're the one that wanted to come."

"Way you made it sound, I wouldn't be much safer going back, now would I?"

We sit in frustrated silence. It's like we've forgotten how to communicate without fighting. This should be simple. I love her. I want to express that. But the words won't come. They'd probably just make me feel even worse if they did.

"So…Luiz is really dead?" she asks.

I wince at a sudden kaleidoscope of memories. "Yeah."

"He was always nice to me. I liked him."

"Me too."

"I'm sorry too, Rudy, I really am. That all this happened, and that I accused you of being part of it."

"Thanks. That means a lot."

Silence again. Finally, I ask, "If you didn't love Chris, what was this all about?"

"Jesus, you have a one-track mind!" she bursts out. "Do we have to do this now?"

I feel my own anger flare in response to hers. "If not now, then when? Until last week, I thought everything between us was okay. Better than okay. Then you left and I had no idea why, because you've hardly spoken to me since…that night."

She puts a hand on her cheek right over that hateful bruise and rubs. "Just tell me what you want, Rudy."

"I wanna know *why!* The other guys you just fucked! *Him*, you left me for! I need to understand!"

She lets out a tired chuckle. "You just don't get it."

"Then help me! You're my *wife*, for Christ's sake! I think I deserve some answers!"

Brynn inhales the last of the cigarette and flicks the butt out into the weedstrewn land around us.

"And I don't know if I have them to give."

The driver's door opens with a squall. Dutt comes up behind us.

"Found this in your glove box." He tosses a folded road atlas down in front of us. He fixes me with an angry, disappointed stare that I pretend not to see. "Way I figure, we got about 25 hours to Reno. That's if we drive straight through, but I don't know if that's a good idea."

Brynn snorts. "Why not?"

"Cause if we hole up somewhere along the road one more night, it'll keep us fresh, not to mention throw off anybody that might be trying to figure our timetable."

"That sounds good," I agree, bending over the map. The route he traced in pencil takes us up 287 all the way to Amarillo, where we leave off for Interstate 40 through Albuquerque and Flagstaff, US-93 to Vegas, then a series of smaller, zigzagging highways up into the mountains of Nevada.

A road trip that would, under any other circumstances, be exciting.

Turned into a forced death march by the specter of what's hanging over our heads.

And pulsing in my chest.

I drive first.

The sun comes up and hovers in the rearview. There's not much to see, just flat highway and squalid towns less developed than even Withers that flash by between blinks. We scan the radio for news updates. The cops, at least, are operating under the presumption that I'm still holed up in town, but they do call it a 'state-wide' manhunt. There are supposedly even road blocks set up. Dutt believes we got outside their cordon area before they locked it down. After all, they don't know we're going to Reno.

For a while, the ride is silent. The Word thrums through my body, tugging gently, but it's less insistent now that I'm cooperating.

Somewhere along a non-descript stretch of road, Brynn is sleeping stretched out across the back seat. Dutt is against the passenger door, staring out the window, his bald head against the glass. He hasn't spoken to me since we planned the route. Finally, I snap off the last static-laden notes of the only rock station we can get out here.

"We're almost outta gas," I tell him.

"Uh huh."

"You got a plan for that, G.I. Joe?"

"Yep."

I lean an elbow against the door and support the side of my head. "You gonna tell me what's wrong, or you gonna act like a penis all day?"

He turns and jerks a thumb over the seat at Brynn's snoozing form. "Why didn't you just offer your throat to her, huh? She's already got her teeth sunk in, just let her rip it out already."

"What're you talking about?"

"This morning. I heard you, man. Tell me something. You'd *really* take her back, wouldn't you?"

"I...look, I don't know..."

"Yeah, you would. God, you make me sick sometimes. You're so pathetic when it comes to her, Rudy."

I continue the argument in hushed tones. "She's my wife, dickhead. This is my marriage we're talking about. You don't understand, you're not married, you don't even have a girlfriend."

"Oh sure, poor inexperienced Dutt, he could never understand the concept of heartache."

"That's not what I'm saying," I tell him, even though it kind of is. "I just want you to try to understand that I love her, all right? Yes, she's done some shit to me, but I still think she's the most beautiful, intelligent, fun and...exciting woman I've ever known. You don't give that up without a fight."

"Christ, would you listen to yourself? You think you're in a movie, where love conquers motherfucking all. When are you gonna get it? She. Is. Bad. News. An emotional cripple with serious daddy issues. Everyone sees it but you."

My hands turn to steel around the steering wheel. "Dutt, I don't know how else to say this, so I'm just gonna say it: you are not my father. Even if you were, I still wouldn't take your advice on this. So back off."

His lips seal together as he nods. "You're right, I'm not your father. I'm just the guy who's been watching your back for fifteen years."

"Oh really? Cause it seems to me you've been gone for most of that. You jumped up and ran to join the Army and left me here."

"At least I did *something!* I couldn't sit around smoking out forever and watching *every…damn…movie!* You gave up on life at some point and proceeded to waste every opportunity you ever had! That bitch is just the latest in a long line of excuses!"

I hold up a finger on my bandaged hand at him. "I told you to watch what you call her, Lansing. I will pull this car over and beat the shit out of you."

He smacks my hand away. "Oh yeah?"

"Don't touch me!"

He reaches out and smacks my cheek, feather light, more insult than injury.

"Hey, I'm driving!"

He goes to do it again, and I backhand him across the jaw with the same halfhearted force.

"Fucker!"

We explode into an outright slap fight, him swishing his hands like a paddle as he tries to move in, me fending him off with one arm and trying to drive with the other. Finally I yank the wheel to the left, and he falls back against the door with his glasses askew.

I snicker. He snorts. We both start giggling and then it builds into a chuckle. In seconds we're roaring with laughter, so much I have to stop the car so I can hold my aching belly.

Brynn sits up groggily in the back seat. "What the hell is wrong with you gaywads?"

That doesn't help us stop.

About thirty minutes later, just as we're seeing the first signs for Amarillo, Dutt points out a combination gas station-minimart coming up off the side of the road. The parking lot is full, especially considering the little traffic we've seen so far.

"Shouldn't we be avoiding crowds?" I ask.

"If we were pumping and getting out of here, maybe. But since we're gonna have to siphon, we need other cars and distractions."

"You can...you can pump," Brynn says quietly, in a strange voice. "I, um, found some cash in the bottom of my purse. Enough for a full tank."

Dutt shrugs. "Okay. The less laws we break, the better. But I still think we should stop here. Any further and we'll be too close to the city."

I exit the road and drive into the lot. The pump island forms an 'L' shape around the station, and I pull up to one on the side, furthest from the front.

"I'll get the gas." Dutt takes down my sunglasses from the visor and hands them to me. "You two go in and pay, but keep your faces hidden. Especially *your* banged-up mug. Grab some drinks and something to eat if there's cash left over. I'm starving."

I am too. My stomach has been rumbling for the last fifty

miles, considering the last time I really ate was yesterday morning, before Weldon and Fiver showed up. I slip the sunglasses over my eyes and get out of the car. My muscles unkink a little at a time as Brynn and I walk toward the station.

And as soon as we're around the corner of the brick building, she grabs my shoulders, throws me against the wall, and rams her tongue down my throat. Once I get over the shock, I hold her and kiss her back, and hate myself just the tiniest bit for it.

She breaks away first and says, "I don't deserve someone as sweet as you."

And she goes inside without waiting, leaving me to wonder just how asleep she actually was during mine and Dutt's fight.

I go to follow her, but something buzzes against my ass cheek.

I jump and swat at it before realizing it's Dutt's cell phone. I must've kept it last night during my payphone adventures. When I slip it out and look at the screen, the caller ID window displays, ANSWER THE PHONE, MR. COMPTON.

How can you argue with that?

"Hello?"

"Have you been boiling in this stew long enough, son?"

"Hillman."

"I told you, didn't I? I told you far worse than Carbini's men might come sniffing around."

I imagine his craggy face and spiderlike hands. "Who are you, you son of a bitch? You don't work for the FBI."

"No, I do not. I *do* work for the government, just not an agency with such a public face." He breathes deep. "Looks like you got yourself into more trouble since we spoke last."

"*I* didn't get myself into anything! These medieval guys showed up at my job! Some hooded creeps that call themselves the Acolytes!"

"The Candlemaker."

"Yeah! Who is this guy?"

"The head of a concentrated and numerous cult. An elderly emperor of his own little make-believe kingdom who's committed the last of his life and waning power to stopping the activation of the package Carbini has in his possession."

"I'm just taking a shot in the dark here Agent Hillman, but shouldn't that be *your* goal, too? Make with the *24* and save the day?"

"*24?*"

"Yeah, you know. Jack Bauer. Stop the terrorists. God, you're easier to confuse with pop culture references than my grandfather. What I'm trying to say is, don't you wanna stop him also?"

"Of course, that is my primary objective. But a close second is taking charge of the package intact. The Candlemaker's methods preclude that."

"How so?"

"Because if you're still the only person who knows the Word when his Acolytes kill you, the package is useless."

"Oh." I swallow a lump in my throat. "Wait a minute, are you telling me there's no other way to get this password? I'm *it?*"

"Affirmative. As far as I have been able to ascertain, you are the last individual currently alive on the entire planet who knows the Word. That's why your connection to the package is so strong. If you were to disseminate the information, that pull you feel would diminish." He adds quickly,

"I do not, however, recommend that. Each person you tell would only be at the same risk."

That Acolyte called me the Omega. At least something about their rambling is making some sense. "Are you gonna tell me what this thing is yet?"

"Negative. The knowledge itself would only put you in more danger. You would be hunted even further. The police are exhausting considerable resources to find you."

I lean against the wall with my forehead in my free hand. "Can you get me out of this?"

"Probably. You're high profile right now, but I'm sure something can be done to make this go away. The question is, *will* I get you out of this?"

"So will you?"

"That depends. According to this phone's signal, you're on the road. I've taken the liberty of blocking it from the police, otherwise they would've found you long before now."

"You can do that?"

"Mr. Compton, I assure you, that's the least of what I can do." His voice has a dangerous edge for the first time. "I suspect you're on your way to Reno. That would be a mistake."

"We're just trying to—"

"I know what you're trying to do son, and it's foolish. The police couldn't help you even if you did hand them proof. They wouldn't know what to do with Carbini or the package, and certainly not the Candlemaker."

"Oh really? Well then maybe instead of trying to catch Carbini, I'll cut a deal with him. I just want free of this situation, and I don't particularly care how. If he can get this Word out of my head, it's all his. Then there's no need for anyone to come after me."

Hillman's sigh suggests I'm being very stupid. Or very

stubborn. I excel at both, so it's hard to say. "No matter what di Latorio and Dunbrough may've told you, it doesn't work that way. The package can only be activated by a single carrier, and that Word is part of you for good now. Once it's been transferred, they'll have no choice but to kill you."

"*Then what the fuck do I do?*" I yell. The family at the nearest pump glances over and I turn away before they can get a good look at me.

"I want the Word, Mr. Compton. Most of my job is done if I can ensure it's with at least one safe carrier."

"And I told you I don't remember it!"

"Let's work on that. I'll bring you in. Offer sanctuary for all three of you."

"Why didn't you do that before?" I demand. "Do you know what happened because you tossed me out on the street?"

"I thought it might help to lure in Carbini if you were a free agent. I miscalculated the Candlemaker's involvement."

"Yeah, you *miscalculated*. You miscalculated and now everyone I know is dead!"

"Then come in. Voluntarily. Let's set this right."

I want to believe him. That he can be the white knight that makes all this go away. But there's too much about this situation I don't understand, and until I do, I can't trust anyone.

"Thanks, but I'll try it my way first."

I hang up the phone and toss it in the nearest trash can.

The gas station is full of people buzzing in and out. I don't notice anyone watching us, but I keep my sunglasses on anyway while I search for Brynn. She's perusing a rack of cheap, tacky clothing in the middle of the store while two teenage boys ogle her from the fountain drink machine. I breeze by and whisper, "We need to go."

I grab a six pack of Mountain Dew and Dr. Pepper, some chips and beef jerky, and three cold case sandwiches, praying Brynn has the money. At the counter, the clerk rings up the 27 dollars of gas Dutt pumped. Brynn comes up next to me and puts on the counter two pairs of jeans, three t-shirts with slogans like 'Texas Girls Don't Pump Gas,' and a pair of flip flops.

"Are you sure you have enough for all this?" I murmur from the side of my mouth.

"Yeah, yeah, it's fine."

She reaches in her purse, careful to keep it dangling from her other side where I can't see. I lean around her so I can peek, and catch a glimpse of her counting twenties off a thick stack.

"You were holding out," I say. "Hey, wait a minute, is that—? That's *my* money!"

"Rudy…"

"You little liar! How much do you still have?"

"Some."

"Let me see, hand it over!"

"Fine, if all you care about is your goddamned money, then HERE!"

She takes the bundle of cash out and throws it in my face, spraying green all over the counter and floor, then storms past me out of the gas station.

Inconspicuous, right?

I grin at the clerk sheepishly as I start collecting bills.

On the racks beneath the counter, the prepaid mobile phones catch my eye.

"Three of these also," I tell him.

Looks like we're sleeping in a motel tonight.

Chapter FIFTEEN

We drive for a good fourteen hours the rest of the day, taking turns in five hours shifts and stopping once more for gas and a late lunch. We cross from Texas to New Mexico to Arizona. The land becomes dryer, redder, and less flat with each state. I expect us to get stopped at every border, but it doesn't happen. Wherever the police are conducting their search, we've obviously lost them for now. The local radio stations we manage to get don't even have a peep about what's happening in Withers.

During my turn lying down in the back seat, I break open the mobile phones, program in each other's numbers, and hand them out.

Brynn lets go of the wheel long enough to turn and snatch hers. "Great, I gotta call my boss."

"*No*," Dutt and I say together.

"People are gonna be worried about me!"

"People are already worried about you," I correct. "So it's not gonna do any good for you to start making calls the police could trace. These phones are for use with each other only."

She hunches forward and mutters, "There better be a helluva lotta treasure in Reno if I lose my job."

"I think they usually make exceptions for kidnap victims," Dutt says.

Finally, at about 10 o'clock, after nearly 24 hours on the lam, Dutt calls a halt for the night. We're somewhere between Williams and Seligman on the map, and there's a string of roadside eateries, gas stations, and travel motels. He chooses one that has parking away from the road, then goes in to pay for two rooms for the night, taking Weldon's pistol with him. Brynn grabs her key, goes in her room, and closes the door.

I can't help but feel I'm missing an opportunity here.

Dutt and I are both exhausted, but a shower sounds too good to pass up. He goes first, and I watch television until he's out. In the bathroom, I peel myself out of the remains of my sexy ensemble for the first time since yesterday morning. I stand there and examine myself in the mirror.

My nose is far less swollen; there's some deep purple splotches under my eyes, but nothing sunglasses won't hide. My torso is crisscrossed with bruises; compliments of Fiver's interrogation. I unwrap the bandages on my hand, give my pinky a few experimental flexes, and decide to deal with the pain rather than be handicapped.

I almost turn away before noticing a little blood down the back of my right leg. High up on the left hand side of my calf there's a tiny puncture wound, about the size of a pen tip. I have a vague memory of Weldon grabbing me there during the chaos of the motel firefight. I clean the blood off and examine the hole. It's mostly healed, so I forget about it.

After I'm finished, I come out and look at Dutt stretched out on the twin size bed. He's already snoring. If I want to get in there with him, I'm either going to have to shove him over, or spoon with him.

It's that image that decides me.

I throw back on my jeans and shoes, a hoodie Dutt had in the trunk, grab my room key, sneak through the door, and ease it closed behind me.

I go next door and knock gently at Brynn's room. It takes her so long to open up, I'm afraid she might already be asleep. Then the door cracks with the chain on and her bloodshot eye peers out. Even my clogged nose catches the sweet flavor of ganja on the air.

"You have *weed?*"

"Jesus, Rudy, let the whole place know." She closes the door, slides the chain, and then opens up all the way. Quiet radio rock drifts out. "There's a dealer around the corner. I still had enough for a dime. And before you tackle me to the ground, it was my money, not yours."

"Can I...come in?"

She chews the inside of her lip as she considers and then walks away, leaving the door open. I follow her inside. She's wearing one of the t-shirts she picked out earlier, a clingy, long number that reaches just below her ass cheeks.

And I'm pretty sure nothing else. Her smooth, bare legs begin just under the hem of the shirt. Through the open bathroom door, I can see her only pair of panties hung up on the towel rod to dry after being hand washed.

I am instantly at rock hard, full mast, Defcon-5 status. I can't remember being this aroused since I actually went and peeped at Ms. Hampton after Dutt told me about her sunbathing habits, way back in fifth grade. Brynn looks like a tiny model as she crosses the room. Hips rolling under the shirt. Flopping on the bed beside a glass ashtray that holds a smoldering roach. Lying on her stomach so her perfect ass forms a curve so convex you could go sledding down it.

As I have so many times, I think, *I'm married to this woman.*

Yeah. For now.

I close the door. Redo the chain. Stand there watching her. She takes a deep hit, holds it in. Smoke dribbles from her nostrils. Even that's sexy.

I motion toward the weed. "You mind? It's been a long day."

She shrugs and pushes the ashtray toward me.

I come and sit on the bed with her. Take a few puffs off the little tokerette. It's good stuff. I instantly feel a little less heavy.

I roll over on the bed and pass it back. We take turns until it's down to a nub, her staring at the wall and me staring at her. Trying not to let my eyes slide down to where her bare ass is showing a little more every time she moves. Marveling at the fact that she's a foot away, but it might as well be the moon. I feel like I have to be Sherlock Holmes to understand her.

How does that happen? How does a person you knew so well—so fucking *intimately*—become a stranger? Lost through a veil of time and separate experience.

On the radio, that old Smashing Pumpkins song "Perfect" plays, and I don't think there could be a more fitting soundtrack for our lives.

I want to say something. Something that expresses the complex web of emotion she and I are caught in. A testament to that blazing bonfire that rages in the center of me every time I think of her.

"I love you," I blurt. What can I say, I'm a lousy fiction writer, not a poet.

"I love you too," she answers.

I shake my head. "No you don't. You can't. Those things you said in that email. You told him you had *feelings* for him."

She takes a breath so deep, it could fill the Grand Canyon. "I thought I did. At first. Felt like we had a connection."

I picture that troglodytic asshole, a guy whose two remaining brain cells were used only to fuck and fight. "A *connection?* What does that even mean? The operator was able to complete your call?"

She ignores my quip. "I was wrong though. Guy was an asshole. Hell, the sex wasn't even that good."

"Can't begin to tell you how sorry I am to hear *that.*"

"God. Your sarcasm is so caustic. That's why you and Dutt get along so well. Never mind."

"No, no, I'm sorry," I say. This is the most she's talked to me since she left, and I want to hear it all. I need to understand. "So, he was an asshole. No big surprise there. You see that now, you have all this out of your system, so why can't you just...come home?"

"I want to, Rudy. I almost did a couple of times. I never planned for this to happen."

"Then why did it? I need some kind of answer here that makes sense."

She shrugs her narrow shoulders. "Chris. He was just...a means to an end."

"What end?"

Brynn moves the ashtray to the bedside table and rolls onto her back on the bed next to me. She stares up at the ceiling and says, "To get me away from you."

"Was I..." I have to stop and try again. "Was I that bad? That horrible?"

She sighs. "No Rudy, you were perfect. Perfect boyfriend, perfect husband. But I just couldn't be perfect anymore. I couldn't be stuck in this rut."

"Rut? What rut?"

"It's like...where were we going, Rudy? We acted like we were eighty-years-old, sitting on the couch watching TV every night. And don't say, 'having kids!' That would've just made things worse."

"And you thought fucking another guy would make it better? Oh, excuse me, *guys?*"

She wilts. "Yes. No. I don't know. We were both going in different directions when we met, and then we just sort of put our lives on hold. I can't help wondering where we would be if we hadn't."

I lie on the bed, the room swirling around me, all those little stippled dots on the ceiling blurring, and feel helpless. Insignificant. Insufficient. "Is this because...of last week?"

"No. Not that." She reaches out, caresses my cheek. "That wasn't you. We both went a little nuts. But anyway, these are *my* problems. All that shit that happened to me growing up...it just left me hollow. I don't know even know who I am. I never have. I just go with the flow and for a while the flow was about being your shadow."

"That's ridiculous!"

"It's not even your fault though," she cuts me off. "I never told you how I really felt. God, about anything. I just told you what you wanted to hear."

"But…why?"

"Because I was afraid to tell you the truth. I have this… this need for acceptance. And I was afraid you wouldn't love me anymore if I upset you or disagreed with you."

"So let me get this straight: you're leaving because you never told me what you really wanted. And the reason you did that is because you were afraid of losing me, which is exactly what you're doing by leaving me."

She smiles. "I'm a girl. I'm allowed to not make sense."

"Baby…I just want my Brynny-winnie back."

A look crosses her face, something pained and unpleasant, and my stomach knots at what I'm afraid is coming. "What if your Brynny-winnie never really existed? What if she's just someone I pretended to be to make you happy? A character I made up, like in one of your books?"

And that's when I realize Chris has nothing to do with she and I breaking up. He never did, and neither did anyone else she slept with behind my back. They were just symptoms of a bigger disease, one I was too self-absorbed to see. I've been trying to blame it on her childhood, but it's more than that.

My parents have two dogs that eat other other's feces, fresh and steaming out of the gate. The vet said they did it because of a vitamin deficiency, that they were trying to get the nutrients they needed from each other's effluence. In that moment, I realize the same thing is true of my adoring wife: she's just been eating shit to try and get what she needs out of this relationship.

~ ~ ~

I break then, utterly and completely. I cover my face and bawl at everything I've lost, and everything I never really had in the first place.

She scoots up close and puts her arms around me, then kisses away one of the tears rolling down my cheek. I turn to her, pull her even closer, needing to feel her. My hands roam across her nearly naked body, my lips brush hers, and that's all it takes. I kiss her desperately, my groin throbbing, and then roll on top of her. My head is still buffered from the weed, and the only thought making it through the haze is that I must have her, must make her mine. She goes willingly enough, but she's not reciprocating, it's like kissing a mannequin, and part of my brain—the Word maybe, or my own shame—is begging me to stop this train wreck before the blood starts flowing.

I unzip, pull my jeans down enough so that the steel drill-bit down there is free. I pull her legs apart with one hand and cradle her head with the other. She gives in, but that's all it is, just giving in, and as I cup her tight buttock and slide into her, I feel sick to my stomach. I've never been pity-fucked before, and it's one of the most dry, demeaning experiences of my life.

But I miss her so much, I'll take what I can get.

I hold her, and do what I need to.

When I finish, I lay against her, and she pets my hair distantly, and murmurs that it's all right, she's there.

But she's not. I don't know where she is, but it's not there with me.

I get up and storm out of the room.

~ ~ ~

Too much.

There's just too much.

I feel like my head's going to cave in from this pressure.

I stomp away from the motel, out into the parking lot, following the buzz of the freeway onramp that runs in front of the place. It's dark now, close to eleven, the sky full of unspoiled autumn stars. Not even the electric light from the string of lodgings, gas stations, and fast food joints is enough to dampen that overhead diorama.

I walk. I'm still high, but the angry blood pounding through my veins is sobering me up. The motel falls away behind me, replaced by one establishment after another. My wedding ring catches my eye, and I finally slide it off my finger and hold it in the palm of my hand. I fight the urge to throw it in the bushes, slip it into my pocket instead, and just keep walking.

For just a second, I consider not stopping. Just strolling into the dark night beyond this huddle of civilization. I could escape into the desert and never be seen again. Just...fuck Brynn and Dutt; my sister and folks. Even Minchi. You want to talk about running from problems? Let's see Weldon or the Acolytes or Hillman find me then.

But instead I turn and duck into the Thorn Rose Tavern with its blinking red OPEN sign.

The Thorn is cozy and dark without being a dive. It's populated by the kind of sparse clientele you'd expected on a—Sunday? It is *Sunday?*—night, a few at the bar and the rest spread out across the tables to the right of the door, all watching a Cardinals game on the TV in the corner, while quiet music plays. A waitress is wandering through, taking drink orders and chatting with the regulars. There's no particular theme, biker or gay or cowboy, so I can blend enough to be inconspicuous.

I take a seat at the corner of the bar. The bartender is a gawky dude with a ponytail, and I order three shots of Jack. I just want to get messed up enough to forget Brynn Cox-Compton ever existed.

The second shot has just made its way down my gullet when someone says in my ear, "That ain't very original, honey."

I'm so high strung, I jump and spin on the stool, setting off a chain reaction of embarrassment. My long knees slam against the seat next to me, and when I reach to grab them, I sweep all three shot glasses off the floor, spilling whiskey in my lap and shattering glass on the hardwood under me.

The waitress raises an eyebrow. "Jesus, babe, jumpy much?"

"Ah. Ah God. Sorry." I start to slide off the stool.

"No, no, stay there, I got it." She grabs a broom from the corner and, in two graceful movements, has the glass wept into a dust pan.

"Uh, what were you saying?" I ask.

She nods at the remains of the shot glasses as she dumps them into a trash can. "Just said surely you can think up somethin more creative than JD."

I shrug as she slides behind the bar. "It tends to do the trick."

"I got better medicine than that, sugar."

She turns to the array of bottles arranged on shelves behind her and starts grabbing a few. I take the opportunity to check her out. She looks somewhere around my age, no older than 30 surely, round face framed by long, curly black hair, a pair of narrow-framed librarian glasses perched on a little bulb nose. She's taller than Brynn, built on a bigger frame with a just a few extra pounds pushing at the waistband of her tight jeans and leather belt, but they work for her. A pair of absolutely mammoth breasts are held high up on her chest and showcased by the dark blue, v-cut sweater she's wearing. Very attractive, in an understated, vixen bookworm sort of way.

"Name?" she asks, bringing her collection back over in front of me.

"Huh?"

"What's your name, babe?"

"Oh. Um, Rudy."

"Annie." She goes to work like a pro, pouring various liquors and other beverages into a mixing glass. "Where you headed? Vegas?"

"Reno, actually."

"All alone?"

"No, I'm with…people."

She bites her bottom lip in concentration. The glass in front of her is three-quarters full, and taking on a pinkish-blue hue. "Any particular reason you're sittin alone in a bar in the middle of the night without these people?"

"…it's complicated."

"Which means it's a girl. A girl blind enough to dump on a cutey like you."

I smile and look down at the bar to hide the accompanying burn in my cheeks.

Annie picks up the now full glass, opens the door of a mini fridge on the back counter, and places it inside. "Gotta chill for a minute before servin." She comes around the edge of the bar and slides into the stool next to me. "So tell me more about this female, Rudy."

"Well, it's not so much female as, you know...*Antichrist.*"

She laughs. It's hearty and pleasant. Easy, somehow. Brynn's always seemed forced. "I thought you were gonna say you're gay."

"Only for Han Solo." I get another of those guffaws for this not particularly funny crack, granting my eternal gratitude.

"Just a fight, or somethin worse?"

"Worse. She's leaving me."

"How many years invested?"

"Four and a marriage certificate."

"Oooooh," she says. "So it's like *that.*"

"Yeah."

"You do somethin to deserve it?"

"I honestly don't know anymore." I wipe at the Jack stain down the leg of my jeans. "But I think she's a borderline sociopath, so, you know, six of one."

Her eyebrows draw down inside her glasses frames. "What, really? Or is that exaggeration?"

"She basically just told me she's been playing a role, and the woman I fell in love with doesn't exist. I mean, is that normal? I'm not too experienced, so help me out here."

"I once had a boyfriend tell me he was the reincarnated spirit of Benny Hill to get outta dating me."

I pause a second to mull that. "You know, I think I'm at the exact right point of inebriation for that to make sense."

Annie swivels on her stool, brushing her knees against mine. "People will say anything when a relationship is collapsing to keep from having to deal with the real problem."

Alcohol makes me chatty and weepy, and I can feel myself pushing toward that edge. "It's like...have you ever been with someone that makes you feel so good at one point—so confident and happy and in love—and then just takes it all away and leaves you thinking that sewer rats have better prospects in life than you?"

She tosses a few locks of loosely curled hair back over her shoulder. "I think you pretty much described every relationship in the history of the world there. And I'm not just talkin about the ones that end in a breakup."

"Yeah. Yeah, I guess so. I just…always believed she and I were something more. Something beyond the norm."

"And I'm not sayin you're not. It just looks like to me—in the full five minutes I've known you, with your swollen nose and that black cloud over you—that this relationship is chewin you up and spittin you out. Maybe it's time to give the roulette wheel another spin and see if a better number comes up."

"But what happens if I end up alone? What if no other woman is ever interested in me again?"

Her hand falls off the bar and lands on my leg just above the knee. She gives it a squeeze. "You'd probably be surprised, babe." She gets up, goes back inside the bar, and retrieves the drink from the fridge. She sets the almost neon concoction in front of me.

I pick it up. The amount of alcohol singes my nose hair from a foot away. Against my better judgment, I take a sip.

My throat seals up. My eyes water. "This is supposed to *help* me?"

"You drink that, and you're not gonna have a problem in the world."

"What do you call this monstrosity?"

She leans toward me, placing an elbow on the bar to either side of the drink, granting me a heavenly view of the cleavage valley between her breasts. "The Bartender Wants to Fuck Me."

Something approximating a giggle escapes me. "You got a restroom here?"

"That depends. You gonna come back and talk to me some more?"

"As fast as I possibly can."

"Down the hall, second door on the left. Don't take the third or you'll end up in the alley."

The bathroom is a dank, filthy hole with one urinal and one stall, currently occupied. I whiz and turn to the mirror over the sink to give myself a once over.

I have no intention of having sex with this woman. Don't get me wrong, I would love to hit that until I get friction burns, but nothing could happen while I'm still hopelessly in love with Brynn, and certainly not while I'm carrying the Word.

But I must admit, I *do* feel excited. And horny again.

This newfound buoyancy lasts just long enough for me to wash my hands, hear the stall door open, and look up to see Weldon leering at me in the mirror over my shoulder.

Then he jams the taser into my ribs, and the only thing I feel is agony.

Wake up Rudes, ol' buddy, ol' pal.

"Hn."

You gotta come to me, dude. You gotta lemme outta here.

"Whuzzat?"

I think things are gonna get, like, a whole lot worse for you, and pretty fast. I'll do what I can to help Rudes, but you gotta do me an itsy-witsy favor and just remember the damn Word already!

Sweaty, stifling darkness. Hard surfaces. Suffocating enclosure. Muscles cramping. Bouncing motion.

I'm pretty sure I know how it feels to ride in a car trunk now.

I feel it when the car stops. The engine shuts off. Two doors open, close. Footsteps.

My lips are chapped to the point of bleeding, and I'm sore from having my knees pinned against my chest. When the trunk lid raises, I blink against the flush of daylight. The air is thin, crisp and cold. Two familiar silhouettes stand over me in a cloud of dust.

"Morning Rudy! Welcome ta Reno."

Weldon and Fiver reach into the trunk and yank me out by the arms. Something in my back screams. Every inch of my body feels like road kill. The only thing I can be thankful for at this point is that my bladder was empty before I was electrocuted.

When my eyes finally adjust, I take a look at the new surroundings.

On the immediate front, their silver Benz is parked in the middle of a narrow gravel field bounded by metal shipping containers of all colors stacked haphazardly, some of them two or three stories high. They form a twisted trail curving out of sight behind us, and lead up to a squat, gray, warehouse in front. Beyond that, against the backdrop of cloudless blue sky, a wedge of sloping mountain ridgebacks climbs towards heaven. Reno seems like a beautiful place.

The Word beats a staccato rhythm in my chest, outpacing even the rapid thump of my heart. I'm closer than ever to whatever has been drawing me here. I don't think it's in this warehouse that Weldon and Fiver are taking me to…but close.

I'm so parched, I can't even talk. My head lolls as they carry me up the stairs to the door. The building is two stories, non-descript metal and concrete, the kind of place Batman villains always use for a hideout.

The security measures, however, are the sci-fi bullshit that movies always want us to believe the government keeps on its most vaulted secrets. Weldon places his palm on a scanner next to the steel door, and I realize that neither of his hands bears the gaping wound one would expect from being shot with an arrow two days before.

Then again, with a dead man on the other side of me, why should I be surprised that he's all healed up?

A metal panel in the wall slides open, revealing a device that looks like the machine the optometrist uses to blast air into your eyeball. Weldon leans forward while keeping a firm grip on me, rests his chin on a cup, and stares into a cylinder.

It gives an angry beep.

"Goddamn it," he curses. "I—*ES!*—told ya dere was something wrong wit da sequencing on dis skinbag."

"Lemme do it."

The two of them switch places, spinning me 180 in the process. Fiver lowers his square head and looks into the microscope. The door gives a more pleasant tone and heavy latches release. Weldon opens it and the two of them pull me inside backward, heels dragging.

The interior is dim, and my eyes have trouble readjusting back the other direction. Weldon and Fiver stand me on my own two feet and let go while they seal back up the door. I wobble around on shaky legs and take the place in as sight returns.

A long, open warehouse floor stretches away, lit by hanging bulbs overhead. On both sides of us are rows of cylindrical glass tanks mounted on steel bases packed with dials and gauges, each one eight or nine feet tall and at least five in diameter, filled with some kind of murky, fluorescent orange liquid. Through the narrow spaces between, I can see even more rows behind these, sprawling across most of the ground floor of the building. Electrical wires trail from the back of each and run across the floor in bound bundles. Definitely breaking a few safety regulations, but I get the idea no inspector has ever visited this place.

A blurry, human-shaped outline is visible in the tank closest to me. I try to step toward it, but my legs give and I end up lurching forward and bringing my hands up to the glass to catch myself. My weak arms collapse. My forehead smacks against the slightly warm surface. Inside the tank, that shape drifts closer to the glass. A human face swims out of the murk almost nose to nose with me.

And I'm not too far gone that I don't recognize Weldon's froggish features.

I recoil, flailing back into Fiver. He and the Weldon on this side of the glass shove me back and forth, snickering at my confusion. I'm so dizzy, their faces stretch out like carnival funhouse terrors.

"Boys, boys," a voice rings out across the warehouse. I look up to see a man coming down a set of metal stairs in the middle of the room that leads to the second floor. He disappears for a moment in the field of tanks and then comes strolling up the aisle toward us. "Don't manhandle our guest. Poor kid looks ready to crash out. Five-Spot, get the man some water."

"Yes, boss." Fiver leaves my side.

Sullis 'Eels' Carbini looks pretty much as he did in his surveillance photo. He has to be pushing fifty, but he's got the face and body of a demi-god, lustrous brown hair coiffed into gentle waves on his head. Nice suit, a charcoal gray Cavalli number, and a pair of shoes that probably cost more than my car. He gives me a shiny smile around steel cheekbones and holds out a hand when he finally reaches us. "Sullis Carbini, Mr. Compton. Nice to finally meet you."

"Likewise," I rasp, accepting the shake with limp fingers.

"I trust you had a pleasant trip?"

"Last few miles were a little rough. You might consider an in-flight meal."

Carbini shows even more teeth. "I'll take that under advisement."

About that time, Fiver comes back with an open bottle of ice water. I consider that it might be drugged, but then decide I don't care. They didn't bring me all this way to poison me, and doping me up isn't going to accomplish anything their torture didn't. I drink greedily, then ask, "Brynn? Dutt? What did you do to them?"

Carbini looks a question at Weldon, who explains, "Dey weren't wit him when we caught up. Thought it might be better ta get 'im here and deal wit dem later."

"Or hopefully not at all, if everything goes well. But that's entirely up to you, Rudolph. Can I call you, Rudolph?" Carbini claps me on the back, squeezes my shoulder, and doesn't give me a chance to tell him that nobody's called me Rudolph since my grandmother died when I was in seventh grade. "You know something kid, only a handful of people have ever come into this place. Everything I value most is right here, in this building. And that's coming from a man with four kids."

I finish the last of the water and Fiver snatches the bottle. "Does that include the guy in the fishbowl? The one wearing fat boy's face?"

"In a way." He winks at his associates. "You know much about cloning, Rudolph?"

I take another look around at the rows upon rows of orange-hued tanks. Think about Fiver coming back from the dead. Weldon's missing wound. The fact that he looks years younger than a picture I saw two days ago.

And just when I thought my life of late couldn't get any weirder.

"Man…you gotta be shitting me."

Carbini slides his hands inside his slacks pockets and strikes a GQ pose. "Let's take a tour."

"The drug trade is a fickle business. Times change, tastes change, manufacture centers change. Used to be, your urban coastal centers were your moneymakers. You got the coke or weed or what-have-you down south from the producers, dreamed up ways to get past customs into New York, Miami, L.A. Great return, but high risk, low volume. And the manpower! Jesus, I had twenty different crews running trips to South America at any given second. That's a lotta little time bombs waiting to go off and steal from me. Or get themselves arrested and cut a deal to sell out the person above them who does the same thing to the one above them, on and on, one big ladder until it eventually reaches me. But then middle America gets a taste for the stuff, so we have to expand to meet demand. Which means *more* manpower. I had my own little triangle trade running from NY to FL to right here in Reno, which is surprisingly easy to use as a west coast hub. We got better at inventory distribution than goddamn Wal-mart."

Carbini leads the way through the passages between the tanks while he talks, stopping every few steps to kneel and check the instrument panel at the base of one or another. Part of this story I know from Hillman, so I walk along behind him and try to figure out what I should do. Like I have much choice. Fiver and Weldon follow at my heel, the latter muttering choice selections from the alphabet.

"But evolution happens, just the way it always does. People get smart. They find new drugs, stuff they can make right at home. Meth, crack. The old ways are out. The drug trade has to shift to keep from belly-flopping, and, ultimately, it's a good thing. No more customs, cheaper product, higher volume. Problem is, the blacks are in a much better position to manufacture and distribute. And they don't want to share. Wop dinosaurs like yours truly got left with their dicks in the wind, empires crumbling around them, and a lot of hungry mouths to feed. I watched good men—colleagues, if you will—get swallowed up. Figuratively *and* literally."

He stops and pats the side of one of the tanks lovingly. "But I lucked out. Twelve years ago, I send Weldon to initiate some...*creative encouragement* for this egghead nerd type who missed more than a few loan payments. He gets there, finds the basement littered with a bunch of sciencey crap, and calls me. Turns out the guy had come up with a revolutionary new cloning method, quit his job at some government lab, and decided to scrape the money together to patent the research himself behind their backs. And the process worked, too. Quick-grown, full body clones in just a few days. He called them 'skinbags.' So I took the thing as payment on his loan."

"And started making your own little army of Jersey psychopaths," I surmise. Weldon steps on the back of my shoe for punishment. Guess that's what I get for using a pleonasm like 'Jersey psychopath.'

"Oh no, I didn't do anything, not then. Didn't see the implications. I just wanted to sell the thing." Carbini leads us up the rattling stairs to the second floor. "Took some doing, but I eventually found a guy who dealt in this stuff. He bought the designs, but I kept the tank for myself. Figured it might make a good conversation piece. Anyway, this guy asks if I want a commission for another job along the same lines. Well, I'd been my own boss for so long that it didn't exactly appeal, but I saw the writing on the wall for my triangle trade and besides, this shit fascinates me. Turns out, there's a whole other universe of this high-tech junk that'll never see the light of day. Somebody invents it, and then the race is on by every government and private dealer in the world to get to it first and keep it under wraps for themselves."

We reach the top of the stairs. Carbini enters a code on a keypad to a pressurized door, and we step inside a long vault of open rooms that leads along the second floor. The otherwise white, sterile walls are covered with mounted gizmos and doodads. Some of them have the clean, plastic look of mass-produced items, but most seem to be held together by spit and gum, with wires hanging out everywhere.

Carbini waves around at them proudly. He obviously loves showing this stuff, and probably doesn't get too many chances. I figure that's the only reason I'm getting the third-act, overly-talkative, Bond villain treatment. Something about him reminds me of a museum curator. Or maybe Willy Wonka, showing us around his zany factory full of shit that looks awesome, but could probably kill me. He continues his story.

"So the guy gets me involved. I start making new contacts. I love it so much, I scale back on the trade, turn my guys toward helping with new acquisitions. Set up a whole new black market. And let me tell you, I have seen some crazy shit. Shit you couldn't imagine. Shit you wouldn't *want* to imagine. I sell enough to stay comfortable, and keep what I want for myself. Like these little beauties."

He reaches into a rack hanging from the wall filled with these four-inch-long steel cylinders. Carbini pulls one out and tosses it to me. It looks like a roll of dimes up close, and feels about as heavy. There's only a single, unmarked button on the side, and a hole on the top where these little discs the size of cadmium batteries slide out. The thing reminds me of a Pez dispenser.

"Picked these up a few months ago. Low-yield, non-biological mass retrieval units." Carbini reaches into my palm and pops out one of the little discs. He takes a lighter from his shirt pocket, sets it on the table, and stacks the disc on top. "Okay, hit that button."

I do. There's a hum I know only too well. And then the lighter disappears from the table, leaving the metal Pez hanging in midair for a split-second. It reappears in my hand, right next to the cylinder.

Carbini beams and smacks the tabletop. "Handheld teleporters! Those things can bring any object you've tagged to you from halfway around the world, provided it's not living and weighs less than 10 pounds! The applications are limitless! They're already surgically implanted in the palm of every skinbag!"

I close my eyes and let my head hang until my chin touches my chest. "Yeah, I'm sure they're great for smuggling knives and ropes into a locked jail cell."

I hold the device out, but Carbini sticks up a hand. "You keep that, kid. Souvenir."

"Um, thanks." I drop the thing in the pocket of my jeans as we move on, and Carbini finishes telling me how he came to be the mogul of a sci-fi laboratory that would've been Phillip K. Dick's wet dream.

"So anyway, I get into this new life far enough, and make a whole new set of friends. People who know how to put some of this stuff to use, and I start thinking about that clone tank that started it all. How maybe it could help my manpower dilemma. I get a guy to reverse-engineer the technology, and set me up with this lab. The only problem was, the skinbags were blank templates. You can grow the bodies, but the brains are empty. Like babies."

I have to bite down on my tongue fast to avoid laughing at the idea of Weldon rolling around on the floor, sucking his thumb, and shitting in a diaper.

"Then some other crackpot figures out a way to upload the human brain via Wi-Fi to a central database, and I'm set. Fired all my people, got rid of those ticking time bombs, and started cloning the ones I could trust."

"Wait a minute, wait a minute," I interrupt. "You mean to tell me you got all this tech at your fingertips, you're cloning people to perfection and uploading brains,"—I hook a thumb at Weldon, twitching his head to the side—"and you can't tweak the-the *DNA* or whatever to get rid of this poor bastard's…"

I trail at the look of death the poor-bastard-in-question gives me. "My—*ES! GEE-DEE!*—*what*, Rudy?"

"Uh…weight problem?"

Carbini looks relieved I didn't finish the way I intended. "Trust me kid, if it were possible, I would've bred a race of supermen by now. But the more you tamper with the sequencing, the more defects can arise. We got enough of those already."

I nod along, making connections faster than he can give them. "Like heart defects that make you keel over when you get a little electric goose from the cops? Or ones that make an eye scanner not read your retinas correctly?"

Carbini lays a fingertip on his nose. "You do catch on quick, kid. Coulda used someone like you in the old days."

~ ~ ~

We move on. I can see the end of the vault rooms ahead, and another thick door beyond. "I usually keep three sets of these guys thawed out at any given time, running various errands for me. In a few hours, I'll be able to replace the Five-Spot that died in the cell with you. The originals—at least, their physical bodies—have been dead about four years. Killed by a rival. But their brains are uploaded every few minutes to the database here, so really every copy is the same person, same thoughts and memories."

The man is obviously intelligent, I'll give him that. Much more so than the two men he's chosen to endlessly Xerox. "What about you? You got some copies of yourself out there somewhere?"

He shakes his head. "Maybe some day, but for now, I'm careful to fight that temptation. Even though they'd all be me, I'm paranoid something would go wrong. Don't want one of them to get any ideas and make a play to take over." He leans close to me where his lackeys can't hear and whispers, "Plus, the whole thing kinda creeps me out."

Under normal circumstances, I'd be eating shit like this up, for my writing if nothing else, but I'm feeling stronger and a little antsy and I want to know what the hell is going to happen to me. "Can we just skip to the part where Mommy met Daddy and I was born?"

Carbini laughs. "There were three skinbag templates originally. My three most trusted: Weldon, Five-Spot, and Lennie Kincaid. I took a job recently, to find something different for some buyers. Something I've never really dealt with before. The deal was for delivery of an object, and the Word that activates it. I won't bore you with details other than to say I acquired the former and was having Kincaid bring the latter. But he was far behind schedule. I suspect he'd been influenced by the power of this Word, and was actually coming here with the intention of stealing this object from me. It tends to have that effect on people. I sent Fiver after him, and, well, you know the rest. Suffice to say, there will be no more Lennie Kincaid skinbags. *That* template was destroyed."

I think of the poor bastard with the stutter and the wall of hair. Was he *influenced?* Did he finally give in to this force that's dragging at me? "So the plan was for Fiver to get himself arrested, take the Word, and...what? Upload it here? Why didn't Lennie just do that in the first place?"

"One thing about this Word is, it can only be housed in a human brain, and passed on by mouth. You can't electronically reproduce it, you can't send it over phone lines, you can't even write the thing down. Pain in the ass, let me tell you. But lucky for me, I got an endless supply of clones to pass it around. Fiver would've held it until Weldon could get a visit in to him at the prison, then that skinbag would've been remotely terminated."

We stop at the next door in Carbini's funhouse. He turns to me. "So my problem, Rudolph Compton, is that, in 36 hours, some very dangerous individuals are coming here to Reno. When they do, if I don't have both the object and the Word for them..." His eyes glaze over with stark, naked fear for a second. "Let's just say, the Filament isn't synonymous with mercy."

"And here I was thinking terrorist organizations had the patience of Mother Theresa."

"Terrorist, huh? That's cute." Carbini punches in numbers on a keypad at this door also. "So Weldon tells me you don't remember the Word. Whether that's true or not, it's in your head somewhere. If we can get it out, then you go home. You cooperate, and I'll even protect you from the Candlemaker."

I shake my head in disgust. "First of all, let's stop with the fairy tales. I know that only one person can have the Word for it to work, so even if I told you, you'd have to kill me for it to be worth anything."

Carbini's pearly smile disappears. "Well, Rudolph... you've been talking to *someone*. Probably an agent from my least favorite covert government agency. Kyler, maybe? No, he's still busy with that mess he made down south on the coast. I think...Hillman. Am I right?" Something must show on my face, because he nods smugly. "Let me tell you kid, I wouldn't trust any Aurora agent farther than I could throw him, but *especially* not that ruthless spook."

"At least he hasn't locked me in a car trunk. Anyway, it doesn't matter. I still don't remember. Do your worst."

Carbini pushes open the door to reveal a white-tiled room empty of everything except what looks like a heavily-modified dentist's chair with lots of straps, and a man in a white smock standing next to it.

"Rudolph...I certainly intend to."

Chapter SEVENTEEN

This is for the best.

After everything that's happened, all the people that have died over the Word, the best thing that could happen is for this to end here and now, before it reaches those closest to me.

I know this.

But damned if something doesn't break in me at the sight of that chair.

I wheel around and try to run even though there's nowhere to go. The mountain that is Fiver blocks my path. I shove against him anyway, hoping to get some of that super strength back, but the Word seems to be playing it cool.

Hell, for all I know, I'm exactly where it wants me.

When he gets tired of me whaling on his broad chest, Fiver grabs me by the throat and forces me through the door. I hold on to the jamb, but Weldon is there to smash my few remaining good fingers until I let go.

They throw me in the chair. Hold my arms down while straps are stretched over my wrists, then do the same for my ankles, torso, and neck. When they get finished, I can't so much as twitch. My heart starts jackhammering and I suddenly really need to visit the restroom. That's my stomach for you; always wanting to shit when I can't.

Carbini's off to my left somewhere. "Rudolph, I want you to meet Dr. Gruenwald." The man in the white smock steps into my field of vision and gives a choppy bow. He's got a bowl cut of greasy black hair and a narrow mustache, and the glasses perched on his little nose are caked with so much filth I don't know what good they could be. But even worse, there appear to be threads of metal and wire meshed with his skin, high up near the hairline. A few ragged, silver veins pulse at his sweaty temples. "He's an extractor."

"Hallo, Mishtah Compton. Ve are going to be gettink zis Vord out of your head, ya?"

"Oh God. Please tell me you mean hypnosis when you say that."

Gruenwald reveals green-and-brown-stained teeth. "Not qvite."

Carbini comes around where I can see him. He kneels in his five-thousand dollar suit and pats my knee. "All be over soon, kid."

"That's what I'm afraid of."

The tech-dealing former mobster stands up and snaps his fingers at Weldon. "Once the good doctor jogs his memory, get the Word out of him however you have to and dispose of whatever's left. I want you to keep it until our guests arrive tomorrow. I'll be at the casino. Call me if there are any problems." He starts toward the door with Fiver in tow.

"Wait, wait, Mr. Carbini, don't go!" I strain against the bonds.

"Sorry kid, I got a weak stomach. Plus, I don't want to be anywhere near you when that Word pops into your memory. That thing gets into my head, and I'm just as expendable as you, trust me."

Inspiration strikes. "Then clone me! Download me into a skinbag and you can kill this body after you have the Word!" At the moment, anything seems better than death, even if the me in this body still gets tortured.

But Carbini just shakes his head. "Even if I wanted to, it would take a week to grow you a body we could code to your brainwaves. We don't have that kind of time."

"*Please*," I beg. "Don't do this, there has to be another way!"

He looks at his polished shoes briefly, then back up at me. "Wish there was, Rudolph. But things are how they are, and this is way bigger than either of us."

Carbini closes the door, locking me into the clinically white room with Weldon and Gruenwald.

There are no windows in here, and just the one door with the keypad. The light comes from naked bulbs overhead, yellow glare bouncing off tile walls and floor. On closer inspection, the porcelain is all clean, but the grout in between is stained the slightest shade of pink. There's a drain in the corner. God knows what this room has been used for.

Gruenwald spins me away from him and starts futzing with the equipment mounted on the back of the chair. He smells like sun-ripened cheese. Weldon stands in the corner and lights up a cigarette as he watches me struggle.

"Can't ya knock him out or something, doc?"

"He needs to be avake for ze procedure. But feel free to be violent vit him."

"Hear dat Rudy? I get ta work out some frustration if ya don't settle down."

I force myself to sit still. To take my mind off the panic, I ask, "How'd you find me at the bar?"

"Ya ain't no genius, huh Rudy?" Weldon smirks at this riddle. "I started ta get dat idea back at da motel."

"But...that wasn't *really* you, right? I mean, I know you're not the same clone from the motel. Are you the one that came to my apartment?"

Weldon shrugs. "Semantics. I remember da whole thing, how ya screamed like a girl and whatnot, ya big pussy. So if it wadn't me *physically*, it sure was *mentally*."

"If? You mean you don't know?"

He releases a jet of smoke. "Carbini makes da whole skinbag setup sound nice and easy, but he don't know shit about what it actually feels like. Me and da other two Weldons, we share a brain, right? So ya get memories of being in three different places at da same time. Kinda confusing. Ya think about it too much, it could drive ya insane." He holds up his left hand in front of his face and gazes at the palm. "Like right now, I could swear dis hand's got a hole in it from dat arrow. Hurts like a motherfucker."

"Yeah, sounds fantastic."

He grins wearily. "What can I say? It's immortality. But it's got a price, just like everything else in life worth having."

Gruenwald interrupts our conversation by coming to my side, holding what looks like the plug to a piece of stereo equipment. A cable trails out behind him, and the tip is a blunt spike with little mechanical pincer arms surrounding it.

"All right now, Mishtah Compton, here is how zis vill

vork. Ze operation is qvite simple und qvick, but it can painful, especially if you resist."

I respond to this by promptly thrashing as much as I'm able in my seat and screaming in high-pitched bursts. By the time I'm done, sweat pours down my face and neck. Or maybe those are tears.

Gruenwald lets me wear myself out and then holds up the cable. "Zis neural cable vill go into ze back of your zerebral cortex. Vonce I jack in as vell, I vill have complete access to your memory banks. I vill be able to search for zis Vord und bring it to ze forefront of your consciousness. I'll see it, but it von't be able to transmit over ze cable. You vill have to give it to Mr. di Latorio orally, preferably vonce I am out of ze room. You understand?"

"I don't understand much of anything you say with that accent, asshole."

His thin lips pull down, his greasy brow furrows. "You know, zere is no cause for rudeness. I have feelings, too."

"Do me a favor and take it up with the henchman union. Until then...just get this over with."

The doctor disappears behind me. He lifts some kind of metal cap from the back of the chair and fits it over my head, restricting movement even further. I feel him place the tip of that cable against the hard point on the back of my skull.

And then those little pincer arms are digging through flesh and bone, tunneling toward my brain.

I shriek.

My vision washes in red. My brain is swept clean of thought by a napalmed inferno. I am made of pain and that is all that is or ever has been.

"Don't vorry, it's nanotechnology." Gruenwald's attempt to comfort me. "Ze physical damage is not permanent, ze nanites vill repair everything zey damage."

If I could form a rational thought, I would tell him that's like mending the horse's leg before you send him off to the glue factory.

The cable finally gets wherever it's going in my head and stops moving. The pain subsides enough that I can suck in a breath without screaming it right back out. I expect to feel blood running down my neck, but there isn't any. Gruenwald comes back in front of me, and there's another cord plugged into an input slot above his left ear, a hole usually hidden by his disgusting hair.

"Let's begin."

Imagine your brain is a filing cabinet.

There's all these drawers, maybe they're arranged in some kind of system but it's so individualized no one outside of you could read them. Some of them even have locks on them. Inside are every thought, feeling, opinion and memory you've ever had, the sum total of your parts. Gruenwald is making like the Flash in my personal storage space, yanking open drawers, rifling through the contents at sonic speeds, and only sometimes bothering to close them back up. I can feel his grimy digits leaving mental fingerprints up there. And everything that he checks out swims to the forefront of my mind: embarrassing secrets, deep fears, shameful regrets. There's a quick, thirty-second montage of every time I've ever picked my nose. It's the single most invasive experience of my life.

Trust me, you can't help but tense up. And when that happens, more of the locks on these filing cabinets are thrown closed. So Gruenwald has to break the locks before he can look inside. And that is not merely uncomfortable, but extremely painful. So much so that within five minutes of starting, I'm weeping openly and shivering in my bonds.

A kid I pushed down in kindergarten. Ten bucks I swiped from my mom in junior high. The first time I masturbated.

"Come on, come on, vhere is it?" Gruenwald has his eyes closed and rubs his pulsing, silver temples as he paces back and forth in front of the chair.

Leaving Luiz at the Meg. Oh God, hitting Brynn.

As that awful memory of my wife floats to the surface of my consciousness, Gruenwald falters. I can sense him cross-referencing files related to her. Suddenly my mind is filled with every filthy position and sexual deviance she and I ever undertook.

"*Get. The fuck. Out of there*," I wheeze.

Weldon holds up his cigarette. "Stick ta da program, doc."

Gruenwald dogears the file and keeps looking. The pain worsens after that. I'm dizzy, sweating and broken. The doctor gets rougher with his search as his frustration grows. And then he pulls open a drawer and an image of Lennie Kincaid comes out and the tiny guy opens his mouth and a single word comes screaming out like the trumpets of Judgment Day.

SEEEEEEDOOOOOOOC!

Way to go, Rudes. Now we're cooking with gas.

The Word—'Sedoc' now, I don't see how I ever could have forgotten—hooks into me like never before. My whole body is lifted up from the chair like it's full of helium, my butt leaving contact with the seat. The straps are the only thing keeping me from floating to the ceiling. From the corner of my eye, I see Gruenwald get hit with the mental feedback from what I'm experiencing. He jitters violently, rips the cable out of his head, and then goes flying backward, smashing into the wall so hard he bursts open like a ripe melon. He leaves a blood smear as he collapses into the floor.

I work my limbs, and the straps across my body snap one at a time. For just a second, I'm levitating. So much energy courses though me, it's intoxicating. I reach back and disconnect my end of the cable.

Weldon stands in awe, unsure exactly what to do.

The Word is pulling, and I so badly want to give in and let it take me wherever it wants. I touch down on the floor and run toward the door before I get dragged to it. When it won't open, I smash my fist down on the control panel until it does. This power is already fading again, so I figure I better put it to good use. Weldon seems to wake up just as I step through into the tech vault. I try to slam the door, but his arm snakes through up to the shoulder.

"RUDY!" he bellows. "You ain't going nowhere you goddamn—*EM-EFER! DEE-DOUBLE-YOU!*—cunt! Gimme the fucking Word!"

I hold on to the steel door handle, keeping the pressure on his arm. I can't let go, or he'll be on me in a heartbeat. He tries to pry my fingers away. When that doesn't work, his hand buzzes, and another large pistol teleports into it.

He starts firing. I dodge to the left of the door, still holding the handle. He can't get his arm turned around to shoot at me, but he's putting holes in the ceiling, walls, and the array of gadgets that decorate them.

I reach behind me and grab at Carbini's hoarded technology. I'm hoping for something sharp. What I come up with is some kind of miniature chain saw that looks like it could be used for carving a turkey. I jab at buttons until the thing starts up with a cute little purring noise.

The rounded blades at the end begin to glow blue as they spin.

I bring them down on Weldon's doughy bicep. They chew through his coat and sweatshirt and into the flesh beneath. Blood flings across the wall in angry slashes. He screams and drops the gun and tries to pull away but I keep bearing down until his arm hits the floor at my feet.

He draws his stump back amid wails that sound vaguely like letters. I close the door, pray it locks, and turn to run.

I half-sprint, half-get-pulled through the tech vault. The Word is hauling at me with the force of an eighteen wheeler. I can hear that other voice in my head like background static, calling me 'Rudes' for some reason, telling me that 'I have to get out of here, like pronto.' The kind of surfer dialogue that instantly reminds me of the Photolab Twins. It's everything I can do just to stay on my feet. If I fall, I'm going to get dragged bodily across the floor.

The exit door of the tech vault doesn't lock from this side. As I push it open, I hear the door at the far end bash against the wall. Weldon is coming.

I charge down the stairs. He reaches the top just as I hit the bottom. I hear the rattle of automatic gunfire and dive into the first row of clone tanks. Glass shatters, some sticky fluid washes over me, and then a clammy, slime-covered Fiver flops into the floor beside me with a row of bullet holes in his torso. I crawl through the puddle of goo, deeper onto the warehouse floor.

"RUDY!" I can see Weldon stumbling down the stairs, the nub of his right arm trailing blood, the left clutching a heavily-modified M4 carbine. "I'm gonna fucking—*GEE-DEE! KAY! EF-AITCH!*—kill ya!"

"You can't!" I yell back, while trying to figure out what curse word starts with 'K.' "I still have the Word!"

"Fuck Carbini, fuck da Word, but most of all, fuck YOU!"

He's sprays machine gun fire in an arc. Tanks crack everywhere, spilling their contents. I hit the deck and squeeze my eyes shut and wonder if it counts as suicide or abortion if you kill your own unborn clone. When I open them, I'm staring at a red warning label on the base of the tank next to me.

CONTENTS HIGHLY FLAMMABLE.

"When I'm done with ya—*AY-AITCH!*—I'm gonna go back and find your pretty little wifey—*EM-EFER!*—and have myself one HELLUVA party, Rudy!"

At this, my jaw clenches so hard, I think I crack a tooth.

I reach into the thick nest of cables and wires that run into the back of each clone machine and rip out a handful. They spark and crackle with live electricity. I grab as much slack as I can and jump to my feet before I can stop to think.

Weldon is lurching through the pool of clone birthing juice and dead skinbags he created with his manic gunfire. His face is pale from blood loss, eyelids fluttering. But when he catches sight of me in his peripheral, he gnashes his teeth and starts to bring his gun around at me.

"Have a party with *this*, you DEE-AITCH!"

I toss the sparking end of the cable into the puddle.

A great big *FWOOOMP!* and a wave of heat force me back. Weldon roars in pain.

The middle of the room becomes a boiling cauldron of flames. Weldon is just visible at the heart of it, running around in weak circles. Flashbacks of the Meg come to me as the fire spreads, blackening the glass of the intact clone jars.

I can see the door of the warehouse. I squeeze between tanks and make my way to it. The first of the units explodes behind me as I burst into sunlight.

The warehouse sits in a little oasis of gravel carved out by the lane of metal shipping containers. I don't waste time debating which way to go, just cut across the lot and slide between two of them. On the other side is a junkyard full of rusted out semis, beaten furniture and broken appliances. I start across it as more hollow booms come from the warehouse interior, and the first tendrils of smoke creep into the air.

Fuck, Carbini is going to be *pissed*. I'm just taking a wild guess here, but I don't think his clone lab or super technology museum was insured.

The Word calms down now that I'm out of immediate danger—it's still indicating which direction to go, but no longer dragging me—and the voice is silent. I concentrate on navigating the junkyard and not thinking about the fact that I just killed a man.

Or clone. Whatever. Either way, it's still my first murder, a big no-no for a Transcendentalist, and I feel like someone's stepping on my stomach with a sharpened pair of cleats.

Pretty soon I hear traffic, and then I reach a chain link fence I have just enough energy to scale. A cab narrowly avoids sideswiping me when I drop to the thin median on the other side. I bend over, clutch my stomach, and try to catch my breath.

This is some sort of industrial park. The light-but-constant traffic flowing by is coming from a large freeway off ramp that arches high overhead and then flows past the junkyard. Some of the faces in the vehicles are turning to look at the column of smoke coming from its center. I have to get out of here before the cops arrive.

Across the street is a sign with an arrow that says, 'GAMBLING THIS WAY!' And below that, 'World-Famous Virginia Street Casinos!'

I need people, I decide. People and a phone. I take off down the roadside as fast as my sore legs will carry me.

The bum eyes me for a long time, taking in the grimy orange stains all over my clothes and skin. Other than that, I don't think I look too much worse than I already did. Just as Gruenwald claimed, the hole in the back of my head from the neural cable completely sealed up.

"You want *what* now?"

"Some change, man. Please." I stop rubbing my bare arms and point at the payphone beside me. "Just enough to use the phone."

We're in the mouth of an alley between a convenience store and a donut shop, just up the street from where the casinos begin. If I poke my head around the corner, I can see that famous sign hanging over the road: RENO, The Biggest Little City in the World. It's about nine in the morning, and the sidewalks are just filling up with tourists.

The Word thuds in my chest, like a dual heartbeat. I'm agonizingly close.

This bum I spotted squatting in the alley scowls at me. Looks at the Styrofoam cup full of his panhandled earnings sitting beside him. Then reaches into the interior of his ragged coat and hands me a cell phone. "Five minutes. And ya gotta stand right here while ya use it."

"Sure thing, thank you so much." Considering how awful that payphone looks, I'm completely sincere.

I dial the number for Dutt's prepaid phone, which I remember only because I programmed it into mine and Brynn's. He answers cautiously on the third ring. "Hello?"

"It's me."

"Jesus H. Christ Rudy! Where the fuck are you?"

"I'm in Reno."

"…you son of a bitch."

"Dutt, it's not like that."

"You fucker. I thought you were past all this going-it-alone bullshit."

"Stop right there. I didn't go anything alone. I got tasered outside the motel, thrown in a trunk, and taken to Carbini's hideout."

"Oh. *Oooooh.*"

In the background, I hear, "Is that him? Let me talk to him!"

The phone sounds like it's snatched from Dutt. "Rudy, are you all right?"

"Yeah, I'm fine."

"You're sure? They didn't hurt you?"

"Oh no, they hurt me quite a bit. But I'm fine now."

"Thank god." She sighs in relief. "Did you, um…did you happen to find the treasure?"

"No, Brynn."

"This isn't some kind of elaborate scheme to cut me out, is it?"

"For the last time, there is no treasure."

She pauses before snarling, "You better not fuck me!"

"Wow, if only you'd said *that* to half the male population of Withers over the last few years." I hear Dutt utter a single, boisterous, *HA!* I can imagine the shocked, pouty look on her face and a small thrill runs through me. Maybe today's that day Officer Reed told me about. "Now give the phone back to Dutt."

After a few seconds, he asks, "Seriously Rudy, what happened?"

The bum is already giving me the stink eye, despite elapsed phone time of barely a minute. "That's a long, mindblowing story, and I'm under a little bit of a time crunch here. I'm safe for now, and I got away from them with only another arson credit on my record to show for it. Where are you guys?"

"Still right here where you left us, man. We got up this morning, saw you were gone, and freaked the fuck out. We were on the verge of calling the police and turning ourselves in."

"Yeah, don't do that. How fast can you get here?"

"Depending on the traffic we hit in Vegas, I'd say we're still about five hours away. And that's only if we don't get pulled over or hit any roadblocks. There was a story on the news first thing this morning. The cops got an anonymous tip that you're heading west, most likely to Nevada."

I grind my teeth. "Must've been Hillman. Be a lot easier for him to get to me if I'm in police custody."

"Can you hang tight till we get there?"

"Don't have much choice, I guess. When you get into town, just find a motel room somewhere and make sure Brynn is safe."

"How will we let you know where we are?"

"You won't. I'll call you back in five hours."

"All right, just be careful, man. Lie low and don't do anything stupid."

"Not making promises," I say. "Oh, and there's one more thing. I know what the Word is now."

"You remembered?"

"I had a little help."

"That's awesome! What is it?"

"What are you, nuts? I tell you, I might as well put a bullet in your head while I'm at it!"

"It's okay, I can handle it! You shouldn't be the only one that knows."

"Carbini said it wouldn't transmit over the phone lines."

"Just give it a shot."

For a second, I consider. But that second is filled with the faces of so many corpses—not to mention a violent wrenching of the Word itself in my head—it passes fast. "Dutt…I'm not making you any more a part of this than you already are. Besides, if you know it too, I don't think I'll be able to track down this Servant of *Sideris*. Whatever it is."

"Okay." He sounds very disappointed. "See you soon."

I hang up and hand the phone back over to my homeless savior. "Thanks again."

He nods and says, "Latin."

I'm already stepping away by the time I comprehend that he didn't say, 'Welcome.' "What's that?"

"*Sideris*. It's Latin." He slips the cell phone back into his pocket as he looks up at my slackjawed expression.

"It means 'desire.'"

I don't know about you, but I could use a recap. Preferably one with some of the relevant dots connected, the ones I gleaned from Carbini's rambling.

A terrorist organization called the Filament is looking for an object of great value. They hire Carbini, since his dealings in high technology have gained him a reputation as a man that can find things. Somehow, he gets his hands on what these people want; I'm still a little fuzzy on those details. He also gets a hold of the password that makes the thing work, by hunting down everyone else that knows it. Lennie Kincaid (or one of his clones, as the case may be) is tasked with physically getting this password from Florida to Reno. He's the only one in the entire world that knows it, and once he hands it over, presumably to a representative from this Filament agency, he'll be terminated.

Except Lennie snaps. Goes off the radar. If Carbini is right, he decides he wants this object for himself. He starts toward Reno with the intent to steal it, but gets tossed in jail for that broken taillight. By this point, Carbini already knows something is up, and has Fiver out looking for him. Toss all these elements in a locked jail cell, stir in a little of yours truly, bake for twenty minutes at bloodbath degrees, and, *voilà!*, I end up as the sole person in possession of the Word.

Two complications worry me about that scenario.

First. The more I learn about this mess, the more I see Hillman might've been right: I can't get rid of this thing now that I have it. I know the Word—Sedoc—and I can't *un*know it. Sharing it with someone else only puts them in the same boat as me and cuts my connection to the object, again, according to Hillman. And even if our plan goes perfectly and I find this object, turn it over to the cops, and prove my innocence, that Word is still going to make me a target.

Second. Back to Lennie Kincaid. I keep thinking about how he was when I met him near the end of his existence, tearing at his head and talking to himself. Comparisons to Gollum would not be out of line.

Is that going to be me? Is that yet another little bonus that comes with being the only person carrying the Word, besides the occasional burst of strength, the magnetic compass in my chest, and the pleading voice in my head?

And if so…how much longer do I have till I'm a drooling idiot too?

I duck into the restroom of the convenience store where I met the Latin-speaking, cell phone-carrying bum. This time I'm careful to check all the stalls. After bathing in the sink, the crusty remnants of the clone juice are off my skin and hair, but my clothes are permanently stained. Can't do anything about that or my hunger until Dutt gets here with my wallet.

Just before leaving, I catch sight of my bloodshot eyes in the mirror. I lean close to my reflection, pull down the lower lid of the one on the left, and look deep inside.

"Helloooo?" I mutter. "Are you in there? Can you hear me?"

Loud and clear, Rudes.

I jump so hard, I almost poke out my own eyeball. That voice sounded like it was right in my ear.

Not in your ear, in your brain. *Right about where Gruenwald stuck his little toy.*

"Who." Swallow. Wet lips. Try again. "Who are you?"

Can't answer that one, dude. Again, I'm reminded of Sean and Kevin, but only distantly.

I lean toward the glass again. "Why not?"

Cause I don't know. I don't know, cause you don't know.

"Are you...the Servant of *Sideris*?"

Lemme tell you how this works, Rudes. We're connected by the Word, you and me. It's trying to, like, bring you to me, and give you a helping hand when you get in trouble, as you've already seen. And I can use it to talk to you by bouncing off your brainwaves. Like an echo. But that means I can't send any information you don't already know. It's really more like you're talking to yourself, with my will thrown in.

"Bullshit," I say. "I didn't know any of *that*."

Don't be a wiseass, dude. This takes a lotta energy. Energy I don't exactly have, like, in abundance.

"Sorry."

Look, somewhere in your subconscious you'd already figured it out, or I wouldn't be able to say it. But that's beside the point. You gotta set me free, Rudes. Come to me, and come fast. I can answer all your questions then.

That voice is fading as he finishes, and I put my hands on the mirror as though I can hold onto it. "Wait, wait, *where* are you? What am I even looking for? Shit. *Shit!*"

It's gone, if it was ever really there in the first place.

Now I know why Lennie Kincaid was arguing with himself.

God, I think I'm going nuts.

Back outside, strolling down Virginia Street.

It's cold out, probably just above 50 degrees, with a slight wind. I'm shivering even in Dutt's hoodie as I wander past one casino entrance after another. Silver Legacy. Fitzgeralds. Eldorado. Harrah's. The garish lights are all off at this time of morning, and the pace of foot traffic in and out of their open doors is lazy but constant, mostly old folks, married couples, and cowboys. Slot machines tinkle and beep. At each intersection, the backbone of the Sierra Nevadas is visible off to the west, a dark ripple of earth beneath a dazzling blue sky.

I put the hood on the sweater up, keep my head down and walk, letting the Word guide me.

It's getting rougher. More insistent. An anxious fluttering in my chest. It feels like a panic attack. Before I know it, I'm coming to a stop on the wide sidewalk in front of the entrance to one of the smaller casinos, a place called 'Slots of Luck!'

Whatever the Word has been leading me to—whatever owns that cajoling voice—is inside this building. I'm sure of it.

I take a look at the outside. Two stories, plain brown brick, marquee-style billboard outside decorated with four-leaf clovers and a sinister-looking leprechaun that promises, 'Loose Slots and Easy Dealing!' Sounds like ad copy for a whorehouse.

I should turn around and leave. Judging by his parting directives to Weldon, Carbini is most likely in there, although I can't imagine him playing keno. My best bet is to go somewhere else and lie low and wait for Dutt to plan my next move.

But the Word wants to go in there. And I find that I do, too.

I pass under the archway with the scowling leprechaun and into Slots of Luck.

The place is pretty dead. A few slot jockeys work the rows of machines by the front door, all women and all old enough to have survived the Depression. Beyond that are blackjack, roulette, and poker tables, only about one in three with a dealer and sparsely populated by players. The air is clear but still smells like smoke, and the lights are dim. I have my head craned around, checking out the interior as I slide immediately to the left of the door.

When I turn back to look where I'm going, I smack right into Sullis Carbini.

Except this Carbini flops over limply to the gaudy carpet and lies there all two-dimensionally and before I can scream and bolt I realize it's a life-size cardboard cutout. I stand it back up and check out the front.

The man is wearing a different suit, smiling broadly, and holding out a drink as if he wants to toast me. Near the bottom, across his legs, are the words, 'Slots of Luck Owner Sullis Carbini Invites You to Our Annual Poker Tournament'.

That answers one question.

I slip past the standee and down the outside aisle of the casino, against the wall. The carpet is worn, a black background overlaid by a glowing collection of shapes you'd find in a box of

Lucky Charms. The ceiling is studded at regular intervals with opaque glass globes, behind which a hundred cameras take in every inch of this place. I try not to look at them without *looking* like I'm trying not to look at them and head toward the back, where there's a bar and a several cash-out windows.

I'm so excited, I feel like I'm going to piss my pants. It's like a tab of the most euphoric acid ever. I feel this way, and I don't even know why. The Servant is back, his voice stronger than ever, spurring me on like a crowd near the finish line of a marathon.

A security door in the wall ahead of me bursts open, giving me just enough time to flail away and duck behind it. Someone walks through, and I hear a voice say, "Hey, I just came by to let him know as a courtesy. Nothin I coulda done to keep the fire department outta that place. No need for him to get attitude with me."

"That warehouse had particular emotional attachment for Mr. Carbini." This second voice is inflectionless, deeper, and much more familiar. Fiver. I feel my bowels loosen.

"Yeah, well, he's gonna have to find another truck for his *emotional attachment* to fall off of. I don't know what he had stored in there, but that place burned right to the ground. They're sifting through the ashes, but I hope for his sake they don't find anything."

"Doesn't matter. The property is owned through a dummy front." Fiver sighs on the other side of the door. "We'll need to move fast. The young man responsible has to be found immediately."

"How do you know he didn't die in the fire?"

"Because we do. We need as many men as you can spare to help search."

"I'll see what I can do, but even that's gonna be hard. This is the same kid those cops from Texas are looking for, right? Lotta heat on this. We even got an APB from the FBI a half hour ago."

"It's *not* the FBI, trust me," Fiver growls. "Just keep a watch for him. Once Weldon gets here, we should have no trouble tracking him down ourselves."

"Whatever. No promises."

The door swings shut, leaving me exposed. Lucky for me, Fiver has retreated back in to wherever it leads, and the owner of the other voice is strolling away from me on the casino floor. I get a good look at the back of him.

Good enough to see he's wearing a Reno Police Department uniform.

I give the cop enough time to leave and then fly out of the casino. Takes every bit of my willpower. I force myself to walk and just start off down in the sidewalk in the first direction I see.

The whole damned city is looking for me. Every face that passes seems to be watching. That thing Fiver said about Weldon coming to track me down really threw me for a loop, until I remembered there's two more copies of him out there somewhere, along with another Fiver. Somehow, that doesn't alleviate my guilt over killing him. In any case, I need to get off the street and find a place to lie low until Dutt arrives.

But every step I take away from that casino causes the Word to beat against my ribcage. The sorrow it dredges up in me is painful.

Rudes, Rudes man, don't go! It's sounding further away, but majorly panicked. *I'm right here, you're so close!*

"I know, goddamn it," I say through clenched teeth. "I know you're in there, but knowing doesn't help me get past

Fiver and whatever else Carbini has up his sleeve. What do you want me to do, bust in there Bruce Lee style?"

There's no answer, but judging from the drum solo in my stomach, that's exactly what it expects.

And, God help me, I'm so desperate to get my hands on whatever's up there, I'd almost be willing.

The traffic running on the street has gotten heavier. I get about two blocks from Slots of Luck when a long shadow falls over me. An engine chugs along at the curb, matching my pace. I look over.

A rusted school bus is driving in the closest lane to the sidewalk.

From every window, hooded eyes stare directly at me.

"Oh fuck meeeee," I groan. Another of those complications that just have a way of finding me.

I walk faster. The bus speeds up. I break into a run. The bus roars ahead. I duck right at the next intersection and head down 4th Street. The bus runs a red light and turns after me, the brakes squalling.

The new street is mostly souvenir shops, lighter with pedestrians but a bit heavier on traffic. There's no place to hide, and I don't want to risk going into one of the stores. I have a feeling the only reason I don't have an arrow in my back already is because I'm in public, and there's too many people around for them to slaughter.

The next cross street is Center, and it's one-way. I charge across the intersection and run by the front bumper of the bus as it squeals to a stop. It can't turn after me this time. I hear the doors whoosh open and look over my shoulder.

Three of the Acolytes are stripping out of their conspicuous robes at the top of the bus stairs. What emerges is three young jock types with shaved heads, in white undershirts and dark jeans. They look like Neo-Nazis auditioning for a stage version of *Grease*. The trio looks up and down the street and then comes barreling at me.

I'm already tired and out of breath, but I sprint away, crossing at least two blocks. Feet pound the pavement on my tail. I push through a crowd of Japanese tourists and run into a little bodega on the corner. Don't know if they saw me and don't stop to find out. I pass by rows of bong pipes and smoke paraphernalia and out a door on the adjacent wall.

Back out on the sidewalk, to a tiny little side street. Ahead is Virginia; I've made a big circle. I stop, catch my breath, and hear a horn honking from the other direction.

One of the Acolytes crosses against the light, heading east away from me. The second sprints by the opening of the side street without even glancing over.

The third comes around the corner, sees me, and grins.

Running again.

He chases me back out onto Virginia, right on my ass. I feel fingers scrabble at the hood of my sweater. I'm just about to spin and try to take him on when a cop car cruises by in front of us.

I slow down to a casual walk.

So does the Acolyte.

We couldn't be any more obvious if we both looked at the sky in different directions and started whistling.

But the cop car doesn't pause. By the time it's out of sight up the street, I've slipped in through the front entrance of the Nugget with the Hitler Youth right behind me.

We power-walk onto the casino floor, which is a lot more crowded than Slots of Luck. I used to do this with my sister when our mother would take us to a store and tell us not to run. Weaving through rows of machines, a few people look up at us, especially when I cut right and the guy chasing me plows into a silver-haired grandma while trying to follow, knocking her down and tossing quarters across the floor. While he recovers, I try to lose him around a kiosk of electronic keno machines. He goes around the far side to cut me off. We end up staring at one another back and forth on opposite sides, waiting for the other to make a move.

Two huge men in black suits approach us.

"Is there a problem here gentlemen, or do we need to call the police?"

My tongue hangs.

"No problem," the Acolyte answers politely, without taking his eyes off me. "I was just inviting my friend here to the bar for a drink."

I let him pick the table. It's a back booth in the corner of the bar adjacent to the casino floor, pretty empty at this time of day. I'm hesitant to slide in across from him, but go through with it only because there's no way he could be hiding a bow or mace under his clothes. He sits bolt upright across the table and glares. His young face is criss-crossed with healed scars.

"So are we actually having the drink, or—?"

He doesn't answer. Instead, he gives a full body tremble across from me, his eyes roll back in his head, and his mouth falls open. Before I can run or scream, a voice drifts out of the hole in his face, one withered and dry and as ancient as the Sphinx.

"Boy," it rasps. "You have no idea of the foulness you carry inside your head. Do you?"

These words aren't coming from the Acolyte; his mouth and tongue aren't even moving, just hanging ajar. He seems to be unconscious.

The voice continues while I try to figure out what the hell is going on. "No, of course you don't. Any decent person would've killed themselves long ago to rid the world of that filth. But here you sit, alive and well, staring at me like a half-witted jackanapes."

"You...you're...?"

"I've gone by 'the Candlemaker' for as long as I can remember. That should do for our business. I apologize for the insult of speaking to you through one of my precious Acolytes, but it's the safest way. Can't have you infecting me with that pestilence."

I finally get my mental train back on the rails by reminding myself this is far from the strangest thing that's happened to me today. Also, I *hate* this motherfucker. "You and your *precious Acolytes* butchered all of my coworkers. You murdered Officer Reed. You're trying to kill me."

The Acolyte-puppet gives another few angry twitches before that gravel voice snaps, "Don't say that as if *I* am the villain here, boy. *I* am waging a war for the salvation of all mankind, just as I have my entire life. And victory is so close, I can taste it. Admittedly, you might be innocent in this—certainly not as wicked as that brigand currently in possession of the Vessel—but your life is nothing compared with the prospect of stopping the evil that will come out of it once and for all."

"Vessel," I repeat. "Object. Package. Weapon, treasure, evil. You know, I might be able to understand what's going on if one—just *one!*—of you people would stop talking in code long enough to explain what this thing is."

"T'would do you more harm than good." That disembodied voice reminds me of the old two-paper-cups-attached-with-string gag. "Bad enough you have that Word in your brain, hammering at your willpower, luring you in with its siren song. But at least it's limited to using only what you already know. Thankfully, that's not much. Any knowledge I give you would just be more fodder for corruption. That's how the Servant of *Sideris* thrives, you see: by twisting hearts and minds, making brother to kill brother, laying honorable, decent men low through greed and the promise of power." The Acolyte is jittering now, eyelids fluttering. I glance around to make sure no one is watching us before continuing.

"I don't understand. Is it a person?"

"Your understanding is inconsequential. But perhaps if I impart a bit of history, it might help you see the decision laid out before you."

"I'm listening," I say cautiously.

He starts to tell me a story, and his cadences remind me of a preacher spouting off a well-known and much-loved sermon. "In the earliest days, a monastic society known only as the Order decided the Servant was too dangerous to be allowed to roam free. Many wanted the beast destroyed outright, but another faction insisted it be kept alive, in case the time ever came when it was looked upon as the lesser evil. They thought this creature might one day *save* mankind, if you can believe it. Weak-willed fools." These three words come out coated in disgust. "But...they won out. Or rather, they imposed their plan before anyone could act, and drove away those that argued. They created the Vessel and the Word to contain the Servant, as prison and key."

"But how did the Word—?"

He cuts me off. "For 2,000 years, the Vessel was kept guarded by the Order while the Word was spread far and wide across the world. Each human brain that absorbed it diluted its power. Added yet another tumbler to the lock of the Servant's prison. Meanwhile, the remnants of the Order that were cast out drew together, rebranded themselves the Acolytes, and dedicated themselves to hunting down all who carried the Word. They figured if they couldn't destroy the Servant, they could at least trap it forever. That war between the Order and the Acolytes has been waging ever since. And then along came that ruffian Carbini." The Candlemaker sighs, the sound weary and brittle.

"Yeah, I've met the guy, so I can relate."

"The blame for the current situation can, at least partly, be laid at our feet. The Acolytes have eliminated the Carriers one-by-one for millennia, so, in a way, we made it even simpler for someone to swoop in and do exactly what we all feared, Order and Acolyte alike. With the information Carbini was supplied by his...*employers*...he was able to steal the Vessel from the Order with an army of those science-grown abominations. Then it was just a matter of having one of his many-faced monsters absorb the Word and hold on to it while he finished the work we began."

I nod my understanding. "Killing off everyone *else* that knows it."

"Yes. You are the last. The Omega. The Wellspring of all that potential energy. You hold the key that will open the Servant's prison and set the creature loose once more. There hasn't been one such as you since long before Jesus Christ walked the earth."

I sit quietly, trying to comprehend something that big. All of my problems with Brynn, all of this bullshit I've been calling a life for the past twenty-eight years, just seems so petty now.

The Acolyte is almost seizure flopping by this point, and I can't help thinking of an overtaxed computer with smoke pouring from the CPU. The Candlemaker confirms this by saying, "I don't have long. This faithful boy gave his life just so I could speak to you today. I am here to offer you a chance."

"What kind of chance?"

"To save your soul. Or, if you're a godless heathen, to do the right thing by humanity and everyone involved in this business. Now that I am certain beyond a doubt you have not passed the Word on, we can end this. Once you are dead, the Word is lost, and the Vessel will remain sealed for all time. If you come to me—surrender yourself—then there is no need for your loved ones to be hurt."

"Please." My voice creaks as much as his. I feel sick and cold, but only because he's making so much sense. "There has to be another way. I could spread the Word, tell it to everyone I meet. If we get it back out there again, Carbini won't be able to—"

"No. That sort of thinking got us here in the first place. You could spend the rest of your life spreading it, but someone just as determined would take Carbini's place someday. Eventually we would end up right back at this point. The threat *must* be eliminated, before the vile denizens of the Dark Filament get their hands on the Servant." The Acolyte starts to slide down in the booth with blood pouring from his ears. "I shall give you a few hours to get your affairs in order. But at six o'clock this evening, you must meet my Acolytes in front of this establishment. If you aren't here, or you make any attempt to pass the Word on, we'll be forced to resume our hunt of all you've been in contact with." He pauses, and that sandpaper voice softens as much as it's able. "I swear on my honor, I will make it humane and painless. This is for the best, boy."

The Acolyte slumps over, unmoving.

I get up and leave the bar as fast as I can go.

Chapter NINETEEN

The strippers are hot, but I'm sure they're not Vegas caliber. They dance to angry metal music like Pantera's "Walk," that's not the least bit sexy. Most of them have extra meat on the bones and the first saggage to the tits. But the best-looking one in the place reminds me of the bartending waitress from the Thorn Rose Tavern last night.

Annie. She could've been that mythical girl everyone told me was coming. I wonder what she thought when I didn't come back from the bathroom. Should've had Dutt explain to her before they left. Yeah, Brynn would've loved that.

Then again, who gives a fuck what Brynn would've loved?

None of the girls in the joint are anywhere near as nice as Annie though. Once they figure out I'm not tipping, they retire to the customers at the opposite end of the stage. But that's okay, cause I'm only killing time in this dank hole, keeping my head low.

After the third time one of the waitresses comes by to see if I want a drink—each time accompanied by expressions of increasing disgust—I ask if she has a pen. She takes one from her apron, tosses it in my lap, and walks away before I can ask for some paper also.

I check my pockets. I've been collecting a lot of crap. The first thing I come up with is the gadget Carbini gave me, and I switch it to the opposite side. Next is my wedding ring. I stare at it for a second. Again, I'm struck by the realization that all our problems are dime-a-dozen compared to what we're involved in now, but they're still there. Still lurking. Waiting for me to either put this silver band back on or throw it away. I plead the fifth for now, move it over with the little metal Pez dispenser, and keep digging.

In my back pocket is a deeply creased sheet that turns out to be Brynn's email to Chris. I have a vague memory of reading it back at the apartment before Weldon and Fiver showed up. Glancing over the type again, the pain isn't nearly so bad knowing that the guy she's writing to is dead.

I set the paper down on the edge of the stage. Hover over it with the pen. Something that Carbini said has been turning over in my mind for a while now.

Moving deliberately, I try to print the letters 'S-E-D-O-C.'

The pen won't write. I think at first it's out of ink. But it works when I scribble, or try to spell out anything else. But as soon as my intent is to make a physical representation of the Word, it shuts down. So I push harder, using the blunt tip of the pen to carve the letters into the paper instead.

I get as far as midway through the 'S' before the thing bursts into flames.

Using my palm, I beat the fire out before anyone sees.

Guess I'll call this experiment a failure.

~ ~ ~

I also mull over the Candlemaker's offer while cellulite-dimpled ass shakes in my face. He seems pretty straightforward. Not telling me lies about sending me off into the sunset after he's done with me, anyway. And everything he said only agrees with the conclusion I came to in the Meg: there's no need for those around me to keep dying if I can prevent it. I just have to make sure that Dutt and Brynn are safe from all other parties—including the cops—before I take him up on it.

The Word gives a nervous flutter every time I contemplate surrender. I wait for the voice to come back and beg, but it must still be tired out. I admit, the Servant has my sympathy.

After all, I was only locked up for a few hours, and it was nearly the death of me.

I can't imagine what 2,000 years has been like.

At two o'clock, when hunger is killing me and it looks like the club bouncer is getting ready to toss my ass on the street, I ask to use their phone. The guy at the front window takes pity on me.

Dutt gives me the name of the motel they're staying at. I grab a cab outside and nearly fall asleep on the twenty-minute ride over.

The place is nicer than where Brynn was staying back in Withers, fresh paint with a row of desert palms across the front. My car isn't here, but Dutt probably has it stashed somewhere out of sight. He meets me outside the office, tosses cash at the cabbie, and throws his arms around my neck. I hug him back, but mostly because I'm just about too weak to stand on my own anymore.

"I thought you were dead, man."

"Why don't you cry about it, you big pussy?"

He lets go and steps back. "No, really. Listen, I'm sorry for what I said yesterday. In the car. I didn't mean it."

"It's cool."

"No, it's not. She's your wife, I understand that. I'll butt out."

"Oh shit. This isn't your way of telling me you slept with her on the way here, is it?"

His fist pistons into my upper arm. "Goddamn it, Rudy, I'm trying to have a moment here."

"Okay, all right. Look, I don't want you to butt out. I know you're trying to help. But I want you to back me up no matter what decision I make."

"I will, I will." Dutt nods eagerly, trying to move the conversation along. "Also, I gotta tell you—"

"Save it a minute. Let's get inside before someone sees us."

He takes me into the adjoining rooms they rented. Brynn nearly bowls me over, her eyes leaking. I hold her, smell her, rub my nose against the side of her neck, then drop her when I catch sight of the smorgasbord they have laid out on the room's only table, next to the open door that leads into the next room.

I alternate between double-fisting a sandwich as long as my forearm and drinking from every fast food cup on the table while I talk.

"Clones," I babble around a full mouth. "Carbini has clones, a lot of them, or he *had* them—"

"Rudy," Dutt says softy.

"—And they're looking for me and the Reno cops are dirty and I met the Candlemaker—well, sort of—"

"*Rudy*," he says a little louder. Brynn gives him an uncomfortable look.

"—And you're not gonna like it, but I'm pretty sure I know what I have to do."

"That's great, Rudy, but there's something you should know."

Before he can explain, Agent Douglas Hillman walks in from the other room.

"Glad to see you're all right," Hillman says. Today I get his casual side: ill-fitting blue jean jacket over a fully-buttoned, short-sleeve cotton dress shirt, with dark jeans. And the boots, of course. His whole wardrobe is like IT cowboy, and neither image really works for his creepy persona. "I received notice of a commotion uptown a few hours ago. I assume that's your handiwork?"

"How'd you find us this time?" I ask.

"I had local law enforcement blockading every road into Reno."

"They're all working for Carbini, you know."

"I'm well aware. That's why, when they caught your friends and impounded your car, I came immediately to take them away. After I explained the situation, they agreed to bring me to you. Thank God they have a little more sense than you do."

"Gee, thanks for the Calrissian, guys," I mutter.

Dutt crosses his arms. "You didn't tell us he called while we were on the road."

"Yeah Rudy, he only wants to help."

"Bullshit." I glare at Hillman while I talk to them. "If he wanted to help, he wouldn't be blowing just as much smoke up my ass as everyone else. He would tell me what this is all about. Isn't that right, Agent Hillman, of the super top secret government agency known only as...*Aurora?*"

Hillman is implacable. The only sign that I've gotten to him a minute flare of his large nostrils.

"Tell me, Agent Hillman, who is Aurora? What do they do?"

"I'm not at liberty to discuss that."

"Why does Carbini know who you are? You personally, I mean."

"We've had run-in's over the years."

"He says I shouldn't trust you."

"And what opinion would you expect a criminal to have of an authority figure?" He waits to see if I have any other questions. When I don't speak, he finally says, "Your friends tell me you've recalled the Word."

"Yeah. With some serious help from a greasy German extractor named Gruenwald."

"I met the man back in '96, when he worked for us. Can't imagine the experience was pleasant." He studies me for a long moment. "Now that you have the Word...are you willing to give it to me?"

"What happens to us if I do?"

"I told you, I bring you in, offer protection. We take care of this legal problem. And all three of you go back to your lives."

Going back to the current state of my shitty life isn't exactly a bargaining chip, but I don't say it. "Just like that, huh? You let me go skipping around with this Word in my head for the rest of my life?"

"Oh no, of course not. It would present far too great a danger. We would have to make sure that the Word is satisfactorily erased from your mind after you surrender it to us."

"Riiiiiight," I say, backing toward the door. "You said yourself that I'm stuck with it. So that either makes you a liar or me a lab rat while you figure out a way to do that. I'm outta here."

Dutt goes to block the door. "Just hear the man out, okay?"

"Let's talk about options, Mr. Compton." Hillman comes forward to the table, pulls a chair away, and sits primly. "As in, your appalling lack of them. What plan were you blabbing about as you came in? You've obviously seen that Carbini has no interest in helping you, and I think by now you've figured out the illogicality of relying on the police in this situation."

I breathe deep. "The Candlemaker. He said if I surrendered myself tonight...he would make it quick. Painless."

"Jesus Christ, Rudy," Dutt mutters. I see Brynn's hand go to her mouth.

Hillman shakes his head sadly. "I can't believe you would even entertain an idea like that, son."

"Look...I really don't give a shit about myself at this point. I just want these two taken care of. What else am I supposed to do? Once the Word is gone for good, this all ends and there's no need for anyone else to get hurt."

"Let me assure you, Carbini's employers would still hurt them. If only for spite."

"You mean these Dark Filament terrorists?"

Hillman's brow lowers. "They are...not what you think. My sources tell me a contingent is coming here, to Reno, by noon tomorrow. The package can *not* be allowed to fall into their hands. Better we should do things the Candlemaker's way than for that to happen. This situation is so much larger than you could ever understand."

"Try me."

The gravity in his answer chills me to the bone. "I would not be exaggerating in the least to say that the fate of the world itself depends on the decisions we make in the next 22 hours."

Silence fills the room. What the hell do you say when someone feeds you a line like that outside of a James Bond movie?

"Maybe you should just give him the Word," Dutt says.

"No. Once I do that, I'm completely expendable."

"*Rudy, would you just stop it?*" Brynn is hugging herself while she shakes with anger. "The man just said the *world's* at stake! I'm scared shitless, so stop being so stubborn and let him handle this!"

"Listen to them," Hillman advises.

"Okay, you said your piece, now let me say mine." I come forward again, to the opposite side of the table. "I'm not saying my life is worth more than the world. It isn't. At all. But I think you people want this thing just as much as anyone else. To keep it safe, yes, but also so you can use it yourselves. And you'd say anything to make sure that happens. Including threatening me with a bullshit Armageddon or offering a magical cure-all that's gonna get me out of this situation."

"Are you so sure?" Hillman's tone is full of pity and amazement all at the same time. "I take it you've been in that house of wonders we've always believed Carbini keeps. After all you've seen the last three days, are you *so sure* that I don't have such a solution?"

"No, I'm not. I'm just not willing to give up my one bit of leverage until I'm sure the people I care about are safe."

Hillman tugs at the flap of his jacket, enough to reveal the shoulder holster concealed beneath. "I could just arrest you, you know. All three of you. Getting the Word out of you at this point would just be a matter of applying the right...*pressure.*"

"Go ahead. I've been tortured by the best. I think I'm building up a tolerance."

"I didn't say the pressure would be on you." His eyes flick over my shoulder, to Brynn and Dutt.

Mine, however, stay rooted on his. "If you ever say anything like that again Hillman, our dealings are gonna be over for good."

He sighs tiredly and closes the jacket again. "Fine then, if you won't give it to me, then at least use it to guide me to where Carbini is holding the package."

I think about that a second. It's not a bad idea. I don't trust Hillman with the Word, but I figure this thing—the Vessel—is better off in his hands than Carbini's. Plus I can't see how doing it would hurt my deal with the Candlemaker, if I decide to go that route.

"I already know where he's got it. I'll tell you."

For the first time, excitement comes into Hillman's face as he scoots to the edge of the chair. "I'll need you to come with me."

"No way," Brynn answers before I can. "He's done with this, he's not going anywhere."

He glances at her with obvious annoyance. "I need to find this package, and I need to find it now. The truth, however, is that I have no idea what it even looks like. With Mr. Compton there, Carbini won't be able to lie, bluff, or hide."

"Yeah, and what if you get him killed in the process?"

"There won't be any danger. I'll obtain a warrant and we'll raid the building."

I chew my lip. Check the clock on the bedside table. 3:18. Plenty of time before the Candlemaker's deadline for me to go with Hillman back to Slots of Luck and let him take down Carbini's stronghold.

It has nothing to do with the fact that I'm filled with deep, secret glee at just the thought of going back toward the Servant.

Atta boy, Rudes. Get your ass back over here and rescue me already.

"Okay," I tell Hillman. "I'll go with you."

Who knows? Maybe I really can save the world before I die.

The water is as hot as I can get it. I stand under the stream and let it wash away the dirt and stains and fear and memories, and try to enjoy what I'm sure is my last shower in this life.

Telling them everything that happened—saying out loud about Carbini's skinbags and the Candlemaker using a human being as a bullhorn—somehow makes it all less real, like I'm pitching one of my book ideas.

Hillman remained silent but attentive when I recounted the history of the Vessel and the Word.

When I finally turn off the water and slide aside the curtain, Brynn is waiting by the sink with a fresh pair of jeans and a long-sleeve black sweater. "There's a store around the corner. Dutt got you some clean cloths."

I grab a towel and cover up. I don't step out, partly because there's hardly enough room in here and partly because I don't want to stand so close to her while naked. I've suddenly become modest around her.

She watches me dry off and says, "I don't want you to do this."

"Can't get dressed while I'm wet."

"Not that, moron. I mean go with Hillman to get this… this…Vessel, or whatever."

"Why not? Don't you want your precious treasure?"

She fiddles with the ends of her newly shorn hair. "Honestly… yes. But not if you get hurt. That's never what I wanted."

I grab the jeans from her and slide them on. "I won't get hurt. Hillman will call in the other agents, they'll take down Carbini, and I'll show him to the thing. Then we'll figure out what to do from there."

"Okay. If it's so safe, let me come with you."

"No, absolutely not. I can't do this and worry about you at the same time. I need to know that you're out of harm's way. And feel free to blackmail me all you want. Not gonna work this time."

As soon I step out of the tub, she throws her arms around my bare waist. I stand rigid.

"Don't," I say.

"Don't what?"

"Just…don't." I take her wrists and manually unlock her embrace, then step away as much as I can in the tiny space. "I don't need your pity."

She stares at me like a bug just crawled out of my mouth. "I. I'm not… This isn't pity."

"That's not how it felt last night. You want away from me? Fine. If…*when* we get back, I'll sign divorce papers. Whatever. But don't confuse me. Just…don't fucking do that. I'm too tired for more bullshit."

"I'm…I'm sorry."

Big tears gather at her bottom eyelids. Liquid manipulation. In my head, the distant voice of the Servant shouts, *Aw, c'mon dude, don't fall for the oldest trick in the book!* He sounds like someone hurling commands at the characters on the movie screen.

Brynn looks at the floor. "I said those things last night, but…I was just trying to explain. Doesn't mean I don't love you. I just can't get my head on straight to figure out what I want."

"Yeah, yeah, Brynn, that song and dance is getting real old. There was this girl last night—"

Her head flies back up. "Wait, *what* girl?"

"She was a waitress at the bar next to the motel. She made me realize that we can spend forever trying to solve our problems, but if what we have is real and true and meant to be, then we wouldn't have to. You're not the only one that's been miserable, you know."

Those hovering tears finally spill, trekking down her cheeks. "This morning…when you were missing…I was so scared. God, I. I started thinking of what I would say if I got to see you again. Or what I should've said. And. And I just think. After this over. Maybe…maybe we should talk."

"What does that mean?"

She holds up her left hand. Her wedding ring sparkles from its place on her finger.

"How did—?"

"I grabbed it from the motel in Withers, when I went back in for my purse. Hey, where's yours?"

I pick up my old, scummy jeans from the floor, pull my ring from the pocket and slap it on the counter. "I don't know about us anymore, Brynn. Until I do…I'm not wearing that thing another second."

She sniffles. "I wanna go home, Rudy. I just…wanna go home."

I don't know what to say to that. I'm too exhausted and

scared to have any hope that I'll be alive tomorrow, much less that she and I could get back to the way things were.

If there ever was such a way, and our entire relationship hasn't been something I imagined.

Brynn reaches to hug me again and this time I don't stop her. Against my chest she asks, "So was this girl hot?"

"Smoking."

"I swear to God, if you don't come back from this in one piece…I'll tell Dutt and your sister and your parents and the police and the media all about that thing you like me to do. With my finger and the brillo pad? The headlines will say, 'Withers Psycho Forced Wife to Perform Kink Before Massacre.' How's that for blackmail?"

"Not cool." I shake my head, but can't keep from cracking a smile.

In the motel room, Dutt and Hillman are perched on opposite sides of the bed, watching the local news. My mug shot is plastered across the screen, along with a picture of Brynn obtained from god-knows-where, and a police artist sketch of Dutt. Apparently they also want me in connection with the warehouse fire and the death of a certain shaved-head Acolyte found in the casino bar at the Nugget with his brains turned to toothpaste.

Christ, they're going to blame me for JFK, the Hindenburg, and new Coke before this is over.

Hillman stands. "We need to move. This situation is out of control. The more headlines you make, the harder this will be to clean up."

"Let's get one thing straight." I lock eyes with Hillman. "I'll go and help you find the Vessel. But after it's over, *I* decide what happens to me next, whether it's surrendering to the Candlemaker or not. You try to arrest me or detain me in any way, I start screaming the Word to anybody in earshot. Your agency can try to figure out what to do with all of us then. Agreed?"

"Agreed."

We head toward the door, with Dutt right behind us.

"Where are *you* going?"

"I told you dude, you don't leave my sight."

Brynn says, "Yes, at least take Dutt."

Hillman looks hesitant, but finally shrugs. "Fine, he can ride along. Let's move."

Hillman is driving the same shit-brown Ford sedan I saw him with at the Meg. I sit up front, with Dutt right behind me. Hillman navigates the afternoon streets of downtown Reno like a native, until we're once more rolling up what passes for a casino strip here.

The place has gotten busier as afternoon wanes. The sidewalks are packed. Now the elderly are joined by the drunkards and late night crowds who have finally crawled out of bed for this evening's festivities. The casino lights are just starting to come on up and down the strip, winking, flashing, and strobing. It's different from the pictures I've always seen of Vegas, cheaper and gaudier. Reminds me of a carnival my father took us to when I was ten. A lot more cop cars are parked along the avenue also, either routine after-hours presence or search teams looking for me. As we pass the Nugget, I stare at the entrance where I'm supposed to meet the Acolytes in a few hours.

But I don't even need to look to know when we're in

front of Slots of Luck. The excited pounding in my chest lets me know.

"There." I point at the sly leprechaun outside. The place is lit up with green and yellow pulsing lights. "It's in there."

"Excellent." Hillman pulls onto the next cross street and parks in front of a meter. "Mr. Lansing, you will have to wait here. Mr. Compton, stay behind me at all times and don't speak until I ask for your assistance."

"Whoa, whoa, wait a second, that's it?" I ask.

He blinks. "What do you mean?"

"I mean, we're it, just the two of us? I thought you said a raid on the building! You know, a bunch of SWAT guys and agents in blue blazers with guns all over the place and once it's secure, *then* I go inside. What if he just shoots us or something?"

He says, with a touch of annoyance, "Sullis Carbini is not going to kill a federal agent in his own place of business. We will enter, I will arrest him and any associates inside, and then you will take me to the package. It's very simple."

"Uh yeah, well the guy ordered my torture and execution a few hours ago, so excuse me if I'm not eager to walk back into his hands."

"Any agents from my bureau would take several hours to arrive, and he could decide to move the package someplace more secure in the meantime. Local law enforcement is all firmly in Carbini's pocket. It's us or no one, son."

"What about that warrant?" Dutt asks quietly.

Hillman glances at him over the seat. "What?"

"The warrant you said you were going to get. Don't you want this to be legal? For prosecution?"

Hillman's hawkish face draws up. "Of course. I can have it sent electronically. It will only take a moment."

He gets out and closes the car door, leaving us alone. On the sidewalk outside, he begins talking on his cell.

"Rudy, I don't like this," Dutt says. "I don't trust this guy."

"Then why'd you bring him to me?"

"I honestly thought he could help. Besides, we didn't have a lot of choice. We were caught dead to rights by the cops, then he came out of nowhere and took us out of their custody."

"Then what do we do?"

Before he can answer, the door opens again and Hillman leans down. "All right, everything is set. I have a copy of the warrant on my phone if Carbini needs it, and he'll be presented with a paper copy at booking."

"Mind if I see it?" Dutt's expression is all innocence. "I'm fascinated by that kind of stuff. I'm in the military now, but I'd like to be a cop when I get out."

"As soon as we're finished here. Mr. Compton, please exit the vehicle on this side and follow me."

I look at Dutt. He looks at me. And then I get on my knees in the bucket seat and start crawling across to Hillman. The agent moves aside and straightens up where he can no longer see us.

"Good luck, fucko." Dutt reaches over the seat to pat my back.

Except his hands go *under* my t-shirt, yank open the back of my jeans, and shove a lump of cold steel between my ass cheeks.

I bite down on a yelp and make my face as neutral as possible as I climb out onto the sidewalk.

~ ~ ~

There's a crowd milling around in front of the casino entrance, watching a street performer. Hillman pushes through them, and I try to stay as close behind him as possible.

For the first time since I met him, the government agent looks slightly more alive than a walking corpse. He lopes across the casino floor with purpose, heading toward the back of the place without me even having to tell him. The casino is noisy, full of constant talking and the beeps, whistles, and clinks of the slot machines, but over it all I can hear a heavy backbeat like distant jungle war drums and then I realize it's the Word beating behind my eardrums and against my ribs.

We reach the inner security door. Hillman tries the handle, but it's locked solid.

A manager or pit boss in a jet black three-piece suit comes hurrying toward us with a gang of bouncers. "Excuse me, can I help you gentlemen?"

Hillman whips out an ID wallet and flips it open. I'm sure it probably says 'FBI.' "Federal agent. Is Sullis Carbini in the building?"

"Yeeees, he's upstairs—"

"Open the door."

The pit boss squirms. "I'll need to call up first."

"No, you don't need to do anything! Open the door now unless you want to be arrested for obstruction of justice!"

The guy hesitates only another second before pulling a plastic key card off his belt and running it through a reader beside the door. Hillman yanks it open and steps inside. I give the pit boss an apologetic shrug before Hillmans pulls me through also.

He's moving fast now, on the verge of running. We hurry down a white-tiled hallway past rooms of computer banks. Technicians and security personnel poke theirs heads out to watch us pass. Hillman takes a left so abruptly I can't help but wonder how he knows his way around so well. He flies up a staircase, reaching under his jacket to pull his piece. It's a big semi-auto, something like a modified M9. I cringe a little at the sight of it.

At the top of the stairs is a reception area and a closed set of double doors made of heavy wood. Hillman never slows down, just raises one of his stick legs and slams the worn underside of his boot at the jam where they meet.

The doors fly open. I follow Hillman through into an ornate little office decorated to look like a New York subway stop.

Carbini sits on the far side of a desk made from old track pieces, a telephone receiver pressed to his ear, with Fiver hunkering in a chair just in front of him.

Hillman holds the gun out, aimed at Carbini's chest, and pushes the door shut again with his heel.

"Yes, they're here now," Carbini says calmly into the phone pressed to his face. "No no, that won't be necessary. Tell the boys to stay downstairs. Thank you, Lewis. Feel free to turn in your badge and vacate the premises."

"Hands up, both of you, right now!" Hillman barks. "If I see that big lug teleport in so much as a flyswatter, it's *you* I'm going to shoot, Sullis!"

Carbini places the phone on its cradle but doesn't raise his hands. Neither does Fiver, who's sitting halfway turned toward us, a huge grin across his thick face.

Hillman takes another step forward. "You know what I'm here for. Give me the Vessel. Now."

"And I think *you* know, that's not gonna happen." Carbini sits back in his chair, as relaxed as a man on the beach. "But I have to thank you, Hillman. For returning my little lost lamb."

He turns to me, and I feel the ice in his stare.

"You cost me a lot today, Rudy. More than a shit stain like you could ever understand. And after I get that Word out of you...I'm gonna make sure it *hurts*."

"Keep your mouth closed," Hillman tells him. Then to me, without looking over, "Is it here or not, Mr. Compton?"

The Word is dancing a jig in my chest, begging me, pulling at me, trying to drag me across the room toward where Carbini sits. At the same time, the Servant chants, *Dude, dude, c'mon, come to Papa, just a few more steps Rudes, almost here...*

The excitement is infectious. "Yeah, it's here. Somewhere on that side of the room."

"Get up." Hillman gestures with his free hand to a leather sofa against the left wall of the office. "Sit over there. Both of you keep your hands where I can see them." Carbini and Fiver comply, both with their matching predatory smiles still in place. The two of them barely fit on the loveseat. "Go find it, son."

Feeling like a golden retriever, I head across the office. Every step brings me closer. I give in to the Word fully for the first time and let it lead me like a puppet behind Carbini's desk. There's a knee-high liquor cabinet painted like grime-flecked subway tile against the wall. I fall to my knees and start rummaging through the contents. I have no idea what I'm looking for, but I figure I'll feel it in my bones when I find it.

"Mr. Compton?" Hillman sounds edgy. "Is it there?"

"I...I don't know..." I'm getting desperate, shoving through glass bottles and drink tumblers, knocking over a few of them.

It's close. So close. Finding it feels like the culmination of the last two weeks. Hell, of my *life*. The voice of the Servant is practically singing to me. I want it. I *need* it.

I look up. There's a canvas painting of an antique rail car above the liquor cabinet.

I stand. Grab the frame. Lift it off the wall. Toss it aside.

To reveal a big, steel safe door.

Carbini chuckles. "You geniuses didn't really think I was gonna have it sitting out like a paperweight, did you? Christ, I'm surprised you didn't check the couch cushions."

Hillman takes a step closer, jabbing the barrel of his pistol into the man's eye socket. "Open it."

Carbini never loses his cool. "Make me."

Hillman cocks the hammer with his thumb. "I *will* kill you."

"Whoa, hey, calm down," I say. As excited as I am about the prospect of finally (*reconnectingjoiningfreeing*) seeing the Vessel, this whole situation is making me uneasy.

If this is a government-sanctioned detain-and-search, why do I feel like I'm in the middle of a robbery?

"No you won't," Carbini says. "Not till you have what's in that safe."

"Then I'll torture you."

"What in the holy fuck do you think you could threaten me with that would be worse than what the *Filament'll* do if they show up and I don't have the Vessel?"

Hillman backhands him with the pistol. Carbini rocks

back against the couch with blood running from his forehead. Beside him, Fiver snarls.

"Hillman, Jesus, stop!" I shout. "What are you doing, just arrest them and get them outta here! It's in the safe, and it's not going anywhere! You gotta have someone from your agency that can come in and open it after they're gone!"

Carbini pulls a handkerchief from the pocket of his suit and presses it to the wound on his head. "You can't possibly be this stupid, kid. Do you really think that if this thing was as important as I'm sure he's been telling you it is, that Aurora would let one…*miserable*…*stinking*…*agent*…come after it?"

"Shut up," Hillman growls.

"What are you talking about?" I ask.

"Tall, Skinny, and Ugly over there? He can flash his creds and his security clearance to get just about anything he wants from the small time PD's. But I guarantee, his bosses don't know a goddamn thing about the Vessel, or they would've sent an *army* after me."

Hillman winces like he's just been stabbed in the side. "Mr. Compton, don't listen to him, he's just trying to muddle the issue!"

Carbini grins wickedly. "Hillman's working this alone, trying to get his hands on the Vessel same as everyone else. Aren't you, Hilly?"

"I said shut up, you two-bit Jersey street trash!"

Hillman rears back to strike the mob boss again.

As soon as the gun is off its target, Fiver launches off the couch.

Hillman might as well be a sapling in the path of a tornado as Fiver plows into him. The two of them tumble across the gray carpet, the gun flying from Hillman's spindly fingers. They land in an awkward tangle with Fiver trying to get his hands around the agent's throat and Hillman attempting to sink his teeth into the cloned mobster's side.

"You see kid? Nobody from this bozo's government-sponsored knitting circle even knows you're here."

Carbini stands up from the couch and straightens his suit. The wound on his head is blood-crusted and swelling.

"I could kill you both right now, in this office, and no one would give a shit."

He strolls past the wrestling match in the floor and retrieves Hillman's gun.

"Well, maybe not about him. You and I still have business."

I circle around the desk and back toward the door, with him following. Dread burns the back of my throat. I try to get my sluggish, slow-witted brain working, but the engine upstairs just won't turn over.

He waves the gun as he closes in. "Where you going, Rudy? Let's have a chat."

I reach back, grasp the handle of Weldon's pistol that Dutt shoved in my waistband, and pull the weapon free. I point it at Carbini's chest with a shaking hand.

"Drop the gun and tell Fiver to get off him."

"Kid, you are just too precious. You still think you're the hero in all this, don't you? I don't know how many ways I can tell you: nothing you do is gonna make any difference."

"Tell that to your burned-down warehouse and all your little toys," I taunt. The smile drops off his face. "Now, you're gonna open that safe and give me the Vessel."

"Oh really? And why would I do that for you when I wouldn't do it for him?"

"Because if you don't...*I'm* gonna say the Word."

It takes Carbini a full fifteen seconds to catch my drift. His body stiffens.

From the corner, under Fiver's crushing weight, Hillman screeches, "*Do it!*"

Carbini's eyes lock on mine. "You're bluffing. You don't even remember it."

"Nope, sorry, total recall thanks to one Dr. Gruenwald. I say the Word, and everyone in this room gets infected." My hand steadies. I know I should just get out of here, but I can't leave without whatever's in that safe. "You said yourself, you're just as expendable to these Filament guys as the rest of us. Unless you think they'll wait patiently while you rebuild your clone factory and grow yourself a new body. Bet you wish you'd kept a few skinbags on reserve now, huh?"

"*Do it, just say it!*" Hillman screams.

Carbini's mouth hangs open. His healthy tan skin pales about three shades. "You...y-you wouldn't."

"It's on the tip of my tongue and just itching to come out." When he doesn't move, I open my mouth and make a deliberate and drawn out 'S' sound.

Carbini yelps and jumps away like I was a snake. He drops the gun, jams both index fingers in his ears and shrieks, "*Don't, don't say it, I can't know the fucking thing!*"

"Then open the safe!"

"*I can't! They'll kill me!*"

"Worry about them or worry about me! Once we're gone, you can send whoever you want after us to get it back! But if you don't have that safe open in thirty seconds, you're gonna share whatever I got coming!"

"*All right!*" Carbini runs to the wall and start spinning the lock dial.

I move the gun to Fiver. "Get off him."

The big lug reluctantly lets go and rolls away. Hillman gets up with tears in his jacket and one eye blackened and swelling. "Good work, Mr. Compton!"

"Shut up and stay over there."

He blinks in confusion and sputters, "But...but...you don't actually believe—!"

"I don't know what I believe, I only know you haven't been playing straight with me."

There's a ratcheting clank from the safe. The door swings open. Carbini is blocking my view of whatever's inside.

"Reach in and take it out," I say. "Slowly."

He does. My heart beats so fast, I think I'm going to puke. I haven't been this excited since the loss of my virginity in eleventh grade. Carbini turns around to face us and I get my first look at this thing that so many people have been willing to kill for, to die for.

An old.

Rusted.

Bedpan.

Say it Rudes! Pick it up and say the Word! Lemme outta here!

"That's it?" I ask. It looks like a reject from a medieval history museum, a dingy metal bucket with a lid clamped to the top by corroded hinges. I only recognize it as a shit can from a documentary I watched about the history of toilets. IBS; don't ask. The voice of the Servant babbles a constant stream in my head, louder and clearer than ever before.

Carbini sets the thing on the desk like he's scared to touch it.

Hillman starts across the room.

"Hey! Stay back!"

His gaze flicks from the Vessel to me and back again. He licks his lips like a junkie, but when he speaks again he's striving to regain his dry, uptight composure. "This is what we came for, Mr. Compton. This can clear your name and save the world. Let's take it and go."

He's right. No matter how stupid it looks, this thing is too dangerous to be left here.

God, I hope that's me talking.

Everyone seems to be holding their breath as they wait on me. I finally walk over to Hillman's gun where Carbini dropped it, then kick it under the sofa. "Go," I tell Hillman. "Into the hallway." I almost add *Don't go anywhere*, but from the way his eyes stayed rooted on the Vessel, I don't think it will be a problem.

Hillman brushes past me. I step up to the desk, grab the phone and rip it from the wall, then reach for the Vessel.

"Are you...are you gonna open it?" Carbini is almost panting with restrained eagerness as he awaits my answer.

I don't give one. I pick up the chamberpot instead.

A tingle goes through me at the contact. It's not as exhilarating as when I absorbed the Word, but I instantly feel relieved, at peace, and I never want to let go of it. The voice of the Servant falls silent in my head. I spin with the Vessel tucked under my arm like a football and run for the hallway.

Outside, I start to close the doors of Carbini's office.

"You better kill me, Rudy." Carbini raises a clenched fist. "Cause I'm coming after you and everybody you love with the Dark Filament *right behind me!*"

I close the doors, grab a chair from the reception area, and jam it under the handle.

This time I lead with the gun, and Hillman follows. I take the stairs three at a time and then sprint down the hallway toward the casino floor.

"I'll carry the Vessel!" Hillman reaches for the bundle under my arm.

I yank it away. I feel a moment of breathless panic followed by seething fury at the idea of giving it up. "That's okay, I got it."

Outside the security door, the collection of guards is standing around staring at one another, completely clueless about what to do. Hillman and I charge through them and onto the main aisle of the casino without being stopped. All over, heads turn our direction, eyeing the gun in my hand. The exit to Slots of Luck is just ahead, and I'm sprinting at top speed when a familiar figure bursts into the casino a few yards ahead.

"RUUU—*CEEAYGEEDEEEMEF!*—UUDY!!!!" Weldon comes through the door like a nightmare, face red and fuming but otherwise whole and alive once more. You have no idea how surreal it is to see someone you murdered up and talking, even when you know it's a clone. There's a shotgun as big as a rocket launcher in his hands, and he brings it up and starts firing.

With my current momentum, I have no time to veer from his path. The only thing I can do is throw myself hard to the thin carpeting.

Something hot blasts over my head. I hear Hillman squeal in pain.

The casino erupts. Everyone jumps off their stools and heads for the doors amid screams. Legs stomp all around, hiding me from Weldon. I roll away, then get to my hands and knees and try to crawl while holding the gun and the Vessel. It's all I can do to keep from being trampled.

I bang my head on a slot machine and use it to climb to my feet. Now I can get a better sense of the situation. Weldon's been shoved aside by the people fighting to get out of the casino. I spot Hillman further down the aisle, moving against the flow of human traffic. The side of his jacket is spotted with blood as he tries to escape.

The guards come running, pistols out and pointed at Weldon. They shout for him to freeze and drop his weapon, but he just unloads, cutting two of them in half with one shot. The others either hesitate or try to leap for cover like morons and get mowed down in the process.

The casino is empty and silent now, except for the ever-beeping machines. Weldon steps over the men he's just slaughtered on his way into the place, and I see that, even though he looks unharmed, he's twitching all over. Like with his Tourette's, but much worse. One arm keeps dropping from the shotgun barrel to flail uncontrollably.

In my head, I hear Carbini talking about defects.

I slink further down the aisle before he spots me.

"RUDY!" he shouts again. "Ya cocksucker, ya know how it feels ta get yer arm cut off and den be *burned alive?* Cause I sure as fuck do!" He unloads a round into the ceiling.

Guess he's holding a grudge about that whole setting-his-mentally-connected-clone-on-fire mishap.

I stay low, working my way toward the back of the casino. Weldon follows, looking for me down each row. On the far side of the room, the security door opens and Carbini sticks his head out.

"Jesus H. Christ Weldon, *no shooting in the goddamned casino!* What the fuck're you doing?"

"Killing dis—*EF!*—little pissant!"

"You can't kill him, he's still got the Word!"

"With all due respect, Mr. Carbini—*CEE! AY-AITCH!*— I've had a *really* bad day, so I don't give a shit!"

I can see a fire exit door at the very back of the casino, next to the restrooms and far away from anywhere money would be kept. I reach the last bank of slot machines before I would be exposed. I'd need a miracle to get across that much open space alive.

From my left, someone grabs me.

"The Word, the Word, give me the Word," Hillman wheezes. He leans back against the slot machines while blood pools in the floor under him. I can't see how bad he's hurt, but his clothes are shredded all down the extreme left side of his body and his lumpy face is even paler than usual. "I can fix all this, just give me the Word and the Vessel."

"*Shut up*," I hiss.

Above everything, the sound of wailing sirens grows from outside. All those cops parked up and down the street will be here in seconds.

"*You hear that, you idiot?*" Carbini bellows from the hallway at Weldon. "The cops can only cover up so much! How the hell are we supposed to keep this quiet?"

"Rudy, get da fuck out here so we can finish dis!"

I pull free of Hillman's weak grasp and peek over the top of the machines. Weldon is just a couple of rows away, spinning in vicious, drunken circles, twitching all over like a Parkinson's victim. From the security door, Fiver comes out with empty hands held away from his body.

"Weldon…buddy…put the gun down."

Weldon spins toward him and raises the shotgun. "Fiver, ya don't know what it's like!"

"Then tell me." Fiver's eyes flick over to mine, and one of his hands gives the smallest, 'go on' motion.

I get it. They still need me alive. They would much rather have me out of danger, away from this malfunctioning, homicidal version of Weldon, even if it means me escaping with the Vessel. Since that's what I want too, I won't look a gift clone in the mouth.

Against my better judgment, I bend down, get the arm holding the gun around Hillman, and drag him to his feet. We head for the fire exit with him leaning heavily on me.

"I felt it," I hear Weldon say, "I felt da flames…heard 'im screaming…and now we're cut off! It's tearing my brain apart! *He* did dis ta us, dat little shit!"

"I know, Wel, I know, but we'll rebuild it. Get the network set right back up."

"No, no, don't ya get it? Our original DNA samples're gone! We'll just be copies of dese shitty bodies!"

"Mr. Carbini can fix it. But you gotta play it cool for now and cut this shit out."

I stop at the door with the Vessel under one arm and Hillman hanging onto my neck and look back.

Weldon is still twitching as Fiver eases toward him. His shoulders shake like he might be crying. He allows the shotgun to be taken from his hands.

"There, there now, Wel," Fiver croons, squeezing the back of the man's neck. "It'll be all right."

And then he steps away, puts the shotgun barrel to Weldon's temple, and sprays a fan of blood and gore across the casino floor.

When he looks at me, his eyes are twin cannons of hate.

"Time to go," I tell Hillman. We push through the fire exit as the first police cruisers squeal to a stop in front of Slots of Luck.

TWENTY
TWO

I don't know why I'm saving Hillman.

I only know if I leave him, he's a dead man, and I can't think far enough ahead to know where that will leave me.

Hell, without the Servant chattering in my head and the Word dragging me along, I have no idea what to do next.

There's a corridor beyond the fire exit with a guard post at the far end, in case a would-be robber tries to use this path as a getaway. It's abandoned now, the security detail either having fled or been shot by Weldon in the other room. We hobble down toward it with Hillman using me as a crutch.

Just as we push open the next door to see the last vestiges of afternoon sunlight, a gun goes off behind us. A bullet ricochets off the metal beside my ankle, throwing up a spark. We turn.

Fiver is at the opposite end we just came from, leaning around the corner with a pistol. He aims low and squeezes off another round that comes close to pulverizing my kneecap. Shooting to maim. I raise the gun in the hand still supporting

Hillman and fire off a few awkward shots. They don't come anywhere close to hitting him, but it does make him pull back. We move outside and let the door slam after us.

We're in a narrow alley behind the casino. I maneuver us to the closest end and we pop out on the same side street we parked on earlier. When I turn to the right, I see Hillman's sedan and Dutt standing beside it, trying to see what's happening around the front of the building. I shout his name.

He comes running and meets me a few steps from the car. "What the fuck happened, there's like twenty cop cars in front of the place! Is he shot?"

"Long story! We gotta go! Help me with him!"

Together, we manhandle Hillman into the backseat of the car. He gives a whimper, but I think he's unconscious. His forehead is drenched in sweat.

"The keys!" Dutt reminds me.

It almost kills me to let go, but I make myself put the Vessel down in the floorboard so I can dig in Hillman's pockets.

—ay it, Rudes, you gotta, just say the Word, say it right now *dude, and let me out and I'll do everything I can to help you—*

The second I'm no longer touching the rusted pot, the voice of the Servant comes back midstream, begging and gibbering in the back of my brain. I ignore it and snag the car keys from the agent's jeans.

We close the back door just as a Reno cop car screams past on its way to cover the alley, lights and siren blaring. It gets another twenty yards down the street before braking hard and turning into a tight spin.

"Shit, go, go!" I shout.

Dutt opens the front door and scrambles across the seat. I

leap behind the wheel, jam the key in the ignition, and bring the engine to life.

The cop car turns around and accelerates toward us. Running from the police not only seems stupid but hopeless, but if they catch us, we're as good as dead. I slam the car in gear and floor it.

Ahead of us, traffic is at a snarled tangle where this street intersects Virginia, probably from the platoon of cop cars blocking the road just around the corner. Another alleyway is coming up on our left just before we'll get there. I squeal around the corner, catching the edge of a dumpster in the process. The steering wheel almost gets away from me. Jeff Gordon, I am not.

The squad car shoots in behind us, right on my tail. Its lights paint red and blue splotches across the brick walls on either side of us.

Dutt turns around in his seat so he can see out the back window. "They're gaining!"

The Word, Rudes! You gotta say it before they catch you!

"Rudy, goddamn, you better go faster!"

Dude, I'm, like, telling you: pick the Vessel up, say the Word, and let me outta here!

"Everyone, just shut the fuck up!" I yell. Dutt shoots a confused glance at me.

I floor it through the alley, picking up speed. The cop car, one of the new Charger models, catches up to us fast and nudges our rear bumper. I pump the brakes, causing them to slam us. They back off.

The next street is four wide lanes and looks clear. I'm doing about fifty by the time I shoot out onto it.

Roughly the same speed as the other car when it T-bones our rear driver's side panel.

~ ~ ~

The world spins sickeningly. Pain flashes across my body, from too many sources to catalog. My ears fill with the sounds of metal and glass and plastic collision. Then the motion stops and everything is blessedly still.

Wake up, dude! Snap out of it! Rise and shine!

At some point, my eyes open, but I can't make sense of what I'm seeing. The world is made of shapes that don't fit together right. This is worse than the motorcycle accident. I try to shake the cobwebs out while the Servant yammers with increasing panic.

There's blood on the steering wheel. It takes several seconds of intense contemplation to understand it's mine. I hurt all over. My limbs feel dipped in lead. I'm dizzy and nauseous. But I'm breathing, and nothing seems to be broken. Next to me, Dutt groans in the passenger seat as he peels himself away from the dash, minus his glasses. In the back, Hillman's unconscious body is now in the floor. I look around outside.

The accident spun us around and pushed us a few dozen yards up the street, where we came to rest against the curb. The engine is off and the rear driver's side of Hillman's ride is crushed in. Judging from our trajectory, I think we're pointed away from the casinos. A crowd is gathering on Dutt's side.

My blurry vision picks out the car that hit us on the opposite side of the street. A silver Benz whose trunk I recently resided in. The front end is pancaked where it struck us dead-on. I can see Fiver behind the wheel. Or rather, *around* the wheel, since most of the steering column is sticking through his chest. His head is caught at an awkward angle in the corner of the window frame, his eyes open and staring at nothing.

The Benz came to rest slanted across the mouth of the alley, blocking the cop car from exiting. I hear doors opening, voices yelling for us to freeze and exit the vehicle. Everything echoes in my ringing ears. The cops clamber over the disabled vehicle to get to us. I know we need to do something, but if I move I'm just going to puke and pass out, and maybe not in that order.

"If this POS still runs," Dutt croaks, "then get us outta here."

Yeah yeah, dude, I second that!

I shake off the last of my shock, then try the ignition again. It fires right up. Within minutes, we're speeding down the street, leaving the cops behind.

It's simple, Rudes.

"Says you."

Dude...you just pick up the Vessel, and, like, say the Word. Presto. Couldn't be easier.

I think I'm beginning to understand how this part works. The talking in my head, I mean. The Vessel is a broadcast tower for the Servant, which only the Omega can hear. When I'm far away, the occasional stray signal drifts my way whenever he—it?—boosts the amperage, like radio stations when you're outside a city. The closer I get, the clearer the Servant becomes. But any physical contact causes interference that cancels out the signal entirely.

Well, look at you, smart guy. Figuring things out on your own now, huh?

Still not used to having my mind read.

"So I'm just supposed to let you go without even a second thought, huh?"

Sure! What's the worst that could happen?

We're back at the motel room with Brynn, who's trying to patch up the gash on my forehead while I talk to the rusted pot sitting in the middle of the table. I wince as she dabs alcohol across the cut above my eye and answer the Servant's question. "For starters, I could be releasing an ultimate evil that will consume the earth and destroy life as I know it."

Oh, come on, *dude. Do I sound like ultimate evil?*

"Someone must've had a good reason for locking you up in that toilet."

That's pretty cold, Rudes. The disembodied, Keanu-Reeves-esque voice sharing space in my head sounds sulky. *Like, you don't know a damn thing about me. Other than what those morons told you.*

"And it's real convenient you can't tell me otherwise. All I know is, there's never been an inmate alive who didn't go around claiming he was innocent." My gaze flicks up to Brynn, standing over me. "I got experience with that one."

Brynn picks up the bandages she bought at the CVS across from the motel and pulls one out. "Gotta say, this talking to yourself thing is getting reeeeeal creepy."

"I'm not talking to myself, I'm talking to *this* whiny bitch."

Hey! Uncool, dude.

"So...there's someone trapped in there?"

"Someone or some*thing.*"

"And you can hear it?"

"Damn thing won't shut up."

Talk trash all you want Rudes, but don't forget, you'd be dead by now if it weren't for me and the Word. And you know that's totally true, or I wouldn't be able to say it.

"Yeah, and I also *totally* wouldn't be in half the trouble I'm in right now if wasn't for you and the Word."

Brynn arches an eyebrow as she stretches the bandage across my wound and presses the adhesive against my skin. I've got a bastard of a headache to go with my collection of pains, but otherwise I'm not in too bad of shape from the accident.

"I just don't get it," she says. "This is the treasure everybody's after? What, does it belong in a museum or something?"

I sigh. "I don't know. Now that we have it, I don't understand any more about what it is then when all this first started."

Then maybe you should let me out so I can tell you!

Brynn's not even aware she echoes the sentiment, with a demure downward glance. "Maybe we should open it. You know...just to see what's inside."

See, your whorey wife's got the right idea!

"Shut the hell up!" I yell, and then, at the wide-eyed glance from Brynn, "No, not you."

I'm telling you dude, I can explain everyth—!

"Jesus, would you pipe down for a while?" I rest my hand on top of the lid and enjoy a few seconds of blessed internal silence.

Dutt walks in from the adjoining room. He's a little bit worse for wear than I am—black and blue across the right side of his torso where he hit the dash, lump on his scalp, and the frame of his glasses got twisted so much they barely sit on his face anymore. He hooks a thumb over his shoulder. "Hillman's still out. I did everything I could for him. The shot wasn't too bad, so I got the bleeding stopped, but we gotta get him to a hospital or call his people or something."

"*People?*" I snort. "You might as well call *People Magazine* for all the good that's gonna do us."

"What the hell happened in the casino, Rudy?"

I reach for the pack of cigarettes on the table and manage to get one out and light up while still staying in contact with the Vessel. I'd rather not have the Servant putting in his two cents on this conversation. "Hillman's not investigating this mess. At least, not officially. He's after this thing the same as everyone else. He played me. Got me to lead him right to it. We almost made it out and then Weldon came charging in the front with a shotgun. And he was not happy with me."

"Weldon? The fat one?" Brynn takes the cigarette out of my hand, drags, and hands it back. "I thought you said you killed him at that warehouse."

"They're clones, baby. Try to stay with the program. Anyway, he went crazy, came after me, and shot up the place. There was something…wrong with him. Fiver put him down like a rabid dog."

"Christ. How many more of these Weldon and Fiver guys are left?"

"By my count, one of each. We've just about brought down Carbini's entire empire." I won't say that thought doesn't fill me with smug satisfaction.

"So Hillman's a fraud," Dutt says. "Let's get in touch with his agency then."

"If you have any ideas on how to do that, I'll listen. I don't think Aurora maintains a listing in the phone book."

"Okay, if not them, then someone else in power."

"Yeah, and who would that be, Dutt? The local cops, who wanna turn me over to Carbini, or every other law agency in the world, who've got me painted as Jack the Ripper?"

I actually see him swallow whatever bit of sarcasm was ready to pop out of his mouth. "You've got this Vessel thing now. *That's* your proof. I thought that was the whole point in coming to Reno."

"That was when I thought we were dealing with a nuclear missile. Or anthrax. Something the cops or FBI could take one look at and know who the bad guys were."

"Then let's talk about the military again. My CO—"

"Goddamn it, it's not gonna help!" I pick up the Vessel and slam it back down on the last word. "Does your CO have standing protocols on what to do with warlock cults and telepathic creatures locked up in bedpans and mobsters armed with weapons from the future? No matter who we give it to, I'm still gonna be the only person who knows the Word, and anyone that wants to open this thing will have to get it out of me and then kill me, the same way Carbini was going to. Face it, there's no cavalry coming. There never was."

They're quiet for a minute. Dutt comes over to the table and gives Brynn a look I can't interpret. As he sits down, she gets up and goes over to the bedside, where there are two sacks of fast food and coffee she also picked up after we got back.

The glowing digital clock beside her reads 5:13.

I have only 47 minutes until the last appointment I'll ever make. I wonder for a split second if it will make things easier or harder if I try to get in touch with my parents first.

"Rudy," Dutt says, drawing my attention back to him. "If help isn't an option, what do we do then? What's the next step?"

I swallow and look down to avoid his eyes. "You know exactly what the next step is. I get back to the Nugget and meet the Candlemaker."

He studies me through the crooked frame of his glasses. "That's not an option either."

"It's the only way. The only way to make sure you two and my sister and my folks are safe. The only way to end this."

"You don't fucking worry about us, all right? You're not gonna turn yourself in for this religious nutbag to kill you!"

Before I can answer, Brynn comes back to the table and places steaming coffee in covered Styrofoam cups in front of each of us. I take mine and drink deep. It burns my throat, but I don't care. I want to remember this last coffee. I'll need every bit of caffeine for what's ahead.

When I've drained half the glass, I ask, "Dutt...what if Hillman was telling the truth about how dangerous this thing is?"

"What if he wasn't?"

"Can we take that chance? The whole world at risk, and only one measly guy's gotta die to save it?"

Dutt rolls his eyes. "Cut the Christ crap, man. You being the savior of the world is just another one of your romanticized fantasies."

Brynn speaks up from my other side. "He's right, Rudy. You're not doing this. We won't let you."

"Well, I don't see how you're gonna stop me." I stand up from the table with the Vessel. Bunch my free hand into a fist. "I mean, God, do you think this is what I want? To fucking die at 28, a pathetic loser who never did anything in his life except fuck up his marriage and write some shitty novels? I didn't ask for any of this to happen, but it did, and now I'm responsible for whatever comes next. Why can't you understand that?"

Dutt stands too and jabs a finger in the air at me. "No, this is just another way for you to give up, Rudy!"

"I know what you're doing."

"You're right, you *are* pathetic!"

"I won't let you goad me into this just to keep me here."

"Yeah, well...that's what I said to your mom last night."

I grin wearily. "Goodbye, Dutt." I start toward the door.

"Please," Brynn says. I stop with my hand on the knob. "Don't do this."

I turn back and look at the four of them standing there; two Brynn's and two Dutt's. "I haaaaaaaave toooooo."

The room is a smeared canvas of color all of a sudden. I'm aware of my knees buckling, but I don't actually feel it as I spill forward onto the floor. The Vessel bounces away and even the Servant's voice sounds slurred in my head.

Just before I cash out, Dutt's warped face hovers over mine.

"Sorry man, but this is for your own good."

Chapter

TWENTY THREE

I only walk into the tiny office at the back of the apartment to tell her I miss her. That I love her. To rub her shoulders and kiss her forehead and encourage her to come hang
out with me and Dutt.

I'm not checking up on her or anything.

I swear.

Even with everything she's already done to me by this
point—every betrayal, every indignity—I still trust her, never
suspect anything but the best from her.

Because I love her. I love her so much I'm blind with it,
like being in a sensory deprivation tank where all your senses
are dulled to the point of uselessness, only mine are worn
down by love, and in my deep down darkest of places...I
know I would put up with her shit forever, no matter what
Officer Reed or Dutt or anybody else told me.

When I come into the room, I see the way she jumps,
the way she scrambles to hide what she's doing, and I know.
Even when all this didn't have the vague repetition of a
dream, I know. I may love her, I may trust her, but I know

guilt when I see it.

I ask to see what she's doing.

She says no. She actually tries to block the screen with her thin little twist of a body.

It's panic that rampages through me, fear that turns my veins to ice.

Not anger.

Not yet.

I tell her I have to see. After everything she's done, if she wants to rebuild trust, she can't hide anything from me.

She refuses.

I need to see what's on that screen. It goes from desire to obsession in milliseconds. I step to her and put an arm out, trying to brush her aside. She won't move. I get rougher, grabbing her shoulders and shoving, and then she comes back at me, slapping and pulling. Before I know it, we're in some kind of bizarre wrestling match; her trying to yank me away, me working to escape her grasp and see what's on that computer screen where I sit and peck away at the keyboard for hours on end. It's wrong, I know it's wrong, and it's escalating out of control. Dutt comes running and stands helplessly in the doorway.

Finally I break free and go to the computer, and in this dream I'm terrified because I know I'm going to see the email to Chris that started all this, but instead Carbini's face is leering at me. He reaches right through the glass, grabs me by the throat and says, Why don't you pick on someone your own size?

This time when I open my eyes, the throb in my skull is worse than any hangover I ever had. There's a big, pulsing fireball in the center of my forehead that wants me to know it hates me.

I'm lying in bed with my shirt off. I recognize the motel room even in the dark. I try to sit up and a hand pushes me back down. The lamp on the bedside table clicks on, momentarily blinding me. When it clears, I see Brynn sitting beside me.

"I'm so sorry," she says.

"What did you do?"

"Dutt said it was the only way."

I hold my groggy, aching head. "*What. Did. You. Do?*"

"I got some drowsy-formula stuff at the pharmacy and put a bunch in your coffee. I was afraid I gave you too many. You were barely breathing for a while there."

"You...why did...wait a minute, shit, what time is it?" I grab the clock beside me before she can answer.

11:09 PM.

"Fuuuuuck," I groan.

"Well, what were we supposed to do? We couldn't let you go."

"You have no idea what you've done."

She takes a deep breath. "I kept you from killing yourself, and that's all that matters."

I sit up in bed, ignoring the sloshing migraine that screeches when I move and reach for my shirt on the floor. "Where's Dutt? Get his ass in here right now."

"He's gone."

I stop with my head halfway through the neck-hole of my hoodie. "Where is he?"

A flash of something crosses her face. Annoyance? Anger? Even with the lamp on, it's still too dark in here to tell. "I tried to stop him. I told him it was yours. *Ours.* It could be worth millions of dollars—billions, even!—and he's going to just give it away."

"Oh my God." For the first time, I realize the Servant isn't blabbing in my head. The fact that the Vessel isn't nearby, close at hand, makes my bowels clinch. "Where did he go?"

"He took the pot-thingy and went to meet some Army guys."

I reach out, sink my fingers into her shoulders, and give a shake. "*Where*, Brynn? You have to tell me."

She cringes. At the glimpse of fear on her face, I let my guilty hands drop away. The dream—memory—is still too fresh on my mind.

"I don't know. He called someone, his commander or whoever. He was on the phone for a long time while they transferred him to other people. But someone finally agreed to come. They gave him directions and told him to be there at midnight."

"Okay. Get me one of our phones so I can call him."

"He didn't bring his. He said he didn't want you trying to talk him out of this. He'll either send word or come back himself once everything is taken care of."

"Goddamn that asshole!" I'm up off the bed and tying my shoes. The Servant may be out of range, but I can feel the pull of the Word again, loud and clear. "When did he leave?"

"About a half hour ago. Rudy…can't you just let him take care of this?"

"He doesn't know what he's doing! Thanks to you guys, the Candlemaker is after us again by now! *Dutt's* the one that gonna get himself killed!"

"Well…so what if he does?"

I stare daggers at her. "I'm gonna pretend you didn't say that."

She closes her eyes, shakes her head. "I just meant, you risking your life also isn't gonna change anything. You and me, we can leave and—"

"No!" I stand and jump away from her. "I'm not running away from this, not for you or anybody! Once I find Dutt, we're coming back here to get you and then we're *all* leaving, I swear. Until then...just stay outta my way."

I grab my phone, then check on Hillman before I leave. The Aurora agent is bathed in sweat and shivering even under two blankets, but he actually looks better than before. His bloodshot eyes open in the dim room when I approach. They're twitchy but cognizant.

I ask, "Do you want us to take you to a hospital?"

He coughs. Blood stipples his lips. "No hospitals. I'll be fine in a few hours."

"Um, somehow I doubt that." I shake my head. "Was it true? What Carbini said about you?"

He gives something resembling a nod. "Got a tip the Vessel had been found. Some associate of Kincaid's in Florida who couldn't keep his mouth shut. Always thought it was just a myth. I hid the intel, took a leave of absence from the agency, and came down to poke around."

"You lied to me. From the very beginning."

"I'm sorry." His gaze floats to the ceiling, and he whispers, "My god, that much power...who could turn it down?"

"I thought you said it was a weapon."

"It is. It could be. But I wasn't going to use it. At least, not like they would."

"Spare me your rationale, Hillman. I don't know what to believe anymore."

He reaches out and clamps down on my arm. "I can still fix this. Just give me the Word and the Vessel."

"Yeah, well, that's easier said than done at the moment. The Vessel is…MIA."

"Oh god, you didn't. Not Carbini…"

"No, no, just my idiot friend. He's turning it over to the Army."

"You have to stop him. That thing…in the wrong hands… it really is just as dangerous as I said. I wasn't lying about that."

"All right, well…get some rest. We'll talk when I get back."

Dutt must've taken a cab, because Hillman's smashed-to-shit Ford is still behind the motel where we parked it. A cab is probably the smarter play considering the cops have to be looking for this vehicle, but I don't want to play a game of Warmer/Colder with a driver while I give turn-by-turn directions toward the Vessel. There's an angry squall under the hood when I start the engine, but it runs. The gun is still under the passenger seat.

It's the middle of the night, and most of the streets are empty. I drive at random, letting the Word guide me and trying not to speed. It leads east, away from the glow of neon and glitz that lights up the horizon in the direction of the casinos. I'm almost to the neighboring city of Sparks when I exit a belt of suburbs and enter a more commercial area, with shortstack highrises and a few newer warehouses.

I'm passing a three-story building surrounded by a concrete lot when the voice of the Servant cuts into my thoughts.

Rudes, buddy, so nice to see you conscious again! Think you could come get me?

I park the car a block from the warehouse and come back on foot with the pistol. This entire neighborhood is dark, empty, and abandoned. I stick to the shadows and stand across the street, looking up at the office and attached warehouse. It's much newer and nicer than Carbini's hideout. The sign in front says it's an emergency medical supply and delivery company. I have no idea why Dutt would come here, but the thrumming in my chest tells me I'm at the right place.

I cross the dark parking lot. The lock on the front door is busted. God, I don't like this. Feels too much like a trap. I clutch the gun between two sweaty palms and try to keep my sneakers from squeaking on the tile as I travel down pitch-black corridors, following the Word. I want the Vessel back so bad I'd probably stroll into hell itself. At a stairwell lit only by emergency EXIT signs, I start up.

Third floor. Long corridor with windows on one side looking out at a courtyard in the middle of the building. Moonlight reflecting off the floor as I creep past open office doors. I get halfway when something thunderous roars overhead, and a piercing light sweeps back and forth through the windows.

I scream but can't hear myself over the sudden noise. Try to run, but can't figure out which way. I feel pinned by that light.

Someone comes out from one of the dark offices behind me and slaps a hand over my mouth.

"Would you shut up, shithead?" Dutt says in my ear. "It's a helicopter."

The roof of the building has a helipad at the far end, for air delivery of live transplant organs. The company transports donor material to every hospital in Reno and Sparks. It was the closest place they could send a helicopter without going near the heart of the city.

We stand on the roof and wait for the rotors to stop spinning on the green-and-black machine. The doors on the side slide open. A squad of eight soldiers in urban camouflage and carrying M4s files out. Another man in a dark-colored suit climbs down, takes a place at the head of the line, and leads them toward us. The lights mounted along the top of the chopper cast a glow across the rooftop, revealing the pilot in the cockpit.

In exchange for the gun, Dutt reluctantly let me have the Vessel back. It was the only way I would even agree to stay for this. I'm beyond relieved, but still so jittery I could give Weldon a run for his money. As the troops cross the roof through a sea of industrial air-conditioners anchored to the roof, Dutt whispers from the side of his mouth, "Just be quiet, and let me handle this." He starts toward the newcomers and I slink along behind him, clutching my precious.

The man in the front is older than the squad of men following him, late forties or early fifties, with a weather-beaten face and close-cropped hair peppered with gray. An array of colored bars decorates the left breast of his suit jacket. Dutt stops three feet from him, stands rigid, and slices one hand up to his brow in a salute. I can't help cracking a smile. I've never seen Dutt in full-on G.I. Joe mode before.

"At ease," the man tells him. Dutt drops his hand to his side. "Staff Sergeant Lansing?"

"Yes sir."

"I'm Colonel Donovan Moore. I've been briefed on your situation. You did the right thing by contacting us. Lieutenant Davidson has been walking the floor about your situation." Moore turns to his men. "Gentlemen, full perimeter check and electronic sweep." They fan out around us, most of them with guns up and ready, but a couple pull gadgets off their belts and fiddle with them.

"Colonel, this is my friend Rudy Compton." Dutt stands aside and ushers me forward. I stand awkwardly holding the Vessel and stare up at the military officer.

"I'm surprised. With all the carnage the media is attributing to him, I thought for sure he'd be wearing a turban and have a beard three feet long."

I shrug. "No, but I'll be happy to hide in a cave if you got one."

Moore laughs boisterously. I like him. He reminds me of one of those elderly, turn-of-the-century strong men, minus the handle-bar mustache. "What about your wife? You didn't really kidnap her, did you?"

"No, no, that's all a misunderstanding. She's waiting at the motel until she hears from us."

"Say no more. I've had a few of those marital 'misunderstandings' myself." He points at the Vessel hugged to my chest. "I was told that all of this has something to do with that thing there."

"Yes sir. I don't know what it is, other than a royal pain in the ass. It may not look like much, but there are some very dangerous people after it."

"Interesting. May I?" He holds his hands out.

I hesitate. The thought of handing over the Vessel makes me want to break every last one of the fingers he's offering.

Dutt clears his throat. "You'll have to excuse him, Colonel. We've had a rough couple of days. Haven't really been able to trust anyone."

"You can trust *me*. I don't understand what the hell is going on, but by God, if I have to get out of bed in the middle of the night, I'm going to find out."

"What about us?" I ask. "Can you protect all of us? Clear this up with the police?"

Moore breathes in deep. "I won't lie and guarantee that, because I don't know what you've done or exactly how you fit into this mess." He jabs a finger at Dutt. "But I know *this* soldier's CO like a brother, and if he says Staff Sergeant Lansing is worth a shit, then you better believe I start looking for a toilet. And, as I'm assuming Lansing vouches for you, that's good enough for me. I'll have to turn you over to the FBI eventually, but if you're innocent, we'll prove it. I'll do everything in my power to take care of you. Just the fact that you came in on your own will say a lot."

This is exactly what I needed to hear. I gratefully drop the Vessel into his waiting hands, feeling like a junkie surrendering the needle. Dutt claps me on the shoulder.

Don't do this Rudes, please don't do this to me, oh God, I don't wanna be in the dark anymore...

"What comes next?" I ask over the Servant's pleas.

"Next we get your wife and fly all of you out to Nellis for a full debriefing. Once we know what we're dealing with, General Rayburn is standing by to—"

"Colonel Moore!" One of his soldiers hurries toward us with what looks like a miniature TV in his hand. "We got a bug! Looks like a tracker!"

Moore shifts the Vessel under his arm. "Where?"

"The readings say..." The soldier checks his equipment and then brings his eyes slowly up to me. "It's on *him*."

Moments of clarity can be such beautiful things. Mine have always hit like bolts of lightning, especially in my writing.

Even before the soldier says this, I'm thinking about a dirty tavern restroom in the middle-of-nowhere, Arizona, and how Weldon was somehow able to find me. His cryptic response just before Gruenwald mind-raped me. Fiver at the casino saying that once Weldon arrives, they would be able to track me.

Afterward, I'm thinking about a searing pain in my leg when he grabbed me waaaay back at the motel in Withers, and a little hole in my calf later on.

Unfortunately…those moments of clarity can be too late sometimes.

On the far side of the roof, the helicopter and its pilot explode.

Chapter TWENTY FOUR

A fireball climbs into the chilly November sky, throwing shadow across the entire roof. The shockwave is a rough hand that knocks us off our feet. Dutt and I hit the concrete on our backs next to one another, with the colonel almost in our laps. In the distance, car alarms are going off.

Before we can stand, the air over our heads fills up with sizzling, green bolts of energy, like the pyrotechnics at an outdoor concert. The remains of the helicopter are still burning in front of us, but these neon blasts come from behind, near the opposite side of the roof. I can feel the heat against my upturned face.

"Cover!" Moore bellows. "Take cover!"

"What's happening?" I yell over the noise.

"We're under attack!"

The only shelter on top of the medical supply building is the huge industrial air conditioners spread across the open expanse. Dutt grabs me by the arm and drags me toward the closest one, where Moore is already crouching with the Vessel. He pulls a pistol from a holster on his belt. Dutt has our gun out. The Servant wails in my head, but I'm getting better at ignoring him. All around us, the squad of soldiers finds cover of their own. They lean around the barriers and open fire with their M4's. The rooftop booms with the chatter of rapid gunfire.

I get on my knees, shove past Dutt to the edge of our metal shield, and peek around. With the floodlights from the helicopter gone, the only illumination comes from the shifting crackle of flames thrown over my shoulder. I can make out the far end of the roof, where a decline leads down to a shorter structure attached to this building. The weird energy beams are coming from somewhere down there, just past the door we used to get up here.

In other words, we're trapped.

The lasers get more precise. I see a soldier crouching across the roof get taken out with a blast to the face. The bolt liquefies flesh until gleaming skull is visible. Another takes a hit that burns *through* the metal itself, proving that these things really aren't any cover at all.

Moore sees it too. "Hold your fire!" he shouts to his remaining men. As soon as they stop, so do the green lasers. "What the holy fuck is this? I've never seen weaponry like that!"

Dutt looks over at me. "Looks like you didn't burn all of Carbini's toys in that warehouse."

If there was any question about our attacker's identity, it disappears a moment later when a voice booms out over a megaphone, "Send out da kid wit da Vessel, or I'm gonna wipe you Army dicks off da face of da earth."

"You know who that is?" Moore asks me.

I nod. "His name's Weldon di Latorio. Works for a guy named Carbini. They used to be mafia mooks. Now they're… something else."

"Colonel, these men are extremely dangerous," Dutt adds. "And, as you've already seen, they have access to some pretty advanced tech."

"I don't care if he's got a nuclear bomb pointed at my forehead, the United States Army does *not* surrender to street thugs."

The other soldiers are looking to Moore, waiting for orders. He gives them a complicated series of hand gestures. They ease out from cover and start forward, jumping between a/c units, three swinging left and three swinging right in an attempt to flank Weldon and whoever else is down there.

Something dark sails through the night on an arced trajectory, a black spheroid barely visible against the sky. The left trio of soldiers are just a few yards out when it comes down between two of them, striking their shoulders. I expect it to explode or pound them into paste, but instead it passes through them like mist.

And then it evaporates, along with every bit of flesh it touches.

One second the two men are whole and creeping along the roof, the next they're screaming and rolling on the ground as they clutch at missing limbs and exposed organs. Even with all the horror I've seen in the movies and written about over the last decade, my gorge still rises.

The weapons in Carbini's arsenal could revolutionize warfare overnight.

The other four soldiers fall back in a hurry. The green gunfire starts up again, and only two of them make it back to us.

~ ~ ~

Moore turns and slumps back against the metal, letting the Vessel slip from his fingers. His eyes jitter with crazed, manic energy. "God. Oh God. We…we can't make a stand against that kind of firepower."

Dutt grabs the man's shoulder. "Colonel, does anyone else know you're here?"

"Of course. General Rayburn and a handful of the top brass. They'll raise the alarm if I don't report in sometime in the next few minutes. But any reinforcements will be at least a half hour away. Local authorities should respond to the explosions long before then."

"That's not gonna help us any," I say.

Moore contemplates the burning helicopter for another long second. His gaze is steel when he turns it back on us. "You two have to get out of here with this thing."

"How?"

"There's a fire escape ladder on the far side of the helicopter that will get you back down to street level. Run, and keep running. We'll buy you all the time we can."

Dutt is already up and tugging at me. "C'mon!"

"No!" I try to pull free. I'm so tired of running. I just want to feel safe for five minutes. "Even if we get away… what then?"

Moore picks up the Vessel and forces it into my hands. "Once you're clear, get back in touch with Sergeant Lansing's CO! He'll know what to do!"

"Rudy, let's go!"

I give in and follow Dutt across the rooftop toward the burning helicopter.

~ ~ ~

A ladder is bolted to the roof right where Moore said. The flames have heated the metal, but not enough to burn our hands.

Behind us, gunfire starts up again as Dutt and I prepare to escape the roof. Déjà vu.

"Here, take this!" He hands me the pistol. At some point in our run, he picked up a machine gun from one of the dead soldiers that he slings over one shoulder by the strap.

I tuck the pistol back into my jeans and start down the ladder with the Vessel under one arm and Dutt coming after me. We run out of the parking lot and look back from the street.

The flames are still flickering up there, but the building doesn't seem to be catching. There are no sirens yet, but I figure Carbini probably gave the cops ample warning.

"The car's this way."

We run one more block and reach Hillman's ride panting. Just as I'm pulling out the keys, a new sound reaches us, a rumbling *whoosh* that's steadily getting louder. Dutt and I look around, seeking the source, and finally spot a shape soaring through the air toward us from the direction of the medical supply building roof.

Dutt squints into the night through his bent glasses. "What is that?"

I, on the other hand, don't have to strain to identify the blubbery mass flying directly at us.

"That would be Weldon on a jetpack."

He looks like a bloated sausage, hooked into some kind of harness, wires and pipes sticking out all over, the whole thing suspended by twin jets of roaring blue flame. Even with that much propulsion, I'm surprised the device can keep his fat ass in the air. The technology looks less *Rocketeer* and more *Ghostbusters*.

Dutt fires a quick burst from the M4. "Get in and drive!"

I do, tossing the Vessel on the seat beside me. Dutt hops in the passenger seat for the second time today and rolls down his window to continue firing. We're speeding down the street when there's a heavy *CRUNCH!* on the car roof above our heads. The metal buckles and caves in just before the blade of a glowing knife slices through the cloth interior right between the seats.

Dutt pops the magazine on his gun, finds it empty, and then tosses the whole weapon aside. As the knife starts cutting a neat slit in the roof, he tries to reach under me for the pistol tucked in my waistband.

Wind screams into the car. I look up from the road. Half the roof is torn away; Hillman's poor car is a convertible now. Weldon leers down through the hole he's made. "Heya, Rudy! Good ta see ya!"

I yank the wheel side-to-side, swerving all over, trying to throw him off. He clutches both sides of the frame and holds on for dear life, the rockets on his jetpack helping to stabilize him. The thing on his back looks like a junkyard of parts. Dutt finally gets the gun out of my pants and tries to aim it up, but Weldon belts him across the face, shattering the remains of his glasses.

Weldon squirms into the vehicle, straining to reach the Vessel. Dutt throws himself across it, wrestling with the man who's almost on top of us.

I'm trying to keep the car on the street as they fight next to me. One of the hoses on Weldon's jetpack is thrust in my face. I grab it and yank.

An alarm goes off somewhere in the mess of metal and circuits. The mobster blurts letters and then pulls back, grabbing the first thing he can lay hands on.

Dutt's arm.

My best friend is dragged through the roof of the vehicle and up into the air. I see his feet kicking, make a grab for them, and miss.

I slam the brakes. Snag the pistol and jump from the vehicle. Scan the night sky.

Nothing but inky black and cold, indifferent stars.

Dutt and Weldon are gone.

Hillman's car has a first aid kit in the glove box. There's a razor blade inside.

After driving a few more blocks back toward the motel, I pull over in a vacant lot, roll up my jeans leg, and slice into the meat of my calf where that little round wound is still barely visible.

The pain is…bad. Blood gushes everywhere. I manage to keep a steady hand while I force two fingers into the gash I created and dig around in the muscle of my leg.

I come out with a sliver of metal about an inch long, with a pulsing red light at one end. I throw it out the window and keep driving.

I'm sorry about your friend. Really, I am, dude. But please don't do this. I'm, like, begging *you.*

On the way back to the motel, I cross a bridge over a small mountain stream. I get out with the Vessel and stand at the guardrail with it sitting next to me while I stare into the black water.

I can be rid of it right now. All the awfulness it brought. It can be out of everyone's hands, lost forever, and then I can deal with whatever comes next.

Please, the Servant continues. He sounds desperate and earnest. *I don't wanna be in here anymore. Just let me out.*

"I'm projecting," I say. "You can't tell me anything that's not already in my head, so you're using my own thoughts against me. My own memories and emotions. If I believe—somewhere in the back of my head—that you're miserable in there, then you can put on this little act and use it to your advantage. You're a liar and a manipulator, just like…everyone else."

He's silent.

"Isn't that right?"

Not everyone in this world who needs your help has an angle, Rudes. Sometimes people are exactly what they seem. As for whether you're right…you'll never know if you don't take a chance.

But I'm tired of taking chances. All people do is let you down.

I snatch up the Vessel. I want to open it, I *do*, the same way I always do when I hold it, but it's false, just more manipulation I'm being fed. I hold it above my head, suspended over the babbling water.

And then I stop. This won't do any good, and it certainly won't bring Dutt back. As long as I'm still alive, I'll always feel its pull, always be able to lead someone back here if I'm tortured or threatened.

This is just another way to duck my responsibilities.

My phone rings.

I hold the Vessel and take out the prepaid mobile. The time is just rounding 1:30 AM as I answer the unknown number.

"You little shit," Carbini barks. "I am done cleaning up your messes!"

"*Me?* You're the one firing lasers and blowing up Army helicopters!"

"You've cost me a fortune in bribes alone, just to keep everyone in this city looking the other way!"

"Tell you what, I'll write you an IOU."

"You know kid, you're not so funny anymore. Shut the fuck up."

I say nothing.

"…you still there?"

"Yeah. You told me to shut the fuck up."

Carbini gives a frustrated snort. "I'm not chasing you anymore. You're going to bring the Vessel to me before sunrise. Know why?"

There's a pause and then Dutt shouts over the line, "Rudy, don't do it, just call my superiors and—!"

"You hear that Rudolph? *Do* you?"

I slump in defeat. "I hear it. Please don't hurt him."

"That all depends on you, kid. It'll take me a few hours to deal with this Army situation, so you get a short reprieve. But so help me *God*, if you and the Vessel don't stroll through the door of Slots of Luck by 7 AM, I'm going to take your friend here apart. A piece at a time. I'll keep some of his DNA just so I can clone him and start all over again. Then I'm coming after you and your wife next. Got me?"

"Got you."

"You can't get away, Rudolph. If I don't find you, the Filament *will*. And you're much better off dealing with me." The phone goes dead in my hand.

I limp through the door of the motel. Brynn sees the trail of blood my leg leaves and utters a short cry before scrambling off the bed.

"It's nothing," I tell her. "Get your stuff. You have to take the rest of the money and leave."

"What happened? Where's Dutt?"

"Things went wrong. Carbini has him. They're gonna kill him unless I bring the Vessel in a few hours."

"Oh Jesus."

"Listen to me."

"Rudy, I'm not going withou—"

"LISTEN TO ME!" I pick up her purse and throw it at her feet. "*I want you gone!* Get your shit and go! Don't tell me where! With the rest of the cash, you can survive on the run for a couple of months, at least! Once this dies down, turn yourself in to the cops and they'll tell you if you can go home!"

"Rudy, goddamn it, stop." She holds out her hands. "Let's think through this before we do something rash."

I force myself to take a breath. "I don't know what to do and I don't know what's gonna happen. I only know I can't protect you as long as you're here. You're still technically unconnected to all this. The only reason anyone would come after you is vengeance, and I think all the key players are a little too preoccupied to bother. If you walk away now, get as far from me as possible, maybe they'll leave you alone." I move forward, intending to hug her. "This is the only way to keep you safe."

There's a cough from the other room. Hillman stands hunched in the dark doorway, one arm wrapped around his injured side. I'd almost forgotten about him. "There's another way."

"Hillman, why don't you lay back down? I'm gonna take you to a hospital before I—"

"No." He points at Brynn with a shaking hand and says, "If you want to hear what I have to say, make her leave."

After Brynn takes her cigarettes and steps outside the motel room, Hillman emerges from the shadows. He's dressed again and still holding his side, but other than that, he looks utterly normal. Well, uninjured. I don't know if the guy could ever be described as 'normal.'

"I don't understand, how—?"

"You didn't think Carbini was the only one with miracles up his sleeve, did you? Like I said before, I just needed time to heal." He points. "I see you retrieved the Vessel. Thank god."

"Yeah, but it's going right back to Carbini in exchange for my friend."

Hillman licks his lips. "You can't do that."

"Convince me."

He doesn't speak for a long moment. "Do you trust me, Mr. Compton?"

"Not in the least."

"Put down the Vessel, and give me the Word. If you do, I will set this right."

"*How?* How will you set it right? You've got nothing, none of the resources you promised, and I'm guessing once your agency finds out what you've done, you'll be serving a long stint in the closest federal prison."

He shakes his head. "Aurora usually opts for more immediate solutions."

"Okay, so how do you propose to make all this better?"

"Let me show you. If you want, I will...I will contact my superiors and turn myself in. We can see what help they can give you, for real this time. I-I will do whatever you tell me to do. Just...give me the Word."

"Christ Hillman, I've known crack junkies that sound less desperate for a fix." I shift the Vessel in my arms. His gaze follows it like Minchi when I get out his bacon-flavored dog treats. For the first time it occurs to me that having the Word may not be what influenced poor Lennie Kincaid so much as the *knowledge of what this thing really is.* "It's not dangerous at all, is it?"

"I already told you it could be."

"Yeah, well so's a pillow if you swing it hard enough."

"We've been playing games for too long! This is bigger than you, and you can't surrender to Carbini, no matter what the cost!" He squeezes his arm tighter around his side, cradling his wound. "Give me the Word. Now."

"Sorry Agent Hillman, not gonna happen."

Then I realize he isn't cradling his wound so much as reaching inside his jacket. He takes out a pair of brass knuckles and slips them on. Too late I realize I left the gun in the car again.

"Fine. Let's do this the hard way."

He comes at me fast. I dodge back just as he takes his first swing. His metal-laden fingers glance off my cheekbone, the blow still hard enough to rattle my brains. By the time I recover, he's already coming around to sock me in the gut. Air explodes from my lungs as I drop the Vessel and stumble back, upending the bedside table and breaking the lamp. The Servant starts shouting the second contact is broken.

"Understand Mr. Compton, I fully intended to help you out of this mess before serving my own needs. But now you've made us enemies."

Hillman wades in. I piston out with both feet, catching him hard in the shin. His leg goes out from under him and he sprawls across me. We grapple in the glass shards, but he's strong for a wiry guy. Probably why he was able to last so long against Fiver. I manage to get in one good hit before he straddles me and goes to town on my face with the brass knuckles. My nose breaks yet again. The gash on my forehead opens up, along with several more. My teeth get loose in a hurry.

When he finally stops, he gasps, "You can give me the Word now, or I can beat it out of you. The next step is torture. And I am skilled in that."

"I don't have to be skilled to pull this trigger, asshole."

Brynn is in the doorway, with the pistol trained on Hillman.

He throws the brass knuckles at her.

She dodges aside, and he's across the room in a flash. He sweeps the weapon out of her hand, wraps an arm around her neck, and places the barrel against her temple.

"Or maybe we can start with her, since you'd seem to do any idiotic thing for those closest to you."

I struggle to sit up. Spit out a mouthful of blood. At some point while he was beating me senseless, I had another moment of clarity. I've been going in circles, like a rat in a cage, bouncing off the walls to try and find some hole, some weakness, some way out of this situation, and I keep ending up back here.

Maybe it's time I try the door that's been staring me in the face the whole time.

"You want the goddamn Word, Hillman?"

I lean over, snag the Vessel, and hold it in both hands.

"Here's your Word."

He realizes what I'm about to do. "No, wait! Stoooo—!"

Hoping that I'm not ending the world, I whisper, "Sedoc."

The world doesn't explode or implode or get eaten by a giant squid.

It does, however, grind to a halt.

Literally.

Hillman and Brynn are frozen in their awkward embrace. Statues. All the noise is sucked out of the universe and replaced with a cold vacuum of silence.

I keep holding out the Vessel until my arms get tired and then I realize there's another man sitting on the bed beside me. He's my age, blond hair in braids down to his shoulders, pleasant face, dressed like a surf bum in baggy shorts and a skintight neoprene t-shirt.

"'Sup, Rudes?" he says. "Name's Misery."

He holds out his hand to me on the floor.

"I'm your genie."

TWENTY FIVE

"I cannot—I mean, just *cannot!*—express in words how good it feels to be outta that gnarly pot! For a while there, I was totally afraid I was gonna have to start rooting for that Hillman asshole to get the job done, but you came through, Rudes! You grew a pair and you helped me out and I am not gonna forget that! I am the loyal type, through and through! I just…just… thank you for this, dude! Thank you *so fucking much!*"

After fifteen awkward seconds of me not shaking his hand, the Servant of *Sideris* jumps off the bed and stands with his arms held up in a 'Y' shape, stretching his lean, taut body while he jabbers. A six-pack ripples beneath the stretchy material of his shirt. He breathes deep with his eyes closed, performs a few squat thrusts, dances a little jig, and then, after his face lights up, he runs for the room's only window, throws open the curtains and stares up at the night sky. "Stars! Ha! Dude, I haven't seen stars in, like, two-thousand, three-hundred and forty-nine years! Bodacious…"

"Excuse me." I set the Vessel down and wave to get his attention from the floor, with a hand that flops bonelessly.

There's not an inch of my body that doesn't hurt from the beating I just took, and there's a slim chance I may still pass out. So, understandably, I'm not quite sure this is happening. "Did you say...*genie?*"

He pries himself away from the stargazing. "That is what you crazy kids call us nowadays, right dude? Last I remember, that old racial slur *djinn* was just catching on, but I'm pretty sure I translated correctly."

"Genie," I repeat slowly, tasting the word and testing for concussion all at the same time. "That means all this time, the Vessel was a lamp? And the Word was just....Open Sesame? Kazaam? Mecca lecca high, mecca hiney ho?"

He grins and plops back down on the corner of the bed. "You know dude, you're lucky my entire frame of reference on the modern world is based on what was in your head. Otherwise, there'd be nobody to get your little geek references."

I feel so woozy. I look away and catch sight of Brynn and Hillman still frozen in the motel room entry, her in a hostage chokehold, him caught in an angry shout. "What about them? Did you do that?"

"Guilty as charged."

"Are they...dead?"

"*Dead?* Dude, do they *look* dead? They're fine! You and I just stepped outta time for a sec, that's all. A little fourth-dimensional pause button. Figured we deserved a chance to get acquainted without someone waving a gun in our face, you know?"

I stare at him and blink.

"It's a lot to take in, Rudes, I know. C'mon, we'll talk after you get cleaned up. I knew you were hurting after the week you've had but...*damn*, you look like ass."

~ ~ ~

In the end, he has to help me stand, walk me to the bathroom, and then leaves to give me some privacy. I stand for a few minutes waiting to see if I'm going to black out while I study the now-unfamiliar terrain of my pulpy face in the mirror.

Hillman did a number. My skin is lumpy with bruises and swelling, the worst of which causes one side of my jaw to stick out about two inches farther than the other. My nose is wrecked. Several teeth feel cracked. I try to put all the weirdness in the other room out of my head as I splash water on my face to clean away the blood.

When I finally step out of the bathroom, the guy who calls himself Misery is zipping around the motel room with the curiosity of a two-year-old and the attention span of a hummingbird. He's punching buttons on the dark television, poking his head into the mini-fridge, and tugging at the cords that hang from the ceiling fan. "Dude, you humans have come a long way! I mean, I knew the world had changed just from being inside your head, but this is amazing!"

"You should try going to Wal-Mart sometime." I give him another second of flitting around the room. "So you're telling me…you actually grant wishes?"

He stops punching buttons on the TV remote and rolls baby-blue eyes at me. "Don't get me wrong Rudes, I'm thrilled just to, like, be talking to anyone that's not me, but do we *have* to cover this again?"

"Sorry. You just…you know…don't look like a genie."

"How many genies you met?" He shrugs and strikes a pose like he's balancing on a board, both arms straight out. "I picked up the look from Lennie Kincaid. He liked to surf, you know that? Something about the lifestyle totally appealed. That, and I loooove the ocean."

I walk over and retrieve Brynn's purse from the floor where I threw it, being careful not to look over at her and Hillman. They're really creeping me out. Behind them, through the open door, the night is still and silent. There's a car stopped in the lot with the headlights on, the driver caught in the middle of a turn into a parking space. It's like looking at a painting. Or a paused video.

"So is the whole world...?"

"Yep, pretty much. But it's all good dude, I promise. They won't know a thing."

Hurray for them. Me though, I'm suddenly suffocatingly claustrophobic and wishing the carousel would start spinning again.

I take a bottle of aspirin out of Brynn's purse and dry swallow five, then fill my shirttail with the ice cubes from the mini-fridge and hold it to my swelling face. I feel better, or at least, more conscious.

Misery watches me with a lop-sided, dopey grin. If you met him on the street, it wouldn't take much to convince you he was mentally challenged. But there is something charming about the guy.

"I just can't believe it," I say.

"Believe what, dude? Can't read your mind anymore. That connection was severed as soon as you *spaketh* the Word."

"I can't believe that all this has been about...well, *you*."

"That's because it hasn't."

"No?"

"No," he confirms. "All this has been about, like, an *idea*. A concept. Of what each person thinks I can do for them."

"Like what?"

"The three standards, dude." He counts them off on his fingers. "Riches, power, and the opposite sex. Some folks get creative, but it usually comes back to one of those things."

"Hillman claims you're dangerous. And the Candlemaker, he said…" I hesitate, not wanting to get struck down for saying the wrong thing. Who knows what he'll take offense to, or how he'll react if he does?

But Misery is already nodding his head. "Yeah, yeah, I trick people, turn them greedy, make them kill each other, blah blah blah. Basically I'm, like, the next best thing to the devil. That about the spiel?"

I nod, but I do it from across the room.

"BS, dude. Total BS. Think about it, if you get drunk and drive your car and get in an accident, do you, like, blame the car? Course not. The only greed I bring out in people was already there waaaay before they met me. Why do you think no one would just come out and tell you I was a genie?"

"The Candlemaker said just knowing the truth would corrupt me."

"Oh yeeeah, I'm sure you're totally *perverted* now, or whatever." He widens his eyes and waggles his hands as though shooting imaginary rays from his fingertips. "They were just afraid if you knew, you'd want me for yourself, and that would be more competition. Long as they had you believing I was pure, unadulterated, evil-in-a-bottle, you wouldn't be tempted to, like, take a little peeksie."

I mull that. "I guess…that does make sense."

"Damn right. You know, if you humans wanna fight each other over little ol' me, that's your problemo. I don't *wanna* do this, I didn't *ask* to be this, but I didn't get a choice. I just don't appreciate getting locked up in a toilet for it." His nostrils flare in disgust. "Those old windbags've had a smear campaign going against us genies since, like, the dawn of time."

"*Us?* There really are more of you?"

He lowers himself into a chair backward, rests his chin on the back, and cocks his dreadlocked head to the side as if in deep thought. "There were. I mean, our numbers were a little thin even before I got locked up for a couple millennia. Seeing as how everything you know on the subject was stored in your head under the 'Myths and Legends' category, I'm guessing they're not, like, an everyday occurrence." He lets out a sudden, loud guffaw. "Sorry man, I just remembered, I watched *Ali Baba Bunny* from your memory banks the other day. That Bugs is one crazy motherfucker!"

My head is bursting with questions, and I try to get him back on topic. "Okay, but I don't understand. The Candlemaker told me about these monks that put you in the Vessel for safekeeping, and how the Acolytes tried to keep you there. If everybody else wants you, why does *he* hate you so much?"

Misery comes back to the conversation with a shake of his mangy head. "Rudes...do you know what the single worst invention in all human history was?"

I shrug.

"Religion. I was around hundreds of thousands of years ago when it started, so trust me, dude. Soon as you humans started believing in a higher power, everything that made life worth living—or even just easier—was off limits. You people were totally no fun anymore." He pounds the fist of one hand into the palm of the other. "Guys like the Candlemaker are the same ones who tell you what movies to watch or which races to persecute or which sexes to marry. Or which plants you can set on fire and inhale. And they've been doing it forever. *His* people just happened to decide genies were evil, and I was the Antichrist."

"But surely they realized the good a genie could do in the right hands! End war…cure diseases…"

Misery is already waving my words away. "The Acolytes never saw it that way. They're all about a human destiny being earned. Besides…whose hands are the right hands? And how do you fight past all the wrong ones to get one of us to them?" A dark look crosses his boyish face. "I knew one of these dudes—probably the one that started the Acolytes in the first place—and trust me, they're all a bunch of hypocrites."

I sink down into a chair across from him, still holding the ice against my face. So much of the last week is making sense that I'm actually getting dizzy again. "Hillman said you were a potential weapon. I get it now." I don't express the image that comes into my head: Bin Laden with a genie on 9/11, instead of just some hijacked planes.

Misery sighs. "Look dude, we're only as dangerous as the person who's making the wishes. That's what's most fucked-up about the Candlemaker: he wants to blame other people's choices on us."

"You might wanna consider changing your name then. 'Misery' can't be doing a lot for your PR."

"Once again, that's aaaall you humans. Before you guys, we didn't even need names." He grins and grooves his chin up and down, as though to a beat only he can hear. "Let me tell you a story."

The 'story,' as it turns out, is actually more of a fully-immersive 3D movie. The real world of the motel (and I'm not even convinced that's necessarily 'real' anymore) dissolves away, leaving me sitting in the plastic motel chair in the midst of lush jungle where daylight barely filters through the canopy overhead. Misery never narrates, not out loud, but he doesn't need to. I watch events, understanding intuitively that eons are playing out in front of me, condensed into the span of seconds.

I see Misery's kind prancing through this jungle, the likes of which are probably as close to the garden of Eden as truth could ever come. They eat, they drink, they fuck, they take different forms, they live a life of leisure as only immortal beings can. I see the humans come, see them encounter these creatures, see them gradually begin to understand what they can do.

And then the genies are enslaved.

I see them captured. Stuffed in bottles and vases and jars by powerful magics. Stolen. Bought and sold. Used and abused. Countless wars fought in a thousand nameless deserts. The worst of humanity on display. I see wishes granted, for wealth, for health, for kingdoms, for women, for men, for the smiting of enemies, but nothing as altruistic or compassionate as what I just suggested. I see genies disappearing one at a time as humans find their various weaknesses, all of them immortal but not invincible, some killed for spite, some intentionally extinguished by the Order and other idealistic groups like them, some deciding that death was preferable to their current existence and just...giving up.

And as they become more rare, humanity starts forgetting about them.

I see Misery. He's dressed differently, more Aladdin-ish, but otherwise he looks the same. I see him hunted mercilessly. Captured by men wearing robes like the Acolytes. They think he's one of the last. I see the disagreement in the Order that the Candlemaker talked about, another bloody battle. The victors drag Misery in, kicking and screaming, and perform the ritual that seals him into the Vessel.

And then…darkness. Horrible, stifling, suffocating darkness. I'm in that little chamberpot with him, and there is no way out, no matter where I turn. The years pour on like water as I get to see what Misery endured, until I think I might go insane.

Then, a single beam of light pierces the pitch. Misery, caught in his hellish prison, drinks it in, uses it as a window to see out. Or more like a television, the signal wavering in and out just as I suspected. After getting a few image flashes, I understand this portal leads to the inside of Lennie Kincaid's head, the first person to carry the Word alone in almost two-thousand, five-hundred years.

Misery sucks all he can out of Kincaid's mind, gleaning knowledge about the modern world, learning English, while the Word begins pulling at him. With Kincaid, the temptation is so much easier, since he already knows about the Servant.

The rest of this story I know, so Misery fast-forwards.

The perspective shifts, and I understand that this part is something he was able to pick up from Kincaid. I see the Word spread throughout the long centuries, branching out fast to dilute its power, passed along from person to person for so long that most of them don't even know what it means anymore. Some of them treat it like a family heirloom. I see Carbini working to hunt them all down, across the world, with an army of paid assassins and clones, finally narrowing it down to one guy that Lennie kills after he takes possession of it. And, on the other side of things, I see the Vessel in some kind of temple on a high hillside, guarded by the warrior monks of the Order. An alarm is raised. A call to war. At first I think it's the Acolytes, their ancient enemies.

But at the base of this mountain, an army of Weldons and Fivers are on the march, stretching all the way to the horizon, armed with laser rifles and dissolving grenades, some of them hovering on homemade jetpacks.

The story ends. We're back in the motel room, sitting at the table while time stays frozen around us. I'm surprised to feel tears on my bruised cheeks.

"I'm sorry," I say. "What they did to you…that was awful."

He shrugs. "Now you know why I was begging you to let me out, dude."

"Then…I'm glad I could help."

He turns back to me and smiles. It's impossible not to like him.

"So now that I let you out…is this over?"

"Weeeell, not exactly. Now that the key is turned in the lock, the Word is kaput. But I'm still connected to the Vessel; that's a whole other thing. Whoever owns it, owns me."

The neurons in my brain begin to fire. Like I said, I'm a little slow on the uptake sometimes. "So since I have the Vessel…"

"You're pretty much my master." He hops out of the chair, places his palms together and gives me a curt bow. "I live to serve, dude."

"Wow. *Wow.* This is…" I'm having trouble wrapping my mind around the word *master*, and everything it implies. As in, I have control over this person. Except he's not really a person, he's…

"Holy shit, *you* can get me out of this!"

"Heh. Yeah…" Misery squirms, but I'm too excited to pay attention.

"I can…I can wish to have Dutt back! Oh man, I can wish for

the cops to not be after me anymore! Wait a minute. Can you… bring dead people back to life? Luiz and Josh and Officer Reed?”

"Well, *technically*, yes…"

"God, I can wish for *anything!*" My mind is rolling through a mental list that extends far beyond just my present predicament: a bank account full of cash, a body made of granite, a writing career that's actually going somewhere, and underneath all of that, a petty, cruel part of me is thinking, *If you make these changes, she'll love you.*

And if she doesn't…you'll just wish for her to.

"Rudes…"

"But Hillman's right though, we have to keep you away from Carbini, it's just too dangerous. Wait, what am I thinking, we can just wish Carbini to go to jail…"

"Rudes…dude…"

"Okay, I know, I know, I'm getting ahead of myself. How does it work, do I just rub the Vessel or say 'I wish,' or what? And how specific do I have to be in my wording? I don't wanna wish for money and get a sock full of pennies."

"Rudy, can we chill for just another minute before you get all wish-happy?"

I hear his anxiety for the first time and realize I'm doing what every other human being has ever done to him, falling into the exact trap that Hillman and Carbini and the Candlemaker were afraid I would.

I'm suddenly disgusted by the raw greed consuming me.

This isn't me.

It can't be.

"I'm sorry. You probably want me to wish for you to be free, right? I will, I promise, just help me first and…"

I trail at the smirk on his face. "Don't be gay, dude. I'm a Servant of *Sideris*; that'll never change. It's what I was created for. Don't feel bad though; it's not such a bad life, really. 'Specially when you get that rare master who treats you like royalty."

"Then what...? *Oooooooh*. There's a limit, right? What is it, three wishes? I can work with that."

"Nope, you could wish all day, every day, for the rest of your life, and I would have to grant them...if I could."

A cold disappointment settles in the pit of my stomach, the same feeling you get when you realize you have to order fifteen more CD's at outrageous price to get the five free ones. "What do you mean, 'if you could?'"

Misery smiles sheepishly and twirls one of the narrow blond braids hanging from his scalp.

"I can only grant selfless wishes."

Chapter TWENTY SIX

"What do you want me to tell you, dude? Different genies grant different types of wishes. Some of them only deal with money. Some of them can only touch matters of the heart. Like, there was this one that could only grant wishes for *colon cleansing*. He...he didn't get a lotta traffic. But if you look at it from the bigger perspective, my limits are actually waaaay more open than most of the others!"

"But you said before!" I'm almost screaming as I pace back and forth through the motel. The blood pounding through my veins makes my swollen face throb. I let go of the tail of my shirt, spilling ice across the floor. "You said you give people money and power!"

"No way, I said that what's people *think* I can give them." Misery shrugs. "It's like...a natural law. Some kind of structure and order has gotta be imposed, or some douchebag would've wished the earth into oblivion ages ago."

"Yeah, but *selfless wishes*? What the hell good is a genie that only grants selfless wishes?"

"It was good enough a minute ago when you were all

about saving the world." Misery gives me a glance I don't really care for. "But I guess that totally takes a backseat to getting Rudy Compton out of a jam, huh?"

I ignore that, mostly because it makes me feel guilty. "Okay, maybe this isn't as bad I'm thinking. What even qualifies as a 'selfless wish'?"

He answers as though reciting from a textbook. "The wisher—that's you, dude—may not have even the smallest interest or anything to gain, tangible, accountable or otherwise, from any wish made or any action or consequence that comes about as a result of any wish made, unless said action or consequence was truthfully and honestly not part of the wisher's intent in the first place."

I point at the Brynn and Hillman statues. "So what if I make a wish for her to be saved from him? Maybe just to disappear and reappear back home. Or even just a block away. That's selfless, right? Can you do that?"

"Do *you* want that to happen?"

"Huh?"

"Do you want it to happen? In other words, would it make you feel better knowing she was safe? Bring you peace of mind?"

I see what he's getting at. "I...but...that's not fair!"

He grins sadly and closes his eyes. This argument is old hat for him, which only frustrates me more. "Sorry bud, deal with it. Those're the rules. Has to be completely selfless."

"So I could wish for everyone in the world to never go hungry?"

"Only if you weren't gonna, like, take any joy or self-satisfaction or pride from the end result. And if you were the kinda person who *wouldn't*, then you probably wouldn't make that kind of wish in the first place. Get me?"

"But...but...what if..."

"Rudes, a selfless wish is all about *intent*. You can't argue your case or try to hide your true motivation. The magic *knows*. If there's even a remotely selfish thought anywhere in your head, the wish just won't happen. That's why I've only been able to grant three, and they were all pretty much the same."

"Three wishes? In *hundreds of thousands of years*? What were they, for Christ's sake?"

He shakes his head. "That's kind of a violation of privacy, dude. Like a confessional priest."

"Fuck!" I feel like a kid who's just been given a puppy and then had it taken away. "So you can't do anything for me without one of these selfless wishes?"

"Nope. Otherwise I'd help you if I could, Rudes. I swear."

"What about all the super strength?"

"I told you, that was the Word defending itself. It's pure, raw power. Or at least, it was."

"Well, you didn't have any problem *stopping time*, now did you?"

"All right, I shoulda been more specific, don't have a heart attack. I can't use any magic on behalf of a human or that interferes with human affairs in any way unless it's through a wish. This was, like, a one time thing just to answer some of your questions. I thought you'd appreciate it since you've been everyone's whipping boy since this started. Like I said, when I set things back in motion, you're going right back where you were."

"Great. Just fucking great. What you're really telling me is that all of this—all the pain, bloodshed, and death—was essentially for nothing. You're useless." I throw my hands up. I want to yell and scream and throw a tantrum, but it wouldn't do any good. This isn't his fault. "Do they even know? The Dark Filament and Hillman and everybody else that's after you?"

"Carbini does. I know that much from sharing headspace with Lennie Kincaid. Which means the Filament does too. They just don't care."

"But *why?* If you can't do anything for them, then what's the point?"

"Everyone thinks they can find a way around the whole 'selfless' thing. A loophole. That if they word it just right, I can grant them their wish."

I can't argue with that. As ashamed as I am to admit, there's a linguistic computer running in the back of my head, one that's trying to figure out the perfect combination of syllables to make my selfish needs sound anything but.

He swallows and rolls his muscular shoulders. "I'm gonna be honest with you, Rudes…you don't wanna tangle with the Filament. If I'm the hot potato, then you totally don't wanna be the one holding me when they get to town."

He's got my attention again. "You know who they are?"

"I know about as much as anybody knows, which is just rumors. They've been around a looong time, and they're bad news. Cross-dimensional beings. *Mucho mysterioso.*"

"Cross-*dimensional?*"

"Existence is a big place, Rudes," he says, his voice grave, "and they're from a very dark corner of it. They've been trying to get their hands on a live genie for ages; that's part of the reason the Order started hunting us down. If the Filament's sending who I think they're sending to pick me up… well, these guys are the closest thing the universe has to demons. Like, I don't know what they want me for, but it can't be good. Hillman was right about that."

"Jesus." I bow my head. "This just gets worse."

Misery comes over and grabs my shoulders, forces me to look at him. "I like you, Rudes. Like I said, I'm grateful for what you did. So my advice is, get as far from me as possible. When the Filament gets here and finds out Carbini doesn't have the Vessel, they're going after whoever does first, and whoever messed with them second. So let Hillman take me and you get a running start out of town."

"What about Dutt? Not to mention the rest of the world if the Filament actually finds a way to use you?"

He lets go and holds up a palm. "Gotta say, dude…not really your problem. You can't take these guys on. You and your senorita over there…well, I can't say I think all that much of her from the bits I got outta your brain, but I know you love her. So just take her and walk away."

I think about that. Think about leaving Dutt to whatever Carbini has in store for him. Surrendering Misery—who I think I might like—to Hillman or the Filament.

"I can't."

"Figured you'd say that." He puffs one cheek up with air and swishes it back and forth. "One more thing you oughta know, Rudes: I told you all this stuff because I like you, but there's no rule that I have to. I'm required to grant legitimate wishes, but nothing, like, *forces* me to be loyal to my master. You see?"

"Uhhh, not really. Why does that matter?"

Misery looks over my shoulder at the two statues in the doorway. "Because I totally have an idea on how to deal with your first problem."

~ ~ ~

"—oooop!"

Hillman finally finishes the command he's been caught in the middle of all this time. Brynn struggles in his arms. I'm relieved just to see her moving again.

He blinks at me, sitting on the floor where he left me, holding up the Vessel. I'm back in the same spot I was before my tête-à-tête with Misery, same position, same aches and pains, but at least I'm prepared for it this time.

I try to see it from his point of view. There's suddenly a beach bum standing in the middle of the room, perched on the table. Hillman pulls the gun away from Brynn's head and waves it at Misery. "Who is *that?*"

Misery gives a resigned sigh. "This is always my least favorite part, dude."

"You know exactly who he is," I answer Hillman. "He's what you've been after this whole time."

Hillman's eyes nearly bug out of his skull as he takes in Misery anew. Then he seems to think better and presses the barrel of the gun back against Brynn's temple, hard enough to make her grunt in pain. His forearm is almost choking her. "Mr. Compton, if I so much as hear anything that *sounds* like the word 'wish' come out of your mouth, she'll be dead before you can finish the sentence."

"Relax, Hillman," I say. "We can make a deal. Besides, what good would it do to kill her? Couldn't I just wish her right back to life?"

The look of confusion on his face is almost comical. He aims the gun back at me. "Fine, I'll shoot *you!*"

"Dude...what a brainiac this guy is," Misery mutters.

I hike a thumb at the genie. "He's useless. Can't really

grant wishes. Only selfless bullshit.”

“Rudes, what are you doing, don’t tell *him* that!”

Hillman shakes his head firmly. “No, that creature is useless to feeble, small-minded individuals like yourself, Mr. Compton. I’m confident I can find a way to make it work.”

“So you knew this whole time. You knew and you still went through all this. God, that’s pathetic.”

“We’ll see. Give me the Word.”

“The Vessel is officially unlocked. You don’t need me or the Word anymore.”

Hillman addresses Misery directly for the first time. “Is that true?”

“Totally. But I don’t know why Rudes is spilling it. I thought we had a plan!”

“I can tell you exactly why.” Hillman gives Brynn a jerk. “He’s blinded by love for this woman.” Her face turns blue as she scrabbles at his arm.

“Okay, stop!” I tell Misery, “Get back in the Vessel.”

“Fine. Nice knowing you, Rudes.”

Misery snaps his fingers and pops out of existence. I roll the Vessel across the floor, where it stops in front of Hillman. “There. Take the goddamn thing and let her go.”

He stands where he is, gaze flicking from the Vessel to me, looking for the trick. “The car keys also.”

I toss them over. He releases Brynn, who backhands him across the face before running over to my side. Hillman puts the hand holding the gun against his split lip and scoops up the Vessel.

He gives the rusted pot under his arm a squeeze. “I didn’t want it to be this way, Mr. Compton.”

“I don’t think you ever cared which way it was.”

Neither of us speaks as he slams the door and flees the

motel, taking with him the only chance I have at getting back my best friend.

"Rudy, what the hell is going on? Who was that guy with the dreadlocks and how did he just appear like that?"

Brynn tries to help me up but I don't need it. I head for the bathroom without answering her.

"Where are you going?"

She follows, still asking questions as I do a much quicker job of cleaning myself up a second time. I ignore her. My ring is still on the counter where I slapped it earlier. I grab it and the rest of the pocket contents from the other jeans and transfer them to this pair of pants.

"What just happened?" She blocks the door of the bathroom. "Answer me. What was all that about granting wishes?"

"That guy with the dreadlocks is what everyone's been after. The one who's been talking to me from inside the Vessel."

"But I don't under—?"

I push past her. "We don't have time for an explanation. Just trust me, he's a genie named Misery, and he grants wishes."

Brynn's face lights up as the same realizations hit her. "A genie? A real live genie? And you gave him to *that* asshole?"

"Only to get you out of harm's way. Don't worry, Misery and I have a plan."

I pull open the motel door and step outside, with her right behind me. I realize I don't even have a vehicle anymore, since Hillman took his.

But that really doesn't matter, considering there are five Acolytes standing in the breezeway, in full hooded regalia.

"The Candlemaker requests your presence." The one in the lead drifts a finger across us. "*Both* of you."

~ ~ ~

In school, I was always a back-of-the-bus kind of kid. I headed for the rear seats as soon as I stepped on. It just felt safer with no one at your back, where they could sneak up and pour something on you, or rifle through your backpack, or stick a slimy finger in your ear.

Funny how now, I have just the opposite feeling.

Brynn and I huddle together on the bench closest to the emergency door, which is welded shut. The interior of the rickety, unpainted school bus smells like a sweaty tin can. The few rows immediately in front of us are empty, but the rest are filled with Acolytes, most of them turned around to kneel in their seats and stare at us from under their hoods. Some of them sway back and forth as they chant.

Brynn and I slouch so we can talk without them hearing. I take the opportunity to tell her the entire story.

"This is just getting too weird," she whispers.

"Try living with it in your head for a week, then talk to me about weird."

"If he's really a genie, then we have to get him back! We can't let Hillman get away with him!"

"I know. He's the only chance we have of saving Dutt."

"Nonononono!" She grabs hold of my arm. "I mean, yes, by all means, let's try to save Dutt or whatever, but Rudy, we can't give him away, we have to keep him! Oh my god, think of everything he could do for us! He could change our lives!"

"Did you not hear a thing I just said?" No, of course she did; she heard exactly what she wanted to hear and was deaf to the rest. Just like everyone else. "He's no good to us, he's no good to anyone!"

"But...maybe we can figure out a way, maybe we can—!"

"No." The desperation in her voice makes me sick. "We trade him for Dutt, then get ourselves out of town, and that's that. *If* we get the chance, of course." I nod towards the front of the bus and the collection of eyes on us. Their chanting is a mindless drone.

"Where are they taking us?"

"I have no idea." The windows of the bus are grimy, but I can see enough to know there are no buildings anywhere around us. I see nothing but a gently sloping grass field, and more mountains in the distance. Seems like we went north, maybe even outside the city. Judging by the bouncing of the shocks under us, I don't think we're on paved roads anymore. "If I can just talk to the Candlemaker, maybe I can make him understand that Misery is no danger."

"How?"

My tongue flaps as I try to answer that. Somehow, I don't think the religious zealot that wiped out an entire grocery store full of people is going to see the light of reason.

"Just let me do the talking."

She lays her head against my shoulder. "All right. I trust you."

Just then, there's the squall of brakes as the decrepit bus ratchets to a stop. The doors beside the driver open, and two Acolytes come back to escort us down the aisle and off the bus. I step out onto an uneven dirt road and check out the new scenery.

We're in a cemetery.

It's early morning, probably sometime around 4 AM, but there's enough moonlight to see the somber rows of tombstones and several large mausoleums. It's colder out now than when I went to find Dutt a few hours ago. Probably because we're at higher elevation. The lights of Reno twinkle off to the right below us.

They herd us along, into the graveyard. Brynn stays close, shivering. We stumble through patches of tall grass and around knee-high tombstones until we reach the brick wall of a mausoleum.

I turn to face the one that's been prodding me in the kidney. "What now, kemosabe?"

He says something foreign filled with harsh consonants and steps past me. Where a few seconds ago there was blank brick is now a wide iron door with ornate, base relief etchings of winged angels. The Acolyte pulls it open to reveal a dark maw and shoves us inside. As we cross the threshold, there's the distinct sucking of a sudden pressure drop in my ears.

"What was that?" Brynn asks.

"I get the feeling we're not in Reno anymore, Toto."

"Get moving," the Acolyte growls.

Beyond the door is a stone staircase lined with lit torches. Very old-world, skull-and-crossbones, Anne-Rice-dungeon kind of feel. The temperature must be 30 degrees warmer. We're ushered down an endless series of tiers to a dim corridor, which deadends at a set of thick wooden doors bearing wrought iron crosses. The Acolytes heave them open without knocking and push us through.

The interior of this room looks like the set of a class from a Harry Potter movie. Huge Gothic architecture stretching out and above, made of black stone, everything drab and dreary and dim. The only lighting comes from thousands upon thousands of candles of all shapes and sizes in tall candelabra, lining the walls and floor, and dangling from metal chandeliers suspended over our heads. Rows of empty pews lead to an upraised portion on the far side of the room, like a stage, where there's a stone dais with a bubbling, fireless cauldron beside it. Beyond that is a throne constructed of two intersecting slabs of granite. The grand seat is vacant and steeped in shadows.

As we're forced ahead, I feel like a defendant on his way to the front of the courtroom. Or an altar boy getting ready for communion at the church of Satan. Just to further the image, we're brought on stage, positioned in front of the dais and then something that feels like a caning rod smashes across my calves, bringing me to my knees. Brynn cries out and does the same beside me. I catch her as she falls.

"I gave you a chance, boy...and you wasted it."

The leathery words come from in front of us. From the granite throne. The seat I at first took to be empty is actually occupied by a form pressed far back in the shadows, where the flickering light in this room can't reach. Then it begins to lean forward, and I get my first look at the Candlemaker.

Chapter TWENTY SEVEN

He's even more ancient than his voice suggests.

His form is withered, swallowed in the folds of an ornate, hooded robe made of purple velvet, but his hands look like bones wrapped in flesh-colored tissue paper as they pull him to the front of his chair. The hood is just shallow enough to reveal the lower half of a sandpapery face, framed by limp strands of long, gray hair. He reminds me of one of the old EC Horror Comics mascots; the Vault Keeper maybe, little more than a walking, talking corpse.

Brynn grabs my hand and squeezes.

"I was generous, I believe," the Candlemaker grumbles, more to himself than to us. His timbre is so gravelly, you would never believe it could belong to anything still living. "But you young people today…so caught up in this life, you never stop to consider what comes *after*."

"It's not my fault," I say from my kneeling position behind the altar. I try to stand, but the Acolytes standing over us force me back down. "I was coming to you, I swear, I—"

"Responsibility," he interrupts, his narrow chin waggling, "is one of the few attributes that sets us apart—and above—the rest of God's creatures. You should learn to take some for your own actions."

"I know. I do. I just want to explain. We can still solve this, we can still work something out."

"How is it *we* will do anything, boy?" He slides forward to the edge of his chair, until his slippered feet can touch the ground. It's like watching that old Lily Tomlin bit, where she pretended to be a little girl by using gigantic furniture. "In order for the two of us to reach a solution, *you* must have something to offer. And you forfeited such a position when you chose to unlock that accursed prison and release the atrocity within."

Something in my chest sinks. "You know about that?"

"There is little concerning that Vessel of which I am unaware. It has been the sole focus of my entire life. My power is not what it once was, and what I have left is devoted to constant monitoring. That is the only reason you were able to elude my Acolytes for so long." His skeletal fingers curl into hooks. "Do you honestly believe I would have risked bringing you into my presence if there was even a *chance* you could still infect me?"

"Okay, yes, I opened it, but only because—"

"Excuses, excuses, so many excuses. I care not a whit for the cause, boy, only the effect. As I said, now that you have opened the Vessel, you eliminate yourself from the equation. The Word is useless. *You* are useless. There is no bargaining to be had, only...reprisals."

My skin chills at the sound of that. "Okay, okay, I get that, I deserve whatever you wanna do to me." I put my arm around Brynn. "But she doesn't. She doesn't have anything to do with this and she never has. Just let her go."

"Rudy, I won't leave without you," she says.

"Yes, you will."

"I *won't*."

"Shut up Brynn, now is not the time."

"Don't tell me to shut up, this is—!"

The Candlemaker slaps a palm down on the arm of his throne with surprising force. "I will be the one deciding who stays and who goes, children."

I grit my teeth. "Goddamn it, would you just—!"

"*BLASPHEMER!*" he screeches, flying up from his seat in a flap of purple and gold cloth. His back is hunched, but even upright he couldn't be any more than five-feet tall and weigh maybe 80 pounds. But I'm terrified of him. "Do not sully my temple with such a wretched tongue!"

I feel my old, reliable temper flare, which means my 'wretched tongue' is right behind it. "You call this a temple? I got news for you pal, you're living in a dank, dark hole in the ground because you wasted your life on this crusade of yours! Misery's no threat to you or anybody else!"

He chuckles. The sound is raspy and horrid. "So you learned the beast's name. Fitting, is it not?"

"He says that's our fault."

"Yes, I'm sure he does. I'm sure there's so much he would like to blame on us. And it sounds as though you have become acquainted with him quite well in such a short amount of time. You spout his doctrine as though it were your own."

"I'm not 'spouting any doctrine.' I'm just trying to make you understand, you've been chasing after him all this time without really understanding what he is."

He shakes a fist at the arched ceiling above us. "I know perfectly well what he is. He's the last of an accursed race that Satan himself sent to destroy us. His kind has been inciting wars and murder and hatred and greed for as long as we've shared the earth with them."

"That's…incredibly narrow-minded."

"Is it? Look at what he's done to you, boy, in the two weeks since you were infected. Your life is in ruins, you flee from the authorities, everyone you know is dead, and you yourself look beaten within an inch of the same."

"Hey, my life was already in ruins, but you bastards did the rest!" I exclaim, remembering everything Misery said about this guy. "You and Hillman and Carbini, all falling over one another to get your hands on the Word and the Vessel and not giving a shit who you steamroll in the process! Misery's just as much a victim as I am."

He stands silent, eyes hidden by the hood, perhaps contemplating my latest blasphemes. "You protect him," he finally says, a note of wonder in his decrepit voice. "You feel some sort of kinship with the beast. You see how he persuades you, tricks your mind?"

"No, I just happen to think he's a nice guy." I laugh, but it just sounds like I'm gargling broken glass. "What do you even know about him, except what the guy who had this job before told you? You people have just been blindly passing this vendetta down through the years!"

"Oh, have we?" A trace of coyness to the question.

"Yeah! But I've met him, and he's a genie that only grants selfless wishes!"

"Even if that were true, isn't that bad enough?"

"No, it's not! Think of all the good he could do! You said yourself the only reason the Order locked him up instead of killing him was because they thought he could save the world!"

"The world needs to be saved *from* the likes of him, not by him!" The Candlemaker starts over to us across the stage. "Let me turn your question back on you, boy: what do you know, besides what lies the beast has told you? If he is so harmless, then why does the Dark Filament come to claim him even now?"

I falter, and think about my brief time as master of Misery, the beach bum genie. The Candlemaker has a point: I don't know anything about the guy, not for sure. Yeah, he seemed sincere, and I assumed once he was out of the Vessel he wouldn't have any reason to lie, but how can I know?

Why am I so eager to trust everyone after I'm repeatedly stepped on?

"I see doubt in your eyes," the Candlemaker continues. "Good. Then you are not completely lost. Get him up."

Hands yank me back to my feet. Brynn tries to clutch at me but she's shoved away. The Acolytes bend me over the altar top as the Candlemaker comes forward and thrusts his weathered face into my view.

"Where is the Vessel?" His eyes glitter under the hood with a mad sheen, and I feel all the fight and smart-ass comments drain right out of me.

"I-I don't know. It was taken from me. But I know where it's going to be. I can get it back."

"Tell me."

I manage to turn my head enough in the grip of the Acolytes to see Brynn on the floor.

"Let her go and I will."

The Candlemaker steps back. "I will do better than that. I will prove my mercy knows no bounds. By giving you another chance to redeem yourself."

He nods at his followers.

I'm lifted away from the altar and dragged backward.

"I am tired of throwing my precious few Acolytes away to chase this monster. If you agree to retrieve the Vessel and bring it to me, I will allow both of you to walk out of here right now."

"I'll do it," I say immediately, marveling how someone with that much power can be so stupid. Must be Alzheimer's. "So we can go?"

"Of course."

He grins for the first time, revealing stained incisors in shriveled, black gums.

"As soon as I have some insurance."

The other Acolytes swarm around Brynn, pick her up, and carry her toward the table.

"*Ruuudyyy!*" She screams my name as they lay her across the altar. "Help me!"

"Hey, what are you doing, let her go!" I struggle, but my arms are pinned behind me.

The Candlemaker waves one of his crone claws across the air. "After the respect you paid my last offer, I would be foolish not to impose some measure of control. And your love of this woman seems the best way to impress upon you."

"I'll get the Vessel, you don't have to do this!"

"Oh, but I do."

He shuffles toward the bubbling cauldron next to the stone altar. "Do you know why I am called Candlemaker, boy?"

"Because 'butcher' and 'baker' didn't really fit your decorating scheme?"

He bends over the steam coming from the big pot and breathes deep. "Mankind has been making candles since 3,000 BC, out of just about anything you could imagine. Paraffin, beeswax...even some types of fish."

He reaches into the cauldron and pulls out a dipper of

what looks like molten wax. Considering there's no fire under the cauldron, I have no idea how he keeps it warm. One of the Acolytes hands him a hollow metal tube, open at one end and a hinge at the other. With a steady hand, the Candlemaker pours the wax into the tube.

"That was the Order's original function, long ago, before they started hunting *djinn*. It was how my ancestors made their living."

From the depths of his robe comes a curved dagger. My heart seizes. But he only extends his little finger and draws the blade across it, splitting his papery skin and drawing a trickle of blood. He mutters something foreign and guttural.

"Candles were used for light and time-keeping and religious ceremonies, but they were also useful in harnessing the magics that once filled this world. The molding agent can be infused with any number of incantations and the flame—when it's the *right* flame—can be a wonderful catalyst. The fires you see in this room were all lit from one utterly pure flame, and they've been continuously burning, candle-to-candle, for more than four-thousand years."

The Candlemaker holds his bleeding finger over the metal tube and lets a generous dribble fall inside. He gives this a shake, like he's stirring sediment in a fine wine, then hands it back to the Acolyte, who dangles a long wick into the tube and blows across the top. The whole deft, professional operation has taken about twenty seconds.

"When the Order split, my predecessors devoted themselves to keeping this craft alive. And now...you will see how powerful a candle can still be."

The Acolyte splits the tube lengthwise, opening the hinge on the bottom. Inside is a perfectly formed candle, ashy gray in color, with swirls of blood red throughout. It reminds me of the surface of Jupiter. The Candlemaker peels it out and approaches Brynn.

I fight. Shout. My arms are wrenched back until they're close to breaking. Brynn tries to kick and scream while the Candlemaker stands over her. Her jaw is pried open and the bottom of the tube is inserted into her mouth until she's almost choking. One of the others brings a lit candle from the edge of the room and gives it to the Candlemaker.

"Please," I beg him. "Whatever you're doing...don't."

Without so much as a glance up, he lights the tip of the candle in my wife's mouth.

The wick burns fast, sputtering down through the candle like a firecracker fuse. The wax melts and runs all over her face in reddish brown rivers. She's gagging and crying. When it gets down to her lips, the Candlemaker snatches away the stub.

In the same second, both of us are released. I run to her, help her sit up. She sobs as she clings to me, coughing up flecks of dried wax and trying to wipe the hot residue out of her eyes.

I look up at the man responsible. "You bastard."

No mercy in the Candlemaker's hard eyes, no matter what he says. "In one hour, she will be sick; in two, she'll be unconscious. Three will find her in a coma, and in exactly four hours, she will be dead."

"No," I whisper.

"Yes. You say you know where the Vessel is? Then bring it and your woman back to me and I will lift the curse. Until then...we have nothing more to say to one another."

The Candlemaker turns and glides toward the only other door at the back of the stage, his long purple robe dragging along the floor at his heels.

~ ~ ~

The Acolytes drive us back to the motel and dump us in front of our room. One of them hands me a slip of paper as we walk off the bus, Brynn leaning against me.

"What's this?"

"Directions back to the cemetery."

"Gee, aren't you guys all kinds of helpful?"

The Acolyte puts a hand on the back of my neck and squeezes painfully. "Don't waste time trying to get her help. No force on heaven or earth can save her. If you truly know where the Vessel is, go and get it. If you lied to the Candlemaker..." The hand on my neck clamps until it forces tears from my eyes. "Then you better find her a casket, and then one for yourself."

They shove us off the bus. It rumbles away. We get halfway across the parking lot to the door of the room when Brynn's legs fold. I catch her before she hits the pavement.

"I...I don't f-feel so good."

"Let's get you in."

I scoop her up and head into the motel. The place is still a mess from my fight with Hillman. I crunch through broken glass to put her on the bed.

She looks up at me, eyes wide and wet. "Rudy...it hurts. My stomach. Everything feels like it's on fire..."

I feel her forehead. It isn't even warm. Whatever's wrong with her is far beyond medical science. I bend over her until our noses are nearly touching and brush the short bangs away from her eyes.

"I'm scared," she whispers.

"It'll be okay. I promise. I-I'm gonna find Misery and the Vessel, and everything will be all right."

"D-don't do anything stupid."

"But I'm so good at it."

Her lips pull into a thin smile that disappears a heartbeat later. "I don't wanna die."

"You're *not* gonna die." I reach in my pocket. Pull out the ring. Slip it back on my finger. "See, look? I love you Brynn, God, I love you so much, and I'm so sorry for everything, we can make this work, I know we can, I..."

She's limp, unconscious on the bed. I give her a kiss. Her lips are cold.

I lay my head against my wife's stomach and cry.

Brynn is terrified of manatees.

You know the things I mean? Big, gray, bloated-looking walruses that hang out in rivers and shallow, marshy coastal areas in the southern hemisphere, eating plants all day. I never understood it. They've been known to harm exactly zero humans around the world each year and are some of the friendliest and most curious creatures on the face of the planet. They're nicknamed 'sea cows,' for God's sake.

We went to an aquarium in Dallas once. There was an exhibit on sharks I really wanted to see for a short story I was working on. The path through the place leads you down through this room that's below the level of the manatee tank. One whole wall is made of glass, and these gentle, majestic creatures hang over you and swim around.

Brynn locked up. Wouldn't even go in the room. On the other side were the sharks I had come to see, but she was so freaked out by these floating slugs she insisted we turn around, retrace our steps to the front, and go home. What could I do except agree?

She took one look at my disappointed face, grabbed my hand, and ran through the manatee room with her eyes closed, dragging me behind her, while a bunch of other tourists stared.

That was the moment I realized just how much I loved her, when she proved she was willing to go to any lengths to keep me from being hurt.

Now…I've got to do the same thing for her.

I find the digital clock in the rubble of the bedside table. It's almost five in the morning. The Candlemaker cast his spell…what, forty-five minutes ago? That means I have until around 8 AM to put the Vessel in his hands, or Brynn dies.

And of course, if I don't put it in Carbini's hands an hour before that, Dutt dies.

All I know is…it's time to stop fucking around.

I call a cab, give it ten minutes to get there, then turn off the lights and lock up the room as I walk out, leaving my wife on the bed like Sleeping Beauty waiting for her prince.

Chapter TWENTY EIGHT

The cab driver's name is Pascale. I climb in the back and he asks me which casino I want to go to. That's probably where most people are going this time of morning.

"You know this area very well?" I ask him.

"Been drivin cabs in the city for eighteen years."

"Okay, this is gonna sound weird, but are there any swimming pools around?"

"Yeah, your motel's got one. Freeze your dick off, I bet."

"Probably has to be indoors."

"A few of the casinos got 'em, but you gotta be a guest."

"No, someplace close by. Closest place you can think of."

He looks me up and down over the seat, scrutinizing my face—too lumpy and bruised to be recognizable as Reno's Most Wanted anymore—and then squinting at my clothes, which are less than swimming appropriate. "There's a fitness center four blocks up, but it don't open till 10 or somethin like that."

"Perfect. Take me there."

Pascale sighs and shakes his head as he puts the cab in gear. I hear him mutter, "Takes all kinds."

He drives. I doze, and try not to think about what I'll do if Misery lied to me. Or if I was just plain wrong. Our idea was a gamble, but it was the best we could do. When Pascale finally shouts at me to get up, we're parked in front of a red brick building called T's Gym. The sign boasts a heated indoor pool.

But, more importantly, a bashed up Ford sedan with a missing roof is parked in front.

I slip Pascale bills, with an extra $20 included if he forgets he dropped me here.

"All right, but if I hear 'bout this place gettin robbin or somethin, I'm goin straight to the cops. I don't need to get caught up in no investigation."

I promise not to rob the place and get out of the cab.

Just like at the medical supply depot where Dutt and I met Colonel Moore, the lock on the front door of the gym is busted. I walk right in.

The place is dead silent, so the voices on the other side of the building echo a long way. I follow them through a few workout rooms to a door marked 'Pool' and put my ear against the metal. I can hear Misery's voice saying something about 'just a little longer dude...yeah, keep it up...it's really working now...' I try to slip in quietly, but the hinges squall so I just jerk the thing open and burst through.

And laugh till it hurts at what's on the other side.

Hillman is stark naked, treading water in the middle of the pool with the Vessel held over his head. Misery is at the shallow end, his feet dangling in the water and cheering him on like a coach. Both of them turn towards me when I enter, Hillman in horror, Misery in relief.

"About time, Rudes! I didn't know how much longer I could string this goofball along!"

"Oh my god, I can't believe that worked." I'm trying to get my laughter in check as I start around the pool on the tiles, heading toward the pile of clothes next to Misery. "What did you tell him again?"

"That the only way to get around the whole selfless thing was to, like, purify yourself by swimming in a body of water with the Vessel. Dude was so anxious to make a wish, I didn't even have to suggest the nearest pool."

I nod. "Sounds about right."

"And just so you don't think I wanted to sneak a peek at little Hillman, getting naked was totally *his* idea."

"You son of a bitch." Hillman, realizing he's been duped, paddles toward us until his feet touch bottom, then walks forward with the Vessel held in front of his wrinkled junk. "You can't lie to me, I'm your master! I command you to kill this man!"

"Sorry dude, I still got free will. Wishes are the only thing I gotta obey."

He clenches his jaw and smashes a fist against the water. "Then I *wish* for it!"

"Now Agent Hillman," I say gravely. "That doesn't sound very selfless to me."

"Shut your mouth, Compton!" He heads toward the edge of the pool, sets the Vessel down, and starts to pull his spindly body from the water. "If you and this traitorous creature think you can make a fool out of me, you are about to be taught another lesson."

I reach down into the pile of his clothes and pick up the pistol he took from me earlier, completing the last part of the plan Misery and I laid out. "School's out, Hillman. Get your bony ass back in the pool and step back."

He watches me carefully as he slides back into the water and moves away from us.

"You got no one to blame but yourself," I tell him. "If you hadn't been so goddamned greedy, you would've taken the Vessel and run. You would've gotten as far from here as you could before trying to jump through whatever hoops he held up for you. But I knew you wouldn't be able to wait. God, you couldn't even get four blocks before—"

"Save the sermon. It's human nature. You would've done the same. You will, as soon as you leave here." His heavy brow furrows, creating a Mariana Trench on his forehead. "At least, until I catch up with you again. I granted you a reprieve before, but I will *not* make that mistake again."

I bring the gun up and point it at his skinny chest. "What makes you think you're gonna be alive to do that?"

He doesn't look scared when he answers, just states what he believes to be plain fact. "Because you're no killer Mr. Compton. At least, not in cold blood. You don't have what it takes."

The thing is, last week...he'd have been right. Yesterday, too. I still feel guilty about what I did to Weldon, and that was a clear cut case of self-defense. Against a clone, no less.

But what Hillman's not accounting for is, directly responsible or not, there's already a lot of blood on my hands. If I leave him alive, there might be more. Others I care about. My moral compass can't seem to find north.

In the end though...I really just don't have time to give a shit.

I try to think of it as 'eliminating a complication' as I pull the trigger three times.

~ ~ ~

Outside, the first watery rays of morning are falling over the city. I carry the Vessel to Hillman's trashed car, pausing only once to vomit. I can't stop seeing the look of shock and surprise on his face as he tumbled back into the red pool water.

I'm not sure if I believe in heaven or hell, but murder is a big no-no in the Transcendentalist's handbook.

Misery comes up and puts a hand on my back.

I shrug it off. "Don't touch me. My life has just gotten continually shittier since I met you."

"Harsh, dude."

"Oh, shut up with the dude-speak. You're no surfer, you've never surfed in your life. You're just this worthless thing that brings pain and death wherever you go. Nothing that's happened is my fault. It's yours, all of it."

His back stiffens. "I didn't make you shoot him."

"Yeah, and you didn't do anything to stop it either." I set the Vessel on the trunk of the car and walk up to him until our chests are almost touching. I'm seething, I haven't been so mad since that night at the apartment when I caught Brynn. The night all this started. "That seems to be a common motif with you. People are always killing one another around you, while you keep saying, 'Oh, I'm innocent, I'm innocent!' Maybe the Candlemaker's right about you. *Dude.*"

A hurt flicker crosses his face before he can hide it. "Sorry you see it that way. I thought we were buds, but it's obvious you're just another human who can't own up."

"Screw off." I stalk away, snatch the Vessel up, and head for the driver's door of Hillman's car.

"So what happens next?" he shouts after me.

I get behind the wheel and start the ignition. "Next I decide who to turn you over to: Carbini or the Candlemaker."

Misery appears in the seat next to me, making me jump. "Rudes, no, you can't! You can't turn me over to the Candlemaker, they'll just kill me! Or worse, seal me back up in the Vessel! Give me to Carbini, the cops, Hillman's people, anything but that!"

"I don't have a choice."

"What do you mean? Of course you have a choice, you can get your friend back from Carbini!"

I lay my head against the steering wheel. "The Candlemaker grabbed us right after Hillman left with you. That's what took me so long to get here. He...put some kind of curse on my wife. If I don't give him the Vessel in a little more than two hours...she'll die."

"Ah...*shit*." The concern in his voice is stark. I feel a surge of anguish. Not just for Dutt or Brynn or me, but for him, because I *really* like the guy, given very different circumstances, he could've been a friend, and I have no choice but to surrender him to the zealot or the mobster.

But of course, the real choice is, do I save my estranged wife or my best friend?

Betray Misery, or possibly doom the world?

"Yeah," I say, "So unless you can grant me a wish to save her..."

"I can't do that, dude. I'm sorry."

"What about if I have someone else make it? A third party, someone who gains nothing if she gets better?"

"It's been tried. Most of the times what happens—if whoever you asked didn't just murder you outright and take the Vessel for themselves—is that they, like, assume responsibility for the person they're saving. And if they feel even a kernel of satisfaction that they're doing something good…"

"What about…what about…?" I'm grasping at straws and I know it. It's just entirely too frustrating to have a real-life genie sitting next to me and not be able to use him.

"Rudy, dude." He leans the passenger seat back and stares up through the missing roof, at the last remnants of the stars fading into daylight. "Do what you gotta do."

I will. I always do.
Haven't I proved that by now?

By the time I make a quick trip back to the motel, check on Brynn, then drive through downtown Reno back to the casinos, it's just past six in the morning. I stop off for donuts and coffee, confident no one will recognize me with the renovations Hillman performed on my face. Misery sits across the table and eats like he hasn't seen food in, well, two-thousand years. We watch the TV, which is nothing but news about me, the firefight at Slots of Luck yesterday afternoon, and the battle on the rooftop early this morning involving more 'unknown assailants.' The city is in the grip of fear. False or incorrect tips about me are pouring in every hour. The FBI—the *real* FBI, that is—is taking over the manhunt. The Reno PD is under their jurisdiction now, which means all ties and allegiance to Carbini are undoubtedly severed.

The one bright spot comes when the head of the investigation says they have 'new information from Army intelligence sources to consider.' He makes a passionate plea for me to turn myself in.

My phone rings. It's Carbini.

"You ready to save your friend, Rudolph?"

"Yeah. But we're gonna do it my way."

"Kid, I've been up all night trying to make a military helicopter and a platoon of dead soldiers disappear. I'm in no mood for bullshit. Get your ass in the casino with the Vessel or I'm going to slit his throat right now so you can listen to him gurgle."

"Go ahead. Then you can explain to the Filament why you didn't do what they paid you to do."

He's quiet for a long moment. "I'm listening."

"First off, I opened the Vessel. Pandora is out of the box, and the Word is useless. You don't need me anymore."

Carbini says the last thing I expect. "I know."

"You do?"

"I got a call from my employers. They want the Vessel more than ever, and they don't care about opened merchandise."

It shouldn't be a surprise considering the Candlemaker knew, but it's still nice that I don't have to convince him. "Okay then. Here's how this is gonna work. You meet me out front with Dutt, in public. *Just* you; I don't wanna see Weldon or Fiver anywhere. I give you the Vessel, you let Dutt go, and we both walk away."

"Fine. When?"

"Ten minutes."

This time I hang up on him.

I leave Hillman's car far away from the casino strip. The last thing I need is a cop or the FBI stopping me now. I grab a shopping bag out of a dumpster and carry the Vessel in it.

"Maybe you should get inside," I tell Misery. "I don't need this any more complicated than it already is."

He nods. "Look Rudy, I just wanna say...I'm genuinely sorry for getting you involved in all this."

"Yeah, well...I'm sorry I said those things earlier."

We look at one another for a few seconds. With nothing more to say, he snaps his fingers and disappears back into the Vessel.

I walk down the sidewalk. Another brisk early morning in Reno. There's just enough foot traffic to put me at ease about meeting Carbini.

Slots of Luck is closed down 'for remodeling.' Carbini's already in front of the casino when I get there, with a limo at the curb and a big suitcase by his feet. He's got on one of his snazzy, high-dollar suits, but he's aged at least fifteen years since I saw him last, that rugged face lined with wrinkles, a bandage on his forehead where Hillman clocked him, and huge bags under his eyes. But the sight of me perks him right up.

"Holy hell kid, I hope that hurts as bad as it looks. Who put the beat down on you?"

"Your mother. She thought I was one of her jumbo tampons and sat on me. Now where's Dutt?"

His gaze plays over the bag in my hand. "That it?"

"Yeah, and if you want it, you'll get my friend out here."

He turns and motions to the front door of the casino. It opens, and Dutt is shoved through. He must've been given instructions, because he walks a straight line over to Carbini, who grabs his arm. He looks exhausted and very different sans glasses, but otherwise unharmed.

I set the bag down on the concrete and take a few steps backward. "Okay. Let him go."

He starts to comply, but then yanks Dutt back.

"I want you to know something, you little fuck," Carbini snarls. "I'm not cooperating because I'm scared of you. You're not getting away with anything. Nobody waltzes into my town, puts me through what you did, barks orders, and gets away with it."

"Oh yeah? Watch me."

He grins. "I will. But only because it'll be so much more fun to let the Filament catch up with you down the line."

He lets Dutt go. My best friend walks over to my side and about-faces. "Geez, that guy's a real dick. I'm pretty sure he was hitting on me the entire time I was in there."

I look over at him. "Good to see you, man."

"You too. Thanks for coming."

Carbini picks up the suitcase, places it on the trunk of the limo, and opens the latches. Inside is a foam imprint in the exact shape of the Vessel. He picks up the bag I set on the sidewalk like it's a dead rat and holds it at arm's length. Touching only the plastic, he rolls the Vessel out of the shopping bag and into the foam, presses it down, then closes and latches the suitcase.

I guess keeping himself scared of the thing is the easiest way to ensure he's not tempted to use it.

"What happens to it now?" I ask.

"My employers arrived early, so as soon as I leave here, I go straight to deliver it to them. Then I can finally be done with this fucking business."

"I hope they're paying you a ton."

"Oh, they are, but that's not why I'm doing it. See, another little perk of the job is a seat next to the throne when they use it to bring about Armageddon." His eyes gleam. "Then I get to watch all the fuckers like you burn."

"That's not how it works," I say. "It can't be used like

that. If it could, do you really think you and I would be having this conversation?"

"We'll let them worry about that." Carbini picks up the suitcase and heads around to the back door of the limo. "We're done here, kids. Run along and play, and daddy will be in to say goodnight as soon as he's done with his work."

"Man." Dutt shakes his head sadly. "You are *soooo* gay."

"Just out of curiosity," I yell, as Carbini swings into the limo. He sticks out his head and looks back at me. "What would happen if you showed up without the Vessel?"

"Then kid, I'd be exactly where I expect you're going to be when they find you: flayed alive, boiled in acid, and strung up by your ankles."

He shuts the door, and the limo pulls away in a squeal of tires.

By the time we get back to the car, I've explained the bare bones of the Brynn situation to Dutt.

"Oh my God. Rudy...man...I'm so sorry. I don't know what to say."

"Don't say anything. Just help me save her."

"How're we supposed to do that? You just gave that asshole the thing."

I lift my butt up off the car seat so I can reach in my jeans pocket, and pull out the 'low-yield, non-biological mass retrieval unit' that Carbini gave me. I press the button on top. The Vessel appears in my hands, and, a split second later, Misery is sitting in the back seat.

"Rudes, you sly little devil you."

"Jesus!" Dutt exclaims. "Who the hell are you?"

"Dutt, Misery. Misery, Dutt. Mis, you mind filling him in while I drive?"

"No prob, boss man."

I pull out into traffic as Misery begins to babble.

Chapter
**TWENTY
NINE**

At the motel again.

Brynn's so cold, I think for a second we might be too late, but then I see her chest moving. She's like a stone. Dutt helps me wrap her in blankets, and then we carry her out to the car and put her in the backseat.

Misery follows like a puppy dog, bouncing from one foot to the other. "So you have another plan, right? You're gonna pull a fast one on the Candlemaker the same way you did Carbini?"

I don't look him in the eye when I answer. "No tricks. I'm giving him whatever he wants, as long as he fixes Brynn."

He stops bouncing. His face falls into a flat, dead mask. "Okay then…kill me."

"What?"

"It's not hard. I'll walk you through the ritual."

"I'm not gonna kill you, Misery."

"You have to, dude! I can't go back in the Vessel, I'd rather be dead! Why won't you do this?"

"For starters, I have less than an hour to get her back out there."

"We can do it fast! In the car! Won't take but a minute!"

I grab one of his muscular shoulders and squeeze. "Mis, you gotta be optimistic. You got out once, you'll do it again. A great man once said, 'There'll be another time.'"

He looks at me like I just spit in his mouth. "If that's a reference to what I think it's a reference to, you're an insensitive prick, Rudes."

I let go and shake my head. "I've killed enough people already without starting on the ones I actually like. Besides, if it's any consolation, I'm pretty sure the Candlemaker means to kill you any way. He's too scared of you to leave you alive."

Misery snorts. "Thanks dude. Glad to see where I rank around here." He winks out of existence and reappears in the back seat next to Brynn, sulking.

Dutt comes out of the motel room with the last of our meager belongings packed up and throws them in the trunk. I can't get used to him without glasses.

"You don't have to come with us," I tell him.

"We're gonna save her."

"I know, it's just…you've already been taken hostage. Maybe you should just run for the hills, or get back in touch with your superiors again and get this cleaned up. There's no need for you to risk getting hurt."

He closes the trunk lid and looks up at me. There's actual tears in his eyes. I've never seen Dutt cry about anything, not even when his father died.

"The only time I ever left you holding the bag was when we blew your leg off with those fireworks, and I've never stopped feeling guilty for it. I'm with you until the end. When you gonna get that through your head, you retard?"

He reaches out, grabs me, pulls me to him. I hug him back.

There's nothing more to say.

~ ~ ~

"So what if someone put a gun to my head and told me to make a wish?"

"Well, then you'd only be wishing so you wouldn't be shot."

While I follow directions and drive out of town toward the graveyard, Dutt is working Misery over like a Rubik's cube, and running into the same frustration.

"Okay, okay. So...what if I wished for one of my worst enemies—I'm talking about someone I absolutely *hate*—to get a free wish, with no reservations, no limitations?"

"Depends, dude. What's your motivation?"

"Why's that matter?"

"Cause if you're only doing it so they'll, like, reciprocate, that ain't selfless."

"Let's say I'm not. Let's just say I'm doing it with no expectations whatsoever."

"But *why?* Why would you give your worst enemy something like that?"

"Doesn't matter. I just did it. Now theoretically, could you grant the wish or not?"

Misery wobbles his head back and forth. "If you weren't getting anything out of it...not feeling good about yourself at all...then yeah. I could totally grant that one."

"And then you'd have to grant the other guy's free wish, and it wouldn't have to be selfless?"

"Yeah, that works."

"*Yes!* I knew it! Score one for me!" Dutt pumps a fist through the torn roof.

"But what's the point?" I look away from the road to check on Brynn in the back. "Giving out wishes to people we don't like isn't gonna help."

"I just wanna test the limitations. I refuse to believe there's not some way we can use him to help us outta this. I found one wish that works, now I just gotta find others."

Misery leans over the seat between us. "People have been trying that same thing for, like, a *long* time, dude. There were a few millenia where I just got passed around to the greatest thinkers in Asia. Drove a couple of 'em insane. I've heard it all, and it never works. The best way is the simplest way: an honest, heartfelt wish where the wisher doesn't spare a single thought for themselves in the equation."

"Yeah well, whatever you're gonna come up with Dutt, you better do it fast."

The last of urban Reno drops away as we get closer to the cemetery. Which is a relief, since most of the streets are clogged with police. They must have every officer on the roster out looking for me and my cohorts, along with several FBI cars, a SWAT van, and we even see an Army humvee. Three times we have to take detours because the roads are blocked off with law enforcement responding to reports of my whereabouts. It's everything I can do not to speed as time ticks down.

I'm finally beginning to recognize the area from our late night bus trip as the land opens up ahead. I see the wrought iron fence that surrounds the graveyard. On all other sides is nothing but open plains and rocky scrub leading up to the mountains. I turn in the gate just as Misery slumps back in his seat.

The place looks different in the daytime. I park beside the same mausoleum and give Dutt the Vessel. I carry Brynn. Her skin is ice, her limbs like granite. I run ahead to the wall we entered through last time.

One of the Acolytes is there to greet us. He pats us all down, taking my gun and the hand-held teleporter. He skips over Misery entirely with a disgusted sneer, as though not wanting to touch him, then performs the maneuver to get the door to appear. I don't wait for the others before plunging down the stone staircase with Brynn. I navigate the dank, torch-lit hallways and find my way back to the main chamber.

The Candlemaker is waiting alone. He stands before his gigantic throne, watching from under his hood as I hurry down the aisle and up onto the stage.

"All right, I brought the Vessel!" I lay Brynn down on the same altar where the Candlemaker performed the ritual on her a few hours ago. "Take the curse off her!" And, when he doesn't move, "C'mon, right now!"

"In due time, boy. Once the Vessel is in my hands."

I look back at the door. Dutt is on his way in with the chamberpot, squinting around at the architecture as he comes down the main aisle. Misery slinks in behind him, eyes following the same trajectory, but stops cold when his gaze lands on the figure at the front.

The Candlemaker spreads his robed arms wide.

"Miserea. So good of you to come."

"Auxentius. I see purple's still your favorite color."

"You two know each other?" I ask.

"You could say that," Misery answers. "You see, he's responsible for me getting locked up in the Vessel in the first place."

That's when it dawns on me just why the Candlemaker looks so ancient.

"Yes, I do know the beast," he tells me, as he comes down the stairs. "But you seemed so determined to believe otherwise, I thought it amusing not to argue."

I raise my eyebrows at Misery.

"Sorry Rudes, I woulda told you, but when you kept talking about the Candlemaker, I figured it must be a successor." He looks from me to the old man. "All that power you sucked up just mummified you alive, didn't it Auxentius?"

"Do not use that name here, defiler! Auxentius Decima died long ago!"

"Yeah, but his hatred of me apparently didn't." Misery gives one of his patented goofy grins. "Dude...you mean to tell me you couldn't find anything better to do with two-thousand years of prolonged life than to keep chasing down little ol' *me?*"

"I'm confused," Dutt murmurs.

"Me too." I hold a hand out to Misery. "What does this mean?"

"What it means, Rudes, is that none of this had anything to do with a Christian-slanted cleansing or any belief that I might actually be dangerous."

"Silence, beast!" the Candlemaker thunders.

"What it means, is that it's all been about a very personal vendetta—"

"*Quiet!*"

"And a wish from an angry little Roman sorcerer that just couldn't be granted."

The Candlemaker glides forward and yanks the Vessel from Dutt's hands. "I said shut your lying mouth, demon!" Misery's lips clamp shut. His eyes smolder. Literally; little curls of smoke drift from the irises. This is the first time he's ever been angry.

"Is that true?" I direct the question at the Candlemaker.

He flusters and crooks a withered finger at Misery. "He…
h-he is an unnatural abomination!"

"But that's not why you wanted him, is it?"

The Candlemaker flies into a rage. "I should have ruled
the world! *Me!* But he wouldn't grant my wishes no matter
how I phrased them! I was forced to resort to dark arts, living in the shadows to lap up power when and where I could!
I saw firsthand what the unfilled promise of that creature
causes, how it destroys lives! So yes, I recommended to the
Order that he be put to death, as we did so much of his kins-
men! And when those fearful fools locked him away instead,
I dedicated myself to finishing what they couldn't!"

"You know, someone once told me that responsibility is
all that sets us apart from the animals." I glare at him point-
edly. "Maybe you should take some for your own actions."

He comes forward and snarls in my face, "One more word
from you and your woman will *die in agony while you watch.*"

I shut up.

He goes around the table to Misery and stands in front
of him like a drill instructor. He raises the Vessel between
them. "How was it, Miseria? All the years spent in this tiny
construct. Did you enjoy them?"

Misery's nostrils flare. When he speaks, all traces of the
surfer accent are finally gone. "I was sealed up fully conscious in a lightless hole. What do you think?"

"And do you regret not cooperating now? All you had
to do was give me the power I sought! We could have ruled
together, could have crushed the world beneath our heels,
but you—!"

Misery interrupts the upward-spiraling rant. "If it's all
the same to you, Auxentius, I'd rather just get on with killing
me than listen to you whine anymore."

"Kill you?" The Candlemaker's puckered mouth stretches into a grin beneath the edge of his cowl. "For so long that's all I dreamed of. After the Order took you from me, I spent so many lifetimes trying to ensure you never got free, and then, when you finally did, all I could think of was destroying you. But the passionate words of your new friend over there made me realize, you haven't suffered nearly enough. There are punishments far worse than death."

I'm not sure if Misery's appearance as a human works on the same flesh and blood principles as the rest of us, but his face does pale about ten shades. "No."

"Yes. I will seal you back up in the Vessel, re-infect the boy with the Word…and then kill him, so that you will *never* escape. Then I will take your prison to the deepest ocean trench and sink it for all eternity."

"*Please, you can't!*" Misery breaks completely, clutching at the sleeves of the Candlemaker's robe. "I can't grant your wishes, it's not my fault!"

"*Back in your cage, creature!*"

Misery vanishes.

"Goddamn you," I say. "We had a deal, you old fuck."

The Candlemaker spins to us. "Our deal was that I would remove the curse from your woman." He puts a hand over Brynn's unconscious face and snaps his fingers, producing a burst of flame. She sits bolt upright, gasping for air. "And I have done so. Lock these three interlopers in the catacombs while I prepare the ritual."

Acolytes swarm over us, hoisting Brynn over their shoulders and dragging Dutt and I toward the door.

"This is bullshit!" I shout. "You will NOT get away with this!"

"My boy…I think I already have."

~ ~ ~

The poetic humor is not lost on me that this is all ending right where it started.

With me in a cell.

This one is even less nice than the Withers county lockup. It's just as dank and dark as the rest of the Candlemaker's humble abode, but with a stench like cat piss. Cold stone floors and three walls, with the fourth made of metal bars so corroded they look black.

"Where is it now?" Brynn asks, as she paces in front of us. Dutt is stretched out on the floor. I'm squatting on the only seat in this room, a hard concrete boulder with a flat top, pushed over in the corner.

"*He*. He's not an it, he's a person. Sort of."

"I don't give a shit if he's a…a…a flying Tyrannosaurus!"

From the floor, Dutt muffles a tired-sounding chuckle. "That's kinda weird. How'd you come up with that?"

"Shut up, this isn't funny! Rudy, *where is the genie now?*"

"I don't know. The Candlemaker took the Vessel. Misery goes where it goes." I shrug. "But he couldn't get us out of this even if we had him."

"I'm not talking about that! I'm talking about the fact that it's a real genie, and you handed it over like it was garbage! God, you're such an asshole!"

I would feel guilty—or guilt*ier*—if I thought she had Misery's well-being at heart. Or if she was even worried about our present predicament. But she's actually more concerned with the fact that Misery is in someone else's possession than she is that we're locked in a dungeon awaiting execution.

"Excuse me, I was trying to save your life! You said you didn't wanna die!"

"Of course I didn't wanna die dummy, but that doesn't mean I wanted you to give it up! We could have done anything with it! *Anything!*"

I stand up. "Jesus, Brynn, when are you gonna get it through your head: *it doesn't work like that!* He can't just give you whatever you want!"

She starts panting, like panicked hyperventilating. "There…there has to be some way—!"

"The Candlemaker was convinced of that, too. Look how he ended up."

"But…b-but…"

She can't understand. She's just as blind as so many other people who felt their dreams slipping through their fingers once Misery entered their lives. I felt the same initial disappointment and desperation. In that respect, the Candlemaker is right about him. Some people will destroy themselves to get a free pass in life, and they can't deal with the truth.

"Brynn…I'm sorry," I plead. I've got to bring her back from this edge. "I did what I had to do. I couldn't bare the thought of losing you."

She looks confused for a second, almost sick, but then she nods, slides into the floor next to the bars, pulls her knees up, and buries her face in them.

"I don't suppose we have a plan?" Dutt asks.

"Sure do. Go through with whatever the Candlemaker has in mind for us, and pray it doesn't hurt when he kills me. I'll see if I can talk him into letting both of you go."

"And I'm too tired to argue and tell you not to."

I walk over to Brynn and sit in the floor beside her. She leans against me.

"All of this…it's my fault, isn't it?"

"How do you figure?"

"If I hadn't...you know...with Chris...you wouldn't have gone to jail, and none of this would've happened."

Even though she's kind of right, I cup her chin and tilt her face up to me. "It may sound selfish but...I'd rather be right here *with* you than anywhere else *without* you."

"Yeah, well no one ever accused you of being a genius," Dutt grumbles.

"Rudy," she whispers. "I just thought...if we had the genie...it could solve everything. You know, between us. It could...make things better for me. So I wouldn't be so...so...."

I stop her with a kiss on the forehead. "I know. Me too. But it won't. There are no easy answers."

We all close our eyes and wait to see what happens next.

This rage, this blind, seething animal, is taking control of me, one muscle group at a time. The words on the computer screen burn into my retina as I realize she's cheating on me.

Again.

How could you? *I ask. We're both panting from our wrestling match over the computer. Dutt stands in shocked disbelief.*

Now that she's caught, her face is expressionless. She looks at the floor and shrugs. Shrugs, as though answering what she wants for dinner instead of how she could be capable of adultery.

Say something, goddammit! *I've never felt so alive with anger, it's running through me like an electric current, corkscrewing my vision down to a pinhole, overriding and shutting down all of the fail-safes in my head that could've prevented what is about to happen.*

In that moment, I'm pretty sure I could've killed her.

My hand is out before I stop it, cracking across her cheek with a sound as ugly as any racial slur. It hangs in the air, unsure what to do with itself next. Her head rocks to the side and when it comes back, a trickle of blood oozes from the corner of her shocked 'O' of a mouth. I feel sick.

But still dangerous. Still very, very dangerous.

Dutt gets between us, pushes us apart.

Call the cops, *I tell him. Mostly because I don't trust myself.*

Rudy, are you sure—?

Just do it.

You know how the rest goes.

One of the Acolytes kicks the bars beside my head to wake us up. "Let's go. All of you."

We stand. There's no talking; we're just too tired for that. A group of the hooded lackeys usher us back to the Candlemaker's twisted, black chapel.

The place is packed. Every pew is filled with Acolytes. The entire candlemaking cult in one room. They're turned around to watch us enter. The candles change them into a congregation of flickering ghouls.

At the front, the man himself stands behind his stone altar holding the Vessel. Misery's at his side, shaggy head bowed. "Bring me the boy. Chain the other two up, so they may watch."

The Acolytes move to separate us. Brynn grabs my hand as they drag her away to the right. Dutt puts two-fingers to his forehead and sketches a brief salute as they take him left. There's shackles chained to the wall, and the two of them are bolted on opposite sides of the room with their arms over their head.

I'm led down to the Candlemaker. Up on stage. I stand in front of the altar while he turns his back to me and the rest of the audience and holds his arms straight out. Two of the Acolytes remove his purple robe.

I gasp at what's beneath.

The Candlemaker is naked. He's so thin, so impossibly, Ethiopian-thin, nothing more than bones floating in shriveled, wrinkled skin. The back of his head is like a skull with ragged clumps of hair. He has so little body fat, his ass is concave.

They bring him a different robe, one pitch black with gold embroidery, and a mass of dark feathers down the back. Once he's dressed, he turns to face us.

"My brothers, my sons," the Candlemaker calls out. His creaking voice echoes from the arched rafters. "We have fought long and hard…seen so many of our brethren fall… all in the service of one sacred goal: to rid the world of the abomination you see standing beside me. Today…we see that goal at last achieved!"

It seems as though a cheer should go up, but these guys have had their brains so washed, there's not much left to think with. The Candlemaker continues, beginning to sound like any evangelical preacher I ever heard.

"Satan sent these creatures among us to *tempt* us! To lay us *looooow!* For thousands of years, the Order served the Lord's will by eliminating them, and we continued after they lost their resolve!"

"Why don't you tell them the real reason for all this?" I interrupt. "How the only will they've been serving is yours?"

"Silence his insolent tongue before I cut it out."

A strip of putrid cloth is tied tight around my head and across my mouth.

"Lay him out."

The Acolytes lift me up and throw me on my back on the stone slab. I don't struggle, but they hold me down anyway.

The Candlemaker sneers down at me beneath his hood before gesturing to Misery. "Now my Acolytes, gaze upon the last *djinn* this world has to offer. Know that, though he does not die, his fate will be far worse, and his influence out of the world forever." To Misery, he whispers, "You see what you get for defying me? Enjoy eternity in darkness." And then, back in his stage voice, "Enter your prison, beast! Be gone from our presence!"

Misery looks up. His sad eyes catch mine just before he vanishes.

There's a big brass stand behind the Candlemaker, ringed in lit candles. The Vessel goes in the center. He places his hands on the lid—being careful not to set his long robe sleeves on fire—and begins to chant in a language of harsh consonants. Just the sound of it makes me queasy; if there's one thing I've learned from my recent adventures, it's the power of the spoken word. A murmur rises from the congregation. I turn my head on the altar to find the Acolytes repeating his chant and swaying back and forth.

He takes one bony palm off the Vessel and places it on my forehead. Then he bends next to my ear and whispers the same Word that started all this in the first place.

An electric trill rockets across my nerve endings.

Rudes, can you hear me?

Loud and clear, Misery.

I am once again the Omega. If I wasn't gagged, I could scream the Word and infect everyone in this room.

Could really use some of that super strength about now, I think at him.

I'm trying dude, but it ain't happening!

The Candlemaker smiles knowingly, reading the desperation on my face. "He won't be able to help you. This altar nullifies any power he could impart to you."

From his new robe, the Candlemaker takes the same dagger he used to cut his hand earlier. "This boy is an accomplice of the beast. With the extinguishing of his life, we ensure the creature can never harm our world again. One life, for the lives of many."

Rudes, I'm sorry, so sorry I got you into this...

The Candlemaker hefts the knife over my chest. I can hear Brynn sobbing. Dutt shouting.

I close my eyes.

And then open them as the chapel doors at the far end of the room slam open.

The entire congregation spins in their seats to look.

All the torches in the hallway are out; a thick, cold darkness waits beyond the chapel threshold. Something stirs out there, and a round, hairy object comes rolling through. It bounces up the middle aisle like a bowling ball bound for a strike, past the pews of Acolytes, and stops just a few feet short of the stage.

The severed head of Sullis Carbini stares up at me with glassy eyes.

Oh God, Rudes, you gotta get outta here. Like, right now.

The Candlemaker grasps the significance before even I do.

"They found us," he says, more to himself than anyone. The hand holding the knife over my delicate innards drops to his side. He screams to his followers, "*The Dark Filament is here!*"

From the pitch black hallway beyond the chapel doors comes an ungodly chorus of screeches that makes my stomach clench.

And then I get my first look at these 'representatives' of the Filament.

They hurtle through the doors in an unending wave. Misery said they were the closest thing the universe has to demons, and I can think of no better term for the jet black nightmares that come boiling into the room. They're nothing but hunched, shadowed wraiths, so dark they absorb the candlelight; the only bit of color is the mouthful of gleaming fangs in the middle of what passes for their heads. They howl and screech and slash at the air as they charge the Acolytes.

"STOP THEM!" the Candlemaker roars. "DO NOT LET THEM THROUGH!"

The room erupts. Acolytes jump from their seats and clamber over pews, producing bows, maces, and axes from god-knows-where. They meet the incoming demons in a crush of bodies. The din of hand-to-hand combat fills the church.

The ones holding my arms are just as distracted by the fighting. I jerk free of their grasp and sit up.

At the sudden motion, the Candlemaker raises the knife in a panicky backswing. I grab his wrist before he can perform some pre-Thanksgiving carving on me. His brittle bone shatters like glass beneath my palm. The knife clatters across the floor.

He stumbles backward, holding his crooked hand, and croaks, *"Kill him!"*

I kick and twist free of the Acolytes holding my feet, tumbling into the floor. The second I'm off the altar, the strength of the Word courses through me, more power than ever, and *god*, did I miss it.

The Acolytes come at me, pulling broadswords from sheaths on their belts. I break one's jaw and the another's ribs before they can even take a swing. As the last two close in, I dance around their blades and maneuver one into impaling the other. All it takes is a backhand to the face to put out the last one's lights.

The Candlemaker is backing away from me in horror with the Vessel hugged to his chest, heading toward the door at the back of the stage. I rip off my gag as I stalk after him.

"Stay away! *Away!*" The Candlemaker's dead voice begins to crack. "You're nothing to me, boy! A gnat! I've lived a *thousand* lifetimes!"

"Yeah, and you wasted them all, you self-righteous hypocrite!" I yank the Vessel from his stick arms and lift him up by the front of his robe. His frailty combined with my super strength make the act no more strenuous than picking up kindling.

"This is my destiny! *You can't do anything to stop meeeee!*"

"We'll see. This is for Reed and Luiz and everyone else you murdered for your revenge!"

I toss him through the air, putting every inch of strength into it. He travels only a few yards at roughly the speed of light before slamming against the back of his granite throne.

Imagine a water balloon thrown at a brick wall, and you get the idea. His wasted body seems to collapse in on itself, and what lands in the seat is nothing but broken bones wrapped in a blood-soaked robe.

The Candlemaker gives a last shudder before growing still.

~ ~ ~

I spin around and take in the situation.

There's a war waging in the church. Pockets of armed Acolytes stand their ground across the chapel, demarcating a line of resistance against the screeching invaders. They use swords and axes to chop at the demons or stand on the pews to shoot them with arrows from a distance. The black monsters go down in droves, but three more pack into the room to replace each that falls. Every few seconds they overwhelm an Acolyte and either drag him kicking and screaming out the chapel doors, or tear him to pieces where he stands. The defenders are steadily being forced to retreat toward me.

Against both walls, Brynn and Dutt struggle in their shackles. They're yelling, but I can't hear them over the howls, cries, and wet thuds of impact. For now, they're behind the Acolyte line of defense, but not for much longer.

Let me out, dude, I'll help!

"Sorry," I tell Misery, "but right now I need the Word a lot more than a genie who can't grant wishes."

I stash the Vessel deep beneath the altar, grab two swords from the Acolytes I knocked out, and leap off the side of the stage into the fray.

I hurtle pews and push between Acolytes. Most of them are so focused on the Filament, they don't even notice me. One turns to take a swing as I pass by, and I put him on the ground. I reach Dutt just as the front line of Acolytes jostles back into me. I undo his chains and push him out of the way before an arrow goes through his shoulder.

"*The Vessel!*" I tell him over the din of battle. "*Get to the Vessel and keep it safe! It's under the altar!*"

"*What about you?*"

"*I'm going after Brynn!*"

"*I'll come with you, watch your back!*"

I fork a peace sign in the air in front of him. "*How many fingers am I holding up?*"

He nods. "*Good point.*"

I hand him one of the swords and he turns toward the stage. The crush of bodies is so thick, it's everything he can do to keep from being smashed against the wall. I see him swing the sword when he gets stuck just before he's lost in the crowd.

I shove aside anyone that gets in my way as I cross the chapel. The Acolytes fall all around me. The candles on the floor are either being tromped or kicked over, and the room is slowly getting darker. The idea of being trapped in this insanity without being able to see makes me move even faster.

One of the Filament demons slashes out and takes a chunk of my arm as I pass a thin place in the defense line. I stab it with my remaining sword. The blood on the blade is nothing but black ichor.

The opposite side of the room is in worse shape. The line is weakening, being pushed back. Brynn is exposed just as I reach her. I cut one of the smaller creatures in half as it springs, then release the shackle on one of her wrists and hold back the others closing in while she frees herself.

"*Head to the back of the stage! There's another door!*"

She clutches my arm. "*The genie? Where's the genie?*"

I shake her loose in time to chop the head off another demon as it comes at us. "*Dutt knows! Both of you just go, take Misery and get outta here! I'll stay here to fight and give you as much of a head start as possible!*"

I expect an argument. I expect a kiss. But this is no movie.

Brynn gives my arm one last squeeze and turns to go. The crowding is less on this side of the room, so she has an easier time. She might even make it there before Dutt. I watch until I'm convinced she's safe.

I give myself fully to the Word, let it control me like a puppet, and throw myself into the battle. I feel invincible, swinging my sword at these living shadows and hacking off every leathery appendage that comes close to me. Once the Acolytes see I'm helping, they accept me into their ranks. With me, the odds get a little better, but we're still losing. People are dropping and the ranks of Filament reinforcements show no signs of slowing.

What hole did these things crawl out of?

After what feels like an hour of fighting but is surely no more than a couple of minutes, I back up into one of the pews and tumble over it, sprawling in the seat. One of the demons vaults over behind me and lands straddling my chest, ragged claws at my throat.

"*Little human fights so strong,*" it rasps, in a voice that sounds like a hundred children crying. Its breath is rotten meat and sour milk and something rich and ashy, like the smell of a forest fire. I'm instantly more terrified of it than I've ever been of anything in my life. "*You are the one Carbini spoke of. The one who causes our master so much trouble.*"

"*I'm also the one disemboweling you, asshole!*"

I ram the sword up through it and get sprayed with fluid the consistency of maple syrup. It goes limp on top of me. I toss the corpse to the floor and jump to my feet.

The battle is ending. We lost. The few remaining Acolytes are being isolated and mobbed. I have to hand it to them though; not a single one turned tail.

I look out across the room, toward the higher landing of the stage. Dutt is just now climbing up beside the altar. He squints across the church, looking for me, then picks up the Vessel and gives me a thumbs-up. I start to wave back.

And then I see Brynn emerging from the shadows of the stone chair right behind him.

There's a glint in her hand, from the last of the four-thousand-year-old flames in this room.

The Candlemaker's dagger.

And a split second later...I *understand*.

"DUTT, LOOK OUT!"

He never sees it coming. The confusion is still on his face when she rams the knife into his back. He stumbles over against the altar and then falls into the floor with the Vessel, out of sight. Brynn scoops it back up and runs through the door at the rear of the room without looking back.

I run. Shove through the last of the Candlemaker's cult. Slaughter every demon that gets in my way. Vault onto the stage.

He's lying on his back, in a pool of blood. His eyes get big when he sees me.

I fall to my knees beside him. He tries to talk, it sounds like my name, but then he's coughing and trickles of scarlet run down the side of his face.

"No, no, no, no, no." I try to think of words. The right words. Anything besides 'no.'

But they aren't there.
So I grab his hand. He squeezes.
And then my best friend dies.

Chapter
THIRTY
ONE

Black rage.

It burns through me like gasoline-fed flames. Spreads along every muscle. Licks at my heart.

Compared to this, what I felt before, back at the apartment…that was just a rain cloud in the face of a hurricane.

I leave Dutt and run for the door at the back of the stage. The battle is breaking up, and in a few seconds, the entirety of the Dark Filament will be concentrated solely on me.

The door is locked. The Word feels exhausted, the last of its borrowed power draining out of me, but before it goes, I put my fist right through the wood and undo the latch on the other side.

Another stone hallway lit by candelabras on tall stands. The first of the Filament demons is scrabbling onto the stage when I slam the door again and use two of the metal holders to bar it. The screeching and animalistic battering on the other side sends me running.

"BRYNN!" I roar. Part of me hopes she doesn't answer. I don't know what this fury inside me will do if I see her. The hallway has a few doors that open onto it, but ahead is the glow of daylight. I fly up another long staircase, through a door, and out into the cemetery behind the mausoleum. The sun blinds me after so long in the dark. When I look back, the doorway I just came through is gone, disappeared along with the Candlemaker's magic.

Hillman's car is missing, also. In the distance, I hear sirens. Who knows how the cops found this place, but I can't be here when they arrive.

I sprint, heading around the corner of the mausoleum, and run straight into a huge arm that clotheslines me hard enough to knock the air out of my lungs.

While writhing on the ground, I hear, "*EF! GEE DEE!—* Payback time, Rudy."

"Jesus," I wheeze, after I catch my breath. "I figured you two would've gone the way of Carbini by now."

Weldon di Latorio and Martin 'Fiver' Dunbrough—the last delegates of a once-great clone fraternity—look down at me. To think these two clowns used to scare me is, after everything I've seen, pretty laughable.

But it's somehow fitting that this should end with them.

"Sorry ta disappoint, but we got us—*AY-AITCH!*—a new boss now."

It takes me a second to interpret his smirk. "What, you're working for the Filament? Taking orders from those animals in there?"

Weldon shakes his head. "Dose things? Dey're nuttin but hunting dogs. But deir master...da guy holding da leash... *he's* big-time. Makes Carbini look like a street-corner crack dealer. And he needs good people who don't fuck things up."

"So he tagged you two? Does he know your track record?"

Fiver reaches down, grabs a handful of my shirt and chest hair, and lifts me off the ground. Weldon rears back to hit my already tortured face.

"Wait, wait!" I hold up my hands. "I don't have the Vessel!"

"We know. Your wifey just tore outta here wit it. We'll deal wit her after we find a fresh grave for you."

"You can't kill me, I have the Word again!"

Weldon's grin shows every tooth in his head. "Not gonna save you dis time, Rudy. Da Filament don't care about da Word. Having it was a plus, but dey don't need it for what dey got in mind. Which means you just became *very* expendable."

Fiver throws me. I hit the packed dirt of the graveyard and something in my side gives way. I cry out.

"Save some of dat, Rudy. We got a long way ta go."

The sirens in the distance swell. They're either in the cemetery or just outside.

"And don't worry 'bout da cops interrupting. We called 'em, in case we needed help cleaning out dese cult fuckers. Dose're *our* boys again. Funny how fast things got back in line once da Filament blew inta town."

I crawl into the graveyard. Weldon follows, kicking me in the side but missing my cracked rib. He and Fiver laugh at my whimpering.

The hum of a teleporter precedes the click of a revolver hammer. "Maybe dis'll teach ya bout setting me on fire and blowing my head off."

"Oh," I gasp. "So you didn't tell him the truth then, Fiver?"

"What're ya talking about?"

I roll over. Weldon stands over me with the gun, but Fiver is a few steps away with a look of horror on his slab-of-a-face. "So they told you *I* shot your other clone at the casino?"

"Yeeeeah…"

"Sorry, but that was your big buddy over there. Blew your head off with a shotgun. Saw him do it. Carbini's orders."

Weldon hesitates, wanting so badly to kill me, but he can read the truth in my eyes. He turns his head while leaving the gun on me. "Did—*CEE! EM-EFer!*—*did* ya, Fiver?"

Fiver's backing up with his hands out. It's all the confirmation Weldon needs. The gun swings away from me and points somewhere at the ground in front of his partner.

"Aw man! How could ya? Every skinbag counts now!"

"Wel…you were going nuts. Shooting up the casino. I had to put you down."

"And he also said your Tourette's was annoying," I add.

Weldon puts a round through Fiver's chest so fast, I don't even think *he* knows he did it. At the same time, I grab a heavy stone engraving from the nearest tombstone and smash the edge across his shin. He goes down in a huge blubbery mess, screaming more consonants than a Wheel of Fortune contestant.

I roll on top of him and wrestle the gun out of his hand. He gnashes his teeth, tries to choke me, but after I put a bullet in his face, he just lays there and bleeds.

Then I put two more in him and three in Fiver.

You know, just to be sure.

I leave the cemetery by the opposite direction as the sirens. I have just enough energy to climb the fence around the place. There's nothing on the other side except open hardpan and mountains in the distance. I walk out into it.

It takes almost twenty-four hours to circle around Reno on foot—slinking through the hills, hiding from the helicopters that graze by overhead—and reenter the city from the west. I can barely walk, but I have to get to her before the Filament does. That piercing rage stays with me every step, replenishing me in a way even the Word can't. When it gets dark, I keep the glitter of lights to my left at all times. I end up sleeping in the dirt under a hollowed out tree stump, shivering from cold and the pain in my side.

All my nightmares are about Dutt.

Misery talks to me occasionally, telling me how sorry he is, asking me what I intend to do. As if I have a clue. Since he's not connected to Brynn the way he is to me, he doesn't know where she took him. Even if he did, he wouldn't be able to tell me over our mental walkie-talkies.

But that's okay, because I have the Word again.

And it will lead me where I need to go.

Traffic is being redirected on nearly every street as the search for me goes on. I catch today's newspaper, with a headline saying the body of my accomplice was found, and that it's suspected I attempted escape through the Sierras, a suicidal undertaking this time of year.

But just in case, they're canvassing all of Reno and Sparks.

I don't dare try to get any food, even though I'm starving. I just follow the tug of the Word all the way back to yet another motel in the middle of town, on the outskirts of the casinos. As I limp through the parking lot, a man standing in front of the office does a double take and whips out his cell phone as he runs away.

I won't have long before they come.

The Word leads me to room 21. I bash a shoulder against the wood until the flimsy lock breaks and step inside.

~ ~ ~

Ralph Waldo Emerson once said, "Passion, though a bad regulator, is a powerful spring."

He's right. Passion is such a dangerous, double-edged sword. It pushes and pushes and pushes, until you're lost in it and you can't swim but it feels so good to drown. It's the freshest, most delicious apple you ever tasted, but it goes sour fast if you're not careful. It lifts you until your head is in the clouds, but that just means you have farther to fall when the show is over.

You can't contain it, you can't control it. You can only channel it into something constructive.

And hope the scars aren't too bad when it's finished with you.

Brynn shoots me in the shoulder. Not by accident either. She takes a half second to check my identity as I come through the door and then aims far enough to the right not to kill me. If I'd been anyone else, I'd be dead.

I stumble back against the wall and clutch at the hole. For my first gunshot wound, it hurts surprisingly little.

"Rudy," she says. She's sitting on the bed cross-legged with the Vessel in her lap, gun still on me but shaking uncontrollably. Her eyes are wild and red. "I'm sorry. I'm so sorry..." I'm not sure if she even knows what she's apologizing for.

"*You bitch*," I growl, forcing myself away from the wall. That bruise is gone from her cheek now, but I know I have the capacity to do far worse. I want my hands around her neck, I want to feel the pulse slowing there as I squeeze. All this fury—this *passion*—demands it.

"S-stay back!" She holds up the Vessel with her free hand. "I need you to open this thing, Rudy."

I show her my bloody palm. "You gonna kill me if I don't?"

She seems to think about that. She's shaking like a hypothermia victim. Finally she lowers the gun, drops it on the bed beside her. "No baby, of course not, I love you. I do. Whether you believe it or not, everything I did, I did for us."

"Really? *Us?* Because if 'us' didn't end when you walked out on me, it sure as hell did when you murdered my best friend and left me to die."

Her fists bunch at her sides, crumpling the bedspread. "Rudy, goddamn it! None of that matters, don't you see?"

"Explain how."

"We have a genie! A fucking *genie!* How many people in the world can say that? I'm here, you're here, and no matter how that happened, it has to be fate! So let's use it, let's do it together! You want Dutt back, let's open this thing and wish for it!"

The idea itself is like another punch to my already sore stomach. "Don't you say his name."

She goes right on with her fantasy. "We can do anything, go anywhere! We can be rich! We can...we can be king and queen!"

"We were already king and queen. You were just too blind to see it." I shake my head. "And anyway, I told you, it doesn't work like th—"

"*NO!*" she shrieks. She tilts her head back and bares her teeth at the ceiling. "No, I refuse to believe that! If it's true, I wanna hear it from this genie! Not from *you*, from *him!* Just...just fucking open it and let me talk to him!"

"What's wrong with you?" I ask. The question is so loaded, I half-expect it to explode. "Why are you like this?"

"*Because I need it!*" All sense of composure and humanity is gone. "*I need this thing, because it's* my *turn to be happy,* my *turn to get what I want! My turn to not be miserable every day of my life and not know why! And if you ever loved me, you'll do this, you'll give me this one fucking chance to be happy!*"

I stare. Words will never work on her; I see that now. Now matter how many 'I-love-yous' I give, it will never heal what's wrong with her.

Outside, the first sirens split the morning. I'm so tired of that sound.

Her eyes flick to the window. "*Please* Rudy! They're coming! They'll take the genie away and they'll take us away and you'll never see me again! If you'll just open it...just let me try...then even if it doesn't work...I'll come home with you. I'll be with you and I'll stay with you and...and I'll never cheat again. I *swear.*"

I come and sit beside her on the bed. Blood spatters the covers from my shoulder. All that rage I've been holding on to just...evaporates, leaving a great, empty hollow inside me.

That's important for you to understand, I think.

That I'm not mad anymore.

Brynn collapses on me, sobbing, more vulnerable than I've ever seen her. Her hand finds mine, the fingers intertwining. Our wedding rings make a quiet—yet still very solid—*clink!* when they connect. I hold her, this stranger in a familiar body, and wonder if we would be here even if Misery hadn't come into our lives.

Something in my gut tells me it couldn't have ended any other way.

"Rudy, Rudy," she cries. "Oh God, I killed him, didn't I? I didn't mean to do it! What's wrong with me?"

"I know. It's all right," I try to soothe her.

But she still stiffens when she feels the barrel of the pistol against her chest.

Brynn looks down at it between our bodies, pointed right at her heart, then back up at me.

"Rudy?" Utter confusion. "But...you love me..."

"And I always will," I assure her, and pull the trigger.

I don't know how long I sit on the bed. The world beyond the drawn motel curtains is nothing but a sea of flashing red and blue lights. For a while, the bedside phone rings, until I unplug it. Someone is trying to negotiate with me by bullhorn, encouraging me to surrender. The minute I walk out the door, I'm either dead or in prison. Even if I somehow get cleared for everything else, there's no way to hide what I did in this room.

Brynn's body is covered with sheets next to me. She's so tiny, that lump could be a child under there. My wedding rings sits on top of the bloodstain spreading from her chest. I sit alone and try not to look at it while my body throbs and the color leeches out of the world.

Then I remember, I'm not alone. The Vessel is at the end of the bed. I touch it with my foot and say the Word for the last time.

And then the Servant of *Sideris* is sitting in the chair next to me.

"You didn't say anything," I tell Misery. "That whole time...you were watching...and you never said a word." Somehow, this is far worse than when he let me end Hillman.

"What was I supposed to say, Rudes?"

"I don't know. You could've tried to stop me."

"Would you've listened?"

"Not when I came through the door. At the end…maybe."

He nods and stares at his feet. "Besides, I think I've interfered in your life enough. Whatever happened…it needed to be your decision. Sometimes you gotta respect boundaries. You know?"

That advice reminds me of my dinner with Officer Reed, in another life.

"I wasn't angry," I say.

"I know."

"I was just setting her free."

"I know, Rudes."

"Fuck. Love is complicated."

"You can say that again."

From outside, the man on the bullhorn tells me if I don't come out or make some attempt at contact, they'll be forced to use tear gas.

"What're you gonna do about them?" Misery asks.

"That depends."

"On?"

"If you can grant my wish."

I tell him what I have in mind. Ask if it can be granted.

"Are you sure that's what you want?"

"Absolutely. Why do you ask?"

Misery hesitates. "It's just that…well, I like you Rudes, so can I offer a warning?"

"Not if it's gonna put some selfish thought in my head that will make the wish ungrantable."

"No, no, relax. Like I said, it all depends on what's actually in your heart when you say the magic words. If your intent is really pure, nothing I can tell you would change that."

"Fine. Go ahead."

"A wish like that...you're talking about creating an alternate timeline. Totally unpredictable."

"So?"

"So in the new reality, *anything* could happen. You could be dead. From something unrelated, I mean. Car crash, food poisoning...*I* won't even know, until it's done."

"Things aren't looking too much better in this reality." I swallow. "Besides...I couldn't care less what happens to me."

He squints. "If that's true, then sure, I can grant that one. Done it three times before, after all."

"You mean...?"

"Ice-T said it best, Rudes: 'Passion makes the world go round. Love just makes it a safer place.'" He shrugs. "I find most people are just faking decency. When it comes down to the wire, they'll pick themselves, even over the most trivial things. But every once in a while...I run into someone willing to give up everything for another human being." Misery looks wistful as he adds, "I think those are the only *true* selfless wishes."

"Okay. I wanna do it."

"I hate to throw one more wrench in the works, but there's another consideration here." He points a finger at his own chest. "Chances are, after I grant this wish, you and I will never even have met. If you weren't in the cell that night, you never got the Word, which means Carbini's plan goes off without a hitch, which means I'll most likely end up in the hands of the Filament."

I sigh and lean back against the headboard. "No offense Mis...but I think I'm gonna have to let someone else save the world this time."

"Then just hold the Vessel and make it official."

I bend over, my whole body screaming, and grab the rusted pot. I hug it to my chest as I settle back again. "Are you even gonna remember any of this?" I ask.

"I will. You won't."

"Gotcha."

"Take care of yourself, Rudes. You're one of the few humans I've met that's actually worth a damn."

"Thanks. Hope you don't get stuck in this thing again."

"You and me both."

I clutch the Vessel and close my eyes.

"I wish Brynn had always been happy."

As I say this, and the world swirls away from me, I think of all the ways she could've been happy without me.

And then I know the true meaning of misery.

Chapter THIRTY TWO

"That's it."

"Where?"

"Right there, the next one." I point at the sign for the highway exit.

"You have no fucking clue where we are, do you? You don't even have a map, Rudy!"

"I don't need one. I told you, I dreamed about it."

"Yeah, well the next time you start thinking you're Joan of Arc, get someone else to be your chauffeur out to the middle of nowhere."

"Joan of Arc didn't have dreams, she had visions, dipshit."

Dutt turns his head from the road to glare at me. "Call me that again, Compton. Go ahead. See what happens."

But he takes the exit, directing my new Dodge Ram onto the access road. It actually took a lot for me to let him drive the thing, but I didn't want to come all this way by myself. I used the money I made teaching summer school last year as a down payment. This summer, I promised myself I'd take the year off to finish the novel I'm working on.

The access road leads us past desert scrub to our right, and not much else. The sun is just setting on the horizon. I sit in the passenger seat and try not to fidget. I'm so excited, and I don't even know why.

These dreams. These weird ass dreams. And during the day, it feels like something is literally pulling me out here, like a hand in the middle of my chest, leading me to this place I've been dreaming about.

"How much farther?" Dutt asks.

"We should see it off the road, any minute."

"You're gonna feel real stupid when you find out this place doesn't exist."

I don't answer, because it's true.

But then, the unending flat expanse of the Arizona desert is broken by a string of gas stations, convenience stores, and motels, scraps of life clinging together to pass for civilization. As we get closer, I roll down the window and point. "Ha! Told you!"

Dutt makes a turn and pulls into a parking space in front of the building I'm pointing at. "Okay. Admit it. You knew. You looked it up online or something. This is some kinda joke."

"No joke, man. I *really* dreamed about it."

"So...what now?"

"Now I go in and see if the rest of the dream is real." I open the door and hop out, but Dutt stays where he is. "You coming?"

"I think I'm gonna let you handle this one alone."

I nod, start away from the car, and then come back to the window. "Thanks, man. I really appreciate you coming out here with me."

He tries to hide his smile. "Just make this worth me taking an extra week of leave."

I walk away, up to the front door of the establishment. The sign in the window of the Thorn Rose Tavern is blinking 'OPEN.' My hands are shaking, but I push my way inside.

I have a bartending waitress to find.

Like this novel?

YOUR REVIEWS HELP!

In the modern world, customer reviews are essential for any product. The artists who create the work you enjoy need your help growing their audience. Please visit Goodreads or the website of the company that sold you this novel to leave a review, or even just a star rating. Posting about the book on social media is also appreciated.

About the Author

Russell C. Connor has been writing horror since the age of five, and is the author of two short story collections, five eNovellas, and fourteen novels. His books have won two Independent Publisher Awards and a Readers' Favorite Award. He has been a member of the DFW Writers' Workshop since 2006, and served as president for two years. He lives in Fort Worth, Texas with his rabid dog, demented film collection, mistress of the dark, and demonspawn daughter.

His next novel—*The Halls of Moambati*, Volume IV of *The Dark Filament Ephemeris*—will be available in 2021.

www.ingramcontent.com/pod-product-compliance
Lightning Source LLC
Chambersburg PA
CBHW030826110726
47900CB00006B/1761